Forty-One's Journey

A car, The dream, Their story

By:
Ronald Forfinski &
John Mathew Farren, Sr.

To Judy,
Who let a dreamer, dream. No matter what, we'll always be together.
R.

To my family, the real Mrs. Maze, and especially to you a traveler in life. May your journey be successful in discovering knowledge and genuine love. May you use your knowledge to better humankind. And when you find your true love, may they love you more. Cherish them, appreciate them, and live a long good life together. The blessed have it forever…
J.M.F.

Table of Contents

Chapter 1 ~ Home Today 1

Chapter 2 ~ Aunt Sylvia 15

Chapter 3 ~ Almost Famous 30

Chapter 4 ~ Village Time 46

Chapter 5 ~ Life's Lesson 60

Chapter 6 ~ Outta Here 75

Chapter 7 ~ Changing Destiny 86

Chapter 8 ~ New Arrivals 102

Chapter 9 ~ First Show 116

Chapter 10 ~ The Note 130

Chapter 11 ~ Hello Eloise 142

Chapter 12 ~ My Ammygam 157

Chapter 13 ~ American Dream 173

Chapter 14 ~ Quick Spin 186

Chapter 15 ~ Honeymoon Car 200

Chapter 16 ~ Beyond Belief 215

Chapter 17 ~ The Homefront 230

Chapter 18 ~ God Willing 243

Chapter 19 ~ Pittsburgh Reunion 257

Chapter 20 ~ X Sticker 271

Chapter 21 ~ Million Tears 285

Chapter 22 ~ My Things 299

Chapter 23 ~ They're Gone 313

Chapter 24 ~ Strange Presence 328

Chapter 25 ~ I'm Home 340

Acknowledgments 354

Chapter 1

Home Today

Walking from her Dearborn Township, Michigan home, Donna Maze turned off Belton Street onto the Telegraph Road sidewalk. She walks with a purpose on her way to Wally's Service Station a few blocks ahead. Today, her errand is to bring home her beloved ruby maroon 1941 Chevrolet… an automobile no one has driven for the past twelve years.

Her stride quickens as she reflects on the solemn promise she made to herself over a decade ago. She vowed then, never to allow anyone to drive her husband's car, including herself. Her late husband Alex had been killed in the war over fourteen years ago, but in a dream two days ago he told her to drive the car home today. Thoughts swirl in her mind as she attempts to understand the reason, and with each of her steps the same question repeats itself... why today?

Unable to find the answer to her question, she tries to remember happier times, smiling as she recalls being a young girl with a temper. To herself, she laughs, thinking of that young person with a competitive spirit. In those days, she was a determined girl who enjoyed playing many sports. Baseball with the neighbor kids, games late into the night, cries of laughter and joy etched into her memory.

Her competitive spirit often caused her amiable personality and composure to vanish. When she lost her temper, her passion and colorful language were put on display for all who were near. She credited these traits of hers for the nickname of Fiery given by her pals which had nothing to do with the color of her hair.

Those names, given in our youth, are sometimes funny and are carried with you forever. Her faithful friends always remembered Donna's nickname, using it to recall their own youth or a moment in time they shared with her. Only a few of her loyal friends still called her Fiery. People now describe her as a mature, charming woman of high moral character and always in control of her temper.

Donna is a stunning forty-two-year-old auburn-haired woman with a flawless complexion. At five-foot-seven-inches, and one hundred twenty-six-pounds, she has an attractive, athletic appearance. Active is how she describes herself. She walks the fifteen minutes by choice this June morning. The overcast sky will make her Dearborn Township destination walk a comfortable one.

As she continues, her mind turns to the event that caused this chaos in her life. The neighbor's enormous Michigan elm tree dropped on her two-car garage a few weeks earlier doing extensive damage. She remembers the date, Friday, June fifth. The same day as her niece Lucy's seventeenth birthday. She has lived with her Aunt Donna since she was four years old.

The elm fell at 6:30 a.m. It had been weakened over the years by Dutch elm disease. She considered the time of the accident a blessing because no one was hurt. Donna's eyes crinkled and a slight grin formed across her face as she recalled the early morning commotion. Several neighborhood teenage boys came over to the house and inspected the damage. In the eyes of those teenage boys, it was Lucy's house and garage. Listening to them talk, the tree was also Lucy's. In reality, Lucy's Aunt Donna owned everything but the tree.

The aunt remembered watching the teenage boys strut around the property. They spent more time swooning over Lucy than viewing the garage's destruction. The day's excitement did not interfere with Lucy's birthday party held that evening with her girlfriends. During the celebration, the same group of teenage boys intentionally stopped by to check out the damaged garage and their true intentions did not go unnoticed by Lucy and her friends. Donna smiled warmly as the whispers and giggles from the girls filled the air.

Weeks earlier, the weather had been very windy. Donna never understood why the elm chose that day to fall on the garage's roof. Upsetting her the most is the tree landed on the side where her beloved 1941 Chevrolet was parked. Somehow the two autos inside avoided being damaged.

She had made two telephone calls that morning. First calling her mechanic, Wally, and then contacted Mr. Bill Kid, owner of a local building company. Mr. Kid's company built the garage eleven years earlier. Later in the afternoon, Wally, the gas station owner, came to her home with his tow truck. He recommended moving her Chevrolet to his shop for safe storage.

Donna did not allow him to take her vehicle. So, he moved it from the garage to the driveway in front of the damaged building. He made sure each canvas tarp was securely in place, covering the vehicle. Earlier, her neighbor stopped over and apologized for the tree falling. She told Donna their insurance company confirmed they would pay for all damages.

For now, she parked her 1948 red Pontiac behind the Chevrolet. Mr. Kid's construction crew came the next day. They started clearing and hauling away the debris. They made emergency repairs and advised her the entire roof and two exterior walls would need complete rebuilding. On Tuesday, the ninth, Mr. Kid called to say they will start her garage repairs on June eighteenth.

She remembered how the start date upset her and recalled telling him that he only had four days to complete the job. Donna Maze explained to Mr. Kid she and Lucy would leave for a trip to Florida on Monday the twenty-second, where she was to be the matron-of-honor at her best friend's wedding. She told him her Chevrolet must be back in her completed garage by the morning of that date, or they would not travel. Few people understood that Mrs. Maze considered the 1941 Chevrolet part of her family!

Donna Maze remembers Mr. Kid promised he would finish the garage by Sunday, the twenty-first. He also told her he would bill the insurance company directly. Once reassured he would complete the work on time, Donna remembers feeling better. Last Thursday, Wally moved her precious Chevrolet to his shop with his tow truck. He kept it at the garage after doing a few minor repairs. The car's absence from her yard was difficult and very upsetting for her.

Once construction started, the building crew worked every day, including the weekend, to repair the damages. The blue laws (Sunday laws) made working on Sunday illegal; however, with special permission, they toiled every day to rebuild the walls, place the siding, and install the new roof. Painting the garage's exterior would be completed while they were in Florida. With the significant repairs completed, Donna wanted her beloved vehicle home today! With that notion, her pace quickened.

Now she was only one block away, and her goal was within reach. Tonight, she and Lucy had a train to catch. In her mind, she knew she couldn't enjoy their trip when her 1941 Chevrolet wasn't back in her garage where it belonged. She knew they could always reschedule their trip, leaving Wednesday and still make the wedding. But her car needed to be in the garage before they left!

With the temperature in the mid-sixties, she dressed comfortably and carried a small purse. She brought her umbrella, just in case the rain started again. Finally, she came to Wally's Sinclair gas station. She looked at the green dinosaurs on the two gas pumps and noticed how faded they appeared. The service station looked similar to other filling stations from the front, but when built, the office was extended in the back for some unknown reason. Behind the larger office, a machine shop was added. There Wally kept a small forge and lathe where he manufactured car parts he could not find or buy.

His large office offered a convenient place for people to stay while he repaired their auto. Clean was not a word used to describe the waiting area, but it kept customers out of the weather. He had a private junkyard of prewar wrecked cars in the back of his station that covered six city lots. Since it was impossible to get replacement parts, he used the yard to salvage the parts needed to keep his customers' prewar vehicles running.

She walked past the gas pumps and only stopped when she reached the office's open door. Donna watched Wally with his back to her from the doorway, putting a black X over the red number twenty-one on the hanging wall calendar. That meant today, June twenty-second, was the day she and Lucy would leave for Florida.

Like many shop calendars, the top half pictured a woman holding a tool, advertising the company's product line. The bottom half had the days of the month. Donna noticed the large 1959 printed above the days. Wally seemed to be deep in thought. He didn't see her at the door. When she cleared her throat, he was startled.

With a broad friendly smile, the burly man turned and greeted her saying, "Hello!"

He was a little embarrassed and glanced nervously over his paperwork. Wally hoped to avoid eye contact with her as he blushed. Finding her bill, he explained her vehicle needed minor maintenance. The bill included an oil change and greasing the undercarriage. He assured Donna her beloved Chevrolet was in good shape for its age.

As he totaled her invoice, he talked about the engine and how it was getting to where it may need new bearings. Years ago, she listened as another mechanic said similar words and went searching for a new one. That is how she found Wally twelve years ago. She knew he was reliable and an expert in repairing prewar cars.

She recognized what was coming next. Right on cue, Wally said, "When they stopped making cars like your Chevrolet, the quality was never the same." As he totaled her charges, he continued saying, "When the war ended, and the seven major automakers resumed building cars, they were never as good as they used to be. The craftsmanship really slipped."

About now, he would prove his theory by opening and closing an automobile's door. Donna zoned out, having heard the same speech every time she came in. But, looking around, she did not see her car anywhere. Wondering where her car was, Donna waited for Wally's "car talk" to end so she could be on her way.

Wally looked Donna Maze in the eye, saying, "Open and close your door. Listen to that satisfying clank like a bank vault door closing. You'll never hear that tinny sound like you do from today's autos."

His favorite pro-prewar car speech finished; he handed her the bill. It was for $14.17! She thought it was excessive and examined the receipt. Her expression communicated to Wally that she was uncertain, but she remembered everything he had done.

Donna caught Wally's eye, "You came to my house and towed my car here. I appreciate everything you did. Thank you."

Wally also worked on her 1948 Pontiac, which her father bought new. She was always satisfied with his work. When her dad passed, it became her main vehicle. Since she drove the Pontiac, this allowed her to store the Chevrolet in the garage. The Chevrolet was more than just a car; it was a time capsule full of precious memories. Donna appreciated the time and care Wally put into his work. She would never go anywhere else for auto repairs. He was the best! She counted out the cash, and then from a small coin purse she brought out a dime, nickel, and two pennies. With her bill paid, Wally handed her the car's key.

The mechanic said, "Your vehicle is outside in the wash bay. I hope you don't mind? I had Jimmy wash her this morning." He then asked, "Are you driving straight home?"

She answered, "Yes."

He replied, "Good, there is less than a pint of fuel in the tank. When you park it in your garage, make sure you keep the engine idling until it runs out of gas. Oh! Be sure to leave the garage doors open until it stops running. She'll be fine for another ten years."

Wally ran in front of her as she left and yelled, "Jimmy, Mrs. Maze is here to pick up her car."

A young teenage boy came around the corner of the building to greet her. He explained how he had finished cleaning her vehicle. Seeing how clean it looked, she gave the youthful boy an appreciative smile.

She took a coin out of her purse and, smiling, handed him the quarter saying, "Thank you, Jimmy; you did a wonderful job."

Jimmy, being mannerly, went running over to the car's door and opened it for her. Taking a deep breath, she feigned a smile as she sat behind the car's large steering wheel for the first time in twelve years.

Jimmy closed her door, saying, "Thanks, Mrs. Maze."

Gripping the wheel, Donna's anguish almost overpowered her. She hoped never again to drive this auto and planned to take the quickest way home so she didn't run out of gas. She drove up to Joy Road and over to her street. Donna enjoyed driving this Chevrolet because it brought memories of innocence and cheerful times. Unfortunately, those fun thoughts, with her husband, were now too painful to recall. She wished not to drive this car today or ever again.

Turning on Appleton Street, she sped up. Suddenly the engine sputtered and stalled. Donna quickly depressed the clutch pedal, which kept the car rolling. She was certain the auto ran out of gas. As the car coasted and slowed, she steered it over to the curb as if parking. When it stopped, she was a block away from home and mad at herself for driving the route she chose.

Looking out the driver's side window, Donna saw her neighbor Jan. The young housewife was looking down watching where each of her steps landed as she slowly crossed the street, and stopped right in front of the car. Her left hand held her belly, the other grabbed the vehicle's hood ornament. For a moment she paused, removed her right hand, kissed it, and lovingly touched the flying lady hood ornament. Donna watched and remembered her late husband Alex, kissing that same hood ornament. Suddenly, she saw him standing beside the woman dressed in his normal work attire, a long-sleeved checkered flannel shirt, and holding their pup, Tiger. He smiled at her, pointed to himself and then to the woman.

In disbelief, Donna blinked her eyes. The vision disappeared, and she let out a loud gasp, which startled her neighbor! The woman smiled at her, and continued her slow walk up the driveway. It was then she noticed Jan was very pregnant, and could have had a contraction. Behind the steering wheel, Donna sat remembering the vision, and sensed it was some kind of sign the woman or her child may one day help her.

Now bewildered by what just occurred, Donna forced her attention to her car's problem. She switched the key off, waited a second, and tried to start it. To her surprise, the motor sprung to life. She wasted no time driving home, stopping only in front of her repaired garage.

Donna thought back to her dream and the vision she had, when she whispered, "Alex, you said, 'I'm coming back for you, and forty-one with Tiger,' but when?"

Unable to answer the question, she sat facing her four new swinging garage doors. Mr. Kid had done an excellent job completing the repairs. Donna allowed the car to idle as she got out, opened the garage's left side bay doors, and noticed the workers had cleaned the entire inside of the building. Carefully she pulled her ruby maroon two-door 1941 Chevrolet Special Deluxe sedan onto the wood-planked garage floor.

Once the car was parked, Donna set the emergency brake. Softly she whispered, "Alex, your car is home. Now, come back for us."

Then she remembered Wally's words, "Be sure to allow the engine to idle until she runs out of gas." She sat there for a moment, thinking about breaking her promise, and driving Alex's car. Suddenly she realized she had left the car idling; exhaust fumes were filling the garage. Understanding her dilemma, Donna went looking for a solution.

From behind the garage, she grabbed a rusted old four-foot-long round metal flue pipe. With the metal tube in hand, she had just placed it over the vehicle's exhaust pipe when the engine sputtered to a stop. The vehicle ran out of gas, and she was out of danger. Donna turned the car's ignition off and pocketed the key. She opened the hood exposing the engine, and took one loose cable off the six-volt battery, which her mechanic recommend-ed. Donna closed the hood, walked around, making sure the windows were closed and doors locked. She took a canvas tarp from the shelf and covered the auto's back half to the middle. Donna did the same thing on the front half with a different tarp.

Finished, she stood in front of the now concealed vehicle. When she looked down at the garage floor, Donna noticed the four and seven carved in the wood floor. She thought to herself, that's wrong. That should be forty-one! Then she remembered. They built the garage in 1947 when both of her parents were still living. Her parent's garage was the old chicken coop in need of repair.

Donna remembered how Mr. Kid came to be the builder. He was the son of her father's neighbor, Mr. William Kid. Young Bill Junior was a returning war veteran who wanted to go into the construction business. He had no experience, but they trusted the brawny veteran. Their first and only meeting, they hired Bill to build the garage, which was his company's first construction job.

He recommended constructing this garage to the left and further back in the lot. The new location allowed cars to pull straight into the modern two-car garage while still using the old one during construction.

Bill told Gilbert Bak, Donna's father, "Dirt floors are out. You'll need a concrete floor in a modern building."

Gil did not like the concrete floor. Donna hated dirt garage floors. It reminded her of the chicken coop it once was. But, since his daughter was paying for the new garage, concrete floors, it would be!

When the time came to remove the old garage, Bill had an idea he hoped could change her father's mindset towards the floor. He suggested they reuse the good one-inch oak siding from the chicken coop garage and cover the concrete surface with that wood.

Donna smiled, remembering how she only paid young Bill thirty-seven dollars to tear down the old garage and install the thick old oak siding on top of the new concrete floor. Donna's father loved the wood garage floor. She now thought to herself young Bill found a brilliant solution and did an excellent job. Donna stomped her foot on it as if giving it her seal of approval.

With his first job under his belt, young Mr. Bill Kid could start his renovation and building company. Donna always recommended his business to her friends. He never forgot how she helped him, and he always took the time to thank her. He showed his thanks to her again when he repaired her garage.

Out of the corner of her eye, she saw her niece Lucy bounding out the house's back door. She watched as the neatly dressed young girl leaned over the porch's rail, cupped both hands to her mouth, and yelled, "Is everything okay, Auntie?"

Donna waved and smiled, showing everything was fine. Lucy had been living with her since March 1946. That's when Maureen, Donna's sister, and her daughter, Lucy, moved in with her. In September 1946, the state committed Maureen to a mental hospital. Lucy and Donna moved in with her parents in their Appleton Street house in May 1947 to adopt their granddaughter.

A widow, Donna legally could not adopt her niece, but she had cared for the little girl since she was four years old. Fortunately, her parents' adoption of their granddaughter became legal before they took ill in 1948. In August of that year, her mother passed away, and three months later, her father followed. In just three short months, Fiery lost both of her parents and became her niece's legal guardian.

She inherited her parent's home, and the two continued to live there. Through the years, Lucy had grown to be a pleasant young girl with a slim figure, auburn hair, and a ready smile. Donna loved Lucy's caring and fun personality. She raised her hand and waved for Lucy to come into the garage.

Lucy ran down the porch steps and into the garage. "What are you doing, Aunt Fiery?"

Gazing at the tarp-covered auto, she replied, "I was just thinking, do you know we've lived here for twelve years?"

The niece looked puzzled, asking, "Is everything okay with forty-one?" She referred to the car by the beloved name her aunt always used.

Donna continued, "You were turning five when we moved here. I remember the month and year, May 1947. I sold my house, and we moved in with my parents. They were getting older and I wanted to help. They built this garage a month before we moved here. Later that year, your grandfather's name came up on a dealer's list, and he could buy his 1948 Pontiac brand new."

Pointing to the red car parked in the other bay, "He had that vehicle only nine months before he died. I never realized how ill my parents were until we lived here."

Donna went on talking more to herself than to Lucy, "My father acted too slow when he tried purchasing a new automobile before the war. He endured those war-time years with his old 1936 Ford. It was a rusted-out unreliable heap, a real jalopy, by the time he got rid of it. When the war ended, dealerships started new car waiting lists for their customers. Manufacturers had to switch from armament production back to auto manufacturing.

"A few dealerships became unethical. For an extra charge, customers could move their names up the list. Your grandfather found this out when the salesperson asked him for a 'filing fee'. He was adamant telling the man, 'I'll push my old Ford around before I make a deal with you pirates!' My father had been partial to Fords, and he was offended by the salesperson and his extra fee. Well, that day your grandpa walked up and down Michigan Avenue and placed his name on every dealership's list, which had no filing charge.

"It didn't matter who the manufacturer was, he went to everyone and came home with their car brochures. I don't know if you remember, but you played with those pamphlets for weeks." Fiery went on, "One day at the Pontiac dealership in the small town of Wayne, your grandfather's name moved to the top of the list. He could finally buy his new car. I began sharing the monthly payments with him. Later in that year, he had his heart attack.

"With his health failing, I took over his car payments, parked forty-one in our garage, and started driving the Pontiac. Your grandfather enjoyed his vehicle for only a few months before he died. Forty-eight was not the best year for me. I can't believe they've been gone eleven years."

Lucy interrupted her aunt, "Is that the reason you don't drive forty-one?"

"I will admit, the new highways with their higher speeds frighten me. Since the war ended, more cars are on the highways. It seems like they each want to go faster than me in their V-8 cars. I'm used to driving forty-one at the war-time government-mandated speed limit of thirty-five miles per hour. Besides, she is bigger than the newer cars. I compete for parking spaces with those two-tone, chromed-up, new automobiles. But, what I'm afraid of is that someone will run into my car."

Lucy again broke into her aunt's one-sided conversation. "What did Wally say? Is anything wrong with forty-one? Did he give you his 'When they stopped making cars like this speech?' Did he?"

"Well, yes, he did."

Her aunt's answer made Lucy giggle.

In a deep man-like voice, Fiery continued, "Wally said, 'This 1941 Chevrolet has a touch of bronchitis.' Its big stove bolt six-cylinder engine isn't running the way it should and might soon need an expensive rebuild. He claimed the new post-war engines were lower quality and not as durable. His opinion is that automakers are using less nickel and iron in their steel. He talked like he was the only one who loved the beauty, and engineering, in those vehicles. That's when he again made his offer of 'when I want to sell my Chevrolet' to call him."

Lucy couldn't stop laughing when she heard her aunt trying to mimic the mechanic's voice.

Aunt Fiery paused for a moment then continued saying, "You need to understand, Lucy. Men like Wally forget the significant impact the war had on women, too. During the war, women maintained their vehicles. We changed the oil, lubed the grease fittings, back-flushed the radiator, rotated the tires, and cleaned and gapped the points and spark plugs. We did all those things and worked in the war plant too!"

"Men can't imagine women doing those things today. When I try to do those tasks now, men treat me like I'm incapable. My girlfriends complain to me about their husbands who won't let them have a job now. I tell them to speak up, let them know how you feel! If I encouraged more of my friends to stand up for themselves, many of their divorces would not have happened."

Lucy now walked around the car and pulled the tarps down to the hubcaps. She looked back at her aunt, asking, "Divorces? Wally's a good-looking guy. Does he like you or the forty-one? Would you go out with him? When I get a job, I could buy a car and park it right here, if you sold forty-one."

Fiery grinned at her, saying, "No, I can never sell Alex's baby. He told me never sell forty-one. It is part of our family. You know, I just realized that for the past eleven years, I haven't even driven her on special occasions, let alone for daily use."

Years ago, Fiery drove the car to visit Alex's grave on Memorial Day, his birthday, and their anniversary. In the summer, her aunt took it to the beach with her girlfriends and Lucy.

"Now I'm happy to keep forty-one, my memories, and my dreams here safely with me." Breaking into a broader smile, Fiery continued, "Remember when I showed you how to cook a meal on the forty-one's manifold? Your uncle wired a juice can to the manifold years ago, so the car could cook the meal while we traveled. We could warm up a can of soup or beans anytime. Lunch would always be ready when we arrived at the beach. How original is that?"

Moving over to the passenger side of the vehicle, Fiery lifted the tarp onto the roof. She reached into her sweater pocket, pulled out the key, unlocked the door, and put it back in her pocket. She slowly opened the car's door, looked in, and said, "Many of my neighbors and friends were used to seeing me driving around town with forty-one. Since I don't drive it, they think I should sell her."

"Many people have offered to buy this car. Some of their proposals were for more money than she's worth." Fiery's tone shifted, solemnly she explained, "Buyers think this automobile is just another vehicle in the garage. When your Uncle Alex bought forty-one, it was a wonderful and eventful time in our lives. We drove forty-one to places and did things that changed the way I lived my life."

Lucy felt the emotion move through the garage as her aunt spoke lovingly of Uncle Alex. "Alex loved this car, and I loved him. When he died, I was a lost twenty-seven-year-old widow. The forty-one here made me feel like your uncle was here. Over the years, a powerful bond developed between me and this vehicle. It has never let me down. If a car could be a loyal friend, I have one here."

Lucy changed the conversation, asking, "Aunt Fiery, are you going out with Wally?"

Fiery understood the deeper meaning of her niece's question, recalling the times her friends asked her why she stopped dating and never remarried. These nosy inquisitors often receive the same analogy and answer she was about to give her niece, saying, "I remember my old baseball coach telling me, I will get one pitch that's worth swinging at each time at-bat. If you swing at the other pitches, you'll probably foul them off or miss them completely. Lucy, in my life, I've dated a few foul balls. But should Wally invite me out, I would consider him a bad pitch and say no. Besides, I believe he's married!"

Fiery now sat in the Chevrolet's passenger seat and brought her feet inside the car. She stared at the tarp-covered windshield, remembering a ride through the long winding country roads. Lucy could hear Fiery's deliberate soft voice say, "We were only married three years. We filled them with memories full of love and joy. I know, if he continued to live until our golden anniversary, each year would have been more wonderful than the last. I am thankful to God for the time we had together."

Fiery reached for a clean paper handkerchief from a tissue dispenser under the glove compartment as she had done thousands of times before. She brought the tissue to her cheek, catching the one tear running from each of her eyes. In a soft tone, she said to herself, "Thank you, Alex, for making the correct decision of not leaving me with a child." With the same tissue, she caught more tears. Again, she whispered other questions to him, "Why did you want me to drive forty-one today? Did you want me to see you and our neighbor? Is she going to help you come back for me?"

As Lucy walked past the open passenger door, her aunt turned her face and body away, pretending to arrange something on the driver's seat. Fiery composed herself, got out, closed and locked the passenger door. Then she pulled down the tarp.

Once satisfied the auto was wrapped to the hubcaps, Lucy said, "Okay, that's done." As she double-checked her work, Lucy stopped, faced her aunt, and asked, "When are you going to tell me all about Aunt Sylvia's marriages and divorces?"

Fiery ignored the question and did a last check of the tarps. The two ladies walked out the garage. Her niece closed the door, and discovered the new side hinges made the doors easier to swing. Fiery handed her a large thick lock that appeared to be more suitable for a bank vault than their garage.

Lucy placed the padlock on the hasp and locked the forty-one's garage doors, convinced her beloved 1941 Chevrolet was home, safe, and secure. Mrs. Donna Louise Fiery Maze stared for a moment at the locked door. She again tried to understand the question, why today? What was the reason she had to drive forty-one today? Lucy nudged her, which broke Fiery's trance, and they both turned, walking towards the house.

For the third time Lucy begged her, asking, "Now, tell me about each of her divorces? And, how many times did Aunt Sylvia marry?" While they walked to the house's back porch, the aunt put her arm under her niece's and grabbed her hand.

Fiery looked at her niece, saying, "When I was seventeen, I never wanted to know about divorce or had the opportunity to take a train to Florida; tonight will be fun. After you've packed, we'll talk about Aunt Sylvia's many relationships." Pausing a moment, she said, "I believe this may be the fourth time I am Sylvia's matron-of-honor. Oh, my! I better get that number correct. Please don't repeat what I tell you to anyone at the wedding."

Lucy giggled, which made her aunt laugh. Still holding each other's arm, they walked up the porch steps into the house.

Chapter 2

Aunt Sylvia

From the rear porch, Lucy and her Aunt Fiery walked into a coatroom that also served as a hallway to the kitchen. Three of the walls had wire coat hooks for hanging coats, sweaters, or any odds and ends that found a home there. A wood bench had long replaced the original icebox. Now you could sit while removing your wet shoes or boots during the many seasons of Michigan weather. In Michigan, it's not a far fetch to have snow in the spring or eighty-degree weather in October. Fiery loved that about the Mitten State; it was feisty, a quality she also liked about herself. As she moved into the kitchen, Fiery turned to her right and hung the Chevrolet's car key on one of the tiny brass hooks.

With the key in its proper place, Fiery placed her purse on the dark green top of the small kitchen table. Two matching chairs with chrome metal legs that complemented the tabletop were pushed in at opposite ends. Fiery walked past Lucy and into the small living room. Lucy hummed as she went about making lunch, grabbing the quart glass jar of milk, the luncheon meats, and cheese. She thought about the night to come and what she might learn from Aunt Fiery. Curiosity had always been a close companion of hers. With the last of the bread, she made several generous sandwiches and called Aunt Fiery to join her.

She poured all the milk into two glasses, making them equal. The empty bottle she rinsed out and placed on the countertop near the back of the sink. Fiery stood in the middle of the small kitchen. She had a blank stare on her face as if she had forgotten something. Without saying a word, Fiery walked over to the backdoor, making sure it was locked. Then, she took the hallway chair for extra protection and slid the high back under the inside doorknob.

Before sitting down at the kitchen table, she went over to one drawer and removed a pink envelope with blue writing. She brought it to the table and sat opposite of Lucy.

She read aloud from a single page in the packet, "We depart today, Monday, June 22, 1959, from Michigan Central Station at 11:20 p.m. for Cincinnati. That's where we board the New York Central's Royal Palm (train) from Cincinnati, Ohio to Jacksonville, Florida."

Lucy smiled, and her eyes opened wide. This is Lucy's first visit to the south and her excitement was hard to control! Aunt Fiery had said that they could spend a few days on a real vacation after the wedding. She was looking forward to Florida's sandy beaches, swimming in the ocean, getting a good suntan, and checking out what Florida had to offer in the department of "young men".

Pausing Fiery sipped her milk then continued, "Would you like to have dinner tonight at the finest restaurant in the Michigan Central Depot? Smirking, she asked, "What do you think?"

Lucy's eyes were wide open with anticipation because she never dined in a fancy restaurant; she shook her head, "yes" while biting into her sandwich.

Fiery went on, "We should plan to arrive at Michigan Central station at seven. There is no dining car on New York Central's Detroit-to-Cincinnati train, and I reserved two spots for us in the sleeper cars. Make sure you pack those extra sandwiches in the brown bag on the counter, and then put them in your makeup case." Winking, she said, "In case we need a snack."

Fiery took a bite of her sandwich. As she finished, Fiery said, "At 8:15 tomorrow morning, our train will arrive at Cincinnati's Union Terminal. There we'll board Southern Railroad's Royal Palm coach to Jacksonville and travel in real luxury. On that train, we have a compartment with two sleeping berths and a private bathroom."

Lucy's eyes widened as her face lit up, a wide grin forming, "Wait till I tell my girlfriends; a private bathroom!"

Smiling to herself, Fiery said, "Lucy, consider this trip as next year's graduation present! We have fifteen minutes to change trains before departing at 8:30 a.m. We'll eat lunch and dinner on the train. I'll telephone Aunt Sylvia when we arrive in Florida. Then we'll take a taxi over to her restaurant."

"Really?" exclaimed Lucy. "I can't thank you enough, Aunt Fiery. This trip is a dream!" Lucy picked up the schedule that fell out of the envelope and started reading the railroad timetable out loud, "The train departs from Cincinnati at 8:30 a.m. EST (eastern standard time), comes into Lexington, Kentucky, at 9:35 a.m. arrives at Chattanooga, Tennessee, at 5:25 p.m. hmm-Atlanta, at 9:35 p.m. Wow! Macon, Georgia, 12:35 a.m. on Wednesday. We even go through a town in Georgia called Valdosta at 5:13 a.m. Finally, we pull into Jacksonville at 8:15 a.m. on Wednesday. I don't think I'll be able to sleep!"

Lucy paused for a moment to look at the timetable and said, "We could have breakfast in Lexington, at 9:30 a.m. — Lunch in Chattanooga, Tennessee, at 5:35 p.m., and dinner in Atlanta, Georgia, at 10:00 p.m. When we get to Florida, we can go swimming in the ocean!"

Fiery looked at her niece and, with a warm smile, saying, "I'm sure there will be reserved times in the dining car, or better yet, let's just eat when we're hungry. I promise before we return to Michigan, you will swim in the ocean."

Fiery looked out the window, thinking about the long night of travel ahead while trying to ignore the other thoughts vying for her attention. Lucy noticed her aunt daydreaming and interrupted, "What are you thinking, Aunt Fiery? And, when are you going to tell me about Aunt Sylvia's marriages?"

Ignoring that last question, Fiery reminisced. She began telling Lucy how most of her friends went back to being mothers and quiet homemakers when their husbands returned. She explained how the husband was the boss of the family during those times, and whatever he said was gospel.

"The military veterans didn't understand that while they were in combat overseas, their wives were fighting for their survival on the homefront. Women didn't always know where they could buy food or gas or how to grow their produce. But we learned because we had to. The war years were tough and to help end the war, countless lonely homemakers began working, so their husbands might return home quicker. Women became independent and self-reliant.

"Uncle Smitty and Aunt Marge may be the only couple I know who married before the war and are still together today. By the 1950s, most of my married friends were divorced, including your parents. Many of those couples married before the men went off to war, and when they came home, their relationships didn't survive. You're old enough now to understand how divorce ruins a family and their children.

"Your dad was in the Navy when he married my sister. Unbeknownst to her, he was an alcoholic. When your father drank, he had unpredictable mood swings. On their wedding night, he drank himself into a stupor and passed out on the bedroom floor.

"Your mom and I put him in bed, still clutching an empty bottle of Napoleon brandy his brother had given him as a wedding gift. Your father, well, he was full of rage when he came home on leave. He drank any liquor just to get drunk, and then he would hit your mother. She forgave him many times for the way he hurt the two of you. But Maureen always wanted to honor her marriage vows.

"The only thing that saved your mother during those early years was his return to the Navy. But once released from the Navy, the situation took a dark turn. When he drank, he often hit your mother, calling her stupid and other names I won't mention; of course, he would apologize the next day and beg her forgiveness, and promised to quit. But he always broke his promises of sobriety. Maureen divorced Joey after only six years of marriage. That's when you and your mom came to live with me. A few years later we moved here to Grandma and Grandpa Bak's house, and your life became even better."

Fiery looked over at Lucy as if to ask, 'should I keep going?' When Lucy returned Fiery's stare with steady resolve, Fiery continued, "Your mom suffered from depression. She told me she often imagined that one day your dad would finally wake up and say, 'I'm never going to drink again.' He continued his drinking binges and hitting her. I believe your father's alcoholism and abuse caused her rapid decline and loss of hope. I can't imagine the mental toll it takes on a person to endure physical and emotional abuse. I want you to know your mother loved you very much and was one of the strongest women I've ever known.

"Less than a month after the two of you moved in with me, your mom attempted suicide by swallowing sleeping pills. When I discovered her, both of you were lying in bed, and she was still holding you. She loved you so much. Please don't ever think she didn't. She was just too sick. I called an ambulance in the nick of time. She recovered from having her stomach pumped, but she never quite healed. Her depression became so severe the doctors recommended committing her to the state mental hospital in Kalamazoo.

"Your father only came to see you and your mom when she received her government allotment check. When she wouldn't give him a dollar for his drinking money, he hit her. I saw him do that once and threw him out of my house. So, Lucy, that is the reason your dad could not enter my home. It was your father who gave you up for adoption during one of his drunken binges.

"As a single thirty-year-old working woman, the state wouldn't allow me to adopt you. It had to be your grandparents. You reminded them of your mother. In their eyes, you became their little Maureen. In 1947, you were five years old and a child in the middle of a divorce.

The best thing I did was meet with a lawyer who drew up the papers to become your legal guardian should something happen to my parents. That's when I sold my house, and we moved here. It was just a year later when both of my parents passed. I was still grieving their loss when I found out your father Joey died in a drunk driving accident. His alcoholism ended his life, and I never found out where the crash happened."

Lucy said, "Thank you, Auntie, for telling me the story again. I know it's hard for you, but each time you tell me, I remember more."

It hurt Fiery every time she told the story to Lucy, but she had to. Lucy deserved to hear the story of her mother and her father. She had no right to keep that from her. Her eyes drifted back to Lucy's sweet face, where a warm smile caught her gaze, "When we come back from Florida, we'll go visit your mother. I always hope that one day, she will recognize us. Listen to me! I sound just like your mom! She was always telling me what to do when we were growing up." Fiery's eyes turned downward again, hmph, I miss her.

Without speaking, Aunt Fiery left the room to make a telephone call and returned, saying, "I called for a cab, and it will be here at six. What are you going to wear on our trip?"

Lucy responded, "I'll wear what I have on. And, when are you going to tell me the actual truth about Aunt Sylvia's marriages?"

Checking the clock, which read 12:30, Fiery replied, "We'll have plenty of time to talk on the train. Now, go put on the dress you wore for Easter, and finish packing your suitcase. Florida is hotter than Michigan this time of year, so don't forget your bathing suit and shorts. I'll see you and your suitcase in the living room when you're done."

Giggling with excitement, her niece ran to her bedroom. Fiery laughed to herself; it was good to see Lucy so happy. Fiery went to finish packing her luggage. It didn't take long because she didn't need much. She placed the worn leather suitcase by the front door and then went about checking her house, making certain each of the windows was locked, the water turned off, leaving none of the toilets running, and even checked the refrigerator setting.

After she had checked everything twice over and couldn't flip any more switches or click any more locks into place, she sat on her tweed patterned living room chair. The cushion gave way beneath her weight and she allowed herself to sink into the comfort of the chair like an old friend. Silence filled the room. In moments like this, Fiery often thought about the ups and downs of life, how it flows like a river, sometimes so quickly and exciting that you can't keep up, but that's all you want to do; chase the current. At the same time, other moments seem to trawl on and sweep the worthy and true feelings up and away, leaving you empty-handed.

Lucy broke her trance, dropping her luggage onto the living room floor with a loud, "thud." Seeing the quizzical look on her aunt's face, Lucy automatically got her luggage and laid it in front of Fiery. She unlocked and opened the suitcase for inspection.

Fiery checked Lucy's luggage, but it only took a quick peek to know she was missing several things. They had gone over what they would need for the trip for weeks. Fiery stopped and looked at her, saying, "I see your bathing suits, but where are your shorts and halter tops?"

Surprised, Lucy darted back into the bedroom. Embarrassed, she returned with the items. "They were on my bed. I was sitting on them!"

They planned to check their bags with the porter and carry their makeup cases on the train. After making sure they securely locked their suitcases, Fiery had Lucy place them near the front door while she went through her written checklist, making sure everything was in order. After all, they were going to be gone twelve whole days. She put her list down and called her neighbor, Mrs. Black, thanked her for watching their house while they were out of town, and assured her she would receive a Florida postcard.

It was still four and a half hours before the Checkered Cab arrived. Sitting in the living room, they wore their best traveling clothes. Respectable people traveled in their finest clothes, which had to be modest, clean and pressed. Women always wore dresses, and men wore a suit coat and tie.

Speaking more to herself than to Aunt Fiery, Lucy quietly said, "I'm disappointed I can't visit New York City."

"But you will see the Queen City, you know the ever famous, Cincinnati, Ohio," replied Aunt Fiery with a wink.

With a slight eye roll, Lucy replied, "I really wanted to fly in an airplane. Have you ever been in a plane?"

"No," said Fiery, continuing, "I was looking forward to my first plane ride too. When I called Capital Airlines, they told me we could travel through New York for no additional charge. I even requested reservations on one of those new jet planes! That's when the reservation agent told me the jet service to Jacksonville wasn't available until December."

"To think I could have flown on a jet airplane," Lucy wistfully remarked. "That sounds like a big tickle." Lucy knew her aunt disapproved of her slang, but Aunt Fiery could handle it; after all, her name was "Fiery"!

Fiery ignored her use of the phrase and continued, "The representative told me we would fly on a Viscount Turboprop aircraft and stay overnight in New York. Then, a similar plane could have taken us non-stop to Jacksonville. The Capital agent proudly told me that the aircraft was the newest in their fleet. Well, that didn't seem to matter."

Fiery went on, "When I heard last month a Capital Airlines Vickers Viscount plane crashed in Maryland, I changed our plans. Thank goodness the airlines refunded our money so that I could make our travel plans with the railroad."

"I'm excited to visit Cincinnati." Lucy added, "But for one month, I read library books about New York City. The next week, I had to ask the librarian for information about Cincinnati. I laughed when she asked me if I knew where I was going."

"At least Sylvia gave me a three-month wedding notice. In the past, she only gave me a week or two."

There was a long pause in the conversation before Lucy commented, "You promised to tell me about Aunt Sylvia's divorces. Can you start now?"

Fiery checked the time on her silver wristwatch. It was ten minutes to three. They still had three hours before their cab arrived. In a strict and harsh tone, her aunt replied, "Okay, but absolutely no repeating these stories to anyone. Understand? Especially your Aunt Sylvia!"

Excitedly Lucy murmured, "Cross my heart, hope to die, stick a needle in my eye." While saying those words she made the sign of the cross over her heart.

Her aunt chuckled, commenting, "We'll hope nobody dies, or whatever, but where should I begin?"

Without hesitation and in one breath, Lucy answered, "Of course you have to start at the very beginning. We have lots of time, so give me all the details."

Fiery leaned back in the worn living room chair, saying, "Since we'll be traveling a few days, I'll start at the real beginning." After pausing for a moment to think, she began telling her story. "In the fall of 1941, your Uncle Alex worked at Buehl Sons Company as a master tool and die maker. There was a great demand for skilled tradespeople like him. They manufactured the essential landing gear component for the B-24 Liberator bomber airplane.

"The B-24 airplanes were being assembled over in Ypsilanti Township. They considered parts like the ones Alex manufactured, part of the war effort. Sometimes he worked twelve and fourteen hours a day, six to seven days a week; I worked as a bookkeeper in their accounting department. Some weeks I worked ten hours a day which included Saturdays because they were mandatory."

Lucy carefully listened. Glancing at her watch, her aunt continued saying, "I belonged to the Daughters of Isabella at our Catholic Church.

During those times, one of our major projects was to sell war bonds; later, I would also sell war bonds when working at Buehl Sons. My friends from church helped me load the forty-one with flags, buntings, and patriotic posters. We'd drive to a war armament plant for a scheduled bond drive. Guys too young or old for military service set up a long table with chairs for us and also brought in our materials.

"The plant employees would hang a giant banner above our table that read, *Buy a Share in America... Defense Savings Bonds and Stamps*. Four or five of us girls would sit at the tables offering free coffee to the factory workers and sell them war bonds. The U.S. bond organizers always gave me money and ration coupons to buy any available coffee or tea for these events. On rare occasions, they gave me ration coupons for sugar. My mother-in-law had beehives and always filled up a container with honey for me to use at the bond drive. I'd let everyone know they could get a squirt for their coffee or tea if they purchased bonds.

"Workers who bought war bonds with at least ten percent of every paycheck became Ten Percent Club members. Those individuals always got honey squirted in their drink. When a factory's total workforce was Ten Percent Club members, the government gave their building a special minuteman flag. Those flags flew over a plant to display their employees' patriotism. We sold many bonds during those drives."

Lucy interrupted, "I'm not trying to be rude, Aunt Fiery, but what does that have to do with Aunt Sylvia?"

"I appreciate you referring to her as your aunt, even though you're not related. You're a respectful young woman, always have been." Fiery leaned over and patted Lucy's knee as a gesture for her good manners.

"Sylvia is my best friend who is a year older. Be patient, and let me explain. You'll see this has everything to do with Aunt Sylvia, especially since she looks a lot younger than me."

Fiery readjusted her position on the chair and continued saying, "There were three girls in her family, and she was the youngest. Sylvia was born in 1916 in Cleveland, Ohio. Her mother worked in the principal's office in one of the city's elementary schools. A carpenter by trade, her alcoholic father seldom worked. When Sylvia was two years old, her father hopped a freight train leaving Cleveland and abandoned his family.

After three months of waiting for him to return, her mother moved the girls to her parent's hometown of Toms River, New Jersey. Once Sylvia's mom settled in Toms River, no one ever heard from her father again.

"Her mother was poor but proud. When her girls direly needed food, her mom would put a bow in Sylvia's long blond hair, dress her up in her most threadbare clothes, and give her a note for a store's owner; her mother told her where to go. In the store, she handed a piece of paper to the proprietor. The note read, 'Please, Sir, could I have any extra food that's going bad? My family is hungry.' When the owner was reading the note, her mother told Sylvia to look up at him with her sad big blue eyes."

"She was six, but she knew what begging was, and it embarrassed her. Most times, she left with a large bag of food. You know, Lucy, that made an impression in Sylvia's life."

As she thought about what her aunt said, Lucy walked over to the window and looked outside, hoping to find a waiting cab.

Her aunt smiled and said, "We've got near two hours."

"Go on with your story, auntie."

Fiery continued, "One afternoon, while selling war bonds, she told me her life story. In New Jersey during the 1920s, roller skating was popular, and she was a talented skater. Her skating helped her to escape poverty. During those years, the city's dirt roads were being reconstructed. The streets soon became modern cement boulevards. Skaters glided on those new streets, unaware of cars, trucks, motorcycles, and streetcars.

"Sylvia remarked, 'Skaters like me felt that these new cement roads were our domain, even if we panicked the motor vehicle operators.' Large groups of men, women, and children met in downtown Toms River. To show who owned the road, they made human chains across the width of the roadway while skating. They rolled along at their own pace, ignoring the blaring horns of the drivers and their angry shouts. The skaters took over the road.

"One time, a driver trying to maneuver around the skaters nearly hit one of them. She told me, 'That is where I learned how to yell out curse words!' Business owners complained to the city council when automobile traffic avoided the downtown streets because of the skaters. To keep them off the streets and promote public safety, the city fathers had a solution. They converted an old unheated wood floor warehouse into a skating hall."

"Wow! She sounds a little wild," Lucy said.

Her aunt grimaced, saying, "Wait, the best is yet to come! Sylvia told me how the city put overhead ceiling lights in the warehouse. Then everyone could also skate in the evening. They added a few potbelly stoves for heat during the winter months, making the dome operational year-round. Everyone she knew skated there. The 'roller dome' became the place to skate anytime of the day. Whether it rained, snowed, or was freezing outside, they could skate. Toms River roller dome's staff set up skate dancing competitions for individuals and couples. She entered both types of contests. That's when she met John, her couple partner.

"Sylvia was fourteen when she met the handsome, tall, muscular framed John. He was three years older. According to her, she was a slim girl who he could hoist and twirl high over his head. She said, 'That always impressed the judges,' and they won many couple contests.

"The following year, she married John… which was her first marriage. One year later, their son, Johnny, was born. Her husband, John, worked for his father, who was a successful building contractor. In her sixteen years, Sylvia finally felt content with her life. Her happiness was short-lived. In July 1933, the Great Depression peaked, her father-in-law's business failed, and cash became tight. They often had arguments over money, causing them to separate in November 1934."

Her niece asked, "She was a mother at eighteen?"

"Wait," said her aunt. "Six months later, they reconciled and soon found out she was again pregnant. In February 1936, she gave birth to their second son named James. Because John was without work and no income was coming in, he left. They were a burden to him, so instead of doing the right thing, he abandoned them. That's when she filed for divorce. Divorced at twenty years old with two small boys and no income, they moved in with her mom, who lived alone.

"Sylvia's mother worked at a cannery, and she soon joined her. The two women also took in washing and ironing to make ends meet. On the evening of May 6, 1937, she heard tragic news on the radio. In nearby Lakehurst, New Jersey, the Hindenburg airship crashed. Everyone rushed to see the accident site except Sylvia. She had a brainstorm. She told her mom her idea and took the twelve dollars and thirty-seven cents she had saved. The following morning, she woke up very early and went to the corner grocery store. There she purchased different hoagie meats, assorted breads, mustard, relish, and pickles. Arriving home, she started making an assortment of sandwiches.

"Her mother woke little six-year-old Johnny to help. Soon the three of them were busy making hoagie sandwiches and wrapping them in the white butcher paper she bought. With a butcher's pencil, they wrote on the wrapper the kind of sandwich. Finally finished, they packed all their hoagies into two large picnic baskets. A neighbor agreed to watch the boys while they boarded an overflowing train to nearby Lakehurst. When they arrived, the two women popped open their picnic baskets and sold sandwiches to the throngs of hungry gawkers who rushed to see the airship's burnt frame."

"Aunt Sylvia saw the burnt airship?" Lucy asked.

"Yes, and after only two hours, Sylvia's hoagies sold out. She made a profit of thirty-four dollars! Her mother wanted to take a taxicab home, but your aunt nixed that idea. She told me that story many times. I remembered her saying, 'It was the first time I felt rich.' She liked that sense of security money brought."

"Wait a minute, was she really there by the blimp that caught on fire? Are you making this up?" Asked Lucy.

"That question you can ask your aunt," said Fiery. "In June 1940, she read in the *Toms River Newspaper* the Lend-Lease Act had ramped up production at war armament companies in Detroit. Factory jobs there were abundant. This new employment opportunity for higher wages caused her to consider moving to the city. Sylvia and her two boys had moved from her mother's house to a small one-bedroom apartment when she found a better job making donuts at a local bakery. She still didn't make enough money to support them."

"Leaving her sons with her mother in September, she made the trek. In Detroit, she found a cheap *ladies-only* boarding house, moved in, and bought a *Detroit Times* newspaper. Searching the want ads, she found the DeSoto plant had several openings for unskilled factory workers. She applied for the job. Three days later, they interviewed and hired her on the spot."

"So, is this when you met Aunt Sylvia?" asked Lucy.

"Soon," said Fiery. "Her first job was drilling out rivets in an airplane's wings the inspector circled as bad. Right after her, the riveters came to install new ones. She was bored, but kept reminding herself how much she earned, especially with all the overtime. After two months, they promoted her to making the bottom bay segments of the bomber. Assembling those sections required the women to stretch and kneel in confined spaces, and not all could do that work. Managers knew athletic young girls did these jobs best.

"Your Aunt Sylvia was a perfect match for that work. She and all the other girls, working on the bay sections, received a special increase in their hourly wage. She often recalled how well that job paid. In May 1941, the DeSoto plant started to sell United States government war bonds. Her boss walked up to her one day and said, 'You're pretty, you like to talk, and I bet you could sell a lot of war bonds.' She said to him, 'What are those?'"

Lucy wondered, when she'd learn the spicy details? She rose out of her chair and looked out the window for a waiting taxi. Seeing none, she sat in a different chair, asking, "What does this have to do with you meeting her?"

"Everything," said her aunt. Not to be interrupted, Fiery continued, "Her boss informed her, 'We'll be in the war soon, and wars are very expensive. Money raised from selling bonds will win the war for us.' She told him, 'I'm willing to try it, but I still don't understand what a war bond is?' So, he gave her a quick lesson. Two weeks later, Sylvia started splitting her time between the bomber bay section gang and selling war bonds. While doing both jobs, she received the same high pay rate.

"I remember meeting her right after Labor Day 1941 at the DeSoto-Warren Plant. The factory workers there were building fuselage sections for the B-26 Martin Marauder Bombers. I was told to meet a woman there named Sylvia. She was to sell bonds with me. Unlike me, she worked there. People described her as having a frank personality, beautiful, and zany."

"We had one crazy fun time selling war bonds! She laughed, hearing how I bribed the 'ten-percenters' by giving them a squirt of honey. Then Sylvia admitted how she persuaded them with a kiss on the cheek and hugged some of the 'great' looking fellas. Standard bond drives were usually a constant flow of people. The men came in waves, and the time in between, we always welcomed.

"During one of those slow periods, she told me her life story. That's when I knew she could be a wonderful friend. Right after another wave of laborers, she caught me gawking at her, and she looked annoyed. I smiled at her, saying, 'Do you know who you look like?' Irritated by my question, she blurted out, 'No, who?' Not intimidated by her, I looked her up and down, and said, like Carole Lombard.

"Other employees listening to our conversation agreed. They described Sylvia as prettier. Carole Lombard was the movie screen's latest sex-symbol. Her beauty and acting skills made her a famous actress. It didn't hurt that her husband was the actor, Clark Gable himself a heartthrob to countless women.

"Sylvia looked just like her, and was eight years younger. She could easily pass for Carole's baby sister. On her way home that evening, Sylvia stopped at a newsstand and bought a copy of *Photoplay Magazine* because it had pictures of the actress. The next Saturday afternoon, she went to a beauty shop taking the magazine with her. She told the beauty operator, 'Do my hair like Carole's.' The following week, I returned to the DeSoto Plant to help sell war bonds, and that's when I saw Sylvia's new hairdo. I told her she looked beautiful, and our friendship was born."

Fiery paused for a minute and looked at her wristwatch. She said, "It's only 5:31 p.m., We still have a half hour."

At that moment, someone knocked on their front door, and Lucy bounced to her feet and rushed to open it. There stood a gentleman wearing a yellow barracks cover. His hat had a band of small black and white checked squares around the bottom edge. He tipped his cap saying, "Did you call for a cab?"

The cabbie in his early forties had a medium-build, but moved with the finesse of a station porter. He removed the four bags from the house and placed each on the front stoop. He picked up each piece of luggage with skill, placing them under his arms while holding the makeup cases in his hands. He jumped past the steps with one hop and landed on the ground, walking towards his cab.

The cab operator put their luggage in the taxi's trunk. Fiery was upset the taxi arrived a full half-hour early. She then thought how an early dinner might help settle their travel jitters. She took her handbag from the coffee table, opened it, checking for their train tickets. In another pocket, she confirmed that her cash and traveler's checks were there.

Satisfied she had everything needed, Fiery took a house key from her red purse. She walked to the open front door while placing the handbag under her arm. Turning around, she looked over the room. Seeing her niece's sweater and beige purse lying on the couch, her aunt called Lucy back to the house; seeing the items, she blushed, picked them up, and with excitement walked out the front door like a princess. She glided down the steps to the waiting cab.

After locking the door, Fiery turned the knob, making sure it was properly closed. Satisfied, she walked to the waiting green and yellow Checkered Cab. She settled in the spacious rear seat, saying, "Michigan Central Depot, please."

The taxi driver was uncertain of their destination, for the city of Detroit had two train terminals. The name Fiery had given, Michigan Central Depot, no longer existed. Three years earlier, the depot had acquired a new title, Michigan Central Station. Passengers traveling on New York Central trains boarded at this station. He needed clarification and asked, "Ma'am, are you traveling on a New York Central train?"

In harmony, both women answered, "Yes!"

Their destination confirmed, the driver said, "Michigan Central Station, here we come."

He placed the vehicle in gear. The taxi moved forward and continued to gain momentum as it sped along Appleton Street. The two women turned and watched their house become smaller, then looked at each other chuckling. As if reading one another's mind, together they said, "We're off!"

Chapter 3

Almost Famous

In the cab, the women looked out their separate windows. Each watched the daily lives of strangers passing by. On the advice of her neighbors, Fiery planned for a one-hour ride to the Corktown Station. Corktown was the neighborhood located west of Detroit's downtown district. Many Irish immigrants settled there after immigrating from Ireland's County Cork.

Most commuters arrived at the terminal one hour before their train's departure. Fiery wondered how they could pass the time. Their train didn't leave for five more hours.

Still upset that the cab arrived early, Fiery vowed to remain positive. Her thoughts turned to the Morris-Markin Company-built taxi they rode in. The cab's spacious rear interior reminded her of the large back seat in Alex's forty-one Chevrolet. However, this taxi was newer and more comfortable. It made her feel like she was riding in a fine coach.

"Excuse me, ma'am," said the taxi driver.

Startled from her thoughts, she answered, "Yes?!"

"Do you have an angry neighbor always in a hurry?" the cab operator asked.

The blunt question surprised Fiery. Sarcastically she answered, "I'm sure we do; I just don't know who they are."

"Ma'am, sorry, the way my question came out. It's just someone pulled out of a driveway in a new pink and white Ford on your street and almost hit me! Then he rode my tail until I got to your house. And, passed me like a bat out of h--- you know what I mean!"

Lucy looked at her aunt. They both knew it was the husband of their pregnant neighbor, Jan, but said nothing. In the distance, they saw the eighteen-story office tower of the Central Station. It was 6:15 p.m. Turning off at Fourteen Street onto Vernor Avenue, the taxi continued through Roosevelt Park, stopping at the station's west side entrance.

The meter read two dollars and forty-five cents. Fiery handed Lucy three one-dollar bills and told her to pay the cabbie after he placed their luggage on the sidewalk.

"Be sure to say thank you as you give him the money," her aunt instructed, "And don't ask for change."

The driver opened Fiery's door, and they exited the cab. He continued to the trunk and unloaded their bags onto the sidewalk.

Lucy stood by the curb, looked at her aunt with wide eyes, and whispered, "A fifty-five cent tip?"

That amount was considered a generous tip. Fiery was certain the driver would signal the red cap, that they were big tippers, and the baggage handler would want to help with their luggage. Lucy paid the cab driver as instructed.

She received a smile with a loud, "Thank you, Miss," from the driver. Fiery noticed the casual high hand salute the cab driver gave to the porter. A head nod was the red cap's reply. In a blink of an eye, the red-capped porter was there. The porter confirmed their destination while stacking their luggage on his two-wheel dolly. Once done, he started walking towards the depot and over to New York Central's passenger check-in counter, making sure both women followed. Lucy turned to follow, and her eyes grew wide as she saw the main entrance to the building.

They walked into the grandiose building through the sizeable mahogany-trimmed bronze doors. They found themselves in the main concourse, which led to a massive waiting area with marble walls, white-colored tiled bricks, and massive soaring arches held up by fourteen marble pillars. Both women gasped at this majestic structure. They soon arrived at the ornate ticket counter. Fiery received a pleasant thank you as she tipped the baggage handler a quarter. Once checked in, the two women walked out into the middle of the main hall five hours before their train's departure. Her niece stared up and around at the vast interior of Michigan Central Station.

Many shops bordered both sides of the large concourse. There was a snack bar with marble counters, a men's smoking room, and the ladies' reading lounge. On the other side were rows of windows for the railroad's ticketing office. Further away was a restaurant with a high vaulted ceiling and other businesses. Lucy studied the elaborate ceiling while slowly turning around.

She was in awe of everything. The far end of the immense concourse was two hundred twenty feet away. The space was one-hundred feet wide. It had a sixty-foot-high arched ceiling with copper framed skylights. Built forty-five years earlier, the depot was sadly past its prime. Fiery's eyes could see a magnificent building sadly needing maintenance and cleaning.

Rows and rows of dark walnut wooden benches ran the length of the concourse. The niece never spotted the chipping paint, the wear on the wood seats, the cracked marbled walls, or the cobwebs on the ornate light fixtures. Fiery tapped her niece on the shoulder and pointed to the restaurant on the concourse's west-side. After dinner, they would have more time to explore the cavernous building. On their way to the restaurant, the women stopped in the ladies' room to powder their noses.

They walked into the large and elegant bistro. With its vaulted ceiling, Lucy noticed the floors made of Welsh quarry tiles. Like the concourse's pillars, they made the counters of the same white marble. The restaurant, which could accommodate two hundred people, looked empty. Fifteen individuals were dining at several white linen-covered tables. Her niece enjoyed the atmosphere and ambiance that surrounded them. Fiery kept her comments to herself, not wanting to diminish Lucy's experience. The service and food quality she later rated less than satisfactory.

After an hour and a half, they finished dinner and discussed where to meet in the waiting area after Lucy's self-guided tour. Once agreed upon, her niece departed to explore the depot on her own. Her aunt walked outside and stopped left of the bronze doors. She stood there in the evening light, staring at the front parking lot.

Her mind traveled back to when Alex came home on leave, and she met him here. She had parked the forty-one Chevrolet with its hood up in the air in that parking spot. She recollected how her husband taught her how to do that and smiled. He told her, 'Police will never ticket a woman with a broken car.'

Hundreds of uniformed soldiers were there. Yet, she picked him out at once. Fiery remembered how they embraced, the kiss he gave her, and what he whispered in her ear.

Tears rolled down Fiery's cheek, and she sternly told herself enough! Drying her eyes and cheeks with a handkerchief, she walked back into the concourse. She made her way over to where she agreed to meet Lucy; Fiery sat on the dark wooden bench to wait.

This was the exact spot where she met Alex many years earlier. Fiery stared up at the cobweb-covered ornate brass light fixture as her mind drifted back to a happier time. Her thoughts were soon interrupted by Lucy's who was sitting on the bench across from her.

Lucy exclaimed, "Wow, this is some pad!" Seeing the look on her aunt's face, she corrected herself, saying, "I mean building."

Although it felt like a few minutes, she was gone for half an hour. "Well," asked Fiery, "What did you see?"

With hands pointing to each part of the station, Lucy was eager to explain. She said, "That's the arcade, this is the passenger waiting area, down that hall, there's a women's bathroom with bathing facilities. You send telegrams at the Western Union office over there, buy postcards at that stand, use one of twelve pay telephones all on one wall over there, and around that corner, there are twenty private payphones booths. You can close the door and make your call sitting down!"

Finally stopping to catch her breath, Lucy continued, "There's another newsstand over there by a drugstore next to the cigar shop, a barbershop, and a private men's smoking room. I looked inside, and nobody was in there. The ladies-only reading room has big soft chairs. Let's go sit in the lady's reading room!"

Her aunt smiled, saying, "I'm fine right here, thank you."

"When I came back, you had a funny smile on your face. What were you thinking?"

Startled by the comment, she replied, "Just remembering the dream I had two nights ago. My…" She abruptly stopped talking, not wanting to share her secret.

Lucy chimed in, guessing, "I wondered why you called Wally, telling him you would drive forty-one home. You told me; you would never drive that car again."

Her aunt responded, "Well, enough of my dreams. We have over three hours before our train's departure."

Her niece said, "Good, tell me about Aunt Sylvia's hairstyle and divorces."

Remembering where she left off, her aunt commented, "Let's start again where Aunt Sylvia had her hair done so she would look like the actress Carole Lombard."

Lucy interrupted, asking, "Are you making this story up, or did this really happen?"

Fiery grinned, saying, "Lucy, let me finish my story. There are things I can't believe myself. Now, where was I?"

"Okay, December 1941, Sylvia and I made a great team. We were outgoing, good-looking young women selling a lot of war bonds. Everyone wanted us at their bond drive. After the attack on Pearl Harbor, we found out Carole Lombard began doing bond drives. She even did a couple in her home state of Indiana. The bosses thought it might be a great publicity stunt for Sylvia to meet the actress in person and sell war bonds with her, especially since she looked so much like the actress!"

"When her boss told her of the idea, she was so excited that, after work that day, she took a streetcar to Hudson's Department Store in downtown Detroit and blew a week's pay on a couple of fashionable dresses. She made sure to choose dresses that Carole would be proud to wear. The meeting between them was the idea of someone at the war bond office and not Sylvia's boss.

"As Sylvia tells the story, they gave her ten dollars to take a cab to Michigan Central Depot, meet a war bond official, and hop a train to Fort Wayne, Indiana. To Sylvia's surprise, the cab driver knew exactly where to drop her. She wore one of her new 'Carole' dresses and hairdo. They would do a bond drive the next day, and she would return home.

"While waiting on the platform for the war bond guy, she heard whistles and catcalls. She turned around to see soldiers boarding a train car two tracks over. Seeing them, she gave a big smile, a hand wave, and blew them a kiss. She almost caused a riot when many of the boys started yelling and screaming. They even tried to jump off the train!

"She wasn't sure what to do. The war bond guy appeared out of nowhere, with two red caps who gently grabbed her arms. They guided her through the crowd, escorting her to the train. Onboard, she noticed other passengers straining to get a glimpse of her. Someone said, 'Who's that?' She heard another person answer, 'I know, it's Carole Lombard!'"

"Wait, are you saying Aunt Sylvia looked like a movie star?" inquired Lucy.

"Yes, and there's more. The government officials wanted to surprise the public with the two look-alike women selling bonds. So, they arranged private travel accommodations for her. She took a seat in her reserved personal coach, thinking this will be fun! Arriving in Fort Wayne, Indiana, she was nervous and started to doubt herself. She thought maybe this wasn't such a good idea. What if people insulted, mocked, or didn't like her? How should she act or react?

"She was dropped off at her hotel and told to go to the front desk. She gathered up all of her courage to approach the front desk and explained to the clerk her reason for being there. The hotel's manager came running out of the backroom. He looked her over and grabbed her arm, saying, 'Come with me.' He took her to a first-floor private suite, hidden from public view, and knocked on the door. When it opened, she saw Carole Lombard sitting at a table, reviewing the rally itinerary with a couple of government representatives.

"Still clutching her arm, the manager walked her over to the actress and said, 'Excuse me, Miss Lombard.' Before Sylvia could even say hello, Carole jumped up and squealed, 'Where's that snapper?' She hugged your aunt and gleefully said, 'I'm so glad you're here! I have no idea what the hell I'm doing!' The photographer arrived and started snapping pictures.

'No,' your aunt protested, saying, 'I just got off the train!' She forgot who she was talking to and bit her tongue.

"Carole smiled, saying, 'Nonsense, honey, you look great. And, I love your dress!' The actress put her arm around Sylvia's waist and told her to do the same. Carole had several carefully posed pictures taken from different angles. The actress had a scar on her left cheek from broken glass during a car accident that almost ended her career. Plastic surgery, makeup, and skillful posing made her scar invisible on film."

Fiery paused for a moment, then said, "Sylvia told me this story a hundred times. Carole sternly told the snapper, 'Get those developed now, and bring them back to me.' She then asked your aunt about her trip and how things were in Detroit. Carole introduced Sylvia to her mother and her press agent, who took a liking to her. After about an hour of small talk and laughter, Carole's agent whispered something in her ear.

"Carole nodded her head and giggled, saying, 'In my next picture, there's a part for a girl to play my younger sister. We both agree you're perfect for the role. Do you think a project like that would interest you?' Stunned, your aunt could only say one word: 'Sure.' The agent replied to her, 'We return to Hollywood on the 16th. I'll set up a screen test, wire you the date, location, and arrange for transportation.'

"The actress told her she would make sure the studio bosses knew she approved. Sylvia told me later, 'Even if it was bull crap, she loved hearing it.' The photographer walked in holding a big yellow manila envelope. Pulling photos from the folder, she scrutinized each one and asked your aunt which she liked best. After inspecting them, she finally chose one. Carole picked up a fountain pen and scribbled on it, *double your trouble, Love, Ma.*

"She firmly said, 'Have a wire photo made and send it to the studio in care of Clark.' The snapper nodded, putting the picture in the envelope, and hurried out the door. Sylvia couldn't believe what she was seeing and hearing. He had sent the picture to Carole's husband, Clark Gable, the famous actor. Your aunt read in a fan magazine that they had just bought a farm. Since their farm purchase, they delighted in calling each other Ma and Pa.

"Soon, a server brought dinner in for Carole, her mother, and her press agent. She asked your aunt to join them, but Sylvia declined, saying she did not want to intrude. Carole insisted and ordered dinner for her. While they ate the two continued to talk for several more hours. Interrupting them, Carole's press agent said, 'If you two are going to look glamorous before the cameras tomorrow, you better get some sleep.' Reluctantly, they agreed. After Carol gave Sylvia a peck on the cheek, they said goodnight. In her room, your aunt thought no one had ever called her glamorous."

Lucy looked in disbelief at her aunt, who grinned and continued, "After arriving at a plant for the bond drive, Carole showed Sylvia the telegram she received from Clark. It read *just what this country needs right now, two little identical screwballs running around loose.* She chuckled, saying, 'Shit, I love that big son of a bitch! I can't wait to get back and see him.'

"Fan magazines wrote how she was wacky and notoriously foul-mouthed. She exposed her true self, saying those words, in front of Sylvia. The actress was comfortable around your aunt. Sylvia told me how wonderful it was to see the real person instead of a prim and proper movie star! Carole insisted she stay an additional day for another rally, and the bond guy made the arrangements. The two women became inseparable. Each enjoyed the other's company. The rallies exceeded expectations in sales and excitement.

"When leaving for California, Carole embraced her, kissed her cheek, and thanked her for coming to Indiana. She winked at her and said, 'I'll see you in Hollywood, little sis. Don't forget that screen test. We're not bullshitting you.' Sylvia thought, how could I ever forget that, and hugged her back, saying, 'Give Clark a peck on the cheek from me.'

"She reminisced how she nearly floated to the train station and remained in a fog on her way back to Detroit. When home, she called me saying, 'Fiery, how would you like a movie star as your best friend?' She told me everything, and we spoke for hours. I told her, that's great, and wished her luck."

Fiery's face turned solemn as she shifted herself on the bench. She took a moment to gather her words before saying, "The next day was January sixteenth. The headline news was that Carole Lombard's airplane had crashed, and no one survived. Everyone, including the actress, her mother, press agent, and fifteen servicemen, perished. The plane hit a mountain in the Nevada desert. From California, Clark Gable flew to the crash site to identify the bodies.

"Rumors surfaced saying Nazi spies had shot the plane down by hiding in the desert, but there was never any evidence which proved that theory. The reason for the accident had been listed as pilot error! When Sylvia heard the news, she burst into tears. Feeling as though someone sucker-punched her in the stomach, she called in sick at the factory and stayed in bed for two days."

Lucy's expression turned sad. In a low tone, she whispered, "Did the actress really die? In a plane crash?"

With a solemn tone, her Aunt Fiery responded, "Yes, and yes. They scheduled Sylvia and me to work a bond rally on the third day. Later, she told me, Carole would've wanted her to be there. While sitting at the bond table, she absent-mindedly watched the stream of people stroll by. Your aunt, hearing the low murmur grow louder, was jolted back to reality. Someone pointed at her, and a portly woman in the crowd shrieked and fainted. One bond organizer ushered her out into the hallway. She broke free from their clutches and ran into the ladies' restroom crying. I ran after her.

"She was bent over a sink, wiping tears from her eyes. 'When Carole died, my future went with her,' she declared. That's not true, I told her, you're still young and beautiful, besides you have your two boys to think about. 'You're right, I miss my children.' She wished her sons could live with her. But, with so many war workers in Detroit, decent, affordable family housing was impossible to find.

"She proclaimed, 'All I want is what you and Alex have, love. But, if you say I'm beautiful, I will use my looks to get ahead.' We talked for a long time in that ladies' restroom. That day I learned that a best friend is a good listener who keeps your secrets in their heart forever. Two days later, she showed up for our next bond rally with a new hairstyle, and her hair dyed flaming red. 'You inspired me,' she blurted out, 'And… if anyone says I look like Rita Hayworth, I'll clobber --!' She was grinning and only half kidding when she told me that."

Lucy asked, "So how many times did she marry and divorce?"

Fiery kicked off her shoes and stretched her legs across the long wooden bench. With a beaming smile, she said, "I'm getting there. I told you she was a zany woman with many crazy ideas. It was April of forty-four and your Uncle Alex was in the Army. In the Detroit Times, Sylvia read an article about how the USO needed women between eighteen and thirty for hostesses. The United Service Organization clubs provided a wholesome meeting place for servicemen.

"The USO opened a club near the corners of Fort and Third Street by the Fort Street Union Depot, which was the Pennsylvania Railroad passenger station in Detroit. We always referred to it as Union Depot. Applying to be a hostess was your aunt's idea, and she talked me into going with her. When the man running the club found out I was married, he kindly advised me I wasn't allowed. Boy, did I get mad at him! I asked him, what kind of entertainment did he have in mind? He really got under my skin.

"The USO boss wanted her to volunteer. He knew I was her driver, and if he took her, he had to take me. He told her, if I wanted to help, I could work in the kitchen. His comment made me reach my boiling point. I was just about to give him a piece of my mind when Sylvia stopped me. 'Fiery, don't be so sensitive. Besides, maybe they'll let you cook on your car.' We both busted out laughing.

"We laughed so hard and for so long, the manager thought we were crazy. She knew how Alex and I cooked picnic lunches on forty-one's engine manifold during our day trips. With the car's small cooking space, we were only able to prepare two hotdogs and one container of beans at a time. She was mocking me, knowing it would take me days to feed all those USO soldiers using forty-one's manifold to cook on. That's why we laughed.

"On Wednesday, we started volunteering at the USO. While she served and danced with the troops, I did dishes in the back. She had overheard the boys saying, 'I wish I had a picture to send home to my folks.' The next time we volunteered, your aunt brought her Brownie box camera.

"That is when your 'almost famous movie star aunt' became the unofficial club snapper. She went around to the various groups of servicemen; Sylvia asked if they wanted their photo taken. Aunt Sylvia received some unexpected responses. Most said, 'Sure you can take my picture, only if you're in it… or if you sit on my lap… or give me a kiss.'

"Soon, she became the most photographed person in the club. Each night she delivered the film to the drugstore across the street and paid for the developing and processing cost herself. The prints were usually back within three days. She pinned them up on the club's walls, where the soldiers grabbed their pictures or took their friends' photos to them. Sylvia understood that was the least she could do for the war effort. Most servicemen wanted one last photo before being shipped overseas."

Lucy interrupted, remarking, "She did that for the servicemen? I mean, take and pay for the pictures?"

"Wait, the best is yet to come," Fiery said. "When someone didn't pick a photo up, she tried to find out who the soldier was and, after finding them, mailed their picture. She became addicted to the attention they gave her and dated a few, even though that was not allowed. She couldn't get enough of their devotion.

"When she wasn't at work, Sylvia spent more time at the USO, and military men became her main priority. Every few days, countless military personnel traveled through the city, many looking for companionship. They needed someone to listen to their stories one last time. She told me they required a lot of hand-holding, hugging, and sometimes necking, but never sex. That was off-limits and saved for marriage.

"They would show her pictures of their parents, girlfriends, and even their beloved dog or cat pictures which made them feel good. Some talked about how they were afraid of going off to war. Others broke down and cried. Quite a few believed they were never returning. Many servicemen wanted a photo of Sylvia and asked her to write them.

"Your Aunt Sylvia kept a file of all the boys she wrote. At her peak, your zany aunt was writing to over thirty-three military men. Some letters came back undelivered; they were the ones who died. Sylvia grieved over several having become attached to them. Others she could not remember, only knowing they met once.

"I recall her telling me, 'They all had hopes and dreams for the future.' When she learned one had died, she remembered his dream, 'That's the guy that wanted to go to college, become a doctor, buy a fishing boat, design cars, and now he's never going to get the chance to do any of it.' We cried.

"Her bond with others lasted through the mid-1950s. Through the years, she received many Christmas cards from them. When the greeting cards stopped coming, she joked, 'I bet their wives put a kibosh on the card!'"

Lucy was becoming eager for the spicy parts of the story, asking, "Did she ever jump-on, I mean marry any of these service guys?"

"Oh! I forgot about Bert," Fiery said, "Why do I remember that name? Sylvia connected with him years before we volunteered at the USO. I met him twice. That was my first time as her matron-of-honor. Relationships during the war years were extremely intense. She cared enough to marry him; Bert became her second husband during a brief ceremony at the justice of the peace.

"Bert was a handsome man. He held the rank of sergeant in the Army, and they married a few days before he shipped out. After they married, Alex and I took a road trip with forty-one to Michigan's Upper Peninsula. We wanted them to have a shot at a honeymoon, and while we were gone, they lodged at our house.

"I was on the front stoop of our house when I met Bert a second time. He left for one of the overseas theaters of war later that same day. Three months later, Sylvia received a telegram stating her husband died. I don't think she cried. Sylvia told me she felt it was her duty to marry a soldier before leaving for foreign shores. Many women married for that exact reason during war times.

"Sylvia resentfully described her husband Bert's death to me, saying, 'He was killed in action. I don't even know what job he had in civilian life.' After a few years, she met another serviceman and fell in love. Before Robert left for overseas, she became his wife. It was her third marriage and my second time as her matron-of-honor.

"As the spouse of a serviceman, she received a twenty-eight-dollar monthly allotment check. Patriotic women seldom married servicemen just to receive a check. We sometimes referred to them as allotment Annie. No one, including Sylvia, wanted that name. The radio news reported one dishonest woman was married to six servicemen at the same time.

"Sylvia rarely wrote to Robert. She confided to me, 'With the distance between us, I wondered if I made the right decision by marrying him. I've met another soldier, and I know I really love him.' Sylvia wrote to Robert and requested a divorce. When listening to her true confession, I became disgusted with her. But her lifestyle captivated me.

"Federal government laws made it impossible for women to divorce overseas servicemen. She had to start divorce proceedings when Robert came home on leave in February 1945. She was married three times, widowed once, and now divorced twice. Here was my best girlfriend fooling around with everyone in brown shoes.

"Later, she found out Robert held a grudge against her for not writing to him while he was overseas. They never met when he returned from overseas. She divorced him within a month. Once her divorce was final, she decided to not carry through with her marriage to the serviceman she had 'really loved.'"

Lucy's face couldn't hide her shock as she repeated, "Widowed once, divorced twice."

"On VJ Day (Victory over Japan Day, September 2, 1945), the DeSoto Warren plant where Sylvia worked called a meeting for all the women employees. The bosses thanked them for their factory service work then announced they were laying everyone off. The news shocked her! She lost the best job she ever had. Now jobless, she made plans to leave Detroit and move back to New Jersey.

"Five days later, I drove Sylvia right here to Michigan Central Depot. We cried out there in the parking lot when we said our goodbyes. She invited me to come live with her, and her family, in New Jersey. I told her, 'I come with the forty-one.' She said, 'That's okay, but there's no garage.' I told her, 'You know me and forty-one! I could never live anywhere without a garage.'"

Fiery looked at her watch and then laughed to herself, finding they still had two hours to wait. She continued saying, "Lucy, here's the funny part. Two weeks later, Sylvia wrote to me, 'Don't come to New Jersey.' She had already moved south to Florida. It turns out she couldn't abide by her mother's rules and hated the thought of another miserable winter in the north. Only her youngest son, Jim, would go with her. Sylvia's oldest child, John, refused to go and wanted to live with his grandmother.

"When I read her letter, I thought that's what I loved most about Sylvia… her spontaneity. Right after Thanksgiving in 1949, she sent a letter asking if I would be her matron-of-honor. That's why I sent you on a New Year's vacation to Uncle Smitty and Aunt Marge's house. Your holiday coincided with Sylvia's marriage. She was getting married for the fourth time, New Year's Day in Jacksonville! I traveled to Florida and back by Greyhound bus, just to be my girlfriend's matron-of-honor for the third time.

"Sylvia had found a waitress job at a beach diner in Jacksonville when she moved to Florida. Over the next five years, she became good friends with the owner of the restaurant, Roy. Three months after his wife died in a car accident, he proposed to her. Upon accepting Roy's offer, she fired two waitresses because of their catty comments about her marrying the owner. He was a generous man and bought her a new Cadillac convertible as an engagement present.

"Having no children of his own, he adopted her son Jimmy and promised to send him to the best private college prep academy in the state. When I arrived for her 1950 New Year's Day wedding, she told me, 'This is the happiest I've been in my life!' In July of fifty-five, Roy died suddenly at seventy-three of a massive heart attack. That's when Sylvia's happily ever after ended."

Pausing for a moment now in deep thought, Fiery continued saying, "You know, Lucy, I never realized until just now, your Aunt Sylvia was widowed twice and divorced twice at thirty-nine. Whenever she divorced or became a widow, your aunt always took back her maiden name. She had spent five happy years with Roy. When he died, she kept his surname of Pompenali. I think she really loved him.

"A year after he passed, she wrote saying how she loves owning and running a business. The restaurant gave her the sense of security she never had. That security gave her son Jimmy his chance to go to college. I believe he graduates next year, and I'm sure you'll meet him at the wedding. He's studying to be a doctor.

"It surprised me when Sylvia wrote she was marrying again. Her new husband is another older gentleman named Mike. So, try not to look too shocked when you meet him, okay?"

"So, how old is he?"

Her aunt responded, "Well, she is a year older than I am, so that makes her forty-three."

Lucy's mouth dropped, saying, "Married five times at forty-three. Wow! She is a zany woman Aunt Fiery; how come you never married again?"

"I don't know how old Mike is," said Fiery. Answering her niece's question, she said, "But I can tell you why I never remarried. Alex was a real guy. He loved the world. He was proud to be an American. He believed in God and his country. We believed in the same things. I loved your Uncle Alex, and he loved me. I feel lucky and blessed to have found him.

"He once told me when he looked at me, he saw a halo surrounding my auburn hair. When I saw him looking at me with his small grin, I would melt. He had a classy chassis."

"True love is a thousand things one person does for another because they want to. It's the person you share your most guarded secrets with, knowing they will never reveal them. Love and devotion are secret bonds you share. Alex's love and devotion made my dreams a reality. "

Fiery paused to get Lucy's attention, saying, "But I never understood how great that love was until he died. My true love was gone. I didn't want to live without him. That's when I learned our death and special dreams are forever. What has kept me alive is my dream of reuniting with my husband, our dog, Tiger, and driving the forty-one to our special green space. I believe the Almighty gave me the courage and strength to survive. God may have taken Alex away, but I truly believe He will give him back to me in the next life."

Fiery started putting on her shoes. She looked and smiled at Lucy. With a lighter tone, she said, "I believe we have no control over when we are born and when we die. The only person we are guaranteed to spend the rest of our life with is ourselves. So, we better get along with ourselves."

"I chose to live my life as healthy as possible, and I hope to enjoy my entire lifetime. Memories of my past I preserve, but I keep informed of the things going on in the present. I need to be flexible when planning future events because things I can't control will always be there. And, I make an effort to bring happiness to others every day." She smiled at her niece, saying, "We still have one-and-a-half hours left."

Fiery stood, stretched her body, and retrieved the pink envelope from her purse, and said, "Oh! And, thank you for not saying anything to the cab driver about the driving skills of our neighbor, Mr. Bryniarski. I saw his wife Jan today, and she looked like she is ready to deliver anytime. Now let's see, departure 11:20 p.m., Monday, June 22nd, 1959. Lucy, what do you say we go get a Nehi at the soda counter? Then you can take me exploring! Okay?"

Lucy acknowledged the compliment with a nod, and said, "Yes!" to the soda shop.

Returning the itinerary papers to her handbag, Fiery looked at her niece and said, "Which way to our new favorite soda shop?"

Her niece looked and pointed to the far end of the concourse. Meanwhile, Fiery turned sideways, and in one flowing action, lifted her skirt above her knee! Lucy looked back at her aunt to see her actions and dropped her jaw in disbelief! Then she realized her aunt was imitating the soft drink advertisements for Nehi soda. Those ad campaigns always showed a woman's nylon-clad leg with her skirt pulled above the knee. Imitating her aunt's sense of humor, Lucy also raised her skirt to her knees.

They looked at each other, and together shouted, "Knee-high!" The two giggling women linked arms, and started walking towards the soda counter.

Chapter 4

Village Time

Thaddeus and Janette Bryniarski moved into their home on the 8600 block of Appleton Street in Dearborn Township in 1956, just before their daughter Denise was born. Each of their parents was first-generation Polish-Americans. They grew up in similar homes where they only spoke the Polish language. Each understands, speaks, and writes the language. Their parents always stressed the need for them to assimilate into their new American culture. One way was speaking only English when out in public.

They used the English names of Ted and Jan so that they would fit in. He drives the twelve minutes from his house to the Ford Motor Company in Dearborn daily. While at the office this Monday, the twenty-second of June 1959, he received his wife's message; she's going into labor. Weeks earlier, he arranged to leave work when this happened. This afternoon, he bested his commute record by two whole minutes.

He later boasted that his superior driving skills were the reason he arrived in time to anyone who cared to listen. Jan felt her first contraction that morning when walking across the street. Four hours later, she knew she was in labor when her contractions were closer together. Then she called her neighbor friend, Mrs. Speiwack, asking her to watch their daughter, Denise. Arriving home, Ted helped his wife into their car and focused on his only goal, getting Jan to the clinic.

He backed his new pink and white, two-door Ford Fairlane sedan out of the driveway without looking and just missed hitting the green and yellow checkered taxi. Ted looked at his watch; it was five-twenty-six in the evening. In front of him, the cab was slowly traveling at twelve miles per hour in the middle of the street so that he couldn't pass. Frustrated at the taxi's pace, Ted rode his bumper.

Without signaling, the taxicab moved over to the left curb, stopped, and parked. The crazed father-to-be sped up his car, passing on the cab's right side. It was at that moment he heard his engine misfire and sputter. Ted looked at the car's fuel gauge to see the needle pointed to E… empty. In a hurry to arrive home, he had forgotten to stop for gas!

He knew the Fairlane's engine might soon quit, so he pulled into the first service station he came to on Joy Road. To his surprise, Jan was understanding. The gas jockey ran to greet him as he jumped out of the car. He explained his need to hurry. Ted purchased one dollar of regular fuel, knowing the three gallons was more than enough. Finally, they were on their way to Dearborn Medical Center, only stopping once for one traffic light.

During her contractions, his wife was a little less understanding. Her colorful vocabulary included a mixture of obscene Polish and English phrases. Each related to him stopping for gas. He remembered his World War II Navy Boot Camp instructor using many of those same words. He also heard them on the factory floors and in the men's room. Ted wondered, where did his wife learn such language? Jan's contractions stopped once they arrived at the medical center.

Her physician credited the cause of her contractions to false labor pains. Doctors were cautious and admitted her for a few hours of observation. That evening, which promised a bundle of joy, was about to end in disappointment. But, to everyone's surprise, later that night, Jan's contractions started again. At 11:20 p.m., she delivered a baby boy.

The new parents named their son Donald F. Bryniarski. He and his sister had loving parents. They gave their children a comfortable life growing up in an idyllic neighborhood. The family would always live on Appleton Street, but their city's name did change. In 1963 Dearborn Township added other parcels of land and incorporated them as the City of Dearborn Heights. That's when the residents began saying they were from Dearborn, a famous next-door city, home of automobile tycoon Henry Ford and his motor car company.

They attended the Catholic elementary school in their neighborhood. Don was an above-average student who loved to read and write. During junior high school, he took on minor jobs. He cut grass while on summer vacation, and during the Michigan winters, shoveled snow-covered driveways. Working these jobs taught Don the lessons of hard work, the value of a dollar, and how to manage his money, which he shared with his family.

Living in Dearborn, they often visited Greenfield Village and Museum. Ted loved attending the village's organized car shows during the summer months. He sometimes volunteered to help at Ford vintage auto shows so he and his family could get in for free. When Don turned fourteen, Ted started taking him along. The village was only five miles from their home, so getting there was easy. At sixteen, he started volunteering by himself at these antique auto shows.

While volunteering, he met many friendly vintage vehicle owners who proudly introduced him to their pride and joy. He became fond of classic automobiles, like his father. He loved the innovations that each new automobile brought to the public. Most of all, he sought to understand what drove their improvements in new models launched each year. He learned many life lessons during his summer days at Greenfield Village.

During his junior year of high school, Don still loved writing, so he took a class in shorthand. He had hopes of becoming a journalist. That same year, the faculty chose him to be on the school's newspaper staff. This resulted in him becoming serious about his note-taking and writing when working on a story. Now, whenever he volunteered, he brought his notepad and documented the wonderful stories the car owners provided.

In the summer of 1977, the tall brawny Don turned eighteen and took a part-time stock boy job at the local hardware store. On the side, he continued to mow lawns for his seven neighbors, making sure he cut the grass on Wednesday through Friday. He always wanted to have open days for what he enjoyed doing most, volunteering at The Greenfield Village's vintage auto shows. Though he only worked two days at the hardware store, his days and times changed weekly. He learned to adjust his lawn mowing schedule to accommodate his other job. As a boyish man, who would soon be a high school senior, he developed a sense of flexibility, independence, and responsibility.

Don volunteered at a unique car show that summer, featuring only Ford Model T and Model A vehicles. It was Ford Motor Company's seventy-fourth anniversary. Earlier in the year, he read a Model T book and requested to work more hours at this show. He was eager to learn more about the vehicle from their owners.

Don thought an antique car story told by the owner is better than the hardcover facts. He read that some car enthusiasts referred to Model Ts as Flivver, Leaping Lena, Jitney, and the famous Tin Lizzie. Ford manufactured this model from October 1908 to May 1927. They kept the car affordable to the American middle class. Interchangeable parts and a moving assembly line were two reasons for the low cost. The book credited this automobile with introducing travel to the nation.

The day of the car show started beautifully — a warm mid-June day. In the late morning, a sudden cool gust of wind rushed across the faces of the volunteers and exhibitors. Chilly breezes soon turned into a sustained frigid wind, blowing harder and harder. Everyone felt what was coming, but no one believed it. The forecast that day mentioned no rain.

In less than a minute, the heavens delivered a biblical deluge. The downpour caused many patrons to scurry for shelter in the park's museum building while some tried to cover their precious antiques. The driving winds blew their large canvas cloths aside. In vain, a few men and women attempted to raise their Flivver's black leatherette top. Some tops almost blew away. They were best left down. Still, others sought to cover their antique autos with what looked like bath towels.

Everything was chaotic as the driving rain continued. In the center of the Model T display were two twenty-foot square creamed-colored tents. These canvas shelters were for the judges and show officials. Don was already in one tent with a judge. He saw the rain-soaked people seek protection under the canvas. The tents soon filled with wet exhibitors, volunteers, and spectators.

Don stood near the tent's middle and heard one gentleman say, "You see that Jitney over there?" Pointing to a ubiquitous black Model T parked thirty feet away, he said, "That's my… Me-Car." Everyone who heard the man looked perplexed. They did not understand what he meant by the phrase, Me-Car. He responded to their curious looks, saying, "That automobile and I were born the same year."

A second man inquired, "What year is your Tin Lizzy? Is it original, or rebuilt?"

He answered, "It's a 1914, like me, an original other than the two conversions I had done. I had 1915 electric lamps installed."

Everyone was a Model T expert inside the tent, and many knew 1915 was the first year Ford used electric lamps.

The Me-Car man continued, "I have an electric starter too."

His statement started everyone talking at once. The experts agreed that crank starting their Jitneys could be a chore, which was probably why women did not drive them. A few Model T perfectionists tried to clarify the term, original antique, to anyone who wanted to listen. Don listened to different discussions and found himself lost in the world of classic cars.

A third gentleman broke into a heated conversation, saying, "What did you do when you were a kid and saw an unattended Model T parked? I'll tell you what I did! I raised the crank handle up, then ran and jumped on it. The handle kicked back, always launching me high into the air. Those were the greatest times I had!"

A fourth man shouted, "Boy! Do I remember doing that!"

"Yeah! We did that too," said another fellow.

A different person responded, "I never knew that!"

Don saw sheets of heavy rain from his place in the group continue to fall and be blown by the gusting winds. A bolt of lightning struck nearby, accompanied by a loud boom! He turned to see where it hit when he noticed a handsome man carrying a little blond-colored puppy enter the discussion group. He thought to himself; this guy doesn't belong here. The man was dry. He wore a long-sleeve checkered flannel shirt and dirty pants more suitable for a shop floor.

The dry man with the pup declared, "I owned a Model A because I need a closed cabin. *Everyone should own a Model A!*"

The third man spoke again, saying, "Is it true, the only reason a Tin Lizzy has an electric starter is because a guy died trying to help a woman start her car?"

Busy writing his notes and without looking, Don heard the dry man state, "Good, you're writing the story down. Always write it down--."

He recognized the man's voice as the dry man with the puppy. Suddenly a flash of light, followed by a booming sound, declared the lightning strike was nearby. Everyone stopped talking. Slowly, the conversations started again. Don moved away from the group's inner circle but still close enough to hear their discussions. He looked for the flannel shirt man with the puppy who commented on his writing notes but he didn't see him.

Don attempted to write every word in shorthand, but his notepad, damp from the rain, made that quite difficult. With rain still falling, an astute-looking gentleman in a wet green-colored shirt joined the group stating, "That is a good question. Yes! A man died trying to help a woman start her automobile. And, that accident caused an automaker to invent the electric starter."

The man spoke like a general and took control of the group's discussion. He said, "Seventy years ago, many auto companies called Detroit home. One of those early manufacturers was the Cartercar Company. A man named Byron Carter founded it. One day in March 1908, he was driving across the Belle Isle Bridge when he saw a young woman sitting behind the wheel of her stalled Cadillac. Mr. Carter pulled over and offered his aid to the stranded woman. What followed is legendary. The young lady stepped out of her Cadillac and stood by her automobile.

"Now facing Mr. Carter, she started speaking with him, and thanked him for his help. That is when he noticed the women's long flowing Victorian summer dress. She innocently moved to shade him from the bright sunlight behind her. Unbeknownst to her, she exposed a silhouette figure of herself through her dress.

"When Mr. Carter recounted the story to a newspaper reporter in 1908, he said, 'I have crank started automobiles hundreds of times. But, when cranking her car, I became transfixed by her shape, and ignored what I was doing. The Cadillac backfired. The crank handle jerked back and hit me in the jaw, breaking it.' So, here's the kicker, excuse the pun! While recovering at home, gangrene developed in his broken jaw. It proved to be serious, and he died a week later."

A woman in the group whispered, "That's terrible!"

Another man uttered, "Does your story have something in common with the electric starters?"

As the monsoon continued, rainwater flowed through the tent and caused puddles to form. Some people moved inside the shelter to higher ground. Several men rolled down two of the sides of the tents to prevent the windblown rain from entering. However, rainwater flooded under those canvas walls. Some watched two volunteers get soaked as they tried to roll down one more side curtain.

The gentleman needed the group's attention. He would take control by asking them a question. But first, he looked the group over. Confident he had their interest, he asked, "What does that have to do with the automobile's electric starter?" Not waiting for an answer, he said, "Everything! Byron Carter's Cartercar Company was in Pontiac. He was a prominent person in Detroit so famous that General Motors bought the company a year after his death."

"Mr. Carter had been a good friend of Henry Leland, President of the Cadillac division. He was angry with Detroit newspapers reporting how a Cadillac killed his friend. Mr. Leland called in his engineering staff and told them, 'I want no more Cadillacs killing people.'

"Mr. Leland instructed his engineering staff to come up with a solution. He put his best electrical engineer, Charles Kettering, in charge. In 1911, Mr. Kettering and his staff invented the automobile electric self-starter. The 1912 Cadillacs were the first cars in America fitted with the device."

The man had the group's attention. So, he continued saying, "Mr. Leland wanted his company to promote goodwill and safety. That is the reason he shared the automatic starter's patent with every automaker. Most companies soon had the electric gadget on their automobiles. Who knows the name of the last auto company to install the electric starter on their cars?"

"I bet it was Ford Motor," said the woman who spoke earlier.

"You're right. Mr. Ford thought the self-starter added too much cost to the price of his Model T. That was near twenty dollars back then. In 1919, Ford Motor customer's perception of electric starters was changing. The electric gadget switched from being a luxury to one of necessity. Based on customer demands, the 1920 Ford Model Ts became the first Ford Motor cars to have an electric starter… as an option. Now you know the story of a stranded young lady, who caused an accident, and the invention of the automobile's electric starter."

A lightning bolt crackled in the air, and a gust of warmer wind blew through the shelter. The heavy rain turned to a drizzle.

A woman commented, "Thank goodness, at least it's a warm rain."

The raindrops were lightly tapping the top of the tent. The wet volunteers had finally completed fastening down one more canvas wall. The shelter became comfortable, and few people noticed the water pools forming on the roof. Volunteers with a pole pushed up on those pools, causing a flood of water to run down the tent's side, making a big splash of water and creating mud on the ground.

Don raised his hand and, looking directly at the astute gentleman, asked, "Excuse me, sir. Can you tell us why there is no bank building in Greenfield Village? And, is the car's electric starter story somehow connected to the reason for no bank?"

"Here at Greenfield Village, we try not to speak about our competition. This, however, may be an exception," said the astute man. "Let's go back to 1903 when the Ford Motor Company first began. At the turn of the twentieth century, local bankers considered Henry Ford just another backyard inventor. A mechanic trying to manufacture and sell a newfangled contraption called the automobile. He sold a few of his first Model A automobiles.

"Mr. Ford went through the alphabet with his models, coming up with the Model T in 1908. His company was struggling to be a functional automaker. Now, on his third try at car manufacturing, he was banking everything on his Model T. The Flint bankers understood the Detroit bankers had already refused Mr. Ford's attempts for loans. His motor company had been in business for six years and was on shaky financial ground.

"The bankers believed Mr. Ford would not survive in the automobile industry. They thought he lacked the essential business expertise. Those were the crazy, fledgling years of the auto industry. Although some recognized his Model T was ready for the market, Henry held them back. The car didn't meet his benchmark for high quality, and he knew the price was too high for the average American consumer.

"Finally, his business manager, James Couzens, convinced him to sell the cars 'as is' or a cash crisis could wipe out the financially-strapped Ford Motor Company. A few months later, Mr. Ford agreed to sell his company to General Motors President Billy Durant. This was before the Model T became an enormous success. Henry Ford wanted cash, but, at the last minute, they offered him stock in the new General Motors Company, which he refused.

"General Motors' stock value had been declining. At the same time, they were trying to start a new division called Chevrolet. Durant couldn't get a loan to buy Ford. The bankers considered both companies too risky, and no one wanted them to fail. Mr. Durant needed to purchase land for Chevrolet's first assembly plant. The experimental factory was on an old lamp factory on West Grand Boulevard. He needed a larger, more permanent home for Chevrolet.

"Billy was interested in a 160-acre parcel of vacant land in Highland Park (Michigan). That parcel was across the street from The Ford Motor Company's Model T assembly plant. Mr. Durant wanted that property. Unbeknownst to him, Mr. Ford was a majority shareholder of the business which held the parcel. It appeared Henry Ford would finally get the cash he needed. Then, at the last hour, Durant reneged on their agreement.

"The bankers offered a sweetheart deal to Mr. Durant and his General Motors Company to buy the old Flint Wagon Works in Flint, Michigan. Billy took the banker's unbelievable offer and built his Chevrolet plant in Flint. When Mr. Ford found this out, he was livid. In less than two years, this was the second time that Billy Durant and General Motors reneged on their agreements.

"In 1909, Mr. Ford began his dislike for anything to do with Mr. Billy Durant, General Motors, and bankers. Those defaulted agreements made his abhorrence towards them greater. So great he refused to use any automobile improvements General Motors came up with first. Ford never implemented items such as dealer financing, Philips-head screws, or the electric starter. Only when consumer demand was so great did Henry Ford yield. A good example is the electric self-starter. When first offered in 1920 on the Model T, it was an extra cost option.

"Mr. Ford's business manager recommended the company sell those early Model Ts 'as is.' They did, and from those vehicle sales, a cash flow came and was used to make the needed changes, which made the Model

T's a phenomenal success. Money was no longer a concern. This one model saved his company and made Henry Ford an icon in the automotive industry. Years later, with all his achievements, he never forgot what the bankers had done to him in 1909.

"The outdoor history museum here at Greenfield Village is Mr. Ford's romantic notion of a rural American village at the turn of the century. I think he intentionally left out a bank, because it was his concept. Now, you know why Ford Motor was the last to install the electric self-starter on their cars. You also have the answer to the young man's question, the reason we have no bank here at the Village."

Finished with his impromptu history lesson, the general spoke with individuals. The rain had stopped, and gray overcast skies gave way to a blue heaven and puffy white clouds.

Going off in different directions, the exhibitors started drying off their rain-soaked antique vehicles. Still, inside the tent, Don looked to his left and observed the general in deep conversation with one of the Tin Lizzy's owners. He walked a few steps closer so he could hear their conversation and stopped.

The gentleman said, "You have to understand, we're talking pre-World War II vehicles. Prewar cars needed to withstand the rough country roads and to last. Cars made after the war are different in style, function, and manufacturing."

The Tin Lizzie owner responded, "Well, that answers that question. But before, you made a statement that Mr. Ford went through the alphabet naming the various models for his cars. If he did that, what is the reason we hear about his Model T, before the Model A?"

"Good question!" The general cleared his throat with a ready answer, "Between 1903 and 1904 Ford Motor Company produced and sold 1,700 Model A automobiles. Did you know a dentist from Chicago bought the very first one? The other Model A, the one the man with a puppy loved so much, was manufactured between 1928 to 1931."

The general saw him listening. He smiled at him and continued saying, "When Mr. Ford reviewed the design of the 1928 automobiles, they were different from the Model T, he considered a name change. The vehicle varied so much, he decided, starting at the alphabet's beginning again.

That's the reason we hear of the Model T and then the new Model A. Both models had a production run in the millions."

The two men finished… and set off on their separate ways. That was it! Don thought to himself, I'm nobody until I own a Tin Lizzy with an electric starter, a Ford car, and a Me-Car. That's it; my Me-Car will be a 1959 Ford. The 'Me-Car seed' idea planted itself somewhere in his eighteen-year-old brain. Being young has a way of making our desires seem dreamlike and achievable. So, we move them to the back of our mind for safe keeping, sometimes to recall later.

During his five-mile walk back home, he considered everything he saw and overheard during the day. He reflected on the people he met today and placed them into three groups: talkers, listeners, and doers. They each accomplished their dreams and had more. He pondered his dreams stored in his brain, owning a Me-Car, and a Tin Lizzy.

He calculated how to achieve those dreams. Never did he tell anyone about them. Today he learned to listen and seldom speak. Don forged a bond that day between himself, Greenfield Village, Ford Motor Cars, and the City of Dearborn. For the rest of his life, he always proclaimed he grew up in Dearborn.

Months later, his path crossed with the general when he volunteered at the museum. It was then he learned the man is an automotive historian and employee at Greenfield Village. During the year that followed, he tried to make friends with him several times; however, each time, his attempts failed. Don heard the gentleman tell someone they should not associate with the volunteers. It wasn't long before he witnessed the historian treat other volunteers with arrogance. Don acted like so many others did, ignoring and avoiding the man. Other individuals stopped volunteering.

In June 1978, he graduated from high school. He would be nineteen soon and was making plans to start college in the fall. Financial reasons caused his plans to change. He tried to join the military, but the armed forces had begun downsizing with the Vietnam conflict over. He took the physical for the Marine Corps but did not meet their new stricter standards. With his college education on hold, he took on other part-time jobs, earning and saving for his education. He took several night classes at a local community college, assuring he could transfer those credits to the state college system.

While keeping busy with work and night school, Don continued to apply to different colleges. In the spring of 1979, Ferris State College offered him a partial scholarship starting that fall. At the end of August, he traveled to Big Rapids, Michigan, to attend the fall quarter classes. The third week of October, he had a long weekend with no classes. At his sister's insistence, he caught a ride home with a classmate to celebrate his mother's forty-second birthday on Saturday, the twentieth.

The following day, Greenfield Village was hosting a private evening party. Most of these events included a reception and dinner for the attendees. To celebrate an event that occurred at Menlo Park, the guests will tour the building. This building is the workshop and laboratory used by the inventor Thomas Edison. Needing help at this event, and aware Don was home, a manager at the Ford Museum called him asking if he could help. He agreed to work that evening.

When the high-end event was over, the manager asked him and another man to stay and clean windows inside Menlo Park. The two men agreed to stay. They took their window cleaning supplies to the laboratory's second floor, where they started cleaning. When his co-worker went for more clean rags, Don continued cleaning windows.

Don heard men talking as they walked into the workroom. Never looking around, he kept working. Their words seemed jumbled and incoherent, but they sounded happy. In the glass window, he saw the reflection of a gray-haired gentleman in a white suit and vest.

The smell of burning tobacco wafted towards him. While facing the windows, Don said, "Sir, excuse me, but you are not allowed to smoke in this building."

A man's voice replied, "In-can-de-scent."
The one word made no sense, so he turned to challenge the individual. He looked around to see no one and became dumbfounded.

The other volunteer walked back into the room and at once approached him, declaring, "You cannot smoke in here!"

Don, disturbed by his experience, yelled in a high-pitched tone, "I don't smoke! It was that gray-haired guy in the white jacket and his friends that are the smokers."

Shaken and pale, Don and the other man stood in the workshop's center discussing what he experienced. A night watchman soon entered the workshop, looked around, and walked over to them.

"You men are aware smoking is not permitted in this building, correct?" asked the guard.

Startled, the volunteer asked the man, "What do you smell?"

"Cigar smoke!" he replied.

This encouraged them to tell the watchman what happened to Don and how they both smelled the cigar smoke odor. The three men standing near the room's middle agreed. Each smelled a burning cigar. The guard again inspected the area for a smoldering fire. He returned to where they stood after finding nothing.

With a serious expression, he said, "It must have been Mr. Edison." The guard studied the workshop once more, paused for a moment, and continued saying, "Old Tom does that sometimes. He enjoys smoking a cigar."

The guard shrugged his shoulders and left the workshop. Don did not believe in spirits, apparitions, or ghosts. But, he knew what he saw and heard. The two volunteers soon followed the night watchman out of the building. Many years would pass before Don volunteered again at the museum.

Back in college, he did some research on the Menlo Park building at Greenfield Village. In 1928, Mr. Ford spared no expense in moving the original building from Menlo Park, New Jersey. He had the building reconstructed in his Greenfield Village in Michigan. Mr. Ford wanted the building to be as authentic as possible.

He even had the topsoil from the original site brought to Greenfield Village. Laborers placed that ground around the restored workshop. During reconstruction, they used most of the original building. Framing timbers and other wood items too rotted or damaged to reuse were remade. Thomas Edison invented many things in the building, including the incandescent light bulb, one-hundred-years earlier.

During his first two summers at Ferris State, Don returned to Dearborn Heights during the summer months, living with his family and working at his part-time jobs. His school was four hours away, and, at the end of his third year, he stayed near campus to take summer classes. To the great dismay of his loving parents, he would never live in their Appleton Street home again.

Chapter 5

Life's Lesson

Don started his last year at Ferris State College in January 1983. After taking all those summer classes, he wouldn't graduate until the winter quarter in February 1984. All he wanted to do was attend class, pass his exams, and study in the quiet of his dorm room. His long-term dormmate, Allen, had other ideas for him.

The roommates met two years earlier. They formed an immediate bond when they discovered each had the same hometown, Dearborn. Allen's relationship with his girlfriend was becoming more serious. Their need to be closer put a strain on the roommate's friendship. Finally, the two reached a compromise that benefitted both men. Allen allowed him the use of his nine-year-old red Pontiac and gave him ten dollars for gas money. In return, Don had to leave the campus for the weekend.

The Pontiac had a few rust spots, but it was very dependable. He could use Allen's automobile to go anywhere he wanted. Together they schemed to get extra food from the cafeteria for Don's weekend trips. With his roomie's car, money for gas, meals, and his books, Don started leaving campus on the weekends for adventures to places unknown.

On his first trip away, he discovered one of Michigan's nearby state parks, which set the pace for future trips. Each weekend adventure began on a Friday afternoon or evening, and Don would drive to a different state park. There he rented a campsite. He set up a tent to store his supplies while sleeping in the Pontiac at night. Don was a city boy;

he learned a lot about primitive camping and how to enjoy the outdoors while on his trips.

He would use the campsite's fire to warm his cafeteria meals and started walking the park's hiking trails on these excursions. Those walks were a welcomed respite from his studies. On one particular summer weekend, there were no classes scheduled between Thursday and Monday. Allen wanted his roommate out of the picture a little longer, so he offered him a few extra dollars and extra food to have him leave.

Don viewed this as an opportunity. It was late June 1983, when the long weekend came, he drove Allen's vehicle one-hundred miles to the town of Traverse City, Michigan. He never told his roommate where his adventures took him. This one coincided with the city's Annual Cherry Festival and classic car show. Don was hoping to attend both events.

When entering the town, he went directly to the car show's office. There he met the receptionist and inquired about volunteering for the event. He mentioned his previous experience at Greenfield Village. She explained there was one spot available as part of the clean-up crew. He knew the show's staff seldom bothered those volunteers and agreed to help.

After some discussion, the office volunteer provided him a list of state and privately-owned campgrounds nearby, where he could stay. She recommended using her name to receive a discount when registering for the three nights he would be in town. Determined to find an inexpensive campsite, he left the center and drove three miles to the state park. At the park and several other private campgrounds along the way, he discovered there were no available campsites. The one site he found was too expensive for his meager budget.

At another camp, he found out that a campground further west may have a few vacant sites. Don drove there and met the proprietor, Bill, who was ten years older than him. The only campsites he had available did not have electricity. The cost to rent one of these sites was half his regular rate.

Desperate and familiar with primitive camping, he agreed to rent one. He then explained that he was volunteering at the classic auto show, hoping for a greater discount. The owner laughed and explained that he thought Don was an exhibitor as he pointed to the old red Pontiac. Don laughed along with him.

Most local merchants took part in the Cherry Festival, and Bill was no exception. He explained to the young man how he was responsible for the auto show clean-up on Monday. The two men laughed when he told Bill he was on Sunday's litter crew. They soon struck up a friendly conversation about cleaning the litter, antique cars, his college studies, and Bill's campground. Don learned during their talk how Bill was alone on Monday's litter detail.

With his last dollars dwindling faster than expected, Don had to watch his expenses. Even with the campsite's reduced price, gas money could be tight. Suddenly, an idea came to him! He would try to negotiate a free Sunday night stay for helping Bill clean up on Monday. He needed to be back on campus for a Tuesday morning class.

Telling the camp's owner his gas fund was short, Don started bartering. He offered four hours' help with Monday's cleanup in return for a complimentary night's stay.

After a moment, Bill agreed, saying, "I'll return your money after Monday's clean-up."

Thrilled that his negotiation technique worked, now he could plan on having a few more dollars, somewhere to camp, and a reason to stay until Monday. They shook hands to seal the deal. Later at his campsite, he made a small fire, set up his tent, and warmed up one of the pre-cooked cafeteria meals. After eating, he studied and fell asleep on the old Pontiac's backseat with the windows rolled down.

Saturday, he woke to blue skies and lots of sunshine. It looked to be a wonderful day. After a quick breakfast, Don left the campground to explore the Traverse City area and met the camp owner near the entrance. Bill had just lost another group of customers because his campsites had no working electricity. The two men spoke, and soon the proprietor disclosed his troubles. He told how last fall; he hired an electrician to rewire his campground. The man was to install new safer outlets called ground fault interrupting. He referred to them as GFI outlets.

The owner confided in him, saying, "I did not hire a business but bartered with an electrical contractor's employee. He was doing maintenance work on the high voltage towers in the area. I bought and paid for the supplies. He stayed here for free with his large tent and big company truck. When he wasn't working for his employer, he was to rewire my campsites. It appeared to be the perfect arrangement. Well, before he could finish, they sent him and the entire crew to repair storm damage in another state."

Bill remarked, "Since I bought the tools and supplies, I made sure he left everything, including the spare uninstalled outlets. I opened in April to discover fewer than half of my campsites had working new outlets."

He listened to the owner's plight. Don explained he was currently taking electrical engineering courses and offered to help solve the camp's electrical problems. The owner agreed and gave him a tour of the camp and access to his treasured tool barn. With some essential tools from the barn and his knowledge of the principles of GFI receptacles, he was eager to put his education to use. He found a new four-foot ground rod in the shed and replaced the one that was suspect.

He established a functioning ground with the new ground rod in place and a simple rewiring of the power grids ground in the electrical boxes. He then began disconnecting, moving, and reconnecting wires inside the two electrical boxes. He worked for several hours, correcting the issues, and discovered and fixed additional problems with the ground fault outlets at the campsites.

Within four hours, the electrical boxes and all the ground fault receptacles were wired and done! Don and the proprietor visited each camp's site, testing the now working electrical outlets. There were no more electrical problems. He even taught the owner how to troubleshoot these new outlets himself. Bill found himself enamored and impressed with the young man.

To Don's surprise, Bill showed up at his site early the following day, Sunday, with a five-star breakfast of ham, bacon, eggs, pancakes, toast, and coffee. Thanks to Don's work yesterday, Bill rented six campsites while the college student explored Traverse City. He thanked Bill for the delicious breakfast. Afterward, he drove to the car show, arriving one hour before opening as instructed.

The young man reported to the event's registration tent to find Bill and others there to greet him. Many people thanked him for volunteering. He thought it unusual to thank a volunteer before they worked, and he knew they were setting him up for a surprise. The board had changed Don's volunteer duties to the event's security staff. He soon learned of his new reputation, which preceded him, for fixing the camp's electrical grid. It turned out Bill, the camp's proprietor, was an influential person on the show's governing board.

In the afternoon, the two men met and walked around the car show together. They talked of classic cars and the event, comparing it to other shows Don had attended. In many ways this event was much nicer. There were over five hundred exhibitors, which only reinforced Don's interest in vintage vehicles and their owners.

While on their tour, the college student recognized an exhibitor he met several times in Dearborn. The man was there displaying his 1931 Ford Model A coupe. It was dark green with black fenders. Don went over to the gentlemen, where they reacquainted themselves. He then introduced Bill. The three men struck up a lively conversation about classic cars, which soon changed to this car show.

The exhibitor complimented Bill about the organization of the event. While they spoke, a show official needing Bill's advice showed up and took him aside. A spectator stopped to admire the Model A and started chatting with the owner. Just then, a man wearing a flannel shirt and carrying a blond-colored puppy stopped to examine the vehicle. The flannel shirt guy briefly inspected the Model A.

He then blurted out, "*Everyone should own a Model A.*"

As quickly as he arrived, the man and his puppy left. Don thought how strange the man appeared, and yet he seemed familiar. Turning to observe the man in greater detail, he was nowhere around. The rest of the day, Don walked the show, visiting with other attendees and acquaintances. He returned to the campground that evening and began packing the Pontiac in preparation to leave. The following day, he left the campground at 7:30 a.m.

Bill woke to find the college student gone. He attributed the young man's actions to his age. Later, to his surprise, he found Don waiting for him in the city at the deserted festival grounds.

He greeted the camp owner, saying, "I have to drive back to campus, so my four hours starts now."

The two men finished much earlier than expected. Bill insisted on buying him lunch. They ate at a local Union Street diner speaking on various topics, but always returned to antique automobiles. Before he left, the proprietor again thanked him for repairing the camp's electrical grid. Neither Don nor Bill knew that they had set the foundation for a friendship that would last a lifetime.

Don graduated in February 1984 from Ferris State College. He left with a degree in electrical engineering and two associate degrees. One of his minor degrees was in journalism, the other in business administration. Before he had graduated, he accepted employment as a technical writer. His new employer designed and manufactured corporate security products on Detroit's east side.

Within a few months of his employment, he wrote each of their product's manuals. To write these manuals required him to learn many details about the products. Armed with this knowledge, he began making many money-saving recommendations to the business. Although they never considered his suggestions, he received a promotion to supervisor.

Don rented a one-bedroom apartment near a local university and work. He was not very social, had no social life to speak of, and decided to spend his free time continuing his education. He applied to the university's computer program and soon found himself accepted. The former college student was now back in school. The following several semesters, he attended bachelor courses and then graduate classes.

In October 1987, he earned his master's degree in computer engineering. His new degree earned him a promotion to computer room supervisor. He would report to the telecommunication manager. One day Don saw the division's director in the hall. She was the former chief telephone operator who worked her way up the corporate ladder. She was now an influential company director. He asked her if she knew the reason the computer room reported to the telephone department?

Irate by the subordinate's question, she rudely responded, "Because they both needed wires!"

The executive's flippant answer suggested to him that she knew little about computers. He was now convinced computer technology would play a minor part in this company's future. To improve his employment opportunities, he met with an executive recruiter. He understood he had great value for the right company. Don understood the future of computers. However, he doubted if his director understood how fast change was coming.

During the summer of 1989, Don received confirmation about his ideas. The president, Mr. Stone, called him to his office. There he found a new personal computer (PC) on the president's desk. A local business installed it. The president admitted he had no idea how to use it or even turn it on. Don admonished him for not consulting with his department and for his terrible choice in choosing this computer model.

Surprised by such frank talk from a subordinate, the well-dressed executive said nothing. Don felt slighted and hurt, and recommended the company hire a consulting firm. Soon after, he abruptly ended the lesson and left the man's office. The following week, he returned with a new computer and connected it to their company's small network. Mr. Stone now had access to company data in actual time.

The company did hire a technology consulting firm, never telling their computer room employees. The consultants did interview several vital people within the company. With the information gathered, they were to present their finds. On the day of their presentation, Mr. Stone gave them an unannounced tour of the company's computer room. When the three consultants walked into the computer room, they were surprised to see Don worked there. During their brief conversation, each addressed him as Mr. Bryniarski.

Days later, after their consultant's presentation, the president asked Don, "How are you acquainted with our consultants?"

He pondered his response, answering, "They were each in the computer networking class I taught at the university."

After the consultant's presentation, Mr. Stone often visited the computer room. There he questioned him about computers. Don later learned one consultant asked the reason Mr. Stone hired them. Commenting, you have professor Bryniarski on your staff. Don told no one he only taught that one semester's class as a student-teacher. He also learned the consultant's recommendations were the same as he had made months earlier.

Weeks later, the board terminated the consulting firm's contract. Instead, they agreed to Don's recommendation and installed electronic mail. After implementing the e-mail system, productivity increased.

Accountants would link an increase in corporate profits and productivity to forty employees. Each of them used the new e-mail system.

The labor-intensive mailroom now had less work. Some mailroom clerks found new jobs in the higher-paying manufacturing department. The company's mail distribution room now functioned with half the employees. For his contributions, they promoted Don to manager with a generous salary increase.

Bored with his social life, he needed to do something. To move out of this rut, he signed up for a master's degree in business administration. The local university accepted him into the program in the spring of 1990, and he made the two-year commitment to attend. They designed the degree for executives, which required him to attend classes on weekends. His education and career were consuming his personal life.

At thirty, with money in the bank, he grew tired of studying and weary of the city's apartment lifestyle. Often, he thought back to his college days and his trips to state parks, where he found peace and adventures. Now, on rare occasions, he drove the rural country roads. He was looking for his ideal parcel of land to build a house.

On a country drive in April 1990, he noticed a small farm that matched his needs. The eight acres were on a private road in a semi-rural section of Brighton Township, surrounded by wetlands that looked perfect to him. Included was a century-old farmhouse in need of major repairs. Don saw beyond the overgrown weeds and peeling paint. After negotiations with the listing agent and owners, he closed on the property six weeks later, paying cash, and became a homeowner.

Instead of demolishing the old farmhouse, his contractor, Jerry, made another recommendation. He knew Don wasn't ready to occupy the property. So, he recommended a less expensive alternative, completely remodel the century house. The owner considered his options. He hired a local architect to draw the plans and Jerry's company to do the work. They agreed the contractor could work on the farmhouse in between jobs.

By allowing Jerry's building company to work this way, Don received a discounted rate for his work, saved money, and could now pay cash. In addition, Jerry would work for his crew in between jobs; each party benefited from their mutual agreement and planned for completion during the next two years.

Don received a generous company bonus in February 1991, based on his company's performance. He set aside half of it to finish paying for the farmhouse that was now half completed. With the remaining bonus, Don wanted to treat himself and buy an antique car. Less than nine days later, he purchased his first "new" old vehicle. The next day, Don called Jerry, asking him to finish the inside of the garage within the next seven days. He wanted to store his car in the remodeled garage. A minor setback pushed the date for the garage's completion from seven days to ten.

On the tenth day, Don proudly drove his antique automobile into the farmhouse's driveway. He shared his excitement with his sister, Denise, her husband, and their two children. Denise told Don the vehicle fit him; it was destiny. His niece and nephew couldn't wait for a ride from their uncle, and he told everyone to hop in. He pulled his vintage white, two-door, 1959 Ford convertible out of his newly insulated and drywalled garage. With the top down, they went on a slow drive down the old country roads.

The evening was unusually warmer for a late February evening, but it was still a cold jaunt. Shivering cold and exhibiting a broad, cheerful smile, he was happy to have his sister's family there to share his special Me-Car moment. He couldn't contain the joy he felt pulling his car into the garage for safekeeping. Rarely in his life did he have such joy, and he savored the feeling. He had a local antique car specialist complete a couple of minor cosmetic repairs the following months, which made his Me-Car ready for his first car show as an exhibitor!

Changes were coming to business, computing, and Don's career. The company's board recognized the need for a computer department renaming their computer room, The Information Technology Department. The name changed, but there was a lack of opportunity for Don, so he plodded along with his studies, waiting to graduate, and hoped for a new employer. Finally, in December 1991, he graduated with his master's degree in business administration.

With his MBA degree, his chances for new employment expanded. He understood the needs of business for people with his computer networking experience and education. Potential employers were lining up to interview him. But, he was selective. Rumors of his leaving the company had been a common topic at the water cooler, and Mr. Stone heard these same rumors. He always respected Don's honest, blunt professional views and met with him often. Mr. Stone wanted to discuss his future with their company.

The president did not want to lose the loyal employee. With the board's permission, he offered him a promotion to the position of company director. He would be responsible for all aspects of their Information Technology (IT) Division. Don had his attorney negotiate the company's offer for him, which he accepted. It came with a generous salary increase. Their telephone department would now report to the IT division and him.

Don's computer hardware and software recommendations were coming at a personal cost to him. He and his modern ideas were alienating some of the old guard managers, directors, and vice-presidents. They often challenged the need for his recommendations. He never defended himself. Instead, he moved a new project and the work to their departments.

One such project created a company home page on the Internet, and few understood the idea of having a company website. Don recommended the mailroom's manager be the project leader; she accepted the challenge. With the board's approval, and some trial and error, their first website went online. Everyone on the internet could access information about the company and its products.

Meanwhile, his staff was busy installing over two hundred computers throughout the company. Each connected their users to the company's expanding local area network. The local network was sharing more information on production timeframes and delivery schedules. Several employees even had secure access to sensitive information on the same network.

In early March 1992, a wedding invitation arrived for Don, reminding him he did not have much of a social life. It had been six years since he heard from his college roommate, and he was surprised by the invitation. Allen's romance with his college sweetheart didn't work out, and neither had his first marriage.

He was unaware of his divorce until receiving the wedding announcement. The RSVP card found a home in a drawer while he debated whether or not to attend. Two weeks later, Allen called him. They reminisced about their college days, and how time had passed. Finally, Allen got to the point of his call.

He said, "Don, I want to see you at my wedding reception. Attend, and I promise you'll have a wonderful time. Be my bartender; you'll get to meet everyone."

Don didn't smoke or drink and thought it would be a good distraction from work, and since finishing his classes, he thought it might be fun to "people watch." Working the bar also gave him an excuse as to why he was alone.

He agreed, telling his old roommate, "Yes, I'll be at your celebration and work the bar for you!"

That evening, he filled out his RSVP. On the card, he marked 'one' for dinner and mailed it the next day. As the late May wedding approached, Don decided not to go. He never enjoyed these types of events. Then, earlier in the week, Allen called him, asking if Don could get there early to show him the bar. Now he had to attend!

He dressed in his dark blue pinstripe wool suit, a white button-down collared shirt, and a classic navy and red striped silk tie. He arrived early at the reception hall, meeting Allen and his soon-to-be bride. The two old roommates moved aside privately, talking and laughing about their college days. The groom introduced him to Harold, who would help mix and pour drinks.

Allen reviewed with them how to prepare the four most popular alcoholic drinks they would probably serve. The groom insisted his bartenders each make sample drinks and taste each one. Don reluctantly sipped small amounts of each cocktail. The green bartenders became skilled in their trade as guests came over requesting a beverage.

During dinner, the bar was closed. So, he and Harold went to their assigned dinner seats. They sat with Harold's wife and the five other guests. Each person at the table was a Ferris State Alumni, and their conversation ranged from funny to sometimes uncomfortable. After dinner, he excused himself and returned to his bartending station.

The band's steady background dinner music quickly changed to lively dance songs. Traffic at the bar slowed as the small dance floor became packed with guests enjoying the night. He noticed a well-dressed young woman smiling at him from the near side of the crowded floor facing the bar. She appeared to be alone. Then he remembered serving her a whiskey on the rocks.

Automatically, he smiled at her. Then, holding a bottle of Old Crow whiskey, he lifted it high while pointing to her. She read his raised bottle gesture as a witty invitation to refresh her cocktail and walked over to the bartender. While refreshing her beverage, they started a conversation. He discovered her name was Ann, a guest of the bride. She learned he was Don and not a paid bartender but an acquaintance of the groom.

The two spoke in between his duties. As their conversation continued, Ann encouraged him to drink with her, but he refused. Don explained he does not imbibe. She boldly asserted that she too doesn't drink and is only drinking at the bride's insistence.

Becoming comfortable with her, Don poured himself the same small cocktail. She finished her drink, then shared his. Her speech became candid, describing how she came with a girlfriend. Ann explained how her friend departed the reception after dinner, leaving her with no ride home.

There was a brief pause. Ann looked at Don and told him, in a pleading voice, she had no ride home. There was a long silence. He did not recognize the blatant hint and opportunity. As the lull continued, she placed her right hand on his to gain his full attention.

She looked him in the eye, saying, "Well, are you taking me home, or must I telephone a taxicab?"

He never experienced a woman who was so blunt! Not wanting to embarrass himself or her, he could only agree to take her home. So, after the reception ended, he drove Ann to her apartment. During the drive, he found her open and honest, with an appealing style.

He learned she was three years older than him, and at six feet was three inches shorter than him, which only added to her mystical charm. She told him how she had received her Ph.D. in veterinary science six years earlier. And how, before receiving her degree, she worked at a local Brighton area animal clinic. Still working at that clinic, she was planning to buy it from the retiring owner.

The couple developed a friendship and, during the summer, started dating. For Don, this was a novel experience, balancing his work and social life. He kept trying to tell himself his career always came first, or he tried to believe that.

The company's management team was grasping the real potential of computers. The tide was turning in Don's favor. Computer technology was proving to be a good fit for their company. By late summer 1992, Don had guided his company's IT division through some rough times.

His staff was now busy training employees on the next generation of software and how to use a computer's mouse. The training classes were a grueling experience for everyone involved. It was around this time when Don was reviewing a programmer's work. He discovered the individual wrote a line of code for backdoor access. This code with the password allowed unapproved entry into the company's software programs. The programmer soon used this access to move company funds to a private account. The IT management team notified the police and charged the programmer with embezzlement.

Their corporate attorneys found the case easy to prove by his team's meticulous documentation of the event. A lengthy court case ended with the programmer being found guilty. The courts made the individual pay restitution and ordered them to serve probation. However, several programmers considered the company too harsh when charging the former employee.

A few of them chose to leave for other employment. Morale sank to a new low. Hoping to improve everyone's spirits, the director instituted a casual dress day, soon followed by flexible work hours. His employees loved these new and more current guidelines.

His technology division was working with other departments to automate the manufacturing processes. With automation came more production which in turn made expenses and billing became more accurate, and the company became more profitable. The board of directors recognized him and his department's achievements. They compensated him well. He received an increase to his six-figure salary with a bonus.

Meanwhile, Don's personal life was blossoming. He and Ann attended plays, concerts, and University lectures on the weekends. He suspected she was a city girl at heart, but his plans were different. Often, he missed her during the week. He occasionally called her just to say hello, asking how her day was going.

Cheerful, friendly, with a buoyant, outgoing personality, Ann had all the qualities he considered ideal. But was she right for him? Having her say I do, only to discover he was wrong, is not something he wanted to chance. So he convinced himself the easiest thing was to break off their association and stay friends. The question is how to do it?

While having lunch in the cafeteria, he heard a male co-worker say, "I told her the truth, and she broke up with me. Did she want me to lie? I was honest with her! So now she hates me."

He thought, what a magnificent idea. I'll be straightforward with her. Tell her everything about me, and then she'll hate me, but we can still be friends. In his mind, he set their breakup to happen Friday night at her apartment. Ann called him during the week to inquire if she should plan something for the weekend, maybe a movie. He insisted she make no plans.

Late Friday evening, he called to explain software update issues required him to work into the night. He asked if they could meet on Saturday, and she agreed. Ann suggested they consider doing something on Sunday. If he wanted, he may bring an overnight bag and sleep on the couch.

Dumbfounded by her words and knowing what he had planned, he said, "We'll see, I'll call you tomorrow."

The planned software updates failed miserably. Working through the entire night, he and his five programmers finally finished the job at 6:05 a.m., Saturday morning. He invited everyone to join him for breakfast as his thank you. He asked them to call their spouses to join them.

At the diner, Don spoke to each programmer and how they contributed to solving the problems. He then thanked the team for their successful implementation of the scheduled upgrade. While waiting for their partners to arrive, one husband quietly thanked him for inviting his wife.

He then whispered, "My wife is always suspicious. She thinks I was partying all night and only came to see if I was working." The candid comment shocked Don. Nevertheless, the man continued saying, "I love her. I always tell her the truth, and she still thinks I'm lying."

The husband's remarks solidified Don's strategic plan for later that night. He heard that comment before, women thinking men lie to them and hate them. So Don decided to tell Ann the truth about himself, of course, she'll assume he's lying and will hate him. But, he kept telling himself, this is the right time to end their four-month relationship.

When the spouses arrived, Don thanked each of them for coming. He took a moment during breakfast to recognize the partners for being understanding and allowing their spouses to work all night. Throughout breakfast, Don listened to the one wife's distrustful tone towards her husband. He used her words to convince himself that a relationship with Ann would not work. He smiled at everyone at their table. But, in his mind, he was thinking tonight I will break up with Ann!

Chapter 6

Outta Here

With breakfast finished and the bill paid, everyone departed their separate ways. As Don drove home, he diverted his attention from his planned breakup to the gusting winds buffeting his vehicle. To gain control of his vehicle, he had to slow down and keep both hands on the wheel until he finally reached his apartment. Once inside, he fell asleep.

Don woke up hours later than planned and immediately called Ann to apologize. He promised to be there within three hours. She said she understood. A flash of fear came over him as he hung up the telephone. Finally, he admitted to himself how much he liked her and even cared for her. Then soon reminded himself that such a feeling cannot be, for today was about breaking up, not moving forward with this relationship.

He arrived at Ann's around 8 p.m., sitting on her couch; he struggled to find the courage to speak. She immediately knew something was wrong as she sat near him on the sofa.

Mustering all his courage, he said, "I haven't been honest with you and need to end our relationship." Then with a quivering voice, he explained buying a house and he was remodeling it, and would soon be moving there. He understood how she liked worldly and cultured things, and he was just the opposite — a blue-collar guy who likes the country.

Shocked, Ann looked at him, saying, "What else?"

A twenty-minute speech came from him detailing his purchase of an antique Ford automobile. She never interrupted him. When he finished, she thought to herself, so? There was a long, uncomfortable silence between them.

Ann bluntly asked, "Are you married? Divorced? Do you have children you haven't told me about?"

Don couldn't believe she was asking these personal questions. So instead of answering, he continued to tell her how different they were.

Ann struggled to keep her anger in check. Finally, in a low gentle tone, she said, "I don't live in the city you do. I prefer the rural country life."

She began her own ten-minute explanation about him being the refined one. Ann described how he loved living downtown. The reason they attended plays and lectures was that he wanted to stay in the city. She tried to make him see what she saw in their relationship. It was difficult for him to listen to her genuine comments.

Ann probed harder, asking, "So you bought a farmhouse and an antique white car two years ago? So where is this house? A couple of hundred miles away?"

In his brilliant mind, Don, staying true to himself, acknowledged her, the only way a genius could, replying, "The house and auto are here."

The doctor of veterinary science listened to his words and could not understand them. Finally, she slowly asked, "Where is here?"

In a high-pitched tone he yelled, "Here!"

While wanting to explode, Ann looked into his eyes, and calmly she replied, "Your farmhouse is here?"

In a matter-of-fact tone he answered, "Well… yes!"

Thinking he is an idiot or lying, she decided to try a fresh approach with him. Still wondering about his house, she looked at him, asking, "Donnie, does your house have a street number and name?"

He defensively answered, "Um, I forgot the address, and it is not a street; it's a place. About five miles from here."

Relieved to know his farm was not in Michigan's Upper Peninsula, Ann grabbed his car keys from the table.

Standing up, she declared, "Let's go! I'm taking you and me wherever here or that place is now! And I'm driving your car, Mister! Point the way!"

She drove down the dark country backroads for an hour. His directions kept changing. She thought, "He's crazy. He's lying!" I have been driving on these same country roads at least twice, traveling in opposite directions."

He finally told her to slow down and shouted, "Turn here on this dirt lane." The street sign read Barkley Place.

She remarked, "This is a street?"

He commented, "I told you it is not a street; it's a place."

It was so foggy she could barely make out the dirt track. As she drove on the private dirt road, Don directed her to pull onto a paved asphalt drive. The vehicle's headlights outlined a farmhouse's shadowy silhouette. Still uncertain he was telling her the truth, it surprised her when he offered to take her inside. The house key, he mentioned, was on the same ring as the car key.

She declined, saying, "It's too late; I'll see it tomorrow. Tonight, you're sleeping on my couch."

The following morning while eating breakfast, they both laughed and joked about their late-night journey. Don apologized for getting them lost, having never traveled that way before, and commented on the lack of streetlights.

Ann only laughed harder, remarking, "Welcome to the country."

They attended an early Mass at Ann's church. It surprised her girlfriends to see her with someone. Her friends wanted to know who he was? She explained they were busy this morning and could not stop for coffee after the service, which only added to their speculation.

They set off for his house after the services ended. After driving by Barkley several times in the daylight, they finally found his farmhouse. Key in hand, Don opened the front door. Ann walked in the front door and was speechless. The walls were new and primed white, waiting for painting.

Everything was wonderful, including the white vintage Ford convertible in the garage. They wandered the property's perimeter. The couple spent an hour roaming and examining the outbuildings. Ann had the interest of a veterinarian in his small two-stall horse barn. The building was at the far edge of the Brighton Township property.

When walking towards the house, she smiled at him, saying, "I am sorry I doubted you. If you enjoy the country this much, I love you even more."

In the middle of the lawn, she stopped and kissed him. He kissed her back. Reaching the house's empty kitchen, they kissed again. Much to his surprise, instead of breaking up, they happily left the farmhouse engaged. That evening, Don gave her a key to the property. That night, unable to sleep, Ann couldn't believe how her life had changed. Out of sheer joy, she cried to herself. Finally, she understood how incredible love felt that day.

Several days later, he asked her to help with the house renovation. As fate would have it, the veterinarian knew Jerry, the contractor, and his entire family, including their dog Mazy, a goldendoodle. Mazy was one of Ann's patients who just loved eating clothing. Not the best diet for a dog!

Ann suggested a few changes to the project, and Don readily agreed. They added a 1,100 square foot addition, rearranged walls, increased the master bedroom and bath size, and eliminated another room all in one week. More work made Jerry happy. But he had to finish the remodeling before their marriage, and he did.

Ten months later, on July 24, 1993, the couple walked down the Saint Patrick Catholic Church aisle in Union Lake, Michigan. Her parents married in the same church three decades earlier. After the ceremony, the couple hosted a small backyard reception at their Brighton Township property.

Don loved his bride's matter-of-fact, straight-to-the-point, impatient doctor voice. He also adored her romantic, softer tone she used only when they were alone. Those little phrases always melted him, and she knew when to say them. That's what love is all about, a moment you remember forever. His wife told anyone willing to listen that there was a generous, soft teddy bear at heart under Don's grumpy exterior.

The couple enjoyed their remodeled country retreat. Don and Ann's house sat on a small rise in the middle of the property's 1,259 feet of street frontage. Don attributed this perfect location to the original homesteaders. He knew a century ago that settlers always chose the ideal spot for their dwelling. The first homestead for this property had three hundred and twenty acres.

The post office's official designation for the private two-lane dirt road was a 'place.' This dusty road accessed twelve parcels. Nine of those lots had houses and other outbuildings occupying them. Parcels varied in size, each between eight and eighteen acres.

Don and Ann had eight acres, and the couple felt like they owned a large farm. Their serpentine driveway was thirteen-foot-wide and two hundred six-foot-long — a boulevard of black asphalt that widened in front of the garage doors. A local contractor paved the driveway a month before meeting her, thanks to his bonus.

Three rows of young and mature indigenous white pine trees ran along the front and sides of their land. The backline overlooked a broad wetland that extended around their property. Don would say, "It's swampland, and yaa can't build in the swamp." But, no matter how negative he sounded, Ann knew he cherished this place. It was their perfect home.

A large green lawn surrounded their farmhouse, and they both enjoyed its covered wraparound porch. Don and Ann kept the outbuildings and two-stall horse barn with its wood-fenced paddock. Occasionally Ann did board animal patients in the outbuildings. She tried not to make this a habit, as Don disapproved. But, being a vet, she had two choices, spend the night at the clinic or come home with an animal patient. It wasn't always an easy decision.

In early 1994, she bought the veterinarian clinic where she worked. Don discovered they could get a tax deduction when her clinic used their property. This newfound tax break changed his position toward her overnight patients.

Don's new role as husband and gentleman farmer brought a renewed vigor into his professional career. Forward-thinking was the one thing he had in his favor. In the spring of 1994, he instituted a policy to have his programmers add a four-digit year code when rewriting their software programs. This action seemed unnecessary to his team, but he demanded it. This change allowed programs with two-digit year codes to work beyond nineteen-ninety-nine getting everyone and software programs prepared for the year 2000.

It was April 1998, and Ann thought she and Don needed a change. While looking through Don's antique auto magazines, she came upon an article on the Old Towne Classic Car show. The event in Michigan began at the end of June during Traverse City's Cherry Festival. His wife thought he should enter his vintage Ford in the event. Ann thought it would be fun to spend a few days in the area and made plans to celebrate Don's June birthday and their July wedding anniversary during this trip.

Ann had never been to Traverse City. She was unaware he had visited the show while attending college. Much to her surprise, he agreed to go. With the show happening in only two months, he called the registration center the next day. The representative asked him if he ever attended the festival. Don told him about volunteering at the event when he was younger.

The volunteer interrupted him, saying, "Donnie, do you know who this is?" The man then said, "It's Bill. You fixed my campground's electricity when you were in college."

The two men spent the next twenty minutes getting reacquainted. Then, with his vintage Ford registered, a cabin booked at Bill's modern camp, the two men promised to meet at the festival. At the show, he introduced Ann to the neatly dressed Bill and his cheerful wife, Kathy.

Their oldest daughter and son-in-law were helping to manage their old but modern campground, giving Bill time to volunteer at the event he loved. During the event, Kathy stopped by and agreed to watch their 1959 Ford convertible while Ann and Don toured the festival grounds. The show had over five hundred exhibitors.

While touring the grounds, they came upon one particular car they both adored. It was a burgundy and gray 1930 Studebaker automobile model called the President. Don spoke with the owner, but he did not want to sell his pre-World War II vintage vehicle. Leaving for home the next day, they decided to take their time and drive the scenic route.

With the sun shining and the top down, they enjoyed the rural country road's scenery. While driving, he declared how he enjoyed seeing the late 1930s and early 1940s American autos at the show. He especially liked the old Packard they viewed the day earlier. Then with time to spare, he described how the big flowing-style fenders added character to that era of automobiles and how each manufacturer had unique design styles.

Don told her of his Greenfield Village volunteer experiences with his father and by himself. He shared his thoughts about how royal it would feel owning and riding in a vintage vehicle from that period. It was a dream he had never shared with her or anyone.

Ann encouraged him, saying, "If that will make you happy, do it."

Thinking out loud, he spoke about how he would search for a Studebaker, a barnyard-find Buick LaSalle, or even a Packard. She remembered growing up, her family had Pontiacs and Oldsmobiles. However, Don was partial to Fords. She reminded him of that. He remarked about how an old Ford Model A, with a flathead V-eight, was something he could envision himself affording and owning. He laughed, telling her how someone once told him everyone should own a Model A.

But how to do it? He recognized searching for an antique automobile might take months or years. Don wasn't settling for just any old vehicle. He needed a particular vintage automobile that could take him back to that bygone era, a time when ordinary people first used motorized cars for everyday transportation. He needed a vehicle that could transport him back generations to before he was born.

To a time when paved roads were called boulevards and thirty-five miles per hour was fast enough. An age when families thought the Sunday drive was a journey into the unknown. He imagined himself in a vintage Packard riding by quaint roadside diners, motor courts, auto camps, malt shops, and even a milkman. That was the era when weary motorists first stopped at motels. (A contraction for motor courts and hotels.) An age when gas stations, service stations, or garages are thriving on every other city block.

He always knew an impressively designed prewar 1930s or early 1940s automobile could stop anyone in their tracks. Don wanted to shock and astound everyone with his choice of a vintage vehicle. He wanted one with grandeur and style. A car people would stop to look at and admire. He broke his daydreaming when he turned their vintage Ford into the driveway. It surprised them to see a sold sign on the vacant property across the street, but neither gave it a second thought.

Throughout 1999, Don focused on his career instead of looking for a prewar vehicle. His IT department had little to worry about while other companies dealt with their own year 2000 (Y2K) crisis. Six years earlier, his programmers wrote the software codes for each computer program to prepare for the millennium change. They were way ahead of the game as his software team tackled a unique project.

They were developing a new timekeeping and high-security access system for employees. Everyone on the system will receive a new identification badge. They would be similar in size to a plastic credit card. On the front of the card would be the employee's digitized picture, and embedded inside will be a microchip to identify the user. They would swipe their card at a reader. The system would limit their access to buildings and offices by days and times.

In July, Don's team was busy beta testing the new system's badges with their department and offices. This modern secure entry system surpassed every test, and it wasn't long before other departments wanted to use it for their team members. During these crazy months at work, Don's weekly trips to the local newsstand kept him sane. He bought every auto magazine advertising the sale of antique cars. He scrutinized their ads for each prewar auto that was for sale.

In August, one magazine listed a green and black 1928 Ford Model A coupe. He recalled the man once telling him everyone should own a Model A. So, he and his wife took a drive one weekend to the Village of Holly to see it. But, after viewing a rusted-out vehicle, he learned to ask more questions about a car before they traveled again. Afterward, the few trips they took were pleasant diversions from their professional lives.

Don presented his access system to the board in early October. At their meeting, he recommended the company offer it as a new product line. The board members thought the system needed more enhancements and referred his business case to the marketing department. They would do an internal study and report back to the board.

New Year's Day 2000 came and went with no effect on their company's computer systems. The Y2K crisis was a non-issue for his group. He received a generous bonus for his work. His wife insisted he add those dollars to his prewar automobile fund.

By April, every worker used the new card entry system to keep track of their hours worked and building access. Soon the marketing department's report came back to support the product. Don again presented his recommendations to the board members. They at first rejected his appeal, but then agreed to fund fifty percent of his request.

With the added funds, in four months, his team had refined the system. The project's success soon gained the attention of a third-generation owner. The young woman understood the product's potential. In November 2000, she influenced the board to sell the product to the public. The product line went on the market in January 2001. Pleased with the project's success, Don wrote an article on the microchip card system. The trade journal piece offered no trade secrets. His reputation in the national information technology community soared. It impressed people that he shared his credits with those around him.

On September 11, 2001, foreign terrorists attacked the United States. Government agencies and private companies scrambled to secure their property from attacks. Their company's high-security access system was the product many needed and wanted. By the year's end, Don's company sold fourteen systems. It had become their most profitable product. In March, Don received a generous bonus for his work.

Don's professional life had become cluttered and blurred with sales consulting activities. He needed a distraction. With no suitable antique automobiles for sale, he acted on a whim. He made himself a beekeeper when he bought used equipment from a retiring apiarist. He also became more active in his Knights of Columbus Council and attended every meeting.

But by far, Don's favorite diversion was exhibiting his 1959 Ford convertible at local auto shows and parades. He called it his Me-Car. The real plus to attending these shows was his wife Ann's involvement. She found pleasure and joy in joining him at the events.

She frequently met current and prospective clients who loved to talk about their pets. Ann always listened attentively and sometimes helped them schedule an appointment with her. It was a Sunday evening in mid-August when they were returning home from a local car show that they noticed a new building permit sign on the lot across the street. They gave it little attention.

In mid-September 2002, Don could finally take a two-week vacation. This year, Ann worked while he stayed home to repair items on her house fix-it list. On his first morning off, Don completed three minor fixes and spent twenty minutes on a business-related call. Staring out the kitchen window, he saw his contractor friend, Jerry, drive up. Don hired him to help replace the coatroom's exterior door, which Ann hated.

The men replaced the outdated exterior frame and door in less than three hours. At Don's insistence, the new entrance had a thermal pane glass window. Ann was so surprised when she arrived home from work that evening. She thanked him for remembering her and thought it was the little things he did that she loved.

Don devoted the second day of his vacation to complete other minor repairs on Ann's to-do list. One job included refastening the barn's door hinges. He spent the entire afternoon on several business-related conference calls. As Ann left for her clinic the following day, she noticed a construction crew in the lot across the street. She went back into their house and told Don about the crew and people watching them.

Ann started for work again, while Don walked down to the end of their driveway. It was then he noticed the construction workers were breaking ground for a new house. Walking across the street and over to the group of people, Don introduced himself. He met the excited owners who showed him their newly approved house plans.

Don met eight of their nine children. Their oldest son and his wife also planned on living with the family. The rest of the children ranged in age from three to twenty-one. They needed a large house for their large family.

The owners briefly described their new house plans. After wishing them well, he left the cheerful group. Don walked down the freshly bulldozed dirt driveway back towards his home. Disappointed, he blamed himself for not buying the property. Don knew this new home would put an end to his private, perfect home life. He envisioned cars pulling in and out of that driveway at all hours. The quiet peace he so loved will soon be gone. His sadness turned to anger.

He was so upset that he called his wife at work, and in his high-pitched voice screamed, "I'M OUTTA HERE! THAT IS IT. WE ARE MOVING!"

Ann listened patiently. She calmly told him they could have this serious discussion when she got home. Later that night, she agreed with him that their privacy would be affected. If he wanted to move and build a modern house, they could. But he had to choose the land of his dreams, a new house, or purchasing an old prewar automobile. He could not have both! And his car fund had to be used to buy the land. Ann thought to herself; this was a splendid opportunity for him to consider a career change and for her to ponder early retirement.

The following day he visited a neighborhood real estate company to help him find and buy the perfect vacant property. He left their office armed with several local county maps and a list of acreage locations. Don started his hunt, driving down south-central Michigan's backcountry roads. Over the next few days, he put hundreds of miles on his car.

Don's quest for his special classic prewar automobile had to take a backseat to his present goal. Now he had but one aim: buy several acres of wilderness where he and Ann will build their new house!

Chapter 7

Changing Destiny

Two miles west of Charlotte, Michigan, Don looked at a twenty-four-acre parcel of land to buy. After eliminating it from his list, he started his drive to view another piece of real estate. He was off to look at an eight-acre wooded lot, seven miles northeast of the city. It was becoming monotonous for him, riding alone on the back-country roads. This morning he had driven seventy miles in his antique 1959 Ford convertible and was ready to call it a day.

It was a perfect Saturday morning in late September; Don decided to take advantage of the weather, and hoping to change his luck, put the Ford's vinyl top down. He could feel the sunlight beaming through the clouds, temperature in the sixties, and fresh air in his face. Don reminded himself he wasn't here for a joy ride. He had to stay focused and find the right property but his mind continued to wander from his goal.

He wondered what it would feel like to drive into a 1930s service station where an attendant in a spotless white uniform would pump gas, clean the windshield, and check your oil, all without being asked. They remembered your name, each of your family members' names, and even asked about your pet. Those service stations sold gasoline, kerosene, tires, fixed a flat, and always had a mechanic on staff. Those mechanics were special!

They weren't just parts changers, but individuals who were familiar with your automobile's inner workings. Many of those people could overhaul your car's engine on the weekend. Sitting comfortably on the red and white leather front seat, he slowed his speed to twenty miles per hour as he tried to visualize what this vignette would entail. He lazily closed his squinting eyes; suddenly, he remembered he was still driving the car and startled himself out of his daydream.

A slight grin appeared on one side of his cheek as his thoughts continued. He was obsessed with those impressively designed classic prewar cars that make people turn around, stop, and look. They will pull over just to check it out. He told himself, who could resist the beautiful styling, flowing curved fenders, and meticulous construction on those automobiles? But that would have to wait.

He moved his antique auto funds to a new home account because that had become the priority. Now having passed the street he was to turn at, he continued, making a right turn at the next road, and headed east. Within a few minutes, he came to the small town of Potterville. Turning left and driving northeast, he noticed what looked like a former service station on his left. As he rode by, he watched a man chasing to catch a big old car rolling down the station's driveway towards the street.

The man caught up to the moving vehicle and jumped inside it. He stopped it just before it went into the street and would have hit Don's car. As he was riding by, Don thought he saw a for sale sign on the dark-colored car. With his curiosity aroused, he chose to turn around and inquire what happened at the old gas station? He drove there, telling himself, this is just a leg stretching diversion. Muttering to himself out loud, Don said, "I'm still looking for land!"

The old filling station soon came into view. Don slowed his vehicle, turning into the Phoenix Auto Body parking lot. What he thought was a service station was an auto body repair shop. He deliberately parked on the opposite side of the lot from the vehicle. This act had been deliberate and gave him time to view the automobile during his walk. As he walked, the phrase, *buy land to build a house, buy land to build a house*, kept running through his mind.

He stood there admiring the body lines and detailed trim, the sheer expanse of this automobile's sheet metal skin. It was regal. He could tell the Chevrolet was in excellent condition. A smiling muscular medium-size man came out of the body shop. He was dressed neck to toe in a disposable white painter's outfit. He introduced himself as Johnny O, the owner of the car and the business.

Don, pointing to the auto, commented, "I saw you running after it. Is everything okay?"

Embarrassed, the bearded owner stated, "Yeah, I parked it earlier and just noticed it moving out into the street. I'm certain I set the brake. She's a 1941 Chevrolet Special Deluxe Town Sedan." Johnny O paused for a moment, then continued saying, "The brake slipping like that never happens. She runs great, but you can't drive her with one hand. You are required to keep two hands on this wheel and constantly pay attention to the road.

"There are lots of blind spots, and driving in modern stop-and-go traffic can get awfully tiresome. The original hydraulic drum brakes are up to stopping the car; but, if traffic comes to a quick bottleneck, you may not stop it in time." Continuing with his sales pitch, the shop owner said, "General Motors built these automobiles for cruising the 1940s, open two-lane roads. You have to remember to start your turn a little sooner than you think. I drive this antique slower than most drivers would want me to, but I enjoy driving it."

He never stopped for a breath of air. The man told Don how on the highway, going fifty-five to sixty-five miles per hour is fast enough. How you feel yourself floating at sixty, and higher speeds cause an excess of motor and wind noise which only bolsters your impression of going faster. At seventy-five, the engine is working too hard, and the noise makes you think you're doing one-hundred. There is no air conditioning, so that can get uncomfortable in hot weather.

Don stood dumbstruck, and wondered if the man was honestly trying to sell this Chevrolet?

Johnny O continued, "We competed in and finished this year's Hot Rod Magazine's Power Tour. It's their long-distance car cruise. This 1941's Stovebolt six engine kept right up with modern traffic on the expressways."

Don started walking around the vehicle, looking for flaws.

The shop owner said, "The automobile is original."

Don stopped and asked, "How original is original?"

The shop's proprietor answered, "As in 99% authentic! She's a true World War II survivor from an era long gone, a one-of-a-kind, inside and out. Under the hood, even her engine is an unbelievable time capsule. What you see is what rolled off the assembly line at Flint (Michigan) in August 1941."

Breaking into a proud smile, he commented, "I replaced the tires, belts, hoses, fuel pump, and exhaust system. Then I repainted her to the original factory color. This sedan was one of the last 1941s built before federal mandates shut down car production. The following week, General Motors started to re-tool the 1942 models. Each of those newly manufactured cars was purchased by and delivered to the federal government for the war effort."

Don tried to speak, but the body shop owner kept on talking, saying, "Even with gas rationing, the owner drove this car every day during the war. Remember, no replacement parts were available during those years, and this extraordinary sedan was still running when the war ended. In 1948 the owner parked this Chevrolet in the garage, placed a painter's tarp over it, and shut the doors. The rare wooden floor of the garage saved this vehicle. There she remained for forty years until I came along."

It was then, he realized, Johnny took only one breath during his last statement. While staring at the Chevrolet's front, he noticed the massive die-cast chrome-tooth-grille. It appeared to be grinning at him. Was the special deluxe sedan glad to see him? Inside the car, Johnny pulled a brown plastic knob located under the interior's dashboard. His action opened the hood's center-mounted air vent. Suddenly, two white-painted eyeballs appeared on the open vent's screen, which only enhanced the auto's beaming image. However, Don didn't seem happy to see those staring eyes.

The shop's proprietor responded to his expression stating, "The original owner said one of her friends painted those eyes on the car when the Kilroy was here graffiti was in vogue. They decorated the car while the previous owner was at a war bond rally. She liked the caricature and kept it there."

Johnny saw him running his fingers over the Chevrolet's pristine hood. He declared, "There aren't many hoods around in this fine of condition. During the fifties and sixties, it was a fad for clever guys to buy two of these Chevrolet hoods from the junkyard. They would weld them together to form an inexpensive kayak. On the sides, they added buoyant material such as cork to keep their two-hooded kayak afloat if it turned over. The boulder-strewn rivers of southwest Michigan smashed wooden kayaks to splinters. Even though they were heavy, they lasted longer and were much cheaper than having to buy a new wooden kayak."

Her maroon paint gleamed like jewelry in the bright sunshine when he asked the shop owner, "Is the paint original?"

"No!" He answered and continued saying, "When I bought this Chevrolet, it had no rust. You won't find Bondo on her anywhere. I removed the original paint and only found a few spots of surface rust." Johnny insisted he go over the car's body with a magnet.

Don understood how a magnet could detect any Bondo putty repairs in the body; however, on this point, he did not want to challenge Johnny's veracity. Still ambling around the auto, he recalled his purpose for today's drive. A small grin came on his cheek as he muttered, "Acquire land to build a house, acquire land to build a house."

Noticing what he thought was a smirk on Don's face, Johnny considered it a sign of approval. The body shop owner continued to explain how spray-painting cars was his major business. He described taking trips with the Chevrolet to local auto shows so prospective customers could view the quality of his work.

Don commented, "The vehicle looks nice. But you do know when you painted it? You lessened the value a great deal. Preserved original antique automobiles are more desirable now than those restored or repainted."

To Johnny, the tide had turned. He knew this man was a knowledgeable classic car enthusiast.

Don started another walk around, checking the original stainless-steel trim highlighted with red pinstriping. He could tell the piping had lived up to its rust-free promise. Opening the driver's side door, Don saw the level floor, making it easier to clean by just brushing out the debris. Unconsciously he leaned over, running his hand across the car's carpeted floor, as if sweeping dirt out. He noted the carpet's color was the same as the tan seats.

The owner saw his action and said, "The 1951 Hudson were the first cars that had step-down floors, and ever since all automobile manufacturers followed."

Don nodded approval, thinking he liked this older design better. He noticed the front bench-style seat covered with a thick quilt that matched the car's exterior maroon color. Pulling the protective cover off, Johnny exposed the seat's light tan cloth, still in good shape.

Looking at Don's reaction, he said, "The original wool mohair feels scratchy on bare skin. The first owner placed these quilts on the seats."

Don knew this originated from a time when fabric durability trumped creature comfort. He supposed you might sit four across on the front seat… were it legal. The steering wheel's color matched that of the seats and had a center-mounted chrome-plated horn bar. He slipped behind the gigantic wheel and firmly closed the door. He started taking a mental inventory of the car's interior, noting the vehicle offered plenty of room.

A driver with large thighs could easily slide behind the wheel. The seat went back far enough, accommodating both wide and tall drivers. Once settled in the driver's seat, he experienced a cozy sensation like when entering his grandmother's house. Last updated before he was born, her home remained comfortable and charming. Sitting in the driver seat was like the warm feeling you get when you've crawled under a thick feather blanket by a roaring fire.

The Chevrolet's backseat had more legroom than the front seat. Rear passengers could easily walk in and sit in their seats as if in a movie theater. The painted metal dashboard was the original simulated light woodgrain color. The color made it seem far away, providing a sense of more space. Mounted on the dashboard was a push-button AM radio. It also had the very desirable long-forgotten optional shortwave band.

Next to the radio was a cat's eye lighter. To activate, you pushed in the glass knob and, when ready, the knob would glow like a cat's eye. He found three ashtrays, one for the driver and front-seat passengers and others mounted in each of the backseat armrests. The Chevrolet's dashboard exhibited gauges for water, oil, battery, and fuel. Looking through the steering wheel, he saw a large round speedometer. The odometer on it read less than 40,000 miles.

Johnny O noticed him staring at the odometer and said, "Those are the original miles."

Don looked at the passenger side dashboard, where he noticed a clock similar in size to the speedometer. The optional heater controls were under the radio. There was also a rare factory-installed tissue dispenser, and it was under the passenger side glove box.

While sitting behind the steering wheel, Don looked up at the headliner. He was six feet three inches tall; there was ample space between the top of his head to the roof. He realized this vehicle hailed from a time when everyone wore hats. No fashionista would dare remove their hat while driving. The Chevrolet's split and angled front window allowed better vision.

He looked back at the dashboard where he saw a fixed glass prism device, which the owner told him was called a traffic light minder. A glance at the gadget showed the traffic light's color. He mentioned how the prism came in handy when you stopped too close and couldn't see the traffic light. Don thought, why aren't these gizmos on today's cars?

While stepping out of the sedan, he asked, "So, why are you selling it?"

Johnny's smile left his face. As if embarrassed to answer the question, he turned away. Then he loudly grumbled, "My wife is making me. I love driving this Chevrolet around town and going to local car shows. She says I have to sell this one because I have too many toys."

Again, walking around the vehicle's exterior, he stopped to study the car's balloon fenders. Johnny O stated he was the winning bidder for the sedan at an auction. He had wanted to install a large fuel-injected V-8 and make the old girl a tire-smoking hot rod. However, after learning her history, plans changed, and he only repainted her. He explained how he recently purchased another vehicle for his hot rod project. Turning, he pointed to a far corner in his parking lot, where a 1960s Chevrolet super sport stood like a rusted sentry.

A slight scowl was on his face when he said, "My wife told me, 'You can only do one car project.' Darn those women; they just don't understand! Well, I guess she's right. I wanted a hot rod, so I'm selling my Chevrolet. Let me show you something." He motioned for Don to get into the passenger seat, while he slid behind the wheel. Positive he had Don's full attention; he said, "Let me show you how to start the car."

He started by pulling a beige knob with a black letter C on the dashboard halfway out, saying, "It's the choke." Next, he pulled a beige knob with a T out about one-quarter of the way out, mentioning, "That's the throttle. So, you don't need to prime the carburetor by stomping on the accelerator to depress the clutch during startup. Once the ignition key is on, you must find the starter button; it's on the floor, above the gas pedal."

In an apologizing tone, Johnny stated, "You can't see the starter button from the driver's seat."

After placing the steering wheel's transmission gearshift lever in neutral, Don watched as he stepped on the button with his toe. The electric starter spun, and all two-hundred-sixteen cubic inches of the flathead power plant sprang to life. Johnny pushed the throttle and choke all the way in, as the straight-six engine purred like a kitten.

The plush inside materials softened the motor's sound. It made him think the automobile ran on batteries. The sound was barely noticeable. When the owner pushed down on the accelerator, the engine roared, sounding eager to please. He brought the engine back to an idle; he pulled the hood's release lever located under the dash. Both men exited the vehicle.

They went to the front, where Johnny opened the hood. He took a nickel from his pocket and placed it on the radiator. When he took his hand away, the five-cent piece remained standing on its edge, which proved the smoothness and balance of the automobile's power plant. The Chevrolet's Victory-six engine made an exceptional melodious sound. But what Don heard was the whisper-quiet efficiency of quality engineering. Closing and locking the hood, the bearded owner motioned him into the driver's seat.

Like all 1941 Chevrolets, this vehicle had a three-speed manual transmission with a steering column gear shift lever. His left foot depressed the clutch while his right hand grasped the lever; he moved it through the series of gears: first, second, and third, returning to neutral. Completed, he took his foot off the clutch pedal.

Johnny told him, "The shifter is clunky during cold weather."

He grinned, thinking he would never drive it during winter! The owner suggested a test drive, and he readily agreed.

The car was running when Johnny exited the sedan. He went to his shop, changed the front door sign to read closed, and locked the door. While the man was closing up shop, Don tested the hydraulic clutch, which needed a synchronized motion between his arm and leg muscles. Placing his foot on the clutch pedal, he depressed it and put the car in first gear. Then, he slowly lifted his foot off the clutch. The old Chevrolet responded with a lurch and moved up near the building's entrance.

The shop owner returned to the passenger seat and nodded his approval. Don understood the drive would be a nerve-racking challenge. He tested the brakes before moving to the road. They stopped the vehicle. With no cars in sight, he turned the Chevrolet onto the uncluttered country highway. With no power steering assistance, rotating the wheel required muscle. But he found the column shifter smooth as he sped up through the gears.

At a higher speed, he needed little effort to drive. But when he let his foot off the accelerator pedal, the pedal sprung back, causing the car to slow. Before long, he slowed the Chevrolet only to discover a driver needed two powerful arms to steer when going at a slower speed. Touring at the 1940s war mandated thirty-five miles per hour speed, made the car float, and made your world gently pass.

A modern highway came into view; Don slowed the car and turned onto the higher speed limit road. The Chevrolet's acceleration was brisk for its age. Just as Johnny said, she was happier at vintage era speeds of fifty to sixty. Don continued to press on the accelerator. His action sent the Chevrolet to seventy-five miles per hour. The interior noise increased. He returned her to the more comfortable speed of sixty when the sounds abated. The traffic sped past them. He took the next exit, starting back towards Johnny's shop.

As the owner was ready to speak, Don interrupted him asking, "How long have you been trying to sell this car? And, what do you want for it?"

The owner answered, "It's going on three weeks." He then confided, "Car buyers approve of this old Chevrolet, but at $9,500 most can't afford her."

Turning into the shop's parking lot, they noticed a dirty black pickup near the entrance. He parked the Chevrolet in the same spot they started from, shut off the automobile, and gave the key back.

With the car's key in his hand, Johnny O asked, "Would you mind giving me a minute? That's my wife's truck. She's probably worried about something."

From behind the wheel, he nodded and replied, "Yes, I'll wait."

When the woman saw her husband, she stepped out and walked to the shop. He watched as they entered the building, noting her attractive face had a stern expression. Which prompted him to think, *if I buy this automobile, will Ann give me a similar look?*

While waiting, he realized the car's quality sold him, as he was still excited from his white-knuckle drive. Johnny returned as his wife climbed into her pickup truck and drove off. He apologized to him, explaining his wife, worried that he didn't answer the phone.

Don asked, "Is anyone else interested in buying the vehicle?

The shop owner admitted a new Indiana-based World War II Homefront themed museum had contacted him, asking if he would donate the car. But I told them my price, and the woman advised me their organization may take it under consideration.

Candidly he said, "My wife came to inform me the woman called back, wanting a donation, or to negotiate the cost. After two weeks, she wants to work out an amount."

Don's solemn face changed to a grin as he stated, "Next time she contacts you, tell her you sold it! I'll pay your $9,500. But the banks are closed tomorrow; will you take a hundred-dollar deposit today? The rest paid in cash, say within three or four days?"

Johnny's face lit up with a visible smile and with a nod of agreement replied, "Works for me!"

The two men extended their right hands and shook, sealing the deal. They entered the shop exchanging names and working out the details of their agreement. Upon exiting, he looked at his one-hundred-dollar receipt and thought to himself, how do I tell my wife I bought a 1941 Chevrolet Special Deluxe Sedan? That evening, he sat in their den explaining to Ann how he started the morning with every intention to purchase land in the country and ended up buying his antique dream auto.

He told her, "If I didn't miss my turn, I would have been on the highway and never seen my dream car. It must have been fate!"

Ann was happy for him, which confused him even more when she confessed the new home dream was only his. It turns out the family building the house across the street, changed their driveway plans to enter further up the street. That modification made them content to stay in their current home. They then planned for Monday's trip.

Monday morning, Don made two calls. His first call was to their bank, advising the assistant branch manager of their coming in to make a withdrawal. The second call was to Johnny O at Phoenix Auto Body. He left a message for him with their approximate time of arrival to complete the sale transaction.

At around ten-thirty, after leaving the bank, they were finally on their one-hour ride to Potterville. They were planning to stop for an early lunch before going to Johnny O's shop. But they were too excited to eat and drove directly to Potterville. As Don turned Ann's car into the Phoenix Auto Body Shop's parking lot, they saw her looking like a beautiful burgundy two-door regal queen. Johnny had spent the weekend washing, cleaning, and putting a coat of wax on the Chevrolet.

Ann turned to him smiling and whispered, "Nice car. I like your choice."

The owner greeted them with glassy eyes, stating, "I will miss this automobile." His words were slow and deliberate, which was contrary to what Don told his wife. He continued slowly, stating, "Once you own a classic automobile, it becomes a part of you. Not all old cars survive. This one did because a person with an extraordinary life owned it — a genuine human-interest tale. If you have a minute, I'll tell you how I bought the car and the reason it's not a hot rod. You don't always get these stories. I think you will enjoy hearing about what you're buying."

Don just wanted to leave and pulled the bank envelope out of his pocket. Johnny O took the hint.

When it came time to sign the title transfer inside the shop's office, Don asked his wife to sign the document saying, "Kitten, could you please sign here. We're putting this car in your name."

This was part of his plan. He never told Ann of the man in his dream, telling him to put this Chevrolet in his wife's name.

Ann knew this was important for only on special occasions did he ever call her kitten. Surprised by what he asked, she clowned with him saying, "Oh! You're finally buying me a car."

With their sale finished, Johnny started telling them how he looked for an old car he could build into his dream hot rod. He informed them how he scrutinized auto magazines, newspapers, and those new internet sites for any 1930s or 1940s cars coming up at auction. He had found an estate sale taking place in Dearborn. Finally, Johnny caught Don's interest as he explained how in 1991, he bought the Chevrolet in his own hometown.

The public sale advertised a vintage collection of household goods and listed a completely original 1941 Chevrolet with less than 40,000 miles. The picture showed the entire vehicle. He told them how he could see there was no body damage or major rust issues. The auction service stated the family had purchased the automobile new. In the late 1950s, they placed it in storage, and no one had driven it since.

He arrived early for the auction to find tables filled with all kinds of doodads from a bygone era. The auction tables displayed items such as figurines, ashtrays, depression-era glass, china, and stemware. Clear and blue canning jars filled other boards, along with their zinc lids in every size, and hanging on racks were men's clothes from the 1930s and 1940s. Another table held antique baseball bats and gloves that looked like over-stuffed oven mitts with fingers.

Johnny continued his tale of a well-preserved antiquated Victor phonograph with no motor and stacks of obsolete seventy-eight records and bunches of popular songbooks dating back to the 30s. He described a time-worn walnut cabinet with a Philco floor model radio standing in the corner, and how the radio dial glowed a lime green… hummed but never picked up a station when he turned it on. Other areas displayed Bakelite plates; the kind movie theaters gave out for promotions in the 1930s. Two World War II Civil Defense helmets with their required chrome pitted flashlights hid near a wall. Finally, there was an artisan-crafted oak dining room table and a dinette set with matching velvet tattered chairs.

A loaded wooden box with German metalworking tools and precision toolmaker instruments, dating from the early 1900s, had been mixed in with household goods and appeared out of place. After all this, Johnny explained how he never found the 1941 Chevrolet. When he inquired, he found out it was near the garage. The driveway was cluttered and stacked with items that hid the car. But, as he walked to the backyard, he set his eyes on the dusty automobile. The grimy vintage auto was pulled from the garage bay and stood there as if waiting to be taken home. Someone had tried to wipe the dirt off but stopped halfway through.

This was what they call a true barn find. The shop owner described how cardboard boxes of ancient *Look* and *Life* magazines from the 1950s and 1960s lay strewn nearby. He described how on top of the driver's door, pieces of tattered, yellowed cloth fragments hung down as if torn from the neighboring grounded old dust cover.

Johnny now became more somber, staring, "Looking back, she looked so lonely parked there."

He told them how he inspected the body, finding only a few minor spots of rust. Rough but shiny the chrome bumpers gleamed at him from the dust. The original interior had cobwebs everywhere and had a smell similar to axle grease. Lightly worn with no noticeable moth damage was how he described the light tan mohair seats. The engine looked good and clean. But he couldn't figure out why a rusty half gallon juice can would be on top of the exhaust manifold. He bragged of discovering a speaker behind the front grille and a microphone in the glove box.

He found the trunk contained a treasure trove of items. Inside was the original owner's guide, sales literature, and a repair manual. Johnny stopped to laugh. He then told them about the owner's manual, which had a section on removing blood stains from the mohair upholstery.

A dog-eared copy of the April 1941 Country Gentleman magazine he noticed was lying in there. It was folded open to a full-page ad for the Chevrolet Special Deluxe Town Sedan. Receipts for maintenance dating back to the 1940s from a place called Wally's Garage. Family picture albums of the first owners were there. Everything there told the car's history. What appeared to be the car's original never-used spare tire and a jack completed the trunk's inventory.

Johnny sounded anxious, telling them, "Once the 1941 Chevrolet went up for auction, there were more bidders than I thought, but I wore them down and placed the winning bid. I could not believe I won! Walking over to the cashier's table, I noticed two middle-aged ladies and an older woman in a wheelchair staring at me. I recognized one woman as the auctioneer who conducted the sale."

The body shop owner paused, then said, "I saw her looking at me when she leaned over and cupped her right hand against the elder lady's ear as if whispering something to her. The auctioneer strode over to me and said, 'Excuse me sir, if you don't mind, Mrs. Maze would like to meet you.' She pointed to the lady in a wheelchair."

Ann sensed Don was getting eager to leave and nudged him to continue listening.

Johnny noticed Ann nudging her husband but Johnny ignored her action and said, "After paying the auctioneer, I went over to the elderly lady. I guessed her to be seventy years old, smiled at her, and introduced myself. She returned my smile and told me, 'I'm Donna; I also answer to Fiery. That's what my friends called me, a long time ago.' She introduced a woman pushing her wheelchair as her niece.

"Then she said, 'My late husband and I are the original owners of the Chevrolet you bought. We took that car on our honeymoon to Niagara Falls.' In a cheery voice, she continued to say, 'We loved that car and delighted in driving it everywhere. We went to work in it, on vacations, even to Michigan's Upper Peninsula, and during the war, I drove it to bond rallies. That car went everywhere with us, and we went everywhere with it. We had many camping trips and one memorable trip in Pennsylvania, right before my husband was shipped overseas.' She ended by saying, 'We were young and crazy then.'"

Johnny took a deep breath and, in an emotional voice stated, "She may have been grinning, but when she spoke those words, I saw her tears."

Ann interrupted Johnny asking, "Now, this Mrs. Maze, she was the car's original owner?"

"Yeah! Her name was Metz, Maze, or Mize; I don't remember what it was exactly." Without stopping, he continued, "The woman questioned me when I would remove the Chevrolet. I explained that I needed to make a telephone call confirming the towing company's time. My appointment with them had been tentative, based on my winning. I left her and made my telephone call. Afterward, I walked over, telling the old woman the hauler would be there tomorrow morning around 9 a.m. She told me that was fine. When I started to leave, she grabbed my arm and looked at me. I saw the tears streaming down her cheeks. In an almost pleading voice, she said, 'Please take good care of my car.'"

Once again, Ann interrupted him asking, "Now this Mrs. Mize is her name Donna or Fiery?"

Johnny answered, "I heard her niece call her Aunt Fiery; that's why I called her that name. But, let me finish. The next morning, I traveled back to Dearborn, and the automobile hauler soon arrived. The next thing I see is the old woman and her niece pushing her wheelchair up the driveway. I greeted them and noticed the old woman forced a smile.

"She mentioned, 'You know… you can enjoy a Chevrolet Special Deluxe even when it doesn't run.' Then she asked me, 'Could I sit in my forty-one, one last time… for a minute?' Without hesitating, I said sure and opened the driver's door. She pointed her bony index finger to the bench seat's other side, saying, 'I really would like to be over there.' Her voice was quivering when she spoke."

Johnny paused for a moment to clear his throat and commented, "Both women started tearing up; I too had watery eyes. When the frail woman slid over the long seat to the passenger's side, I watched her clutch a gold bracelet on her wrist as she stared out the windshield. Leaning forward, she pulled a tissue from a dispenser under the glove compartment and began wiping her tears. Mrs. Maze appeared to be mouthing words. It was then, I realized, the woman imagined she was riding with someone else driving.

"Minutes later, the passenger door opened, and her niece helped the woman out. She glanced up at me, smiling, thanking me for allowing her to sit one last moment in her car. Then the old woman whispered, 'I haven't been down that road in a long time.' The two women hugged me, leaving with tears in their eyes. The niece wheeled her around the house and out of view. She never looked back. Right then, I knew my dreams of a hot rod were gone."

Don interrupted him, explaining he didn't want to drive his new auto home in the dark. He asked Johnny if he could stop by sometime and listen to the entire story.

The amiable, former owner agreed, saying, "Yes, but you really should hear the history first-hand, speak with Mrs. Mize or Mase and let her tell you. I don't even know if she's living. She will meet with any person who owned her car."

As they walked outside, Don looked over at his wife and saw several tears rolling down her cheek.

She asked, "Wow! Were you aware of that story?"

He shook his head, telling her, "Never heard that before."

The shop owner ran out of the building trying to catch up with them, saying, "Whoa! One last thing you have to see."

He took the keys out of Don's hand; he walked over to the Chevrolet's back bumper, where he unlocked the trunk. As he raised the lid, he exposed the historical treasures of the automobile and its original owners.

Johnny said, "This is the car's family history. This space holds everything I told you about."

Closing and locking the trunk's latch, he returned the keys to Don. The two men exchanged goodbyes. Don planned for a two-hour ride home on the country back roads. He would drive the Chevrolet, and Ann would follow him in her car. For safety, each had a handheld civil-band walkie-talkie to communicate. Both were silent.

Johnny's story kept repeating itself as he drove his prewar car carefully home. He found himself with more questions than answers. How is it he discovered this automobile? Or, did it find him? Was this God's will for him? And, did this 1941 Chevrolet Special Deluxe Sedan have a providence or destiny in his life?

Chapter 8

New Arrivals

It was 7:30 p.m. when Don and Ann arrived home to Brighton with their new purchase. The sixty-four-mile trip took much longer than expected. With frequent stops to check the car's oil and tires and another stop for dinner at their local Irish restaurant. The overcast night sky created a dark night. As they pulled into their driveway, it was much darker than expected.

A small white flash darted unexpectedly in front of the Chevrolet's headlights. He wondered; did he just see the white albino deer fawn his neighbors told him about? If he had, it was a good omen reinforcing his thoughts of making the right car choice. But Don soon recognized what he had seen as too small for a fawn. Now, he pondered, what did he see?

Ann pushed the automatic garage door openers for each of their garage's three doors and watched them open. She pulled into the right side. Don's beloved 1959 Ford is in the middle bay, and his work car would now be outdoors. As he pulled the 1941 into the open left bay, Ann heard Don let out an enormous sigh of relief with their cars now safely in their large garage, parked at least three feet apart. Don stepped back to admire the Chevrolet while his wife pressed the wall buttons to lower the doors.

Thinking he had seen a flash of white or brown fur as the doors closed, he grabbed a big hand-held spotlight from the wall. Pushing the wall button, he opened the 1941's garage door and walked out into the darkness. It wasn't unusual in their neighborhood to see an occasional fox or coyotes at night on the hunt for deer. As he scanned his light back and forth across the lawn, the beam resembled a spear cutting through the darkness.

His light caught another glimmer of something. He thought, what was that? Over there in the distance, was it a small fox standing outside his light's range? Not knowing, he hurried into the garage when he thought he saw another flash inside the garage and flipped on the two wall switches. The eleven double fluorescent ceiling lights blinked twice, then remained lit. He moved around the garage, shining his spotlight, checking under the cars to make sure no creatures were hiding there.

He even opened the hood of each auto, exposing the engine compartments, to make sure nothing had tucked itself inside to stay warm. Confident not a thing was in there, he pushed the button closing the open door, and went into the house. He soon returned to the garage after remembering how musty the old Chevrolet had smelled and rolled down the windows. Finally, he settled in for the evening and looked forward to a decent night's sleep.

Don woke up refreshed and ready to carry out everything on his to-do list. Before she left for the clinic, Ann gave him a quick hug and kiss, reminding him to plan a relaxing drive for them tonight in their new 1941 automobile. He mentally reviewed the things on his to-do list. They included going to the state's auto license bureau, changing the title for the Chevrolet to Ann's name, paying sales tax, buying license plates, and insure the car with their agent. His wife put her notarized power-of-attorney letter on the kitchen table for him, allowing Don to register the vehicle in his wife's name with no complications.

At the breakfast table, he double-checked his list one last time. It was going to be a perfect fall day, sunny, no rain, low-eighties temperatures, and a drive in his new car. With the license bureau not opening for another two hours, Don had plenty of time to inspect his vintage Chevrolet. He opened the Chevrolet's bay door in the garage and noticed the driver's side door open.

He was sure he only left the windows open last night. As he walked by the old car's door, he closed it and walked outside. He checked around the house and saw nothing unusual. Don went back into the garage to his prewar automobile, where he opened the driver's door and froze! He was dumbfounded; curled up in the middle of the front seat was a large white hound! The trembling furball looked up at him, frightened.

A canine! Don would much rather be facing a rabid fox or venomous snake. His fear of dogs extended way back to his childhood, when the neighbor's little doggy bit his ankle. Country living and being married to a veterinarian introduced him to many unique animals. Dogs, however, were not on his list of likable pets.

Slowly, he backed away and closed the door. He went into the house to call his wife. Ann told him how to remove the dog safely from the car and reminded him there was a wire cage in the garage, some sample packets of dog food, and an extra bowl for water. He protested.

She interrupted him, using her professional veterinarian voice, saying, "Don, I plan to hang up the phone now. So, put your big boy pants on and deal with it!"

He was infuriated. Animals were Ann's responsibility, not his. They had no pets, unless you considered Oscar, the outside cat, a pet. Oscar enjoyed hunting field mice near the farmhouse, and the gourmet treats his wife provided. He followed his wife's instructions, filling a bowl full of water and opening one of those sample dog food packets pouring, the contents in another bowl. With the cage's large wire door open, Don placed both items inside. Then he moved the pen near the Chevrolet's driver's side door.

He put on the thick leather gloves that he used to bring in firewood. The plan was to open the car door, grab the creature, and throw it in the wire crate. Not yet over his nervousness, Don mustered the courage and peered inside the driver's side window. To his surprise, the animal was gone! As he stood between the car and cage, he slowly opened the car's door.

A flash of fur bounded out from the car's backseat between his two open legs into the pen. Don jumped up and screamed as he watched the animal dart into the cage. The leather gloves made it difficult for him to lock the enclosure… but he finally secured the door.

Now, safely locked inside, he threw a blanket over the pen to calm the beast. When he peeked inside, he saw the canine drink the water, sniff at the dry food, and begin nibbling at the unfamiliar treat. Don called his wife to see what he should do next, but she was in surgery. Instead, he spoke to her young receptionist, Sarah. He explained his situation and how he captured this large hound. The young girl made multiple suggestions, and he liked one of them.

He told her he would try it and thanked her. Determined to rid himself of the creature, he went into the garage, put on his big gloves, picked up the blanket-covered cage, and carried it out to the middle of their large side lawn.

Don remembered Sarah said, "The dog found your house. It will find its way back home. Just let it go free in your yard."

He opened the crate with his gloved hands and watched the hound make a dash towards the woods. He let out a sigh of relief. But the dog was running so fast it tripped over itself and spun head over tail, landing with a thud. The creature spun around. Confused, it started running towards him. The dog suddenly stopped to sit and rest. When it turned around to face the woods, Don began walking towards the farmhouse, but the animal followed him. He soon tried another method. Standing there in the middle of the yard, Don started waving his arms, trying to shoo and scare the animal away. He hoped the dog would just go home.

Instead, the tail-wagging hound walked over to him and laid by his feet. His gloves still on; he wasted no time, picking it up and placing it back in the cage. He placed the crate and its contents in the garage and set off to find the neighbor who owned the lost hound. Don spoke to three different neighbors. None of them knew who the stray belonged to, and each promised to pass along the lost dog information.

He had things to do today, and squandering his morning on someone else's lost animal was not one of those items. Don felt totally out of his element. Frustrated, he picked up the enclosure with water, food, and canine inside and placed it in the back of his sports utility vehicle. In the house, Don went to retrieve his to-do list, the car's paperwork, and call his wife. When the receptionist answered, he informed her to tell his wife he was bringing the large hound there. Soon he was walking into the clinic's empty waiting room with a blanketed covered wire cage. He placed it on the floor.

He made sure to use his wife's words, announcing, "Sarah, tell my wife to deal with it."

Sarah, who was in her late teens or early twenties, looked at him with a serious face. She said, "I'm sorry we never make appointments when Doctor Ann has a scheduled procedure." Then breaking into a smiling face, almost laughing, stated, "Okay… okay, we'll see you!"

From behind the counter, she came with her long brown hair bouncing to peek inside the cage and quickly removed the blanket. She opened the cage and, with her bare hands… removed the beast. When she put her index finger in the animal's mouth, Don almost had a heart attack! He watched how she dealt with this strange creature. After her brief examination, she took the canine over to a scale.

Turning and looking at him, she proclaimed, "Seven pounds six ounces." With a hint of sarcasm, Sarah asked, "Mr. Bryniarski, is this the *large* hound you found in your new car?"

Embarrassed, he tried to defend himself by saying, "Well, it… looked bigger."

She picked up the face licking, tail wagging puppy, carried it in one hand to a cabinet where she prepared a water and powder mixture in a bowl.

The receptionist said, "Well, I'll let the doctor tell you what you found. But unofficially, you have a six to eight-week-old puppy. She's… yes, it's a girl. Most likely, someone's prized Golden retriever pup lost from a litter. The breed is friendly, expensive, and a desired pet unless they are sick. She looks a little malnourished, but other than that, she seems fine. I know you want to do errands, so I'll take and feed her. Do you have a name for her?"

Astounded, he could only say, "It's not my dog."

Sarah placed the dog food on the counter and held the pup up with her two hands. She looked into its eyes and set the puppy, along with the bowl, on the floor. Now having had some nourishment and attention, the puppy started running over to him, wagging her tail.

"Well, you found a friend! You must have played with her today. With all that fur, she looks like a little Tiger. If it's okay with you, let's call her Tiger."

The puppy, hearing Sarah say the name, turned and ran to her. She said, "You like that name? Don't you, Tiger? These are expensive dogs;

she may have one of those new microchips implanted in her. Finding the owner should not be a problem, Mr. Bryniarski."

Sarah, with the dog, walked behind the waiting room counter. She placed it on the floor by the bowl, knowing the pup will stay near the food. Don thanked her for taking the dog and started to leave.

She asked, "Could you take the wire pen back to your house? Doctor Ann likes to have cages there just in case."

As he turned to leave with the crate, he tripped but caught himself. Tiger had run around the counter, to the door, and in between his feet. Sarah laughed and apologized as she walked from behind the counter, picking up the dog. The pup looked at Don, wagging its tail, and yapped a few times as if she would miss him.

The outgoing receptionist commented, "I think she wants to go with you, Mr. Bryniarski."

With a smug tone, he replied, "I'm not a dog person."

The pup whined as he prepared to leave. He quipped, saying, "It's amazing what a little food and water will do."

As he went to his car, she stood at the clinic's open door with the pup. He turned, looking back to see the dog yelping, struggling to free itself and follow him.

She yelled, "Gee, Mr. Bryniarski, you must have had fun with Tiger this morning; she really wants to go home with you."

He sat in his car and waved goodbye as they entered the building's waiting room. Don wanted to forget the puppy.

He was finally on his way over to the secretary of state's office with his paperwork. After a long wait, they completed all the paperwork. The automobile received a special plate, which designated it as an antique vehicle. Even though he was late getting home, he put the new plates on the 1941 Chevrolet before entering the house.

When in the house, he noticed several telephone messages on the answering machine. Two were urgent work-related calls for him. He spent the next hour on the telephone with his team of managers, working through a simple client issue. After their call ended, he realized how unnecessary it had been. He blamed himself, recognizing he empowered no one. That would change.

From the kitchen table, he watched his wife drive her vehicle up their driveway and listened as she pulled into the garage. He recognized the sound of the coatroom door opening and heard a strange fast clicking noise which got louder and louder. Just then, he saw the puppy running straight for him. She jumped up on his leg with her tail wagging, begging for him to pet her.

Ann tried to speak first, but her husband's loud voice bellowed over hers as he yelled, "I don't enjoy dogs!"

With the dog's head resting on his left foot, Ann pleaded, "Tiger is only a puppy, about two months old. She requires being fed this special formula every few hours for the next two weeks. In my professional opinion, this pup is a pure-bred Golden retriever. People pay thousands of dollars for a pick of the litter dog like this. Believe me; no one will let this animal get away. We won't have her long."

His wife asked him where he found the dog. Don told her his detailed story of finding it in the Chevrolet that morning.

She listened carefully to his account, saying, "Impossible!"

Pointing to the pup, he answered, saying, "You're the animal person; you tell me how she got in the car."

Ann developed two theories. The pup was born in the woods, and the mother was moving her litter when Don interrupted the move. Or, this happened at the body shop in Potterville, and he drove home with the puppy in their Chevrolet. She asked him to call the body shop owner tomorrow to see if this is his or one of his neighbor's animals.

He stated, "His name is Johnny O. I'll call him because I need to talk to him about the old sedan. So why the name Tiger?"

She responded, "Watch the dog when I call her name." From the hallway, Ann called, "Tiger… here, Tiger… come' on girl."

The pup, hearing her name, got up and started running towards the hallway with her tail wagging. She ran so fast on the wooden floor that she couldn't stop… sliding, she hit the wall. A little dazed, Tiger got up and walked into the hallway, finding Ann waiting for her.

Now from inside the hall, Ann yelled, "Call her, Don."

His wife's test did not satisfy him and he tried his own experiment, yelling, "Okay! Rover, come on, Rover, here Rover."

The pup ambled from the hallway, ignoring him as he called Rover. Through the kitchen, the animal wandered, ready to explore the dining room, when he yelled, "Here Tiger… come on, girl."

The tail-wagging pup immediately ran over to him. There was no doubt the pup's demeanor changed once she heard the name, Tiger.

Ann said, "Don't you understand? Puppies at this age don't respond to names. She is an exceptional animal. Now we need to search our property for the den or mother's litter."

With the puppy, flashlight, and lantern, Don and Ann walked in their woods, hoping the dog's mother might pick up the scent and retrieve the pup. Ann explained how her office staff notified the local authorities, newspapers and posted lost dog messages on their message boards. She was sure someone would claim the dog within the next day or two. That evening they searched the woods and never located a birthing den.

When they returned to the house, his wife stated, "Until we find the pup's den or owners, Tiger is her name! And, I need your help." She handed him a baby bottle, picked the pup up, and placed it in his lap, saying, "Now, feed her." She moved over to him, showing Don the correct way to hold and feed the pup. As the puppy happily sucked the bottle's contents, Ann explained that he had to care for the dog tomorrow. She finished by saying, "With the pup here, you can just take her back to Mr. Johnny, should it be his or one of his neighbors."

Frustrated, Don looked at the pup in his lap; Tiger had finished the bottle and lay curled up, sleeping with her mouth still on the rubber nipple. He reluctantly agreed to care for Tiger.

The next day, Don was busy caring for the pup. Their walk in the woods ended up with Don carrying Tiger. When they weren't feeding, they played outside, only stopping several times to call the Phoenix auto body shop where he bought the Chevrolet. No one answered, so he left several message for a return call. That evening Ann was furious that Don had not spoken with the Chevrolet's former owner. She didn't believe Don tried to make the call, so she tried herself and ended leaving a message too!

The last two days of his vacation had not gone according to plan. Not a single one of Don's projects got completed. His days consisted of either watching or playing with Tiger. The next morning at 8:30 a.m. Johnny O returned their messages.

Don said, "When I brought the Chevrolet home, the next morning, I found a small blond dog in the car. Is it yours?"

Sounding troubled, the shop owner said, "I sold you a car, not a dog. I would never leave an animal inside a vehicle! We don't have a dog, only a cat. None of my neighbor's animals look like what you described. The day before you picked up the Chevrolet, my family helped me clean it. When we finished, I checked the cabin myself, and nothing was inside, other than the history stuff in the trunk, and I showed you that."

Don remarked, "Hey, I hope you understand I had to ask about the dog. My wife is a vet, which compounds this animal issue, and now we settled that. I have to ask you, John, when you purchased the vehicle, what did you do to the engine?"

Johnny, now worried that he may have a problem with the auto, and worst may want his money back. He ignored Don's question and asked him, "How was the ride home? Did you use both hands?"

Don laughed, saying, "Listen, John, everything is fine with the Chevrolet. Can you believe it? My arms are still sore from driving the beast! Now I just want information about the 1941 Chevrolet special deluxe you sold me."

As if needing more time, Johnny O asked him to repeat the question. Don heard him breathe a sigh of relief.

The body shop man remarked, "I'll tell you; at first, I was scared. No one had started that motor in forty-seven years, so I took it slow. I wanted to restore this engine, not blow it up."

Johnny described what he did for three days to the car's engine, which sounded as if he was going through an airplane's pre-flight checklist. He spoke of hiring his friend, a mechanic, who went over the Chevrolet before starting the old motor. When he stepped on the starter pedal, it sputtered back to life.

Johnny declared, "Don, I was cautious; I even considered when to do my first test drive on the road and took it early on a Sunday morning. Remember, this car has not been on the road since Ike was hitting golf balls on the White House lawn. Heading home after my test drive, my neighbors were waving at me, and I waved back. That was something special. Something I'll never forget…"

His last words made Don realize the car's actual age, and Don could tell the words came from his heart. He glanced at his watch to see they had been speaking for thirty-three minutes.

Johnny proclaimed, "What a rush I got driving that automobile. You know what I mean?"

He responded, "I'm getting that feeling. You did a lot to the vehicle, but do you regret doing anything?"

The body shop owner answered, "Yes, one thing. I painted the automobile and took two months to do the job. But I did it right, repainted it in the original color. I became sentimental. While painting the Chevrolet, my emotions got the best of me. That never happens to me; painting is what I do for a living. I paint cars! After I bought the new whitewall tires, I decided she was ready for the local summer charity car shows."

Johnny's voice sounded sad when he said, "But those auto shows came to a quick end, and I stored the car each winter. My wife hated me spending the money on storage fees. If I kept it around here, it just got dusty, so I kept it in a climate-controlled storage unit. Don, I think that car's destiny is to sit in a garage."

Wow! This was more information than he expected, but was glad he asked.

The body shop owner continued, "Did you have time to examine those items in the trunk? It's like opening a time capsule. The car's actual history is there."

Don answered, "No, I haven't; I've been busy with other things around the house, with winter coming and…"

Johnny O interrupted, saying, "When you have time, look. The original tarps that covered the car are there. When I first bought the car, my wife took the dusty covers to a laundromat. She laundered both those canvas covers twice. She washed a smaller picnic or pet blanket too. Everything is there."

Feeling overwhelmed, Don said, "Hey! Thank you for telling me about the car. But there is something…"

Again, the body shop owner interrupted, declaring, "If you truly want more information, start with the trunk and go through that stuff. If you need anything else, speak with the original owner. I forgot her name, but that old lady was sharp. She will talk to you all day… if she's still living."

They ended their conversation, and he remained seated at their kitchen table, looking at their driveway. He noticed the light drizzle had stopped, and pondered what he learned. At his feet was Tiger curled up, sleeping. He wondered, where did she come from? Don moved off the chair to go outside; his action woke the pup who followed close behind. In the garage, he took the Chevrolet's key off its interior visor and opened the rear hatch.

Inside it was just as Johnny described it, a treasure trove of artifacts from what appeared to be the early 1940s. He removed the two large tarps from the trunk and placed them on the clean floor. Meanwhile, the puppy was whining at the garage door, and he understood it to mean she wanted to go outside. He pushed the button to open the automatic door. Tiger darted for the lawn, halfway to the center; she stopped, looked back at him, and tinkled.

When finished, she chased some unseen thing around the yard till she was tired and laid down looking at him. He had hoped she would dart into the woods, but that did not happen. When Don leaned into the Chevrolet's trunk, the pup sprang up and ran into the garage, stopping by his feet, yelping. With the rain gone, he decided to go for a ride. One problem, what about the puppy? He decided to take her along.

The lawn was muddy from the light rain, and the pup's paws were dirty. He grabbed a clean towel from the shelf, picked up the dog, and put her in the open trunk. Tiger was in doggy heaven! She tried to sniff and roll on everything in the trunk, and her tail never stopped wagging!

He wrestled the puppy to clean her paws. And when finished, he placed her in the cabin on the driver's side floor. Don took a folded blanket from the rear hatch, covered the passenger's seat with it, and placed the pup on it. He watched the puppy as she walked off the blanket over to the seat's middle, sitting there as if that was her seat. Not wanting to teach his temporary animal where to sit, he moved the blanket for her.

With the pup in the center, he started the Chevrolet, pulled out of the garage, and drove down their street. Don smiled, driving through the back roads of Brighton, where people gawked, waved, and honked their horns. Individuals reacted when he drove his 1959 Ford, but it was nothing like this. Folks seemed to enjoy seeing this special vehicle. With both hands on the wheel, he turned the automobile north on a rural dirt road, heading to Ann's Fowlerville clinic location.

The pup appeared happy sitting in the middle of the large bench seat. Don took one hand temporarily off the wheel, petting Tiger, who appreciated the gesture. He thought of the many folks who purchased and drove 1941 Chevrolets. They were not the industry titans who made multi-million-dollar deals in the boardroom, but everyday Joe's. Those people got out of bed every morning. They went to a job taking our country's raw materials, making them into finished products sold all over the world.

They were robust people like their cars. Then his Chevrolet hit a pothole in the street, reminding him he was driving. Don knew prewar automobiles were overbuilt, designed specifically for the roadways of their time. The good roads consisted of asphalt, brick, cobblestone, or wooden blocks. They typically ended at the edge of town. Then they became a country road. Those were rough, rutted, and inhospitable, gravel or dirt pathways, similar to the dirt road he now turned on.

He smiled to himself at how this auto responded and rode with no rattles. An absolute feeling of admiration came over him. He sensed himself becoming a genuine vintage vehicle owner — one who loves his memories and automobile. There were over one million 1941 Chevrolets manufactured. He wondered how many cars like this would last for future younger generations to enjoy?

At the next intersection, Don turned towards Ann's clinic. Before the war, wealthy Americans possessed Duesenbergs, Rolls-Royces, Packards, and Cadillacs. Those autos exist today because wealthy owners took care of them. He knew Chevrolets similar to his were rare because they were used each day by working Americans.

People ran these cars into the ground during the war years. Their owners took people to offices, hospitals, schools, stores, and war armament factories. Those people were genuine Americans! He wanted to preserve the history these vehicles created and understood this automobile would help him.

As he and the pup arrived at his wife's clinic, the cordial receptionist, Sarah, welcomed them, saying, "Hello, cutie! I've been busy thinking about you all morning. You look hungry; let me get you something."

Momentarily ignoring Don, she gently took Tiger from his arms. The puppy's tail never stopped wagging. She whirled in Sarah's arms and tried to say hello, as only a puppy knows how, by licking her face.

She added, "Mr. Bryniarski, hello, how are you? It is nice of you to bring the little girl in to visit me." Speaking to the pup, she said, "You must be eight pounds by now."

He responded, saying, "Fine, thank you, Sarah. And, yes, I'll have a glass of water. By the way, what are you doing here?"

Sarah explained how Doctor Ann asked her to come here and watch the clinic while she met with the associates off site. Behind the counter, she mixed a powder formula and water. When finished, she put the bowl and pup down on the floor. With her tail wagging, Tiger licked up the formula.

Going into the break room, Sarah returned with a paper dixie cup full of water. She handed him the water, saying in an almost mocking tone, "So, Mr. Bryniarski, is this what you call a large hound?" She pointed to Tiger, who had licked the bowl clean.

He took the paper cup from her and mumbled, "It looked bigger." He ignored her question and answered much louder, "Thank you for the water. Now, what did you mean when you said, 'You've been busy with her all morning?'"

The receptionist explained the 'dog found' ads Doctor Ann had asked her to place. She spoke of where she was placing those ads and how she even called the local radio station…

He interrupted her, saying, "There goes that theory!"

She responded, "Huh?"

He answered, "I had this theory that my wife put the pup in the Chevrolet. You debunked that, telling me how you're placing the dog found ads."

Sarah offered to take Tiger with her that evening, but Don thought it best to take the puppy home. As they left, he asked her to tell his wife he stopped in. Wanting to avoid the Interstate, Don drove down Grand River, the primary route, from Fowlerville to Brighton. He kept the Chevrolet at the wartime speed of thirty-five miles per hour. Every car on the road wanted to pass him. Many beeped their horn, giving him a thumbs-up; others just yelled for him to go faster! Don would never make that mistake again!

Halfway to their house, he changed directions to take the more rural secondary roads. Tiger sat in the middle of the seat, looking forward and up at the front windshield, reminding him of Nipper, the RCA Victor record's dog. When he pulled into their garage, Don's arms and biceps were sore from their drive. He covered the 1941 Chevrolet before going into the house, using the two canvas tarps pulled from the trunk.

When Ann came home that evening, he told her of his idea of searching for the vehicle's first owner. He repeated his discussion with the body shop owner, telling her how he sensed there was something funny about the man's story seeing the auction ad on a website in 1991? After eleven years, a guy who remembered the owner's name but four days later couldn't, how he talked about the car being stored for forty-seven years and owning it eleven.

He remarked, "I want to believe him, but the dates aren't jiving. Next summer, when we take the Chevrolet to a show, imagine how nice it would be to have a storyboard telling the automobile's history."

Ann saw a passion building in his eyes and heard the feeling in his heart when he spoke of finding the original owner. Ann thought to herself that this Chevrolet might be his needed distraction from work. He stated, "We think the vehicle was stored in Dearborn all those years. Johnny O mentioned a company in Howell that conducted the auction when he bought the auto. I looked inside the trunk, and it had a lot of papers and other items. Our puppy, I mean your dog, loves being inside it, and perhaps we can find the original owner's name in there?"

Then Don said, "No one speaks about the average person and how they lived. This car may have that kind of history. Imagine the tale we could tell. Just maybe they were everyday middle-class working people in Detroit who never needed their car? Or, perhaps they used this car every day during the war. I wonder how those folks survived here on the war's Homefront? Besides, how often does a 1941 Chevrolet show up with our new puppy?"

Ann found herself surprised when her husband referred to Tiger as "our pup." She wondered if he had a change of heart? All this would have to wait. Don's thrilling vacation was over tomorrow, and he returned to work.

Chapter 9

First Show

Ann noticed a change in Don over the last two months since he purchased his pre-World War II 1941 Chevrolet and Tiger came into his life. Nothing had come of the search for Tiger's owner. It appeared as if the dog might become a new family member, just like the prewar Chevrolet. She couldn't determine who had more fun during their evening walks together, her husband or the puppy.

At the office, morale and loyalty remained high in Don's department. They attributed much of that to the success of their company's microchip card entry system. Early in December, their board announced the formation of the Information Technology Division. They appointed Don, Vice-President, of that division effective January one.

His professional life had improved. With his own budget, he planned to reward his team with promotions and well-deserved raises. The card entry system would become a separate department within his new division, and many employees, who Don knew, were being promoted to that department. That made him happy. The card entry system he fought for was becoming an enormous success, and their sales team considered it their business premier product offering.

His wife was glad to see Don's promotion didn't stop him from enjoying his other activities. He finally was enjoying his home life more than work. He leaped into his new personal projects with an uncharacteristic passion and determination. Tiger was next to him, whether he was registering his antique cars for a charity show or making candles. Even when he made wine or planned his spring and summer beekeeping project, the pup was there. The only thing Don didn't do was explore the contents of their 1941 Chevrolet's trunk.

Ann's two veterinarian clinics continued to grow. She brought in two new junior partners to help her, and this soon reduced her hours. Although she was only forty-six, she dreamed about retiring in 2019 when she would be sixty-two. It surprised her that Don could be open to this idea. In the past, he had no interest in discussing retirement. He divulged how an investment group showed an interest in purchasing their company. Don thought if that happened, as a high salaried employee, they may offer him a generous severance package. He explained how he was looking forward to this, if it happened. Ann loved his recent change of attitude.

Christmas was only a few days away, and he finally found what he considered the perfect gift for his wife. He knew how much she enjoyed writing a note each day about her accomplishments, and he hoped she loved the red leather-bound three-year journal he had bought her. He even purchased a new chew toy for the puppy and wrapped it himself.

With the holidays over, it had been thirteen weeks since the 1941 Chevrolet and Tiger came into their lives; Ann noticed her husband appeared happy and content. She started calling him Mr. Wonderful… in her mind! The only time he became cantankerous is when it appeared someone might claim ownership of the pup. The vet thought perhaps she should stop trying to find the puppy's owner.

At work, Don was busy transitioning into his role of Vice-President. The first thing he and his management team did was to write their mission statement. It read: "When profitable, integrate technology within the company and allow each business unit to work in a secure, efficient, and productive environment."

His new position kept him busy at work, but now his evenings were all about making time for the pup. His wife had normally taken care of the pets. But now, he stepped up, helping with those chores. Besides caring for the dog, he also took care of their outdoor cat. Ann welcomed this change in him. Twice a week, Ann would take the puppy to her clinic, but it seemed Tiger preferred to stay home in the garage, roaming around, and playing with her toys.

Some winter days in Michigan are brutal, but the weather never stopped the pup and Don from their evening woodland adventures. Both man and puppy looked invigorated by their thirty to sixty-minute walks. Through snow, rain, ice, or howling winds, they walked. Ann would sometimes find them taking a quick power nap after these walks. One cold wintry weekend night, after their walk, Don pulled back the two tarps covering the 1941 Chevrolet's trunk and opened the rear hatch.

The garage door was open, and the pup was playing by herself in the snow. Don went to look inside the trunk, but it was too dark. He couldn't see anything. He took the three steps over to the light switches, turning them on, illuminating the garage's interior. When he spun around, he discovered Tiger inside the open trunk, sniffing everything in sight.

Don wanted to search for information or clues about the car's original owners: a name, an address, whatever it took; he wanted to know the real story about this car. Wherever he looked, so did the pup. If he moved her out of the way, she would whine. Don began to think that Tiger wanted him to leave the trunk as he found it.

He wanted to create a small storyboard to display with the car when exhibited. Most owners at those shows had a board with pictures telling the story before and after their vehicle's restoration. But he never restored this automobile. It left the factory in 1941, pretty near the condition it was in now. He was certain there was an interesting story behind the car. Don felt challenged now by some unknown internal force to find this 1941 Chevrolet's first owners if they were alive.

In the trunk, he discovered pictures of people with the automobile. He also found magazines, note pads, camping blankets, and other household items, including cooking utensils. A heavy cardstock box hid in one corner. Red Wing work shoes made in Red Wing, Minnesota, proclaimed its label. When he opened the box, he saw the top paper fly out, landing on the trunk's floor, which Tiger promptly stepped on.

As he went through the neatly organized maintenance records and paid invoices inside the shoebox, he noticed they were in chronological order by date, from the early to mid-1940s, with the most recent one on top. Only two receipts had names scribbled on them that appeared to read D M A E G E or maybe M A I G I. He considered this a good omen, but he was sad not to find a copy of the vehicle's title or registration.

Don placed the top on the shoebox, planning to look at it again later. While he continued searching the trunk, he noticed and remembered the pup stepping on the piece of paper under her paw. She sat like a sentry guarding the note so it couldn't blow away. He patted her on the head, and she lifted her paw. Casually he took the paper receipt and glanced at it.

He stopped for a moment, turned, and sat on the rear bumper. Tiger moved to put her head in his lap. Don stared at the sales receipt from Wally's Sinclair Service Station. It was for servicing and towing the car. The Dearborn garage completed the work on June twenty-second, 1959. Whoa! He thought to himself, this is weird!

What a coincidence? What are the odds of this happening? The final receipt for repairs and towing being the date he was born! Looking back inside the Red Wing box, he noticed the top slip dated May third, 1948. He checked the dates of the other papers in the box again. Don rushed into the house to tell his wife the news! He found the original owner's name and what appeared to be their car's last service receipt.

At work, he had spent the last four months getting comfortable in his new position and understanding his different responsibilities. His duties seemed to be a natural fit for him, and he had confidence in his management team. His promotion had been a blessing. He actually had *more* free time on evenings and weekends.

Don developed a passion, as only he could, for wanting to know everything about their 1941 Chevrolet. He wanted to identify and truly understand the initial owners and their reason to take a fine car and lock it away for forty years? And then, to sell it? He will begin his search for the vehicle's first owner from the name found on the maintenance receipts.

After several calls to the Phoenix Auto Body shop, he finally spoke with the owner. Johnny believed he should look for the Macie family, spelled M A C I E. This name varied from what he learned earlier when he bought the car. He also gave him the name for a business in Howell, who he thought conducted the public sale. Don searched the internet for information on the auction company and what he thought was the first owner's name. With no success, he planned a visit to The Brighton Public Library to search the old-fashion way.

Before he could visit the library, the couple found themselves stranded at home. They had no electricity, telephone, or internet communication. This first week of April greeted them with an ice storm that took down many electrical power lines. However, Don had thought ahead and planned for this event during their home remodeling. Don had the electrician wire the house for a portable AC electrical source. He had only to plug in an electrical generator.

Don never got around to purchasing that generator, and now he spent hours keeping both of their fireplaces burning, trying to heat their house. He considered this storm a warning to him. Tomorrow he would prepare their farmhouse for the next outage by purchasing a generator. He finally found one at the local hardware store. It was larger than required, but he wanted electricity!

Once home, he used gasoline from the five-gallon can for the snow-blower to start the generator and had off-grid electricity to the farmhouse within the hour. It thrilled his wife to have the furnace running and heating their house. This storm taught him a valuable lesson that he thought he could use at work.

It was two days before the icy streets melted and four days for electricity to come back on. After that, people trickled back to work. With their life returning to the normal routine, Don spent an evening at the library. He could not locate any data regarding the 1941's owner, but found information on a local auction house. He made several calls over the next few days to the Donlynn Auction Company. No one answered their telephone; after each attempted call, he left a message on their answering machine.

When he returned to work, Don met with his management team. Each had their personal experiences with the ice storm and no commercial power. They now debated using Uninterruptible Power Supply (UPS) units which store electricity with their card entry systems. They planned to wire the customer's card systems into a UPS unit. Then, if their commercial power failed, the UPS unit will turn on and keep the card system working.

All agreed it was the right thing to do, and they needed to act now, adding the UPS units on their present clients' card entry systems. Don's budget could absorb the cost of adding this feature. They would charge new clients a higher price to have this now required UPS unit. If the electricity failed, a client's card entry system could operate for four days. Only their sales team wasn't happy with the decision to increase the price.

Ten days later he received a call from his messages left at the auction house. When he asked the gentleman about the auction records, the man laughed. He told him the business was his parents, and they passed away. When his father founded the company, he was an auctioneer and owned the business for over thirty-five years. He worked all over the country but tried to stay near home here in southern Michigan. Continuing, he explained there were boxes and boxes of his father's paper records saved for legal reasons.

Don explained he was looking for an auction held for a nursing home of household goods in Dearborn. The man explained how his father did auctions for nursing homes and business with "Big Corp.", who owned or managed many of those facilities.

Don asked him, "Do you have a telephone number for this Big Corp.?"

The gentleman said, "Oh! I'm sorry," and continued, "That's not the company's proper name. Dad always called them that. I think the name of the company is Blair Nursing Home Corporation. That's the company you should talk to."

He finally had a lead and thanked the man for his help. The next day he researched the firm and found the parent company's legal name was The Blair Investment Group Corporation. He also discovered their headquarters and employees were in another state.

Several times during the week, Don tried calling the company, leaving a message with a different employee each time. Finally, he called the company on so many occasions he started referring to them as "Big Corp." On his last call, he asked the worker what was so difficult about his request. The explanation he received stunned him.

The representative explained the Health Insurance Portability and Accountability Act (HIPPA) to him. How the law, which took effect six years earlier, protected a patient's privacy and their health records. "Big Corp." couldn't or wouldn't help him; he thought they were hiding behind this law. He became frustrated and put his appeal in writing, hoping they would change their mind.

It was the third week of April when Don started planning the auto shows they may attend between Memorial Day and mid-September. In previous years, they only had their 1959 Ford convertible to exhibit. With his latest copy of *Cruis'news* magazine open on the kitchen table, he reviewed the state's car shows and their dates. With Tiger laying at his feet, he wrote on his list the cruises and shows he was interested in attending.

Years earlier, he had a special rack built to attach to the Ford's convertible trunk. The bracket was custom made to hold five eight-foot poles with flags, one for each of the four branches of service, with the United States of America Flag in the middle. Because of those flags, they often asked him to lead parades with his Ford and its flags waving. It made a wonderful and colorful patriotic display that helped awaken the crowd's national spirit along the parade route. Those people waved, cheered, and even saluted as he drove by slowly.

Don was quickly filling the lines on his *"must-attend auto show and parade list."* His *"may attend list"* was also filling up. He thought of the shows they always enjoyed. The Sunday early September local charity car show at the Ann Arbor Veteran's Hospital. Other local events included the Saint Mary Magdalen Car show held on the Monday after the Woodward Dream Cruise.

The Dream Cruise was a premier show held during mid-August by far the largest car cruise show, with thousands of automobiles from all over the United States and almost a million spectators from around the world. Having attended this event for the past eleven years, he now considered the cruise just a long drive down Woodward Avenue from Royal Oak to Pontiac. He moved that cruise to his *"may attend list."* Other favorites he kept were: the Greenfield Village's Motor Muster car show in mid-June, the late-June Old Towne car show in Traverse City to see their friends and the September Old Car Festival in Dearborn.

By the time he finished writing, he had a list of twenty-one events and many overlapping dates. That evening he and his wife went through his lists and chose only six car shows they must attend. A "would like to attend list" included several one-day shows and parades. They each agreed their choices needed to be flexible. The first show for the 1941 Chevrolet would be in Traverse City.

Late June found Don and Ann traveling with the Chevrolet and Tiger to the Traverse City Old Towne car show. The show overlapped with the city's National Cherry Festival and would be a special event for each of them. It would be the car's first show, the farthest they had traveled with it, and their growing pup's first long road trip. So, instead of the normal four-hour drive, they took a full leisurely day of driving the country roads.

They planned to arrive a day early to visit with their friends, Bill and his wife, Kathy. When their friends saw the 1941 Chevrolet, each remarked how the color looked like a Traverse City Cherry. Bill told them he had to change the car's display location. The following morning Don picked up their new space assignment from the registration tent and asked Ann to drive the vintage vehicle to the assigned space. This was her first attempt at driving it.

She had trouble operating the car. Even backing the Chevrolet on an angle into their street corner space was a near disaster. With the vehicle finally parked, the couple and pup left for an early lunch. As they strolled, Ann vowed never again to drive the 1941 Chevrolet.

Don asked her reason for the comment; she only mumbled, "Too hard to drive."

As they walked to a diner, Ann saw her friend Kathy, and she stopped to chat with her. Don and Tiger went ahead when suddenly the dog stopped on the road's yellow line to look back at the car. He pulled her out of the street. Now, at the curb, Don inspected the 1941 automobile from a distance. He wondered about the owner who cherished that vehicle, how they made certain it survived through the years.

Still observing the vehicle, he pondered how the antique automobile seemed to have some graceful, poetic, and romantic qualities. The Chevrolet was entering its seventh decade; what an accomplishment! For a car, seen by many as cheap, priced for the everyday man, and disposable, it has had a great run! This was the poor cousin to other General Motors manufactured vehicles, and they never viewed it as a symbol of affluence. Ann walked by, breaking his trance, grabbing his arm making sure he and the pup went to lunch with her. He admitted to her, during lunch, how nervous he was, not knowing how people might react to his plain pre-World War II Chevrolet.

Now, wanting to reassure him with his own words, Ann said, "Our 1941 is not inferior to any General Motors automobile of that era, even next to the top-of-the-line Cadillac. Don, we brought a nice auto here, be proud of it."

They had time before the auto show started, so taking Kathy's advice, they walked Tiger to a park several blocks away where she could have a good run. With less than an hour remaining before the opening, all three walked to their staged car. They could see every space filled with pristine classic vehicles and people wiping the dust off, shining the chrome, putting out chairs and storyboards. The pup ignored the activity and discovered a shady spot near the rear tire, content to lie near the Chevrolet.

Don looked at the autos next to him and experienced a funny sensation of everything tumbling out of control. On the one side, he found a 1938 navy blue two-door Ford sedan; on his right was a 1941 two-tone green Cadillac. The very automobile they discussed during lunch! Don smiled at each of the owners and introduced himself, saying a few cordial words about their cars.

During the car show, Don repeated Johnny O's story to every spectator who wanted to know about his 1941 Chevrolet. Not knowing whether or not it was true, he repeated the tale, secretly cursing himself for not having more facts or at least a storyboard telling the unproven facts. As the event continued, the judges came by and assessed, appraised, and ranked each of their vehicle's qualities. When they left, he went over to examine the Ford better next to him.

The 1938 Ford's storyboard told how the vehicle had been at Pearl Harbor, Hawaii, during the 1941 Japanese attack. What made the sedan unique was the never repaired bullet hole in the windshield — allegedly made during the air attack on Pearl Harbor. When talking with the car's owner, Don learned the man inherited it from an uncle, who had passed away. He said his uncle was in the Navy and stationed at Pearl Harbor in December 1941.

When his uncle transferred to the mainland, the government shipped the car to his new posting at the Great Lakes Naval Base in Illinois. His uncle seldom used the vehicle and had stored it for many years. Don learned more during their conversation than the storyboard presented. He thought if I owned this car, the entire story would be on the board.

Parked on the other side of him was a gorgeous 1941 Cadillac Series Sixty-One Touring Sedan. When new, its base price started at $1,500, almost thirty percent more than his Chevrolet. Don wondered what the story was on that two-tone-green vehicle. The owner was engaged with a spectator when Don walked over to read the car's storyboard. On it, he discovered the standard before and after restoration pictures. Also, a detailed listing of how much the owner spent restoring it and the years he devoted to spending his money.

Joey, the Cadillac's owner, came over to speak with him just as Don finished reading the board. He was a talkative and friendly person, maybe five years older than Don. The man commented on how he honestly enjoyed being next to their Chevrolet. Seeing a frown appear on Don's face, the man assured him his comment was not a negative one. He mentioned the two vehicles' similarities and commented how anyone who purchased a new 1941 Cadillac only wanted to impress his neighbors. Joe walked him in between the cars. He pointed out the stout construction and the same robust hardware on both autos.

The Caddy's owner took him to the rear of the car, where he compared the automobiles' trunk latches. Each car used the same latch. The only difference being the Chevrolet had one latch and the Cadillac two. One worked fine. The man's honest comparison amazed Don. They continued their walk around the vehicle stopping at the front bumper.

They stood there looking at the cars when Joey remarked, "Notice the resemblances?" He pointed to the front hoods and said, "If you don't believe me, compare the grille's shape and hood vents, all alike. That's the reason people called it a baby Cadillac. What separated the Caddy from other brands was being ornate, a larger engine, and more luxury options. But they manufactured both brands using the same high-quality standards. As a result, General Motors made more money selling a million of these popular-priced Chevrolets."

He believed Joey's comments were honest and compelling. Which caused him to comment, "So if a car owner didn't mind driving the same auto as his neighbor, he bought a Chevrolet. But if they wanted something less common, with more prestige, and were willing to pay thirty percent more, they bought a Cadillac."

The two men laughed and agreed. They marveled at the simple mechanics of the other's vehicle and how you could service either with a screwdriver, adjustable wrench, and a pair of pliers. Each agreed their vehicle still ran well for being seventy years old.

Joey said, "Don, a restoration expert told me to resist the temptation to restore the survivor. Any vehicle restored becomes a testament to the craftsman. They worked on it, not the manufacturer who originally built it." Joey looked like he was laughing at himself. When he said, "The guy tells me this after I spent the money to re-skin my Cadillac in OEM's (Original Equipment Manufacturer's) sheet metal. Don, that's what gets me upset. Once they removed and installed the newly manufactured front fenders, she was never the same. It even drives differently. It's a different car now. So, what's the story on your Chevrolet?"

Don eagerly volunteered, saying, "I bought it nine months ago, and this is our first car show. The vehicle, as I understand the story, had been stored for forty years. It is pretty much an all-original condition car, except for the paint job by the former owner. He won it at an auction. The auto is not perfect, but it's in excellent condition for not having any restoration. We drove it here because I wanted the experience of living in that era."

Joey replied, "Damn! I know what you mean about driving the vehicle. I sometimes get goosebumps when I drive mine. Your paint looked too nice to be original. But I recognized the authentic ruby maroon metallic paint color. That was a standard General Motors color in 1941. I considered painting my car that color. God, I love that color!"

A solemn-faced Joey stared at him, saying, "Your Chevrolet was in storage all those years, and you had no restoration done? Well, I'm telling you, I'm so jealous of your car, I could spit."

Both men laughed, understanding the indirect compliment given and received.

The Cadillac's owner continued saying, "I noticed the fellow you were talking to about the starter pedal. I'm curious what you mentioned to him, only because last year, the same guy asked me how I started the Cadillac."

Don replied, "Yeah, I noticed him looking inside too at the third pedal; he couldn't comprehend the idea of a footswitch on the floor to start the automobile. I told him, you step on it, and the engine turns over. He said, 'I'd be a lot easier to turn a key.' I reminded him the auto is seventy years old."

Suddenly, Tiger started wagging her tail, jumping up and down, and yapping like she wanted to say hello to someone. This outburst surprised him. Then Don saw someone he thought he recognized from other car shows. The man he knew always dressed in a flannel shirt and carried a dog. But it was not him; the guy he observed had no dog. Ann volunteered to take Tiger for a walk so they could continue their conversation uninterrupted.

Don continued saying, "Joe, one person I spoke with did not believe how my car survived in our state's environment. He assumed it must have been in a desert Southwest climate, not in our swamp-like state. We know you can't go far without seeing a body of water. Our microclimate promotes the rusting of metals!"

The guys talked and laughed. They thought the auto manufacturers conspired with the city of Detroit. Joey commented how few people realized Detroit sits on a huge deposit of salt. It is extracted from mines thousands of feet below the city. During the winters, the county used a mixture of salt and sand to de-ice the roads. The mix promoted rust on the consumers' cars, forcing residents to buy a new vehicle every few years. They spoke of vintage cars from Michigan being a real family heirloom… nearly as rare as a horse-drawn buggy.

They walked to where the officials planned to present the awards. The couple's 1941 Chevrolet won a second-place ribbon for *best vintage pre-World War II original automobile*. Ann took the award in stride, but the honor surprised Don. He wondered how their Chevrolet could win over what he assumed were nicer cars than theirs. He was happy they came to this show.

Later, as they were leaving, Joey ran over and said goodbye. He gave Don a business card saying, "Maybe this will help you find your car's original owner."

As they drove off in the heavy traffic, Don handed the card to his wife, asking her to place it in the glove box. Tiger sat contently on the front seat in between the couple during the drive home. She had grown over the months but still couldn't see outside the windshield. While riding in the car, her height never deterred her from looking forward as if she was doing the driving.

Don found himself occupied driving the secondary roads back home. Ann was in heaven going through the invitations they received for upcoming car shows. Normally car shows charged the owners a registration fee to attend their event. Some shows charged up to fifty dollars. If other auto shows wanted your automobile at their event, they gave you an invitation waiving the fee. Typically, they placed it on your auto's front seat in the hopes you bring your auto to their show.

They received nineteen invitations. Don, busy driving, listened while Ann read aloud the auto shows invitations they received and sorted them by date. Three she dismissed as being too soon, four were on their current *may attend list*, and twelve were actually for next year. Neither Don nor Ann had ever heard of an invitation being offered so far in advance. Ann recognized four shows on their *may attend list*. Both considered the 1941 Chevrolet's display at the Traverse City Old Towne Car Show an A-plus performance.

Not knowing if they would have trouble during their trip home, the couple took the following day off. Ann went into her clinic late morning, and Don was determined to learn more about their Chevrolet's history. For the next three hours, he and Tiger investigated everything in the trunk. Don removed the entire contents of the trunk, and placed everything on the garage floor, including the 1948 license plate wrapped in a shop's rag. The pup sniffed and rolled on everything while Don searched for clues to find the original owner's name. Not finding any information to help his search, he carefully returned everything to the trunk as he found it. He went into the house and wrote another letter to BIG Corp.

In the evening during the second week of July 2003, Ann and Don were sitting in their den, and finished reviewing their auto show lists for the next two months. They revised their plan to do two local weekday and one-weekend auto shows, all using his Me-Car 1959 Ford. He confessed that he did not want to take their 1941 Chevrolet to another automobile show until he found out the car's true history. And the reason the owners stored it for so long.

Ann asked, "Where do you suggest we should look next?' She waited for his reply, but he didn't respond; she continued, "Do you think the Chevrolet was meant to be stored, never seen, and never driven as Johnny O suggested?"

Don answered, "I don't know; I just don't know."

Chapter 10

The Note

Don and Ann drove their 1959 Ford convertible to all the events in July that were on their car show and parade calendar. In early August, they felt guilty not showing the Chevrolet, so they took her for a short ride to a local restaurant.

On his way inside the diner, one of their neighbors stopped him, asking, "How long have you owned this old Chevy? What's its story?"

Don answered truthfully, saying, "I'll tell you everything I heard, but so far nothing I know is based on fact."

At dinner, he told his wife how much it bothered him that they didn't know their car's true story. He vowed, "I'll find our Chevrolet's original owners, or their children, or neighbors! This winter I'm going to spend more time searching for answers or she will sit and rust in our garage."

Ann wanted to change the subject, and remarked, "Can I ask you a question?" He nodded yes to her. She continued, "Would you be okay if we adopted Tiger?"

His face turned into a broad smile, replying, "I thought you'd never ask."

She described how after fourteen days the state normally considers the animal abandoned. But, because she was a veterinarian, she waited ten months. Her associates thought the pup was a pure-bred Golden retriever. Ann thought the same. She also knew it best to write mixed breed on the paperwork when adopting the pet. He told his wife it didn't matter what the pup was he just loved having Tiger around.

He declared, "Did you ever watch her around the trunk of that old Chevrolet? She goes nuts over the stuff in it. I'm not sure who she loves more, me, that stuff, or the car?"

The dinner conversation drifted to their work schedules and how he may have to travel for several overnight business meetings during the next month or two. They discussed how some of those trips might interfere with their planned car shows. Ann commented how she understood and reminded him how blessed they had been over the last two months showing their antique autos and having so much fun together.

Again, he mentioned how determined he was to find the true story behind that 1941 Chevrolet. He needed answers! Was the automobile stored? How long did it linger stowed away? How did the family use the vehicle? Why did they keep it?

She listened to the determination in his voice. He had constantly been doing little things to move in that direction. Don would not be satisfied until he could write a truthful storyboard for their 1941 ruby maroon sedan. Although that is the car's correct color, Ann sometimes referred to it as presidential red.

The following week Don came home and told Ann he had to fly to Washington, D.C. for a meeting on Friday. On Thursday, just past four o'clock, the electrical power failed at his company. A few minutes later, their generator supplied the computer room with power. However, other departments had to stop working. At four-thirty, a rumor circulated that Windsor, Canada was without electricity. He thought that's ridiculous! Don's principal focus was their card entry system, which also did payroll. He confirmed that their system was working without a glitch.

Twenty minutes later, Don verified the city across the river, Windsor, Ontario, had no electricity. Rumors were rampant. Many employees thought it another terrorist attack! A news channel on a portable radio confirmed a massive power grid failure. The electrical outage included eight states in the northeast part of the country. The Canadian Province of Ontario was part of the blackout too. Also, his site for tomorrow's meeting, Washington, D.C., was without electricity.

Don spoke with his sales manager. She delivered his message, which was to contact all clients in the involved states and confirm with each client that their card entry systems were operating. That evening he started his home generator and watched the local news. Eight states in the north-eastern part of the United States, including the Province of Ontario, still had no electrical power. Later that night, Don received a call notifying him the government department had canceled the meeting. He never discovered how that government department found his unlisted home telephone number.

The multi-state power blackout affected millions. Most people and companies had no commercial power for four days. Entry system clients with no electricity were happy to see their upgraded security system function perfectly during the outage. Weeks later, trade journals published articles praising the reliability of their system. Those editorials described his company as forward-thinking and innovative. These remarks only enhanced their company's reputation. New system orders increased, as did corporate revenues and profits.

Over the next two months, Don attended four government meetings in the nation's capital. In between those trips and his work, he found time to winterize their antique vehicles. While working on their cars, he remembered never receiving a written answer to his Blair Investment Group (BIG) inquiries. He always thought BIG intentionally hid their patient information. They used a privacy law, and he needed to do something else to achieve his goal.

Don tried using professional influence to get his information. He made a telephone call to BIG's Director of Information Technology. His call, although courteous, was not welcomed and a complete disaster. His peer gave him a stern lesson in federal law, and he learned something valuable. You should always follow the rules of the patient privacy law.

A return turbulent plane ride to Detroit was in the middle of a winter storm, and he pondered how to find the Chevrolet's information he so desperately wanted. He decided to start over from the beginning. Unable to retrieve his stowed briefcase because of the rough flight, he asked the attendant for a drink napkin. On the small paper cloth, he started jotting the facts he knew about their vintage vehicle. He did this before, but now he would write every detail he knew verbatim. With pen in hand, he wrote:

Johnny O bought the car at auction nine years ago; he then crossed out nine and wrote ten years with a question mark.

BIG Corp.-owned nursing home where owner lived.

Public sale was in Dearborn ten years ago.

Donlynn Auction out of Howell organized the public sale.

Old plate in the trunk.

Pictures, maintenance records, and camping equipment in the trunk.

With the aircraft preparing to land, he placed the napkin in his suit jacket pocket. Two weeks later, during a business meeting, he reached into his pocket looking for a pen and found the forgotten napkin. The meeting vanished into oblivion as he concentrated on his notes and started drawing lines through some of his checked remarks until only two items remained. One a 1948 automobile license plate; the other a Donlynn public sale ten years earlier in Dearborn. It was like a light bulb illuminated in his head.

He thought that's so easy! He never tried the Michigan Department of Motor Vehicles (DMV). After all, it is a state-issued license plate, and the state never throws any records away. That is the perfect place to retrieve the information he so needed. Christmas was in one week, and there was no time to visit the local Michigan DMV office. Don would do this task after their busy holiday schedule.

A few days before New Year's Eve, a huge blizzard was in the making. That day Don worked from home. True to Michigan's changeable weather, the storm never materialized. The roads had only a dusting of snow covering them. With extra free time on his schedule, he got into his car and took the 1948 license plate to the local DMV office. There he only waited five minutes in line before a courteous employee called him to her station. He explained the information, and the employee excused herself to get the help of her office manager.

He remained standing by the counter when the woman soon returned with her supervisor. Both were polite, and the manager explained the standard cost for retrieving the information he requested. However, when Don heard how she said that word, he knew her tone meant to open your checkbook. She continued, stating how current electronic files go back sixteen years. The name and address he sought were in a paper format, and required manual labor to retrieve.

While she was speaking, she handed him a packet. Don learned it contained the charges for the service he requested, and the form he needed to fill out. Since this was a manual search, she advised him it may take months or years to find the information. He examined the rate sheet and thought he could purchase another 1941 Chevrolet for the amount of money he may have to pay for a name and location.

He thanked the manager and employee for being so informative, telling them he would think over the presented process. A few minutes before six that evening, Don decided to try his Option two: Donlynn Auction ten years ago in Dearborn. On a lark, he looked up Donlynn Auction's telephone number and dialed it. He let it ring and didn't expect an answer so late in the day. It surprised him when on the fourth ring, a woman's voice answered. She introduced herself as Sarah and confirmed he had reached their auction business.

She said, "The information you're requesting is from ten years ago and not available. Few of those paper records have survived from dad's time. The files we keep are for taxes, and none are older than eight years."

My brother and I run the company on a part-time basis, and we only work with companies our father dealt with.

Don said, "Have you ever done business with Blair Investment Group?"

"Oh! You mean BIG Corp. That's what dad always called them. We've worked with them in the past, but not so much anymore." Sarah continued saying, "Most of the public sales we do as a favor for our prior clients. We are working less and soon hope to dissolve our parent's company."

Sarah was polite, explaining there was nothing else she could do or suggest. He gave her his name and telephone number, just in case she should discover any information. He then drew a line through the second and last option on his list. Don filed his notes and placed the folder on his desk. Wanting to take his mind off his search, he decided to take Tiger for a walk before Ann arrived home. Before taking the pup outside through the garage, he put on his winter jacket, scarf, and boots.

They were on the snow-covered lawn for nearly twenty minutes when Ann finally arrived. Tiger at once rushed over to Ann with her tail wagging. The dog loved smelling each new animal scent on the Veterinarian and wanted to sniff the dinner she brought home. As Ann tried to calm the excited pup, they said hello with a token kiss. She spoke of seeing a male Golden retriever at the clinic and how Tiger must smell his scent.

Don told her he had organized the car show events for the season and placed the information on the coffee table so they could work on the schedule during dinner. Ann asked him to check the glove compartment of the 1941 Chevrolet, as she may have left some event flyers in there. With Tiger following, he went into the garage, lifted the tarp exposing the passenger door, and retrieved all the papers from the glove box. He replaced the dust-covered tarps over the sedan and returned to the family room with the complimentary flyers.

Ann had gone to take a shower. Ten minutes later, she joined him and their dog. His wife returned feeling refreshed, made herself a small plate of food, and sat down in one of the comfortable chairs as they spoke of their day. Tiger looked for her evening treat and settled down at Don's foot once she had her snack. With dinner over, Don cleared the table and put away the leftovers. When he returned, he found his spouse reviewing a few of the event flyers.

He heard his wife say, "Did you see this?" as she handed him a folded piece of paper.

He took the note from her, unfolded it, and saw a handwritten note. The writing was on a law firm's notepaper with the firm's letterhead and a line stating from the office of Joseph Holloway, Esq. The message read:

Ann and Don, I enjoyed meeting you both and relished our conversation today. Regarding your 1941 Chevrolet, I recommend you look for a civil action in the county where the public sale took place. The corporation needed to file a grievance in the county court to order a seizure of the real estate and other property against the owner of your car. The court had to rule in favor of the corporation and provided a civil judgment, forcing the sale to pay the debt. Good Luck. He signed the note, Joey.

Flabbergasted, Don sat down, not fully comprehending what he read.

He asked his spouse, "Who is this?"

She replied, "I think — it's Joey from Traverse City. The man who displayed his Cadillac next to us?"

Still confused, he replied, "When did he give you the note?"

Ann recalled when they were leaving the display area, and Joe came over to say goodbye. He handed Don the folded note, and Ann placed it in the glove compartment. They had forgotten it since June. For six months, the answer to finding the history of their 1941 Chevrolet was there in the car. Each grinned at the other when their telephone rang.

Ann answered the telephone and handed it to Don, saying, "It's Sarah."

Baffled, he asked, "Your Sarah… from work?"

"No! Another Sarah," she answered.

She watched a smile spread over his face during the call. When it ended, he remarked, "I cannot believe… what just happened! That was Sarah from the auction company calling me back. It turns out she overlooked telling me about county court records and the need for civil action. How a judgment in favor of the nursing home's parent company, BIG, will be part of the court records. When I research the court's rulings, I should start looking twenty-four to six months before the public sale. She said many times it takes a court that long to adjudicate a judgment. Also, the actions become public record unless the courts seal them."

Each considered this a Godwink for them, and they knew it! They were informed where to find the name and address of their 1941 Chevrolet's original owners, in one evening, from two unique sources. During the first full workweek of 2004, Don paid the fee and filed the freedom of information request at the Wayne County Courthouse. He thought… if the body shop owner, Johnny O, had owned the car nine years, plus the one year they owned it, that's ten years. Sarah told him about adding another two years before the auction date. This information provided him with the date of January 1992 as a beginning for the search.

Don wrote the company's legal name of Blair Investment Group LLC. and requested a search range between January 1992 to January 1995. He considered the three-year period an ample time frame. Don checked the box to mail the information to his home address. On Groundhog Day, February 2nd, 2004, a medium-size envelope from the county arrived in the mailbox. Before opening the packet that evening, Don and Ann, who never drank, decided to have a small good luck toast over a glass of his homemade honey wine, called mead.

As they expected, the envelope contained the requested BIG information. Inside the envelope were many civil judgments in the company's favor. To their dismay, they found the company pursuing their right in court to collect any debts owed to them. But they could not find an individual who owned property in Dearborn. Their effort didn't provide the information they hoped for, but both agreed they were on the right track. They decided to try again with a different date range between January 1987 and February 1992. Don planned on going to the courthouse the next week to make another request.

This time he asked them to call him when the data was available, and he would pick it up. A message one week later informed him his request was ready. He picked up his packet of information late Friday afternoon and drove home during rush hour traffic. He dreaded his timing. All the way home to Brighton, cars were bumper to bumper on the Interstate.

One accident made his normal fifty-minute trip a three-hour white-knuckle commute. He arrived home later than expected and was in no mood to review anything. He took Tiger for her nightly walk in the woods and went to bed early. The next morning Ann told him how she reviewed the judgments in the envelope. The overlapping months collected data for only two years and three months.

Ann was determined to find the reason no search information came back before 1989. She explained to Don how she searched BIG on the internet. There Ann discovered they had incorporated the company in January 1989. Finding several civil judgments that may hold a promise, she put them aside for Don to review: one in Dearborn, two in Inkster, and another in Allen Park. Later, he reminded her they were looking for auctions in Dearborn, not the surrounding communities.

Ann rebuked him, saying, "You're the man who always says he's from Dearborn, but you were born and raised in Dearborn Heights!"

Wham! That was personal, and it woke him up like a face slap.

He responded, "Point taken!"

Don spent the entire morning reading through the material in the packet for himself. There were no matches. When reviewing the judgment in Dearborn, he discovered it was for the auctioning of a boat. She reminded him what Sarah said about a sealed decision, which could be why they could not locate the information. Every bit of positive energy was failing fast.

Several days went by as they discussed what they called their 'now what plan'. Ann suggested they consider one more search… with a smaller window and earlier time frame.

He disagreed, saying, "How can they hold an auction after Johnny purchased the car?"

Ann replied, "Just maybe… he bought the automobile seven and not nine years ago?"

Don conceded her point and recalled his gut feeling and suspicion of the body shop owner. Invigorated, he agreed to another inquiry. A third request would have a date range of January 1995 through January 1997. In his hurry to fill out the paperwork and get home, he didn't realize he had made an error in the dates requested. He glanced at his payment receipt, thinking this request was more expensive than the other two but thought it might result from increased processing and mailing costs. He wasn't getting caught in traffic again and checked the box: mail the requested information to the billing address below.

During the second week in March, a much larger envelope arrived. Ann opened the packet. She asked Don to see if he noticed any glaring errors, but he noticed nothing out of place. That was when Ann pointed out he listed the search end date as February 2004.

Her husband said, "Gee, I'm sorry. It usually takes me several months before I get the year change correct on the checks I write. I fouled this up. So, I did an eight-year search instead of the two-year, we agreed upon."

"Well," said Ann, "At least we have more documents to review."

It took them three days to examine the documents, and they found several judgments to be promising. There were twelve civil verdicts in favor of BIG Corp. that were potential matches for them. The two most promising leads involved one auction in 1996 in the City of Dearborn and another in Dearborn Heights in 2000. When reviewing the auctions, each involved all goods, including household properties and real property. The judgments were against Mr. T. Albert Franks, on Francis Street in Dearborn, and the other was Mrs. Donna Louise Maze, on Appleton Street in Dearborn Heights.

The woman's name seemed similar to what Johnny O first told them. To Don, the shocker was the street address. This family may have been their neighbors growing up on Appleton, and the last name was very close to what they wrote on the Chevrolet's maintenance receipts. But the year for the auction was wrong. Well, that's what Don kept telling himself. They reviewed Mr. Franks' case again, finding he did not own a home or automobile and is not a match.

When they returned to the judgment against Mrs. Maze, a public sale date of August twenty-fourth, 2000, that date was also Ann's birthday. The court records showed that Mrs. Maze lived in a nursing facility controlled by BIG. Don felt excited about the owner's name matching and sad Johnny O misled him, and, if true, he would have owned the car for only two years.

The following day, while still light out, Don drove by Mrs. Maze's address on Appleton Street. The drive brought back fond memories from his past. When he came to the auction's address, he found a vacant lot. There were no buildings, grass, trees, or shrubs. Any buildings there were gone. The property had a construction company sign announcing "New Homes" with a modern sidewalk near the street.

Don tried to recall the house that stood there, down the street from where he grew up, but he couldn't remember. He pondered, are any of the family members living? Since he was in the neighborhood, he drove past his parent's home. He thought of the happy memories they made in the house and playing with his childhood friends.

As he went to leave, he deliberately turned around in his family's old driveway. He made this gesture as a goodbye to his parents and added his private somber thought of thanks for their love and memories. Tears were in his eyes by the time he drove past the vacant Appleton Street lot. He remembered the pictures in the 1941 Chevrolet's trunk of it parked in a driveway and wondered if that was the house. Don made a mental note to look closely at those photographs.

Don arrived home late, and it upset Ann. She had to remind him that tonight they were meeting friends for dinner. He quickly showered, dressed, said hello and goodbye to Tiger, and departed their farmhouse. He told her of his trip to Appleton Street while driving to the restaurant.

Ann yelled at him for forgetting their dinner plans, how he should have been home sooner, and gave him every reason he should never have gone by the house without her. He said nothing during that car ride. The Bryniarskis arrived at the tavern before their friends. After a brief wait, the waiter sat them at their table.

While waiting for their friends, his wife ordered a White Russian, and Don got a diet cola. He understood something was bothering his wife, for she seldom ordered an alcoholic beverage. Ann did not wait for their friends. When her drink arrived, she started drinking. Soon she requested another round. Her second cocktail arrived with a change in her demeanor, and she appeared relaxed.

Ann forgot her husband had been late and wanted to hear what he did on Appleton Street. For the next thirty minutes, he told her what he saw, did, and how certain he was that Mrs. Maze and her family were the car's owners. Ann finished her drink and ordered her third.

Their friends, Kim and Connie, arrived at the Z Lake Tavern and Restaurant a full hour late. Connie apologized for how their babysitter abruptly cancelled at the last minute. Connie told them she called their house, but they had left.

Ann, the non-drinker, now finishing her second drink, and with a slight slow drawl said, "Connie, not a problem, no problem, Connie, there's no problem."

Kim looked at him, and asked, "How many has your Ann had?"

Shrugging his shoulders, Don replied, "Two, it was just one of those days."

Everyone had ordered dinner and caught up on what had happened in their lives since their last get-together.

After her third drink arrived, Ann proclaimed, "My husband found the person who owned our old Chevrolet."

He was quick to reply, "We think."

Connie spoke to them and cautioned Don to take it slow and understand that not all elderly individuals are able or want to bring up bygone memories. She said, "It's difficult to comprehend how the individual may react. Like us, they're all different. You may ask to speak with her or them, but why should they chat with you? There is no logical reason they or their family would speak with you, a complete stranger, and tell you about their life or car. It would help if you had an advocate. Someone to introduce you, other than introducing yourself, you know friendly neutral person to start the conversation."

Kim chimed in, saying, "Hey, you don't even know if the nursing facility will allow you to communicate with the woman. Is she still alive, infirmed, or too weak to speak?"

Don took their comments to heart, understanding it was too early to get his hopes up this high. The evening was full of good conversation, delicious food and ended on a cheerful note. As they drove to their farmhouse, he mentioned to his wife what their friends revealed about having an advocate.

She stated, "Oh! I agree with them. You need another individual to intervene for you. Ideally, it should be someone who knows both parties. Call them a guardian angel or advocate, but someone needs to help you break the ice."

Don thought to himself, who wants to help me? And, where does one find… an angel?

Chapter 11

Hello Eloise

Don read the court judgment against Mrs. Maze several times. This ordered the public sale of her personal possessions and caused him to believe this individual once owned his antique Chevrolet. He wanted to speak with her or her children, but Connie's words repeated themselves in his mind. Be discreet, not overt, be friendly, not hostile, and be sensitive to a person's feelings. Have a plan in place to avoid doing something wrong.

He was having trouble hearing the rational voice inside his head. Instead, he felt his desire for information screaming at him, and only heard, telephone now! On an impulse, he looked up the nearest Blair House Nursing Care facility… Dearborn. Without thinking, he dialed the number for their nursing home in Allen Park.

When someone answered the phone, in a stern tone, he said, "Hello, my name is Don. I want to stop by and visit with Mrs. Maze. Tell me your visiting hours?"

The individual on the receiving end of the line took great offense to his irritable tone. They responded, "I'm sorry we have no resident here by that name, good day," and hung up on him!

He considered his human nature, understanding what to do and how to proceed. He took days to draft a strategy and, in one moment, watched his chances go out the window by using a stupid assertive tone. Don became the perfect example of what not to do! The problem, he thought, was his tone. For six days, he agonized over his terrible call.

He and Tiger returned from their evening walk and were sitting in the family room. Don admitted to himself that reasoning and logic had to come first. He screwed up what he thought was his introduction and pondered what he should do next.

Ann walked in on him, and seeing his face remarked, "You haven't been yourself all week; what happened?"

His repentant mood made him confess his Blair House telephone call. He saw the expression on his wife's face change. Ann went into a tirade and lectured him, repeating everything Connie told him.

After three minutes, she stopped to catch her breath and continued saying, "Don, that is what they say at a hospital when you ask for a person who has died. They tell you, we have no one here by that name. They never tell you, the individual you're asking about is dead!"

"Ugh! Don't remind me; I know it wasn't very smart of me," he commented.

She asked, "Do you have that number?"

He knew Ann was furious and gave her the telephone number. She thought, how could this brilliant professional act on his impulse like an idiot! Determined to make amends for her husband's indiscretions, Ann picked up the phone and dialed the nursing home's number.

In a calm tone, she said, "Hello, my name is Doctor Ann Bryniarski; I am calling to inquire about a former client, Donna Maze."

She held her index finger up to her lips, signaling for him to stay quiet as she spoke. On a notepad, she wrote the information confirming the correct spelling and pronunciation of a name. His wife ended the call by thanking the person.

Ann turned to him, saying, "You know… use honey, not vinegar if you want to attract bees. Be careful how you say things. Practice your peaceful voice. Mrs. Maze is no longer in the care of that facility. Some time ago, the family moved her to another home and remembered her as a friendly woman. The operator recommended I call and speak with the director tomorrow. I intend to do just that."

Don knew the reason he called his wife, Kitten. Ann is so sweet and good at taking care of him. He thanked God for having her; she saved his day. But what happened to her last week? He forgot to ask.

To change the subject, he questioned her, saying, "When we were out with Connie and Kim, you had a few drinks. What was that all about?"

She looked at him, cracking a faux smile, explaining, "It was a hell of a day. An animal died during a routine operation. Our associate partner Rhonda left. She thinks she will do better at another practice."

He asked, "So… she quit? And what else?"

Ann answered, "It was not just quitting. She said hurtful things about me and my employees in front of anyone who listened. We'll talk later. I can't deal with it right now."

She left the room, walking into the kitchen, ready to cry. Ann's professional career was a train wreck. He tried to think of something positive. He considered the news of the Chevrolet's owner being alive a few years ago as a positive. Don's emotions were swirling. In his notebook, he wrote, speak with Ann about Rhonda… in bold letters.

Don knew he needed to put himself into a better mood and contemplated what kind of honest, informal board he might create for his car. The story, what would that entail? Should he write of the 1941 Chevrolet or the family? If he spoke with the family or the actual owners, what would he ask them? He started writing questions in his Chevrolet folder, then realized there were too many uncertainties in his situation. He smiled, recalling a unique storyboard he read several years ago when they attended the Motor Muster automobile show at Greenfield Village in Dearborn.

Almost nine hundred vehicles were on display that day. But only one storyboard remained in his memory. It was about a 1923 Dodge Brothers Touring Sedan, plain-looking, unrestored, and much like the thousands manufactured that year. The storyboard told of the original owners being Missouri farmers. The auto endured a practical rural life on their farm. When the vehicle's useful purpose had come to its end, the family parked it in a barn. It remained there for over forty years.

The owner's grandson had the sedan partially restored, leaving an unusual large-shaped crease on the right side of the engine's hood. He wrote on the board in the summer of 1925 that a heavy thunderstorm caught a horse living on the farm outside. So, frightened by a loud clap of thunder, the mare sat on the Dodge sedan's hood, causing the damage. That steed was long gone now, but it left behind its mark… a permanent crease on the car's hood. He chuckled to himself, trying to imagine who would believe that tale today?

What is the story of my car, he wondered? This question continued to haunt him. The following evening when they came home from work, he asked Ann if she spoke with the Blair Nursing Care administrator in Allen Park.

She would only say, "I'll tell you after dinner." He tried to direct their conversation back to Mrs. Maze while at the supper table, each time his spouse interrupted him, saying, "After we finish eating." With supper completed and the table cleaned off, Ann went into the family room where she sat in her chair, he followed. She looked tired and said, "Let's talk after you take Tiger for a walk."

It was a clear and frigid night, and the pooch wanted to stay outdoors. The arctic weather brought both man and beast inside for warmth after thirty minutes. When he returned to the family room, he found his wife napping in her recliner.

He sent their Golden retriever over to wake her, not wanting to do that himself. With wet, cold, and snowy ice balls on her paws, Tiger jumped into her lap, startling Ann awake. The dog wasted no time greeting her. He approached the subject in his mind after a few minutes.

Ann explained how she reintroduced herself to the director, telling the man she wanted to contact and follow up with a former patient. The man advised me he had to phone someone for permission to speak with me. Later, he called me at my office, saying she is frail and would require her family's approval before I could speak with her.

Ann said, very seriously, "Don, before I give you the information regarding her family, you need to reassure me that what you say will be positive. We can talk about this tomorrow. But I want you to consider what you will say."

He understood what his wife was trying to tell him. His earlier approach had been wrong, and he could not repeat it.

She scolded him, commenting, "You can't display your arrogant attitude. So, take your time and plan. I am not giving you the name until Saturday."

Don knew Ann wanted him to be successful, and he had one chance at this. The family's response would depend on his opening words. He had to get this right. This was not a business call … it was very, very personal. To wait four days for a name would be challenging, but he vowed to use his time wisely and plan for the phone call ahead. He wrote several outlines, each with a specific opening statement directed towards a woman or man, the actual owner, or their representative.

Saturday afternoon, Ann found him in their family room gazing out the window, looking at light snow falling in their yard. He was repeating in different distinct tones, "Please tell me, how long did you own the Chevy?"

His wife interrupted him after his third recital of the phrase. She yelled, "Do not refer to that automobile as a Chevy! No one from that era called those cars a Chevy."

That was when she confessed to him. She had told a fib earlier in the week, and she only received the contact person's name yesterday.

Ann declared, "Eloise Graham is Mrs. Maze's legal guardian. The care facility where she lives requires us to have the niece's permission before speaking with her. They would not tell me where she lives."

Don asked, "Who is Mrs. Maze's niece?"

She replied, "I asked the same question and never received an answer. Perhaps Eloise Graham is her niece? You should verify that with her…"

He broke into her words, saying, "What is the nursing home called? Where is it located? When do you think we…"?

She scolded her husband, shouting, "Don, slow down and change that attitude! Remember, that tone of yours is what gets you into trouble. You shouldn't be quick to make an appointment… be that professional, calm person you are. Try to use the advice Connie and Kim gave you. God knows… you don't listen to me!"

Much to his chagrin, he knew she was right. Walking over to his chair, he sat down, rereading the information his wife gave him.

He asked, "How does this sound, Hello Eloise…"

After forty-five minutes and a lengthy discussion about how he should approach his long-anticipated telephone conversation, Ann finally agreed his tone sounded amiable, and he should make his call.

With the telephone receiver in his hand and number dialed, he noticed her watching him. Soon he stated, "Six rings… no answer; I'll call back later." He commented, "Do you remember showing the Chevrolet in

Traverse City? The one guy who came up to us saying, 'This car has providence!' You know who I mean? He was the real animated guy. He talked with his hands. I remembered him saying, 'I can feel it… it has providence.' I wonder if there is something magical about that automobile."

Ann looked up from her magazine to say, "Donald… it's a car… nothing is mystical about an old car." She proceeded in a joking voice, blurting out, "Oh! Wait, you throw dollars at it, and the vehicle makes your money disappear."

He replied, "That's not funny. I was thinking about how people are affected when they see our auto. We've taken our 1959 Ford to fifty more events than the Chevrolet. But we received more compliments during the one show we had the 1941 at than all the other shows combined."

After considering his remarks, as if thinking out loud, she spoke, "Mystical qualities, I remember when we took the Chevrolet to church. The older gentleman was looking at our car in the parking lot. We laughed when we came out of Mass and saw him still staring at our 1941 Chevrolet. He had missed the service completely gazing at the auto."

Don recalled, "Yes, he was in high school during World War II and had a part-time job working at a pop stand. I remember him because he called it pop instead of soda."

Ann answered, "His boss owned a 1941 Chevrolet just like ours. Remember, his favorite thing to do at work was drive the vehicle to a car wash for its weekly washing. What's so mystical about an old man recalling his youthful adventures?"

He responded, "You saw how he smiled when he recalled the story. How his eyes looked when he spoke to us?"

His wife tried to interject humor, saying, "Mesmerized is not mystical."

To prove his point, he stated, "You know what I'm saying. How about the neatly dressed, handsome older man at Traverse City? The guy who stood across the street staring at our 1941 Chevrolet. After ten minutes, he came over asking if the 1941 was for sale? Then telling how in December 1940 he purchased a 1941 Chevrolet Special Deluxe Town Sedan brand new, like ours when he was only nineteen years old."

His spouse, smiling from ear to ear, affirmed, "Yes, and they drafted him in the summer of 1943. That's when he gave me his business card."

"Right," said Don, "He had two wonderful years with his auto. You told me he stared at the Chevrolet with dreamer's eyes staring at a lover."

Ann declared, "You're confusing memories with some mystical notion, Don. My goodness, the man was seventy-five years old, recalling his youth. When I said, I'm sorry, this automobile is not for sale, I watched his eyes well up with tears. My heart ached for him as he scribbled his name, address, and phone number on a slip of paper. He handed it to me, saying, 'Perhaps one day you'll change your mind.'"

Don remarked, "I'm telling you; our Chevrolet makes people reminisce… there is something special about that car."

She interrupted, "Yes, special, not spiritual."

He continued with another tale, "You weren't there when a man came up to me telling how his father and grandfather used a car like ours for their house painting work vehicle right after World War II. How a burning cigar butt tossed out the driver's side window blew back inside, landing on some paint thinner soaked rags on the rear floor. The smoldering cigar butt caught fire, but they were lucky enough to escape uninjured. Their 1941 Chevrolet, however, was a total loss."

He stood up from his chair to stretch, and Tiger got excited as if they were going outside. Don sat down, petting her, and said, "So, why are people compelled to tell two total strangers their life memories when they look at our car?"

She commented, "We get some unconventional stories. I remember the prim and proper gray-haired eloquent woman who shared her earliest childhood memory from the late 1940s. Her uncle stopped at her parents' house with his 1941 Chevrolet to show off his hunting prize. He had tied a large trophy buck to the big pontoon fender on the driver's side. The lady remembered how sad she felt for the animal."

Ann dismissed these tales as a normal reaction to an old car. She said, "They relate to your vehicle, and wonderful old memories come back to remind them of happier days. Those individuals need to express their feelings or relate their memories to someone, and they open up to us because it is convenient. Why don't you try to call Eloise Graham again?"

He said, "I think I will."

He picked up the telephone receiver and placed it back in the cradle before dialing the phone number.

"What's the matter?" She asked.

"Oh! Nothing," he replied. "I just thought of how Johnny O didn't tell me the truth when we bought the car."

Ann, frustrated, looked up from her magazine, saying, "Don, you can't change the past. Forget about it. He didn't have the knowledge you have now. You'll get no glory in shaming him if you meet."

It amazed him that Ann was always right. He understood his spouse was correct, and that bothered him. He inhaled deeply, reviewed his notes, picked up the telephone, and dialed the number. She heard him introduce himself and gave him privacy by going to the kitchen and making him his favorite snack, microwave popcorn. Of course, Tiger followed her, hoping for a dog treat.

After ten minutes, he joined her at the kitchen table. His face was somber.

She asked, "How did your call go?"

He explained how he spoke with Eloise's husband. Reading from his notes, he continued, saying, "Mrs. Graham was out shopping. He wasn't sure when his wife would be home, so he took my name and phone number. He told me his wife is Mrs. Maze's niece, and her aunt, Mrs. Maze, is not in the best of health. I asked him about Mrs. Maze's car. He told me, 'I have no knowledge of a car.' How is that possible? I mean, you're married for many years, and you have zero knowledge if Mrs. Maze owned an old Chevrolet? If Eloise doesn't return my call, I'll try again next week."

The week came and went, and the calendar changed to April. He had not received a return call from Mrs. Graham. After reviewing his notes, Don made another call to Mrs. Graham. A woman answered the phone, prompting him to ask for Eloise Graham. The woman identified herself as she. He introduced himself, explaining the reason for his call. She apologized and in a stern voice asked if he could call back tomorrow evening. She would have more time to speak with him if he called between seven and eight.

The following evening, at precisely seven-thirty, he called Mrs. Graham. Again, he explained the reason for calling her and introduced himself as the current owner of Mrs. Maze's 1941 Chevrolet. It upset Eloise to learn the car changed owners! Eloise explained how she and Mrs. Maze had attended the public auction and what a sad day it was for her aunt. He hoped to get as much information as possible by asking his practiced open-ended questions.

Eloise hesitated when he asked permission to visit her aunt.

She went on to explain her aunt still had her mental faculties but was a very frail woman. Although Mrs. Graham didn't think this was a good idea, she said she would discuss his request with other family members. Other family members? Don asked if Mrs. Maze had children?

The niece immediately took offense to his question and declared forcefully, "I am the only family she has."

He at once apologized and explained he wanted to match her family with pictures in the photo albums he found in the vehicle's trunk.

Mrs. Graham's tone and attitude quickly changed as she whispered, "Were there many things in the trunk?"

Don responded, "It looked like someone had gone through her property, placing certain personal items and things in that car's trunk." After a brief conversation of the trunk's contents, Eloise hinted she needed to end the call. Don asked, "Will it be okay if I call you back, let's say the day after Easter?"

Mrs. Graham cleared her throat and said, "Mr. Bryniarski, you need to realize, my aunt has moved beyond her car and memories… sometimes reminiscing can be bad for a person and their family. I am uncertain she would want to revisit those times. I wish you and your family a blessed holy season. Till next week, goodbye."

A week later, Don called Mrs. Graham. They exchanged stories of their Easter celebration day. The woman described spending it with members of her family and visiting with her aunt. Don held his breath, waiting to hear if they had discussed his request.

Mrs. Graham said, "My Aunt Fiery was sad to discover the gentleman had sold her 1941 Chevrolet Special Deluxe to someone else. He had assured my aunt he would take care of it and never sell it." After a pause, she continued, "Mr. Bryniarski, it is only because of a grandchild that I may allow you to speak to my aunt. However, we must have ground rules for what you may talk about with her. So, let us start by you telling me what you hope to learn?"

He started by saying, "Mrs. Graham, I would like to thank you for the opportunity. I promise you I will be most sensitive to you and your aunt's feelings. I can assure your aunt that my intentions for purchasing her car were most respectful." He took a slow deep breath and continued saying, "What I am most interested in is the history of her 1941 Chevrolet. When did the family buy the vehicle? Why this make and model?"

He listened as Mrs. Graham again cleared her throat.

With no words or other response from her, he continued speaking, "How did they use the auto? Did they travel with it? When was the auto placed in storage, and the reason? Perhaps a safe place to begin is which subjects I should avoid discussing with your aunt? Also, what is your aunt's name… Furry?"

There was another pause in their phone conversation.

Mrs. Graham broke the silence as she remembered what she had said, "Oh! I'm sorry, I sometimes refer to my Aunt Donna Maze as Aunt Fiery. That was her nickname when she was a young girl. And… yes, perhaps there are topics you should avoid. Mr. Bryniarski, do you mind if I call you Don?"

He responded, "That would be nice."

Mrs. Graham said, "You may call me Lucy."

Don considered this an excellent sign and added, "Thank you, Lucy. Which subjects do you recommend I avoid with your aunt?"

Lucy spoke slowly, making sure Don understood her words, saying, "Yes. Please do not bring up the auction of her household goods… it was a miserable day for her. Also, avoid talking about her husband, baseball bats, or gloves, and do not ask questions of their dog. Should my aunt bring up a topic, that's okay, but remember each one is a heartache."

He asked her if she would tell him of the public sale, her aunt's husband, and the dog since he could not discuss these matters with her aunt.

Lucy said, "Try to imagine how you would feel seeing all of your life's possessions being sold, given, or thrown away. And, besides that, the money goes to that nursing home company. Companies have no respect for you when you get old. But, enough of that! My aunt insisted on being at the auction. My aunt wanted to see where her life's treasures were going."

Her speech was deliberate and sad. She said, "The nursing people made sure they auctioned everything, including my aunt's old-fashion Victrola, all of her seventy-eight records, and her Philco radio. She could tell you how she received the war news on that radio. They even sold China plates; the kind movie theaters gave out in the 1940s, her husband's Civil Defense helmet, an oak dining room table, the dinette set I used to sit at, and her automobile.

He listened to the melancholy tone in her voice as she continued saying, "Yes, and even her 1941 Chevrolet Special Deluxe Sedan. Six weeks before the auction, my grandchild and I took Aunt Fiery back to her Appleton Street house. We told the nursing home employees we were taking her to dinner. She hadn't been inside her home in two years, but she remembered the location of each item she wanted. We went through the entire house in less than ninety minutes. Legally we couldn't remove anything from the property. Everything my aunt cherished, we placed in the trunk of her forty-one."

He could hear the tears in Lucy's voice. She struggled with her words, commenting, "So you see Don, each item my aunt valued is in that car. To receive word that a man sold her Chevrolet and removed or threw her items away will devastate her. Aunt Fiery insisted on being at her Appleton Street house to watch the public sale and the next day to see them remove forty-one. I remember her asking the gentleman who bought the vehicle, 'Could I sit in my car one last time?' Then she told him, 'I really want to sit over there,' as she pointed to the front passenger seat."

Her voice broke, and Don heard Lucy sobbing. After a brief pause, in her gloomy voice, she whispered, "I recall my aunt saying to the man that bought it, 'please take good care of my car.' The tow truck driver was in a hurry, wanting to leave, but the gentleman who bought her car was gracious in allowing her time to say goodbye. She sat in the passenger seat, gazing out the windshield one last time.

"I remember thinking to myself she was not alone. My aunt sitting in the car was riding with the memories of her late husband at the wheel. Taking a tissue from under the dashboard, I saw her wipe the tears rolling down her cheeks. She sat there for five minutes, just staring ahead. I wasn't sure what she was remembering. When I helped her from her car, she commented, 'I haven't been down that road in a long time.' Perhaps now you recognize the need to be sensitive when speaking with my aunt."

Don didn't mention her story matched the one the body shop owner told him. He thought it was good listening to something true. He responded, "Thank you, Mrs. Graham, for sharing so much personal information with me. I understand how you wish to protect your aunt and will try my best not to bring up any of those memories." He continued saying, "Lucy, I'm sure everything you referred to is still in the Chevrolet's trunk. I even discovered a receipt for work done on June twenty-second, 1959. I remember that because I was born on that day."

Lucy responded, "What did you find?"

Don repeated his last couple of sentences to her, putting special emphasis on the date.

Lucy said, "Let me think about this. Aunt Donna did not drive forty-one when we lived with her parents. She parked her auto in the garage in 1947 and never moved it. She never told me why."

He replied, "Well, maybe the Wally's Service Station receipts are for another vehicle."

Lucy asked, "What information is on your receipt?"

He repeated the gas station's name, a charge for towing, and listened to her chuckle.

She proclaimed, "You mentioned Wally's garage, I think you must be forty-one's owner. That's where my aunt had her cars repaired. Well, here's your receipt's true story. The last time my aunt drove her automobile, I was seventeen years old. The only reason she drove it was because a tree fell on our garage. Forty-one sat inside there for ages, covered with tarps. But, when an elm tree came down on the garage's roof, she had to remove her auto."

Don asked, "A tree?"

She replied, "Yes, but I'm getting ahead of myself. Let me start again. My aunt never used her vehicle after moving in with her parents... in 1947; I was five. When living at gramma and grandpa's house, she always drove her dad's red car. Her forty-one had sat there forever on one side of the garage, and she never drove it. On June fifth, my seventeenth birthday, the next-door neighbor's tree fell on our garage."

He interrupted, asking, "Did it damage her Chevrolet?"

Lucy responded, "That's the strangest thing… not a scratch was on her car. Wally from the service garage came to our house, pulled it out onto the driveway, where it sat under her covers while carpenters repaired the damaged garage. Now auntie's plan was to have the forty-one pushed back inside the garage, but the construction company insisted the auto could not stay on the property. When they told her that, I thought she would have a cow! What is your receipt's date?"

He answered, "June twenty-second, 1959. The day I was born."

Lucy sounded invigorated, stating, "Well, you had to arrive on a Monday. Wally came over a couple of days earlier and towed the forty-one to his garage. He was to tow it back home on that Monday. But early that morning, my aunt called him, telling him she would drive the vehicle home. I'm sure Wally did some repairs while the car was there. That explains the reason for the receipt. I know that was the day she drove forty-one from Wally's garage to our house on Appleton Street."

Don asked, "So you're saying since 1947 she drove her Chevrolet only once?

She answered, "Yes! Let me think, 1947, she stored it… the auction was in 2000… during those fifty-three years that was the only day she drove her car, and from Wally's to our house was probably a five-min-ute drive."

He asked, "What else do you recall happening that Monday?"

She replied, "After Aunt Fiery parked forty-one in the garage, I helped her with the tarps. At seventeen, what I remember the most is later that day, we boarded a train to Jacksonville, Florida, for my Aunt Sylvia's wedding and a vacation at the beach." Lucy's tone seemed to change, adding, "You reminded me of something. Years ago, when we were covering the car for the last time, my aunt sat in the front passenger seat. She looked similar to when I saw her the day after the auction, sitting there staring at the wind-shield, a grin on her face, dreamy gaze in her eyes, and tears running down her cheeks. You know… like she was dreaming."

Don asked, "You mean she was in a trance or had seen a vision?".

"No… neither!" Lucy stated and continued saying, "There's something loving that old car gives her… that makes her dream of happier times. I saw my aunt with that grin on her face… like a dreamer waiting for her wish to be granted. Sorry for my rambling."

Feeling a need to change the subject, he asked, "Lucy, how is it you came to be your aunt's guardian?"

She responded, "We've spoken for a while, and I need to get going. The quick story is Aunt Fiery raised me since I was five. My true father and mother gave me up for adoption when they divorced after the war. Aunt Fiery could not adopt me because she was a widowed, single woman… even though I had lived with her for a year. We moved to her parent's house, so they could…"

Mrs. Graham cleared her throat, saying, "My grandparents adopted me. Before they died, they made Aunt Fiery my guardian. They passed a year later, and my aunt took custody of me. She was alone because her husband had died."

Before Don answered, Lucy said, "Thanks for listening. Call me on Friday. I'll speak with my aunt and grandchild concerning your request to visit." Then she surprised him by remarking, "You know… I've been around that car my entire life and never remember riding in it."

He interjected, "I'll call you this time on Friday. I'm positive we can arrange a ride for you, your aunt, and your family in forty-one. Thank you again."

After hanging up with Lucy, Don sat in his chair, writing notes in his book and thinking about how to start his discussion with Mrs. Maze. He considered starting with being neighbors on Appleton Street. They could talk about living on the same street. But he understood someone needed to attend with him. An advocate is what he required, and he tried to reflect on who he might ask? His wife wasn't interested in going. He considered their friend, Connie, and her easy interaction with anyone she meets. She could help break the ice and correct him if he said something offensive.

He spoke to Ann about asking Connie to join him. She said, "No! Take someone from work, not my friend, or attend by yourself. You had a friendly talk with Eloise Graham; let her introduce you. I'm going to write in my journal that you spoke to her today." Ann opened her journal to Monday, April twelfth, 2004, and started writing her thoughts.

Don didn't want to impose himself on Lucy. She was her aunt's advocate. He believed taking a female with him would help make the meeting more sociable, but he had no close women friends at work or from college. Don sat there considering the names of who might want to join him? With no idea where to go next, he closed his notebook. He was uncertain where to find his own advocate.

Chapter 12

My Ammygam

Don rushed home early Tuesday afternoon to pack for an unexpected trip to Washington, D.C. He needed to be at the airport no later than 4:00 p.m. After checking his calendar, he quickly called Ann at the clinic and left a message, saying he will telephone her later that evening. Like most Americans who owed tax dollars, he delayed paying their 2003 state and federal income taxes until the last day. He would remind his wife to be sure to mail those letters tomorrow. The other item on his calendar… was to call Lucy Graham, and he would call her from a phone booth in the terminal.

While driving to the airport, he reviewed the received government message. He was only told this was regarding a national security threat, and they recommended he attend. *How can I argue with the government?* With his car parked, Don walked into the terminal and checked in.

His next stop was to get through security and head towards his departure gate. He noticed a change at the security checkpoint. The employee's attitude appeared more serious. With new procedures in place, they struggled with how to check passengers and baggage.

Once he had cleared their process, Don walked down the concourse towards his gate, looking for a bank of payphones. There was plenty of time before he boarded his flight, so he tried to call Ann again. They spoke, and she found it hard to believe that her detail-oriented husband was making this trip, not knowing the reason or what to expect. Don explained how the government agency wanted a decision-maker from their company to attend this meeting, and the only thing his superiors told him was that he "may" be home Friday. Then he called Lucy to explain he had to reschedule their meeting and would contact her when he returned to Detroit.

Don's quick trip turned into six grueling days. These classified meetings were about providing enhanced security for airports and buildings. He returned home late Monday evening, and Ann was eager to hear about his trip. She told him how two FBI agents had come to the clinic and interviewed her and her employers.

Don responded, saying, "They did the same at my office. I guess they just needed to make certain who they invited."

His wife was not satisfied with his response. She continued to question him, stating, "They spent a lot of time with my receptionist, Sarah. Something about you meeting her and having to cancel."

He did not understand what his wife was talking about, but he could tell it bothered her.

She stated, "I want to know what happened… Donald?" A full day of meetings and travel completed, he intended to relax, take a shower, and sleep. But Ann wouldn't let it go; she needed answers! She asked, "Where did you meet up with Sarah? It wasn't at work. I'm waiting for an explanation!"

Finally realizing what Ann was implying, he quietly answered, "Why don't you ask her?"

"I would," she screamed, "But she is… or was … a trusted employee. How do you think I feel… finding out like this?"

Too exhausted to continue this argument, Don replied, "Don't do or say anything you may regret." He went upstairs to bed after saying those words.

His words bothered her. She spent the night in her family room chair sobbing, wondering what brought him to this point in their marriage. Determined not to give up without a fight, his wife became more suspicious the next day when Sarah said she needed to leave early. Don called her later to say he had a meeting and would be home late. Even though it took her forty minutes out of her way before going home, Ann drove past his building. Don's office light was on, and his car was in the secure parking lot.

He stayed late at the office two evenings in a row, so he told her. He and the company's president were the only two individuals who understood the government project. The hard part was he couldn't share any of the specifics with his wife. This morning Don was working from home. A few minutes after eight, Ann joined him in the kitchen. They talked of their busy schedules, each enjoying a rare opportunity to eat a simple breakfast together. She was cool to him as he spoke of his tentative meeting with Lucy and her Aunt Fiery, now planned for Sunday afternoon.

She asked him, "Where are you going to meet? Did you ask somebody to be your advocate?"

He answered, "I'm supposed to confirm the details with Lucy on Saturday. She asked me to be flexible, depending on how her aunt might feel. I'm going to wing it on the advocate thing. I decided to use our Appleton Street neighbors as my icebreaker." Changing the topic, he asked, "Don't you have clinic hours today?"

Ann told how she was leaving for the local elementary school to watch the children plant a tree she donated for their Earth Day celebration before going to her clinic.

Don chimed in, "Hey, that sounds like fun. Mind if I join you? I need the personal time."

His spouse responded, "Since I don't know how many people they invited, stay home."

As they were finishing their coffee, she saw an employee's car pull into their driveway and head toward the barn. She wasn't expecting to see Sarah and was suspicious when Don almost ran to the barn ahead of her. Of course, Tiger beat them both to the barn. As she arrived at the building, he was already walking out. In the building, Ann questioned Sarah asking what she was doing there. Sarah said she didn't know what happened, only that Shelly left her a message asking her to take care of the boarded Shetland pony this morning.

While they spoke, Sarah petted the excited Tiger. The pup soon rolled on her back with paws in the air while the young woman now rubbed the pup's tummy. Ann meanwhile placed a hand under the horse's lips and examined the infected gum.

Sarah asked, "How does the abscess look?"

The veterinarian was indifferent with her response, saying, "Good, and we'll know by Saturday if the pony can go home. You gave him the medication?"

Her employee responded, "It was the first thing I gave him, before his water and oats."

She struggled to be cordial with Sarah. Ann felt rather foolish thinking she could see first-hand what was happening between Sarah and her husband, but she couldn't stop herself. So, she invited her employee in for coffee.

Sarah politely declined, saying, "No, thank you. I need to go to the clinic. Shelly and I have two grooming appointments early this morning."

The young woman drove up the driveway to the street, and tooted her horn, shouting to him, "See you later!"

He waved and smiled back at her as Tiger ran up to him, now wanting to play on the lawn. Ann watched this interaction from the barn and continued to wonder. The next evening, Don called Lucy, confirming the time and place for their meeting. Ann was in the family room writing in her red leather journal. He pulled out his 1941 Chevrolet folder with the notepad and began scribbling notes.

He looked up at his wife, asking, "Do you mind going to early Mass on Sunday? Mrs. Graham wants me to join them at noon, and you'll never guess where I'm going."

In a sarcastic tone, she asked, "Pray tell… where are you going?"

He responded in an excited voice, "South Lyon! Lucy invited me to meet her Aunt Fiery at a place called Home Care at Blair House on Lafayette Street. I told her I'd be alone."

Ann announced, "Going to the early Mass is fine." Then her voice changed to a negative tone, saying, "It's good you're going by yourself, be your own advocate!"

Not knowing what his wife was thinking, he replied, "It won't be a long talk. Besides, it's only twenty minutes to South Lyon from here."

After Mass, they had breakfast at a local diner; Ann asked, "How long did you say you'll be gone?"

He contemplated his wife's question before answering, "I have my notes and questions, so I guess I'll be… an hour or two… maybe three. It's best I go alone."

A quick trip home to drop off Ann, he gathered his notes and was leaving for the Blair house when he met Ann waiting for him at the back door.

Not taking no for an answer, she said, "I'm coming with you!"

Don was too busy practicing his open-ended questions that he didn't notice the lack of conversation on their ride to South Lyon.

They arrived in the parking lot, and he turned to his wife, saying, "Look, I know you're mad about something. I don't understand what is bothering you, but this meeting is important to me. Will you please at least smile and pretend you're happy?"

Ann said nothing; then, she displayed a mock grin. Getting out of their car, she saw they parked next to a vehicle with a familiar dented fender. Inside the lobby, they approached the reception desk but waited as another group of visitors registered. While waiting, they ambled off to their right. There they discovered a vast room beside the lobby with many card tables, each with four chairs. A sign above the door proclaimed a one-hundred-fifty-six-person capacity.

Several scattered groups having quiet conversations. Some sat by the enormous windows, which displayed a panoramic view of the surrounding wetland. Don returned to the desk to inquire about Mrs. Maze and her niece while Ann remained in the room. She stepped further into the room, where a woman sat, partially hidden behind a wall divider. She wasn't certain, but now she recognized the girl.

Ann felt her blood pressure rising. She knew it was her car they parked next to, and today she was coming face to face with her employee Sarah! Surprised to see her, Sarah said, "Doctor Ann? Hi! I didn't know you'd be here…"

Ann wanted to give her a piece of her mind when she blurted out, "Where were you two weeks ago? Because you weren't at work."

What possessed her to speak those words, she never knew but considered herself in the perfect position to lunge over the card table at the girl.

Sarah stood up, saying, "Don't you recall I had finals. I asked you if I might have the week off to study? You said yes. Remember…?"

Like the flash of a lightning bolt in a summer storm, the doctor remembered their conversation. She gathered her composure, and was ready to speak, when two older women joined them at the table. Sarah walked over, hugged, and kissed the lady in a wheelchair, and they exchanged greetings she could not hear. The young woman removed journals from the woman's lap, placing them in the middle of the table. Embarrassed that she thought her employee was here to meet her husband, Ann was ready to excuse herself.

"Gammy, you didn't tell me Doctor Ann was coming," Sarah said to the tall thin lady standing by the wheelchair.

Gammy responded, "I didn't know. He told me he'd be alone."

Her employee continued, "Doctor Ann, I would like you to meet gammy and my Ammygam. This is Doctor Ann, who owns the animal clinic where I work." Suddenly she realized her words made no sense. Sarah laughed, saying, "Excuse me. Let me start again. Doctor Ann Bryniarski, allow me to introduce you to my grandmother, Eloise Graham, and my great-great Aunt Donna Maze. My aunt thinks Mr. Bryniarski may own the car she once owned."

Confused by Sarah's words, Ann asked her to repeat the introductions. Sarah took her time reintroducing everyone. Ann's mind swirled with what was happening. Bewildered, she turned, looking at the older lady.

The old woman was enjoying Ann's confusion and smiled at her, saying, "As a baby girl, Sarah, could not pronounce grandma. Her words came out Gammy. Well, try to utter great-great-aunt when you're that age. My name became auntie grandma. That's where the Ammygam comes from, but you can call me Donna."

The standing neatly dressed woman with salt and pepper colored hair extended her hand, saying, "Hello, I'm Eloise Graham. But please call me Lucy. I understood your husband was coming alone today. Is he here, or should we start without him?"

Ann described how her husband had gone looking for them while she waited. Lucy moved her aunt's wheelchair to an open spot at the table near the window. Everyone sat down while Lucy clarified how they were all related. Mrs. Graham explained how she adopted her grandchild when her only daughter passed away. That is how Sarah Michaels has a grandmother named Lucy Graham. Aunt Donna then clarified how she adopted

Lucy when she was a small girl. The women laughed at Ann's confusion and continued talking.

Meanwhile, from the other side of the Blair House complex, Don returned to the lobby, where the receptionist requested he wait. After waiting for exactly a minute, he made his way into the large room with its stunning vista of the wetlands.

Fascinated by the wilderness scene, he did not notice the woman approach him until she said, "Your wife is over here."

He paid no attention to who she was, but followed her to a table where he saw his wife with two women. One was in a wheelchair smiling at him, and another woman in her early sixties grinning widely. The woman who escorted him, walked around the card table, and sat next to the lady in the wheelchair.

The smiling woman to his left extended her hand, saying, "Hello, I'm Lucy… you must be Don."

He smiled, shaking her hand, and could only articulate, "I am Don."

His wife nudged him, pointed to Mrs. Maze, and stated, "Don, say Hi to Aunt Donna Maze. She wondered if you got lost?"

The smiling Mrs. Maze responded, "No, I did not."

He looked at her and said, "Hello, Aunt Donna, it is a pleasure to meet you."

Finally, focusing on the person who escorted him, Don was lost for words and could only say, "Hi! Good to see you. I haven't seen you since… Thursday!" Everyone laughed as he tried to remember Sarah's name. He peered at Ann, saying, "You didn't tell me you…"

She interrupted him, stating, "I did not ask Sarah; she invited you. Donald, I want to introduce you to Sarah Michaels, your advocate."

He appeared dumbfounded and confused, saying, "My what? You didn't invite her? Who did she ask? What are you talking about?"

The women laughed — especially his wife, who had completely changed her outlook from when they walked into Blair House.

Sarah spoke, mentioning, "I introduced Doctor Ann already, so allow me to acquaint you with everyone."

Don sat in the remaining vacant chair with his spouse on his right and Lucy on his left. Aunt Donna displayed an enormous grin as if she was enjoying Don's confused state.

"Mr. Bryniarski, this is Mrs. Eloise or Lucy Graham, who is my grand-mother. I call her Gammy." Sarah continued, pointing to the other woman; saying, "Aunt Donna is my great-great-aunt. I call her Ammygam. Doctor Ann can tell you later how those names came about. My great-great-Aunt Donna, I also call Aunt Fiery now that I'm older." Looking at the older woman, she remarked, "Did I say that correctly?"

Her great-great-aunt had a proud smile on her face as she replied, "That sounds correct, and you look so much like your grandmother when she was your age."

Aunt Fiery looked over at her niece Lucy, as confirmation. She joined the conversation with his wife and Lucy. Fiery leaned forward, listening to Ann when Don spotted the hearing aid in her ear and silently reminding himself to articulate his words.

Sarah saw him looking at the books on the table and announced, "I hope you don't mind; Ammygam brought those as an icebreaker."

He looked at her and asked, "How long have you been Aunt Donna's niece?"

Sarah's face displayed a mischievous smile. She looked at the other women as if seeking their approval and then at him. With a solemn straight face, she stated, "Mr. Bryniarski… I've been my aunt's niece my entire life."

He then realized what he had said, but it was too late. Everyone at the table erupted in laughter. To concede his blooper, he put a frown on his face and said, "I deserve that." Don, now blushing, looked at the giggling women, stating, "What I really… and truly meant to say, was… Ann, how long have you known Sarah was Aunt Donna's niece?"

Sarah looked at her aunt, snapped her fingers, and in a mocking tone, interjected, "I knew that was exactly what Mr. Bryniarski meant to say."

All four women couldn't stop laughing.

He raised his hands in the air, asking, "Can we start over? Hi everyone! My name is Don."

Ann quickly interrupted, saying, "Now you understand why I only bring him out on Sundays."

The only male at their table, he accepted being made the brunt of their jokes. But their meeting he thought was a disaster and considered changing the subject to their car.

Then, Aunt Donna whispered, "Hello Don, my name is Mrs. Donna Maze, but you may call me Donna or Fiery, whichever you please."

He replied, "Thank you, Aunt Fiery."

She continued saying, "Lucy tells me you have a 1941 Chevrolet Special Deluxe automobile. Can you tell me what color it is? The glove box, what is under it?"

He knew the answers but waited a moment to add suspense and then declared, "My wife calls it presidential red. I believe General Motors refers to it as ruby maroon metallic. You will find a very rare factory-installed tissue dispenser beneath the glove box compartment."

Upon hearing his words, Aunt Fiery's face lit up with a smile, proudly replying, "Those are the two options I picked for our car. How is it you came to own forty-one?"

"Well, Aunt Donna, I mean Aunt Fiery, John O, who you met when he purchased the auto, could not keep it in his shop." Don was happy with himself for not using the word, auction, and continued saying, "And, I was driving by his shop when your automobile almost rolled out onto the street to greet me! Fortunately, I found myself in the right place and purchased the vehicle."

He glanced over at Fiery, who was beaming with delight. Don thought he saw a tear in her eye. He continued praising John O for taking such excellent care of her vehicle. His comments made the elderly lady feel good.

He wanted to hear her story first hand and said, "He spoke a little about the vehicle, and your family items are still inside the car's trunk. I want you to know that your family history will remain there."

He glimpsed over at his wife, who said, "We keep your Chevrolet stored in our heated garage, covered completely with the tarps we found in the trunk. We only drive her on very special occasions or to special events. Don told me he bought the car for me and even registered the title in my name. But it is his child."

"Oh!" Aunt Fiery replied, "My husband put the car in my name too. He really did… but it was his car and babe. Thank you for keeping all our things in the trunk. You won't always have to."

He wasn't sure what Aunt Fiery meant by the words but decided not to question her at this meeting. "I heard you call your 1941 Special

Deluxe Chevrolet Sedan forty-one," he said. "Is that how you referred to your auto?"

Mrs. Maze's pleasant face continued to gaze at him when she commented, "It was a long time ago. My husband, Alex, allowed me to christen our car forty-one. That is what we both called her."

A few seconds of silence enveloped the group, but it seemed much longer. Wanting to extend their meeting, Don asked, "Perhaps you can provide us with information about forty-one, what it meant to your family, how you used and drove it?"

Fiery eyed Ann and him, saying, "I cannot tell you about forty-one…"

Don's heart sunk. He was stunned and said nothing. Sarah's face mirrored what he was thinking.

The old woman continued, "Without telling you about my husband, Alex." Again, Aunt Fiery watched her niece's reaction, remarking, "I don't mind speaking to them about your uncle. Do you mind if I tell them?"

Lucy answered, "Not at all, Auntie."

Sarah selected a journal from the middle of the table as if on cue. She moved her aunt's wheelchair away from under the square table. Opening the book to a marked page, the young woman gently placed it on her Ammygam's lap. Aunt Fiery looked at the open pages on her knees, reading to herself.

Speaking softly, she began, saying, "I loved my husband very much, and I believe that telling you about him, will help keep my memory of him alive. Maeselowski is his proper name: Alex Maeselowski. He was the love… of my life."

Her eyes stared out the window as she spoke as if searching for the words to describe a distant memory.

At first, she struggled to find the right words, saying, "Both of Alex's parents emigrated from Krakow, Poland, and met on the steamer during their passage. They married in 1908. Originally they settled in Buffalo but soon moved to Detroit, where his father became a wheelwright. Alex was born on June ninth, 1913, and was the fourth of five children. During the epidemic in 1919, three of his siblings died from Spanish influenza."

Aunt Fiery resumed her reminiscing, "In 1930, Alex took his first job as a Pure (brand) gasoline station attendant in Dearborn. He pumped gas, cleaned windows, checked the oil and air in the tires of all the cars coming into the station. After four years, he took a sweeper's job at Buhl Sons Company. They were a big business made up of many smaller companies. They did their manufacturing at a large complex in Detroit. Buhl was a well-established manufacturer of iron and steel hardware. Alex knew it was a much better opportunity than working at a filling station."

Fiery's speech continued in a relaxed and natural tone. When she said, "A year after joining the company, he signed up as an apprentice tool and die maker. He intended to be a journeyman in four-years-time. He knew about measuring tools. My Alex was a gifted mechanic and asked many questions! He spent those next years learning everything possible about the trade. Alex had an inquisitive mind. He constantly tried to make things better or simpler.

"My husband, he saved his money. When he had grown tired of taking the streetcar to work, he purchased his first automobile in the summer of thirty-six. A few of his friends had automobiles, but most were open touring vehicles from the mid-1920s, mainly Ford Model Ts. Finding those cars was easy; they were all around the city. Many of their owners worked for the Ford Motor Company. Drivers, who could afford it, didn't want to drive an auto exposed to the freezing Michigan weather. Fully enclosed car bodies replaced open cars by the late 1920s, and Alex wanted a warm vehicle."

Don enjoyed listening to her speak, but he wanted her to talk about their Chevrolet.

As if reading his mind, Fiery said, "Mr. Don and Ann, I understand you want me to tell you about forty-one. But I think it's important for you to recognize Alex as a person before he purchased our Chevrolet. Now, where was I? Oh yes, closed cars had heaters. He preferred a closed auto that had a heater. He told everyone he was looking for a cheap, good used closed vehicle for sale.

"One day an, elderly lady at Buhl, who he barely knew, said her family had a Ford Model A Coupe they had to sell. She told him the vehicle ran well, but they had parked it years ago because it developed a leaky radiator. Her mom wanted forty-five dollars for her Ford. He considered the price reasonable and took a streetcar to inspect the auto that evening. The way he and his friend Teddy told the story, Model A was stylish and popular with first-time vehicle owners. It was a practical automobile for a young man like him.

"This Polish lady lived in Hamtramck, where most of her neighbors worked at the Dodge Brothers Main plant. If not, they worked at a company that supplied its parts. Alex heard stories of Hamtramck residents considering it treason to own an automobile other than a Dodge. He found the house and walked up the worn, peeling gray painted wooden steps to the front door. There a large white Spitz dog appeared at the screen door growling a warning.

"Before he rang the doorbell, a raspy lady's voice bellowed, 'It's out back!' He walked into the lady's backyard and tripped over a rusty mower hidden in towering weeds."

Aunt Fiery's hands and face became animated as she told this story. Don could tell everyone was captivated by her tale, and she was the center of attention.

Not stopping, she continued, "In the backyard, Alex could not find a car. All he saw were vines and weeds covering a mound of used lumber next to a pile of old bricks. He returned to the front door, where the dog greeted him again with a menacing growl. The woman grabbed the dog's collar, flung open the screen, walked over to the end of the porch, and pointed her finger at the vine-covered heap in the yard. With a lit Lucky Strike cigarette bobbing up and down in her mouth, she hollered in Polish, 'It's right there, dammit!'

"Now Alex's family spoke Polish in their home, but they were taught when you were out of the house you spoke English, America's language. His father lectured him and his brother about their new country. Love it, respect it, and if you need to… defend it. He always listened to his father's words but deemed this an exception and thanked the woman in Polish.

"The lady said nothing and disappeared back into her house. Alex began ripping away the wild grapevines and weeds. As he removed the foliage, slowly, a Model A coup appeared from beneath the stacked lumber. Painted dark green with black fenders and wheels, the camouflage easily hid the car. He finally cleared everything and inspected the vehicle.

"The Model A's tires were flat, but they had a lot tread left and just needed filling with air. He opened one side of the hood and removed a mouse's nest on top of the exhaust manifold. When he took off the radiator cap, it was bone dry, leading him to believe the hole was probably too large to fix. Alex opened the driver's door and noticed the odometer had clocked a little over 30,000 miles."

As the gray-haired Fiery Maze spoke, she seldom looked at or turned a page of the opened book on her lap. She recalled this entire story from memory, saying, "Identifying the Model A as a 1928 was easy for him. When the Model A came out in late 1927, they had red rubber steering wheels. The material used dyed the driver's hands red whenever the steering wheel became wet. Ford switched back to black steering wheels the following year.

"He strolled back to the front porch and found the Polish lady waiting for him. She looked at him and snapped in Polish, 'Well, do we got a deal?' He realized the lady wasn't a person to dicker with and said okay. He handed her four tens and a five. She reached into her frayed apron pocket, producing the car's keys and a yellowed envelope which she told him was the car's title. Again, in the Polish language, she replied, 'I'll give you a week to get the damn car out of here'.

"As she turned to go back inside, he yelled at her in Polish, saying he would try to take it out tomorrow. Pretending not to hear him, she just closed the door. The following day he bought a used radiator and a battery from the junkyard. From the service station where he worked, he bought gas, oil, and a gallon of ethylene glycol for the radiator; all the items totaled another twelve dollars. The next day he and his friend, Teddy, traveled there to get the car."

"Alex said Model A's were easy to repair. The two of them removed the original radiator and found a perfectly round one-eighth-inch hole in the bottom. They installed the good used radiator, hooked up the hoses, poured in the ethylene glycol, and topped it with water from the lady's garden hose. Next, they put in the new, used battery, and using a bicycle tire pump, took turns inflating each tire.

"Teddy drained the oil and gas tank, letting the liquids drip into the ground. He figured they would kill her weeds. While his friend poured the new gas into the tank, he filled the crankcase with clean oil. Alex slipped in behind the wheel without thinking, pulled out the choke, and adjusted the throttle.

"He stepped on the starter button, and after a minute, the Model A snorted to life, shooting black smoke out the tailpipe. They let the Model A Ford warm up for a few minutes. While Teddy was busy trying to open up the rear gate which led to the alley, Alex put his tools and the car parts in the back seat. Now they were ready to go, and he placed the Ford in first gear. But nothing happened; it wouldn't move.

"The grooves where the vehicle slumbered five years were deep, and the wheels spun in the dry dirt. He told me how embarrassed he was when his buddy snickered, 'Maybe it grew roots.' Wedged in between the piles of bricks and lumber, his pal had little room to maneuver. But he got behind it and pushed the auto, while Alex stomped on the accelerator pedal. Teddy was laughing when he bellowed, 'You just blew a mouse out of the tailpipe, Alex!' The Model A moved forward, rolled back, and finally lurched forward out of the ruts. His friend had to jump in while he maneuvered the Ford through the alley.

"My Alex will tell you they were both ecstatic. When he pulled up to the first intersection, Alex slammed on the brake; the pedal hit the floorboard without stopping the car. In their zeal to move the vehicle out of the yard, they forgot to check the brakes! The Model A crashed into a curb and bounced off, slowing it down.

"It stunned them for a moment, but they laughed hysterically when they watched a mouse come running out from under the car. He explained how the mouse was scurrying faster than the car and ran into the same curb, bouncing off it. Chuckling, they watched it scramble down the street. After a few moments, he cautiously drove to a vacant field where they adjusted the car's mechanical brakes." Aunt Fiery paused for a minute, shaking her head and giggling.

Don interrupted, asking her, "Are you okay to continue? We can always come back. May I get you a glass of water or juice?"

Aunt Fiery caught Sarah's attention and asked, "Honey, do you mind getting me a little glass of apple juice?"

Sarah left for the self-serve refreshment counter and appeared familiar with the process for getting her aunt's juice.

Fiery continued speaking, "Now that was 1936, he had the auto when we met two years later. That vehicle was his first hint of independence."

He observed how Aunt Fiery's expression changed as she digressed to the Dodge Brothers. She spoke as if she knew them and how they helped to grow the city of Hamtramck. The older woman spoke for another ten minutes about the famous brothers while she sipped her juice.

She ended her individual discussion by stating, "My mother was an acquaintance of Anna Thompson, who married Horace Dodge. Mom played the flute and was in the orchestra the Dodge Brothers started, that story I'll save for another time." Fiery glanced over at her niece, Lucy, and nodded as if to signal her.

Lucy Graham then said, "Auntie, why don't we continue our talk another day."

"I am tired," said the frail looking Fiery. She looked over the square table at Don, saying, "I will give you the information you wish, but you need to understand who we are, how we lived, and how that made forty-one special for us."

She closed the book in her lap. Fiery had a grin on her face when she looked over at Don, mentioning, "When you come back, I'll tell you how Mr. Ford stole Alex's car."

He looked at her before replying, "Thank you so much for sharing your time with us. We look forward to hearing that story, and hope to visit you again soon."

As the aunt said her goodbyes, she leaned over to his wife, and handed her the book from her lap, and quietly asked her to place it in forty-one's trunk. Ann took the notebook, agreeing to put it in their car. Mrs. Graham started pushing her aunt's wheelchair away when they saw Fiery signal and say something to her. She turned the wheelchair around and wheeled her aunt back to Don.

Looking at him, Aunt Fiery apologized, saying, "I'm sorry, I was to tell you something and had forgotten. My Alex enjoyed owning his Ford Model A very much. He would tell anyone who listened, 'Everyone should own a Model A.'"

Stunned by what she claimed, Don asked, "What did he say?"

Slowly, she repeated herself, whispering, "Everyone should own a Model A."

He stated, "I've heard those words before."

"I know," she responded.

As if signaling her niece, she raised her hand. Lucy turned her aunt's chair around and wheeled her out of the room.

Don sat there with Ann and Sarah. He found himself in a speechless dream, trying to comprehend Fiery's last words.

Sarah blurted out, "Wow, Ammygam never told me those stories. Do you think she was making them up? How funny is she, Henry Ford, stealing her husband's car?"

When Lucy returned to the table, Don apologized to her for having Aunt Fiery talk about her husband. Lucy thought her aunt enjoyed their visit. They agreed to arrange future meetings through Sarah.

As they walked out of the Blair House, the three women continued to chat. They said their goodbyes once more. Lucy got into Sarah's car and rode away with her granddaughter. Don started his car but made no move to leave. He was thinking about what Fiery said to him. Ann opened her red journal to Sunday, April twenty-fifth, 2004, and started recording her notes.

When Ann finished writing, she cleared her throat and asked, "Can we go?"

He placed the vehicle in gear and drove out the parking lot. Don wondered, where had he heard those words? Or did he overhear someone say everyone should own a Model A?

Chapter 13

American Dream

On their way home, Ann and Don stopped at the South Lyon Hotel for an early dinner. She was eager to share her private conversation with Sarah when no one was around. His wife wanted him to understand how lucky he was to have been able to meet Aunt Fiery, especially since Lucy Graham allowed no one to see her aunt except for herself and Sarah.

"Without realizing it, Sarah became your advocate even before you made a phone call to Lucy Graham," Ann said. 'It all started when you brought Tiger to Fowlerville in the 1941 Chevrolet. That evening, Sarah had gone to visit her Ammygam and was astonished when Aunt Fiery cried after hearing the story. She described your car and how you found the Golden retriever puppy inside. Her aunt insisted on seeing you before she left this place… whatever that means. Lucy was dead set against your meeting with her aunt.

He sat there listening to his wife's story.

Ann continued, "Before Sarah could arrange a meeting, you had called Lucy. Sarah explained how upset her grandmother was with her. Lucy thought Sarah had told you to call her, and she was furious, thinking Sarah had gone behind her back. And, I saw something else. It surprised me seeing Sarah at the Blair House. I wondered why you never told me how everyone was related?"

He murmured, "I never knew."

He noticed the old book in Ann's lap as they drove home and asked from where it came? She told him Fiery asked her to put it in the Chevrolet's trunk when they got home.

He refused to do it, which caused his wife to say, "Don… just put it in there. You'll make an old woman and your wife happy. The trunk has plenty of room. What can it hurt?"

Later that evening, as they relaxed in the family room, she remarked, "Do you recall when Fiery told us how her husband always said, 'Everyone should own a Model A?' This may sound funny, but I remember someone saying that… but not to us."

Considering his wife's comment, Don agreed and said, "I heard that somewhere, too. I sensed a déjà vu moment. One day something will jog our memory. Just let me know if you remember it first!"

When his wife had gone to bed, he took an old book off the shelf and researched the Dodge Brothers Main Plant in Hamtramck. He wanted to verify Fiery's story about the Dodge Brothers and Hamtramck. His book told how Hamtramck was a quaint farming village on the outskirts of Detroit in 1910. It covered over two square miles with a populace of 3,500 people, made up of mainly German farmers and shopkeepers. Between 1911 and 1921, the village grew to a population of 48,000 citizens and was labeled the fastest growing town in the United States.

At a breakneck pace, sturdy two-story wood-frame houses were built on city lots, thirty feet wide. Paving crews couldn't keep up with road construction for new homes. This incredible growth was because of two men, John and Horace Dodge. At the turn of the twentieth century, the brothers owned the best machine shop in Detroit, learning from their father, who made first-rate marine engines. Their company supplied combustion engines to Ransom Olds for his Oldsmobile automobiles.

Don continued to read and learned how Henry Ford contracted with the Dodge Brothers to build the engines and other components for his 1903 Model A Ford. The brothers also supplied auto components for the successful Model T. Ford, and his partners couldn't afford to pay the Dodges for their parts. Instead, they each accepted fifty shares of stock in the infant Ford Motor Company. Eventually, the brothers made millions of dollars in dividends from their Ford stock.

The Dodge brothers were generous public contributors to the city of Detroit. Their financial support to the Symphony Orchestra made it one of the finest in the country. They gave it a home by their funding for the building of Detroit's Orchestra Hall.

Just as he read the last line, Don yelled out loud, "Holy Cow! Fiery was right; the Dodge Brothers started an orchestra! They also donated land for four state parks in Michigan."

John and Horace Dodge would admit that they drank to ease their nerves in business dealings with Mr. Ford. When they were sober, colleagues would ask the brothers, "Why do you two drink so much?" Both would attribute their blunt and argumentative way to Mr. Ford, who turned them into alcoholics and conceited bullies. The Dodges started to build their car in 1914 instead of relying on Ford for their sole source of income. With their own car company, they were confident the public would finally give them the respect they deserved for the success of Ford's Model T instead of Henry Ford.

In Mr. Ford's defense, he believed his investors made plenty of money off his company. He wanted to buy many of them out, but they wouldn't sell, not wanting to lose what they considered their cash cow. He thought those early stockholders, including the Dodge Brothers, stymied his company's decision-making process. Mr. Ford wanted to invest some company's profits into developing a low-priced farm tractor based on the Model T, but investors blocked him. Instead, he established the Henry Ford and Sons Company for the farm tractor venture.

Mr. Ford floated a rumor in 1918 that he was taking Ford Motor's best employees to a new start-up company to create a new automobile. This vehicle would be better than the Model T. The sham worked, and many stockholders sold their shares before they became worthless. On the sly, Mr. Ford hired an agent to buy his company's stock on the open market, so he would finally own a majority of stock in the company that carried his name.

In another book, Don discovered the Dodge Brothers purchased a parcel of land in Hamtramck's southeast corner, where they built a massive car assembly plant known as Dodge Main. This attracted thousands of immigrants to the area. Many came straight from the mountain villages of Poland. Others came from the mines in Pennsylvania and Ohio. This Polish enclave was devoted to their core employer and validated Aunt Fiery's story for Don. He could see how her husband's Model A Ford, purchased in Hamtramck, may have been sabotaged.

Dodge Main was a major manufacturing complex by 1937 that supported at least a dozen other factories in the area that provided parts to the plant. But the Dodge Brothers never lived to see the complete success of their empire. In 1919, during the epidemic, Horace caught the Spanish flu. He survived several relapses. Then John contracted the flu and soon succumbed to it in January 1920. Horace felt lost without his older brother. He continued his heavy drinking, dying in December 1920 from complications of the disease and cirrhosis of the liver.

It was believed the Dodge brothers became ill drinking tainted liquor, made because of the Volstead Act of 1920 banning the sale of alcohol in the United States. But that was not the case. The brothers' vanity was what the public would remember. They had planned to have their coffins sealed in an elaborate marble mausoleum in the elite Section ten of Detroit's Woodmere Cemetery. Two carved Egyptian-style sphinxes guard the entry to their crypt.

Don sat in his chair, leaned back, and relaxed as he concluded Fiery knew her facts. After consulting his notes from their meeting, Don searched for Buhl Sons Detroit on his laptop. He discovered Buhl was a diversified manufacturer who owned an entire block complex at the corners of Adair and Wright streets in downtown Detroit. In 1937 Buhl Company found a niche in making parts and fixtures for the aircraft industry. During this expansion, it was the perfect time for them to hire and train tool and die makers, like Fiery's husband. Satisfied with his results, Don went to bed dreaming of his next visit with Mrs. Maze.

Wednesday morning, over coffee, Don and Ann discussed what to call Mrs. Maze and when they might meet next. Both agreed Mrs. sounded too formal and Donna or Fiery too casual. They decided Aunt Fiery or Aunt Donna seemed a comfortable alternative while showing respect for her age. They hoped she would agree. Ann was going to check with Sarah to help in scheduling their next meeting with her auntie.

At work, Don's company's airport security project was ramping up at a breakneck speed. Some days he thought of himself as a professional conference attendee. He was constantly reminding team members the project was classified. No one outside their company should know of this project. Their development goal was to allow the good in, keep the bad out, and change the rules whenever.

The big question was, who would be responsible for allowing any changes? The Department of Homeland Security struggled with their decision, so he split his team in two separate directions to tackle the access problem. It would give each team different goals, taking them on a unique path to solving the issue. His thinking was when the government made a ruling; they would have several options to present.

Don worked late into the evening preparing his update to the board of directors scheduled for Monday afternoon. He wondered what he had gotten himself into? How could he help his company develop this classified system while creating a huge profit? He called Ann that evening on his way home from the office and asked if he should pick up dinner. She reminded him it was 9:30 p.m. and told him just to come home. Tiger greeted him alone at the back door as Ann had gone to bed. He fixed himself a quick snack before he hurriedly walked the pup up and down the drive.

The next morning Ann surprised him, stating how Sarah wanted to know if they had time to visit Aunt Fiery at 1:00 p.m. that afternoon. This impromptu get-together was unexpected. They understood if Fiery asked to meet, it must be important. They agreed to change their schedules and confirm everything again at eleven. Don's secretary had been working the morning to reschedule his afternoon meetings. She cleared his calendar from noon to 4:30 p.m. However, he had to be available at 4:30 p.m. for his weekly government call.

When he called his wife, he learned she couldn't leave the clinic but would send Sarah. Don thought that would work. She could meet him at 1:00 p.m. in the Blair House parking lot. As he drove into the Blair House parking lot, he noticed Sarah pulling in right behind him. They walked into the building together and made their way to the meeting room.

She saw her grandmother and great-great-aunt sitting in one of the semi-private areas. Lucy waved when she saw them, and Sarah moved to embrace each lady. Both ladies greeted him, and he watched Aunt Fiery's broad smile became even larger as she listened to Sarah's day at her job. The elderly aunt was genuinely interested in what her niece had to say. Sarah explained how sorry Doctor Ann felt that she had to miss this meeting.

Aunt Fiery then looked at Don, saying, "Tell your wife I missed her. And, please tell her everything I'm going to say today."

He replied, "I will, but my memory isn't as good as it used to be. Will you mind me putting this right here, so my wife can listen to our talk later?"

He placed a black digital recorder, about the size of two packs of cigarettes, laid out end to end on the table. The machine started silently recording their conversation when he pushed the button.

Fiery replied, "That's fine; I want your bride to hear my story."

The elderly lady chose one book on the table, opened it, and began. She leaned forward and saying, "Last time, I told you about my husband. Now, you need to know about me."

He watched as she gathered her thoughts and interrupted, asking, "Excuse me, would you mind if I called you, Aunt Fiery?"

"You can just call me Fiery, but I answer better to Aunt Fiery or Aunt Donna." The grinning aunt continued, stating, "I was born Donna Louise Bak here in Detroit, on April twenty-eight in 1917."

Don interrupted, declaring, "That was yesterday! Happy belated birthday! Ann and I are so sorry we didn't know... wow! That's eighty-seven years young! We will remember you on our next visit."

She replied, "Oh! Hush too many people fuss over me, and... stop interrupting me!"

Scolded by an eighty-something woman, Don laughed inside at himself, and felt his face turning red.

Fiery continued speaking, "Let's see, I am the youngest of three children. My parents were Gilbert and Loraine Bak, first-generation Polish immigrants who came to Detroit to live the American dream. They emigrated from the Kingdom of Galicia, which was near or in Austria. Now, I think it is part of Poland. When they left their families, they were just teenagers. That took courage during those hard times.

"As a child, I was short and scrawny. The neighborhood kids nicknamed me Pee Wee, but my father would yell at them saying, 'Don't call her that.' Dad understood nicknames like that stuck, and he didn't want his favorite child ridiculed. I liked the nickname, I may have been smaller than most girls my age, but I made up for it by being an excellent athlete. I could run faster than most boys my size, and I was the pitcher on my friend's brother's sandlot baseball team."

It was then, Don realized, the baseball gloves and bats in the forty-one's trunk belonged to Fiery.

Without stopping, she said, "Whenever I played baseball, my mother always fixed my auburn-red hair up in curls. She didn't want the fellows to forget I was a girl." She paused for a moment to gather her composure and continued, "When my parents came to America, my father trained as a tool and die maker. He worked at Kelsey Wheel Company, where they made hickory spoke wheels for the new automobile companies in Detroit.

"One of my first childhood memories is playing with the warped wood spokes. Kelsey discarded these every day, and dad brought them home to fuel our family's kitchen stove. Dad taught us all how to use his precision measuring tools. My sisters and I learned numbers by reading measuring tools: Diameter checkers, micrometers, and Vernier calipers. We picked up how to work them. By the time I was six years old, I could measure items using a micrometer to the thousand's place. My mother told me I would wander around the house measuring things. I was awe-struck by a gadget that read increments smaller than the thickness of a hair.

"My sister Maureen played the flute, Jan was the singer, and I was an excellent piano player. When we saved twenty cents, we bought the sheet music for the newest song we liked. We performed all the latest tunes in our front parlor. Neighbors walking by our home during one of our performances thought the radio was playing.

"My favorite show had been *Your Hit Parade*, sponsored by the Lucky Strike Cigarette Company. That counted down the week's top fifteen popular songs. They encouraged listeners to send in their entries for next week's songs. If they were right, they won two packs of cigarettes. I won a lot. When the smokes arrived in the mail, I'd give them to my father. He was grateful because the two packs I earned gave him one day of smoking pleasure."

The woman stared out the room's large windows as if watching her life pass by. She continued, "By the time I was a sophomore in high school,

Pee Wee didn't fit me anymore. I had grown into a lanky redhead. Some people thought I resembled a young Katharine Hepburn, but the girls on our softball team had dubbed me Fiery. I imagined it was for the velocity I threw a ball. In reality, it was for my competitive spirit and short temper."

Like a sonic boom, the ringing of Don's wireless phone interrupted Aunt Fiery's dialog. Embarrassed, he reached into his suit jacket and placed it on vibrate. It was a call from Norah, the president's secretary. He would return her call later.

He whispered, "I'm sorry that won't happen again."

Aunt Fiery questioned him about what made that noise. He explained it was his portable telephone and someone was calling him. He used the word portable, thinking she might not understand cell phones. She considered that unbelievable and asked to see it. When she returned the phone, he noticed three voice mail messages waiting for him.

"Please continue," he said.

Wasting no time, she returned his phone and picked up where she had left off, saying, "Oddly enough, my father didn't object to this nickname and called me that too. When my friends introduced me to unknown people, they would say, 'So and so, I want you to meet Fiery.' I would pipe in saying, 'It's for the hair, not the temperament!' That wasn't true, but I said it anyway.

"I graduated from Detroit's Chadsey High School in 1935, and I thought of becoming a tool and die maker. But my father vetoed that idea. He knew one female in the profession, and she was always the victim of practical jokes. Her male co-workers often nailed her street shoes to the wood plank floor under her machine or placed tacks on her stool when her back was turned.

"So, I chose to attend college, but my mother discouraged me, saying, 'Girls, don't go to college. It's a waste of money because they get married and become mothers.' Finally, my parents and I agreed on a compromise, and I signed up for a one-year certificate program in Bookkeeping at a Detroit Business School. I became an excellent student and an even better bookkeeper. I hope I'm not boring you."

"Not at all," answered Don, feeling the vibration of his phone announcing another new call. He glanced at Sarah and Lucy to see if either had noticed, but they were too absorbed with their relative's story.

"My Father left Kelsey Wheel and had gone to work for the Buhl Sons Company in 1921. By June 1938, he was one of the longer-tenured tool and die makers there. In July of that year, I first met your Uncle Alex," Aunt Fiery said as she broke her trancelike state.

Lucy asked, "Are you okay to continue, or do you want to rest?"

Aunt Fiery responded, "I'm fine; I haven't really started talking about what he came to hear. So just let me continue. Yes, Alex and I met at the Buhl Sons Company picnic in July 1938. I had gone there with my dad and my sisters. In those days, they invited everyone in the family.

"My father knew Alex, but they rarely spoke. Dad thought he was another arrogant, immature kid who figured his new tool-making techniques outshined the old proven ones. He had just gotten his journeyman's card and was eager to impress his bosses. So, he volunteered to roast the hot dogs at the event. Torrential rains placed a damper on the day, not the festivities. With nothing better to do, most picnickers kept busy drinking the free Goebel beer supplied by their company.

"I saw Alex erect a canvas tarp over his charcoal grill to keep the rain off. He stood stoically at his post grilling hot dogs that few will eat. Alex wanted to prove to his bosses that he was a man that would do what he said he would, no matter the circumstances. With the picnic games canceled, many of the boyish men amused themselves by setting cups and buckets under the shelter's roof to catch the rainwater. Then they would chase each other, tossing the rainwater at one another.

"I walked over to grab a hot dog and struck up a conversation with Alex. He stood there under the canvas tarp protecting his grill and hot dogs from the rain. I moved over next to him, knowing no one would throw a cup of water at me. We were the only two sober people amidst the Mardi Gras atmosphere. Every so often, a girl would stop by Alex's grill to get warm. They would soon be splashed with rainwater tossed by a friend and run off squealing."

Don looked to Lucy, who was looking and proudly smiling at her Aunt Fiery. He again felt his telephone vibrating and realized he couldn't ignore it much longer.

Fiery smiled, saying, "The splashed water sometimes hit Alex's grill, causing steam to rise, and as the haze circled his round head, he would yell at the revelers. Alex wanted to be recognized for his reliable grilling achievement but finally admitted, 'They're probably too plastered to see me.' I thought he was funny and told him so. He turned his handsome face and strapping body to stare at me. It was the first time he really noticed me, and I couldn't help smiling at him.

"With his long grilling fork, he stabbed a hot dog, lifted it off of the grill, and in a gloomy voice asked me, 'Would you want my dog?' What he really meant, I knew, and together we broke out laughing. That may have been when I fell in love with him and didn't realize it. I never let on that we had met a year earlier at one of my softball games."

Don's phone vibrated a fifth time and he ignored the call, thinking Fiery's story was more important.

"Alex was coaching his cousin Dennie's softball team that was playing against my team. He walked over to me, gave me the lineup card, and introduced himself. Later, during the game, I overheard him crowing to a few of his friends that he didn't care for softball. He was only managing his cousin's team, so he could smack the girls on their behinds when they made a good play."

"One of his friends says, 'Geez, I wish I thought of that!' I assumed he was like all the other smart-aleck guys I had met at dances. Those boorish young boys always made insulting comments like, 'Stick around kid, maybe I'll give you a whirl.' Or, 'If I said you had a beautiful body, will you hold it against me?' But, after chatting with him at the picnic, I changed my mind.

"His older brother Steve, who changed his first name to Smitty, had recently married and found a house of his own. Alex became the de facto man of their home because his step-father was an invalid. He promised his mom he'd watch out for his step-sisters and make sure his younger step-brother stayed out of trouble. He helped his mother to support his three half-siblings and was very mature for his age."

Don looked over at Sarah as Aunt Fiery took a sip of water. Her fingers were busy twirling a lock of her long hair while she keenly listened to her relative tell her story.

Her aunt said, "To keep things from getting out of hand, Mr. Buhl ended the picnic and sent everyone home. Alex began to take apart the canvas tarp over his grill and asked me, 'Could I stop over your house sometime so we can continue talking?' Not wanting to be too bold, I told him. I'd think about it."

Now it was Don's turn to interrupt her. She appeared uncomfortable, causing him to say, "Are you okay, Aunt Fiery? We can stop!"

She took a few seconds and responded, "Yes, I'm fine. I haven't been down that road — in a long time." After catching her breath, she started again, "The next Saturday afternoon, my father, Gilbert, didn't know what to make of Alex when he showed up at our house unannounced."

My dad was in the backyard painting our wooden outdoor furniture red when Alex walked up to the back gate. He offered to help, and my dad accepted. Then Alex slyly asked my father if I was home. He said he wasn't sure but would check if Alex continued painting for him. He started painting where dad left off. Ten minutes later, I came out with a pitcher of freshly squeezed lemonade. As we talked, he painted. When he had finished painting, a little red paint remained in the can. After noticing two large apples, one on each of our trees. He commented, 'You know, you shouldn't have to wait for the fruit to ripen.'

"He ran over to one tree and painted a few of the small green apples red. I laughed and warned him my father wouldn't be happy. Just then, mother called out that dinner was ready. He asked me to go with him the following Tuesday to a movie, and I accepted. When daddy came back outside, Alex yelled to him, 'See you at work, Mr. Bak.' As he hopped over the backyard gate, he looked so handsome and excited, clicking his heels high in the air.

"My father looked happy that Alex had completed painting the furniture so neatly. But, when dad gazed up at the fruit, the sight of a few bright red apples puzzled him. We became a couple over the next several months and went on many dates. My favorite times with him were going to the movies on dish night. Each person received a complimentary dish, bowl, cup, saucer, or other tableware with each ticket they purchased.

"I was no different from any other woman, who assumed we could assemble a complete set of impressive tableware just by attending the movies. In reality, we got a lot of mismatched dishes that you never used. Theater managers canceled those promotions at the start of World War II, claiming it was because of rationing. I think the reason they stopped was the expensive clean-up they incurred from broken dishes left in the theaters."

Fiery took another sip of water, Don took the opportunity to ask her niece if everything was okay.

Lucy smiled and asked her aunt, "Is everything okay? Do you want to stop now?"

Fiery responded, "I'm fine if he doesn't mind hearing a little more?"

She spoke those words just as Don's pocket vibrated again.

Aunt Fiery looked directly at Sarah, stating, "I hope you do not mind me talking so bluntly. It must be difficult to imagine I was once twenty-two and in love."

Sarah, now smiling, said, "I adore listening to your stories. I never knew my great-great-Uncle Alex or the many things you told us. You're a fascinating woman."

It was Aunt Fiery's turn to blush, for her face was pinkish. Don noticed, at the exact moment, a minor discomfort in her mannerism.

He said, "I would love to hear more of your story, but you women have a much stronger constitution than I. Do you mind if we took a brief comfort break?"

He saw the elderly lady's approving smile and could again feel his phone vibrating. So many calls in such a short period, he knew, meant trouble.

He continued saying, "I need to visit the boy's room. Also, I should check in with my office. Is a break for ten minutes okay?"

His frank comment made Mrs. Maze smile and seem more at ease.

Lucy blurted out, "Let's make it twenty minutes."

Aunt Fiery turned to him and quietly said, "Thank you."

Lucy wheeled Fiery out of the room as Don explained to Sarah that he had eleven calls from his office to return. He excused himself and went outside to find a better signal for his phone. Don tried calling his president's secretary, Norah, but no one answered. He then tried to call the president,

Mr. Stone. Another staff member answered the telephone and told him everyone was looking for him and to wait while she got someone.

After two minutes, Norah came on the line saying, "Oh! Mr. Bryniarski, I am so sorry to interrupt your meeting. A courier arrived here with three boxes for you. They are at the receiving dock, and we are about to evacuate the offices."

He said, "Should you need to leave the building, go now! Don't' worry about my boxes."

She responded, "Don… they're the reason we're leaving the building."

"Why is that?" He asked.

Norah cleared her throat and continued, "Jimmy at the dock signed for your delivery as he normally does. When he found out what was in them, he rejected the cartons. But the special courier left your boxes on the loading dock, saying he accepted them. Mr. Bryniarski, your delivery is from Baghdad… and all three boxes… are explosives… like dynamite!"

Don yelled, "They're what?"

Chapter 14

Quick Spin

Don was on the telephone with Norah, his president's secretary. She had just informed him that explosives were delivered to his office. He requested she add to their call the head of corporate security. As Norah worked to find the requested person, he remembered back twenty-nine months earlier. On September 11, 2001, suicide pilots flew planes into buildings attacking America. Those terrorist acts were still on everyone's mind. No one wanted a repeat of that attack, especially at your business.

The secretary responded, "Don, I have Mick on the line with us."

A man's voice came on the line stating, "Hello Don, this is Michael Embrescia."

The men discussed the packages as Norah listened. Don asked Mick to verify where the cartons were from. The director of security left the telephone to return a minute later to mention they were not from Baghdad, Iraq, but were from B. G. A. D. - A. D. in Richmond, Kentucky. Don then directed him to place his parcels in their company's secure storage facility under lock and key, explaining this delivery is scheduled to arrive three months from now. The men then agreed to meet tomorrow morning.

Norah interjected, "What do I tell people?"

Don stated, "Say nothing about the boxes or their contents. Those items are for a classified project our company is working on. Should anyone insist on knowing, say, they are my fourth of July fireworks. Everyone should be assured the cartons are not from Baghdad, Iraq. You tell them they are from bluegrass… air… aeronautical… display… displays. Yes, say my boxes are from Bluegrass Aeronautical Displays in Richmond, Kentucky."

He still had five minutes before his meeting with Aunt Fiery continued. A little shaken by his call, Don returned inside the Blair House. He didn't mention that BGAD is the Blue Grass Army Depot, a munitions storehouse, and A. D. was their project reference. He returned to the table, happy to see only Sarah was there. It gave him a few minutes to compose himself.

He relaxed and enjoyed Sarah's conversation. She explained to him how she never heard the tales Aunt Fiery was telling. They spoke for ten minutes before Lucy and Fiery returned. When they did, he noticed the elderly lady had changed her dress. Her impeccable but casual clothing appeared to be from the 1950s.

He commented, "Well, you look nice."

Fiery responded, "Oh! Hush now… or I'll forget what I want to tell you."

Sarah took a journal from the table, placing it on her Ammygam's lap. He thought Aunt Fiery looked tired and perhaps distressed by something when…

Lucy asked her aunt, "Do you want to rest?"

She responded, "I relax all the time. Now let me continue. Don, make sure you mention this story to your wife, Ann. Tell her it is all true, and I wanted her to know. By the summer of 1939, Alex and I were still a couple. I was hoping we had a long future together, but I'll save that for later. Ford Model A's were becoming a rare sight on the roads. That's because they were already out of production for eight years."

With the tattered journal on Fiery's lap, she turned to the window and stared outside; she said, "By 1939, the rapid changes in automotive design made a Ford Model A as rare as a horse and buggy. But my Alex loved his Model A. We were going on a picnic one afternoon, when Alex stopped at a hamburger stand on Michigan Avenue to buy two Coca-Colas before he came by my house. As he handed his dime to the cashier, a guy he knew rushed into the store yelling, 'Hey Maeselowski, old man Henry Ford just stole your car.'

"Alex had parked his Model A, along the route Henry Ford took from the Ford Motor Engineering building to his sprawling Fair Lane Estate two miles away. It was not general knowledge, but in pleasant weather, Mr. Ford occasionally walked home for lunch. Alex thought no one would ever want his old rusted heap and usually left his ignition key in the car. He rushed outside and couldn't believe his pal was right, his car was gone!

"He sat on the curb where his car had been parked and pondered what to tell the Dearborn police when he reported the theft. Meanwhile, his friend was sitting on a bench in front of the store, laughing. Alex sat on that curb for fifteen minutes, pondering how to inform the law that a multi-millionaire had stolen his rusted jalopy of a car? He knew no one would believe him! Suddenly he saw his Model A coming around the corner. A slender elderly man was hunched behind the steering wheel.

"Old Mr. Ford pulled right up in front of that hamburger stand and smiled, saying, 'I presume young man, this is your car and I…' Alex interrupted him. He told me he was peeved and gruffly cut him off in mid-sentence, saying, 'Dammit, Mr. Ford, why'd you take my car?' Henry Ford explained to him, he couldn't help himself. He noticed the A on his stroll home, and he just had to check out one of his ladies. With a key in the ignition, and nobody in sight, he figured taking her for a quick spin.

"Mr. Ford informed him how he lost track of time, driving his Model A on a nearby highway, only wanting to see what she had left in her on the straightaway. Before Alex protested anymore, Henry Ford pulled a pencil and a small piece of brown paper, torn from a grocery bag from his vest pocket. He scribbled something on it and handed it to him, saying, 'This is for the gas I used. Show it to my man in the shack.' Just like that, with a smile and a nod, he continued his walk home.

"The note read, 'Fill her up, Ford.' That was it! My boyfriend was helping support his family and didn't have any extra money for gas. His gas gauge reading empty, he took a chance that this was the real Henry Ford and see if he could get gas.

"The shack old Mr. Ford was talking about was actually a shed at the entrance to the massive grounds of his secluded estate. As he approached the guardhouse, a uniformed man came out, and sternly demanded, 'What's your business here?' Alex nervously handed him the note and was surprised when the guard hurriedly opened the gate and politely asked, 'Do you know where you are going, sir?' Alex stated, 'No, I don't.'

"The guard handed him back the note, instructing him to follow the tree-lined private road for a quarter of a mile, turning left at the first road. Alex pulled up to what he thought was a garage. Almost immediately, an attendant in gray coveralls motioned him to pull over to where the fuel pumps were located. He presumed the guard had called the man to tell him he was coming. Alex handed him the note, and the attendant put it in his pocket without even looking at it! He didn't say a word as he filled the car's tank with high test gasoline.

"As he waited, Alex enjoyed viewing the trees, flowers in the meadow, the Rouge River flowing through the estate, and the dam Henry Ford had built across the river. The dam created a small lake and waterfall, which helped a powerhouse supply electricity to the estate. Interrupting his thoughts, the guy told him, 'You're all set.' My Alex started up his Model A and was driving out when he noticed Mr. Ford exiting the woods on the opposite side of the riverbank. He was preparing to cross the dam before walking to his mansion. Alex honked the horn at Mr. Ford, who smiled and waved in return.

"He told me while driving to my house, he pondered what to tell me. The fuel gauge needle was way past full. Alex remembered I knew the gauge was never higher than a quarter of a tank, so he had the proof he needed. When he pulled up, I flung open the front door and yelled, where have you been? You're more than an hour late! I was mad."

Fiery Maze paused a moment before saying, "He stood on the driver's side running board and was afraid to come any closer. When he finished telling me his story, I was furious. I ran off the front porch shouting at him! Do you expect me to believe that auto tycoon Henry Ford stole your old rusted-out rattletrap and filled your tank with gas, just for the privilege of driving it?

"Alex smirked at me and pointed to the fuel gauge. Looking at it I stammered… and was stunned. He never filled the gas tank! I could barely say the picnic basket is on the stoop. He went to the stoop, placed his two soda bottles in the basket, and put it in the A's back seat. I was mad… and he knew it as I sat there, arms crossed, sulking in the passenger seat.

"Alex drove off in the wrong direction, I spoke in a cross tone, you're not going the right way to Belle Isle! He drove on and finally told me, 'I'll prove to you where I was!' and turned onto the drive leading to Mr. Ford's Fair Lane Estate. I gasped! How could he embarrass me like this?

"Alex stopped at the guardhouse near the large closed wrought-iron gates. I saw his face turn white as he said, 'O… Oh… it's not the same man.' But it was too late. The guard was at Alex's window. In a very serious tone, he asked, 'What's your business here?' Alex explained he had visited earlier, but there was another guard at the gate. He continued telling him how he needed to prove to me that Mr. Ford filled up his tank with gas. The guard looked at his car, nearly smirking, then at Alex and me, before saying, 'One moment.'

"He exited the guardhouse with what looked like a log sheet on a clipboard. He glanced at Alex's license plate and checked his clipboard. At Alex's window, in a polite tone, the man said, 'Madam, the gentleman arrived at…' he read me the complete journal where Alex had gone while on Mr. Ford's estate. He finished by telling me his departure time. Politely, he instructed Alex on how to turn his vehicle around.

"Before he could move his Model A, the wrought-iron gates opened to allow a chauffeured driven limousine to exit. Mr. Ford was in the backseat with his window rolled down. The limousine slowed down as Mr. Ford waved at my Alex. Leaning forward in his seat, Mr. Henry Ford himself shouted out, 'Everything okay?' Alex waved and declared, 'We're fine, Mr. Ford, and thank you.'

"It flabbergasted me! He asked me a question, but I was so dumbfounded… I couldn't comprehend it. Instead of answering, all I could say was… did you remember to pack the bottle opener? He always forgot the opener."

Everyone noticed Aunt Fiery's face beaming with joy as she spoke those last words. Sarah excused herself as she went to the self-serve drink counter, as he glanced at his watch to check the time.

Lucy suggested, "Now, auntie, you've been talking for forty minutes; are you sure you want to continue?"

Aunt Fiery responded, "Lucy, people here don't want to listen to your memories. I enjoy talking with someone who is truly interested in my story and what I have to say."

The amiable Sarah returned with five drinks on a tray; looking at Fiery, she said, "Ammygam, this one has ice in it." She pointed to one of the two glasses of apple juice placed in front of her and gave everyone else a drink too.

To give Aunt Fiery a chance to rest, Don, Lucy, and Sarah started a discussion regarding his wife's animal clinic.

After ten minutes, Fiery chimed in, "Now Donnie, make sure you tell Ann this part."

He smiled when she announced his childhood name and responded, "I will."

"In early March 1940," Aunt Fiery stated, "My mother learned my first cousin Mildred's child, Billy, had been killed when a German U-boat torpedoed his ship off the coast of Greenland. He was a cook's assistant on a merchant marine vessel. Mildred's mother, Ruth, my mom, and I planned a trip to Nova Scotia to console my cousin. I told Alex to be good… I'd be gone for two weeks. Mother and I took the train from Detroit to Windsor, Ontario, and on to Truro, Nova Scotia.

"There, we met up with Aunt Ruth traveling together on to New Glasgow. This was my first experience with death. Many stories were going around about seamen being declared lost at sea, then rescued. My Aunt Ruth tried to keep this hope alive. My mom wanted me to realize Billy wasn't coming back. I remember her crying and saying, 'They won't ever find Billy alive. He never had a chance… to grow up!'

"When we got home, one of my sister's friends confirmed she saw Alex out with a girl on at least three separate occasions. I was mad, but deep down, I hoped he had a good explanation for his actions. Sarah, you probably can guess what he said when I asked what he did while I was gone? He told me, 'Nothing, just loafing.'"

Fiery looked at Sarah with intense eyes and declared, "Then… I dropped the bomb! I told him what my girlfriends saw. He stuttered; he always sounded so darling when stuttering. I couldn't believe it, he said, 'Yes, I was.' He admitted it! I asked him, do you have anything else to tell me? He was speechless and only replied, 'No.' His simple answer made me so furious, and my fiery temper got to me. I stated, perhaps we shouldn't see each other for a while. As I stormed out, he muttered, 'Okay.'

"Him going out with another girl didn't make me mad… it was for not giving me a decent explanation. During the three years we had gone steady, I regularly talked to him about finding a better woman. I wished I never said that. My Alex would later tell me how he realized he did me wrong and cared for me. But at the time, he didn't understand how to say it. He felt trapped like an eighteenth-century French nobleman during the revolution, awaiting his turn at the guillotine.

"He knew nothing could change things between us, so he figured why bother to say anything. What really happened was Alex's buddy asked him as a favor to double date. His friend planned to take this girl on a date; however, she would only go if her girlfriend and Alex joined them. I would have forgiven him if he told me the truth, but he didn't. It was that nonchalant way he said, 'Okay,' that caused me to walk out.

"In June 1940, I was working for Mr. Penrowski as his Certified Public Account (CPA), when one day he suffered a mild heart attack, and then he retired. Suddenly I found myself without a job. My father informed me every department at Buhl Sons was hiring workers. But Alex worked there, and I could never work or be near him. A month had gone by, and I had no employment prospects.

"Each evening, I scoured the *Detroit Times* want ads. One day I saw Buhl Sons was hiring a bookkeeper. The week before, I remembered reading they had won a contract to build airplane parts for DeSoto. As part of the Lend-Lease Act with England, DeSoto's Main Plant would manufacture fighter and bomber planes.

"I hesitated to apply but thought Alex works in the shop, and the company is enormous. The way I figured it, the bookkeeping position is in the office, and there would be no reason to run into shop employees. I believed I had a better-than-average chance at getting the job because my old boss, Mr. Penrowski, was an independent auditor for Buhl, and I was familiar with their ledgers. So, I applied, and within a few days, I had an interview.

"I interviewed with Mr. Spencer at Buhl Sons Company. The man was short and stout, with an unlit cigar stub jutting out of his mouth. My first impression of him was that he looked like a plump, wrinkled bulldog stuffed into a brown suit. He ushered me into his office and began questioning me about my qualifications, explaining what he would expect of me at their company. I put my father on my application as a reference. Mr. Spencer knew dad… his reputation was highly regarded, and an excellent Buhl Sons' employee.

"I also handed him a letter of recommendation from Mr. Penrowski. A half-hour into the interview, he looked me straight in the eyes, saying, 'The last girl I hired quit to get married.' I interrupted him, insisting I wouldn't be having a wedding soon. With my proclamation, he smiled and offered me the position at thirty-eight dollars and fifty cents a week. I accepted, and he instructed me to report at 8:00 a.m.

"On my first day, the following Monday, I reported to Miss Graves, a thin middle-aged spinster who took her job as head bookkeeper seriously. After showing me around, she sent me out to the shop with a list of names. She told me to collect their time tickets and to check with the shop's foreman if I needed help. I was happy to see Alex's name, not on my list.

"On the plant floor, I was barraged with catcalls and inquiries of, 'Hey, babe, how about a date?' The one that enraged me was, 'How's it going, Red?' I wanted to yell back, 'My name's not Red, it's Fiery!', but I kept my mouth shut. I spotted the shop supervisor and showed him my list, asking where I could find these men? He looked me over and pointed me to the tool and die area further down the aisle. He said, 'Get their tickets quick and leave. I don't need you around distracting my guys.'

"When I walked around the corner, I ran smack dab into Alex! He winked at me and whispered, 'Well, if it isn't Fiery in the flesh.' Looking at him, I was the one nervously stuttering, saying, wha… what are you doing here? You're not on my list? He beamed at me and answered, 'I'm number three.' I glanced at my paper… three was an 'A. Maze.' He exclaimed, if his brother could change his name to Smitty, he should be able to swap his to Maze.

"Alex was tired of writing Maeselowski on his time tickets. So, he shortened his last name. He said he could write a 'z' faster than an 's' so Maze it became. I had not seen him in three months. I missed him, but I wouldn't let him know. So, I put on my deadpanned face saying, Maze, give me your time records! Suddenly I noticed his eyes glistening as he whispered, 'I realize I upset you, but I love you and miss you. If you give me another chance, I promise… I'll never hurt you again.'

"'Besides, I'm thinking of buying a new automobile. I need you to help me pick it out.' I was staring at him, thinking how much I missed him, and remembered that was my first day at Buhl Sons. So, I said, hand over your damn time tickets. He sheepishly handed them over to me. I swung around, leaving but turned around, asking, 'What car are you looking to buy?' Right then, I knew how much I loved him. I wanted to kiss him right there. Yet, I didn't want to concede that I needed him.

"Just then, I spotted the plant supervisor hurrying towards us. I made a haste retreat, telling him we'll discuss this after work. I saw Alex smile and return to his station before his boss got there. His foreman hollered, 'What's going on over here, and who's that lady?' He confused his supervisor, who was an avid fan of the city's baseball team, by patting him on the back, grinning, and asking, 'How about those Tigers?'

"When I arrived back at the office, Miss Graves asked, 'How do you like our boys out in the plant?' They're fine, I answered. Then I wondered if my visit to the shop was some sort of initiation. I met him later that evening, and it was like we were never apart. We became engaged on July fourth, 1940, at a Belle Isle picnic. He bought me a one-carat diamond ring from Lachman and Company in Dearborn, costing two hundred seventy-five dollars.

"I found out later my chance meeting with him was a setup. He and Miss Graves were long-time friends. For several years they entered and departed Buhl Sons through the same doors, and at night they often walked out together to the parking lot. One day when it was raining, and she forgot her umbrella, Alex offered to get her car from the lot and bring it to the entrance. During snowstorms, he cleaned off her windows and warmed up the motor.

"Alex told me the week before he was walking past Miss Graves' Hudson automobile when she was unceasingly pushing down on the car's starter. He shouted to her, 'Hey Gravey, you're going to flood her, let me help.' Alex got behind the steering wheel, pulled out the throttle lever, adjusted the choke, and pushed on the starter… and vroom-vroom. Her old Hudson's motor sprang to life.

"Thanking him, she asked, 'Why are you so gloomy lately?' She listened to him explain how we broke up, and after three months, he couldn't get me out of his mind. He told her, I wouldn't take his phone calls, and I returned his letters unopened. Miss Graves listened to him and inquired, 'How long were you two going together?'"

"He said, 'Well, me and Fiery…' Miss Graves interrupted, 'Wait, did you say Fiery?' Alex laughing responded, 'Yeah, I realize it's a funny nickname, but Fiery has had it for years, and it fits her.' Miss Graves commented, 'Why? We have a new girl starting on Monday. I was reviewing her application today. In the space for her first name, she wrote Fiery. Then crossed it out.' So he asked her, 'What did she write?' Miss Graves responded, 'Donna.'

"Miss Graves described months later to me how excited he was, saying, 'I bet that's her! What's the position?' She told him, 'Bookkeeper.' Then he merrily shouted, 'That is her, I know it's her. I've got to talk to her.' He begged Miss Graves to do him a favor. He was the one who suggested Fiery pick up the time tickets on Monday morning. She told him, 'If I can do it, look for her about 8:30 a.m.' Miss Graves was really a wonderful person.

"I found out later, they usually sent time tickets to accounting in an interoffice envelope. The department only picked them up in person when things were slow. The ruse went even further. Alex understood if I saw his name on the paper, I wouldn't go in the shop. So, he changed his last name at Buhl Sons but hadn't done it officially before I got there. I wasn't mad at him; he hurt me. I figured, if he could dream up this elaborate scheme to get me back, he must really love me."

Don saw both Lucy and Sarah had tears in their eyes. They felt moved by their relative's story, who when younger fell in love, was hurt, and took a chance to reclaim her love so long ago.

At that moment, Sarah exclaimed, "That's men for you!"

Fiery declared, "Oh! But he was worth it!"

Lucy noticed Aunt Fiery was getting tired and said, "Auntie, you spoke enough today. Maybe we can meet in a couple of days?"

Fiery snapped, "I may not have a couple of days! Let me speak another ten minutes."

The old woman peered at the journal on her lap, pretending to read it. Don knew the words she spoke were all from memory. Lucy looked over at him and shrugged.

"Young man," Fiery said as if forgetting his name while she looked straight at him. "Oh! See what I forgot. I need to tell you something about Alex's family. His mother, Bernice, worked hard to keep her family fed, clothed and tried to give them a decent house to live in. She did her best to raise the two boys, Alex and his oldest brother, Smitty. I already told you about his three siblings dying during the epidemic in 1919. It was difficult raising children back then. His mom did everything… from delivering bootlegged liquor in their baby carriages to cleaning railroad coaches at night."

In a somber tone, Aunt Fiery asserted, "When Alex's father, Stanley, died in 1923, things only got worse. Alex and Steve, I mean Smitty, helped their mother clean the trains. When they weren't helping her, they were scrounging for fuel. In those days, coal heated most of the houses in Detroit. Bernice couldn't afford to buy enough fuel to keep their home warm, so her boys found things. They scavenged for wood and cedar roadblocks or coal that fell out of railroad cars. Oh darn! There I go, getting ahead of myself."

Staring out the window with glassy eyes, Fiery continued with her memories, saying, "Cedarwood blocks covered with creosote were used to pave Michigan Avenue in Dearborn in the 1900s. By the mid-1920s, the creosote wore off the wood, and they replaced them with brick pavers. They dumped the used cedar blocks in large piles by the sidewalk and would later haul them away. Smitty and my Alex always found plenty of those cedar roadblocks to bring home. When the woodpiles were gone, they simply pried blocks out of the street."

Don sat glued, listening to each word. He realized she was speaking of children when they were ten to sixteen years old trying to survive during the Great Depression. He breathed a sigh of sympathy as Aunt Fiery continued, "The locals knew that trains going to Ford's Rouge Plant sometimes lost chunks of coal. As the full railcars rounded a turn or were jarred by a sudden stop, coal pieces might fall out when the engine started pulling again. Adults and children regularly walked alongside the train tracks foraging for coal. Bernice's boys often came home with two full buckets each. Rumor had it that one of her sons was seen on a moving railcar throwing coal out to his brother.

"Bernice knew she had to intervene before they killed themselves or someone else. But she didn't understand how to teach her sons the right things. She decided to visit Father Solanus Casey at the St. Bonaventure Monastery in Detroit. The good friar had a reputation as an inspiring speaker, but he never preached doctrinal sermons. Dozens of Detroit Catholics visited him daily, seeking his counsel and his blessing. When she told Father Solanus her fears for family, he stated she should remarry. He advised her to seek a virtuous man. A person who could help her raise her children into solid Christian citizens."

"Bernice told me she thanked the good Father for his advice. The only eligible gentleman she knew that fit this description was Bill Jastremski. He was a World War I veteran who was exposed to chlorine and phosgene gas during attacks while in France. She had met him at the train depot. He was a passive man, inclined to wheeze whenever he did strenuous work. Bill was a night watchman at Michigan Central Station.

"She married him in late January 1926, and together they had three children. Bill died in 1936, just before I met Alex. He and his brother, Smitty, were helping to support their mom and step-siblings. Alex loved his mother and her children. He worried about how they could survive after we got married. He understood how difficult and expensive it was to raise a family."

Fiery turned, smiling with pride at Don and Lucy. She then moved herself to stare out the window saying, "In late 1940, Alex wanted to buy a modern automobile. But, like most people, he wanted the most bang for his buck. The problem was... Alex was always working. It began in the late summer and continued into December 1940. All skilled workers at Buhl Sons worked six days a week, twelve hours a day, manufacturing parts for the fighters, bombers, and interceptor airplanes.

"Remember, this is a year before Pearl Harbor happened. Alex and his pals could see the United States entering the war in Europe. But, no one thought or considered a war with Japan. On our free Sundays, we went on picnics with our friends. They all agreed this was Europe's problem, and it had absolutely nothing to do with the United States. I recalled one of them saying, 'somebody else can get their head shot off, not me!' Others nodded their heads in agreement."

She paused for a moment as if recalling another distant memory, saying, "In January 1941, Alex asked me to marry him, and I planned to set a marriage date. Thrilled, I couldn't wait to talk to my Pastor at Saint Alphonsus Catholic Church; where was that located again; oh yes, it was on Gould Street in Dearborn. When meeting him, I inquired about setting a late summer wedding date. I asked Father if we might get married after the last Mass, on a Sunday, because many of our friends and Alex worked six days a week. He agreed, and we decided on August twenty-fourth."

Don noticed Fiery's tone changing and looked over at Lucy, who said, "Aunt Fiery, Sarah needs to get back to work. Let's meet again in a few days, okay?"

The elderly lady frowned and stated, "I am tired. Do you mind coming back? I'll tell you how we searched for a new car. And, I want to hear your hound story when you brought forty-one to your house. Sarah told me some of it, but I want to hear your story."

He responded, "You will! And, real soon, Ann and I will visit with you."

Fiery signaled to Sarah to come closer to her. She whispered in the young woman's ear and handed her the notebook that had been on her lap. Sarah smiled and shook her head in agreement. She placed the medium size journal in her large handbag. As Sarah kissed Fiery goodbye, Don casually removed his recorder from the table and slipped it into his jacket pocket.

On an impulse, Don walked around the square card table and knelt down on one knee in front of Aunt Fiery. He leaned in, giving the fragile woman a gentle hug, letting her know both he and Ann would visit her this weekend.

She bent slightly into him and said, "I hope we will meet again. We have so much in common, and I will need your help."

As Lucy wheeled her aunt to her room, the older woman turned, smiled, and waved at him. He looked at his watch and decided to drive home; there, he would make his 4:30 p.m. telephone call. When he arrived home, it surprised him how Tiger wouldn't leave him alone. She was excited about something, smelling and rubbing herself on him. When Ann came home, she commented on how the dog must have smelled a familiar scent on him.

Later that evening, she listened to the digital recording of their meeting. Then, she opened her journal to Thursday, April 29, 2004, and started writing her thoughts on that page. Don interrupted her to say something which she found odd.

Don commented, "After our meeting, Aunt Fiery mentioned she needed my help. There isn't any way I can help her. She's lived a wonderful life, but I have this weird feeling… things will change."

Chapter 15

Honeymoon Car

As they shared breakfast the next morning, Don told Ann he was certain Aunt Fiery would start speaking about the 1941 Chevrolet at their next meeting. He admitted how his original goal was now secondary to hearing her life's story. His wife found this strange and reminded him how yesterday evening he said he didn't think they needed many more get-togethers. He explained how Fiery appeared frail at their first session, but now seemed to have more energy when she spoke of her past.

He said, "It was incredible listening to her and seeing the glow on her face, amazingly, she knows everything from memory. But then I wondered how true her tales really are."

"Well, here's your opportunity," Ann said. As she took an old journal out of a plastic bag and handed it to him, saying, "This one is from Fiery to me." Don appeared puzzled as his wife continued saying, "Sarah came back to the clinic yesterday and gave me Aunt Fiery's writings. She wanted Sarah to give me this to place in forty-one. So do everyone a favor, Don, put this in the trunk."

He took the book, opened it, and realized the faded page was what Fiery had told him, as he read, 'Mr. Ford was crossing the dam and waved to Alex.'

He thought maybe old Henry Ford really borrowed Alex's Model A. Don placed the book on the table, and went outside. Ann met Don and their dog in the garage as she was getting ready to leave for work.

She handed him Fiery's journal, commenting, "Please put this in the trunk. And keep your eye on Tiger as I drive out."

Together man and dog stood there watching Ann drive away. Don walked to the Chevrolet's trunk, but the journal in his hand caused Tiger to get excited, and she continued barking at it. There was something different about this book and Tiger couldn't smell it enough! Don laughed to himself. He thought possibly they had wrapped the diary in bacon!

The antics continued when the pooch jumped into the open trunk, smelled everything, and started acting as if she just found her long-lost boyfriend. Frantically she wagged her tail while roaming the enormous trunk. She finally laid on the journal and appeared to be telling him, 'Go to work; I'll be fine here until you come home.' He had to grab her collar to pull her out.

Don studied his wristwatch, deciding he had a few minutes to spare, and opened the driver's side door. The dog bounded into the vehicle, taking her usual place in the middle of the front seat. He attempted to start the motor with the key in the ignition, but it would not start. Tiger gave him a disappointed look realizing she was not getting a ride today.

As he was getting out, Don heard the dog whining. She was sitting with her paws on the dashboard. It was then he realized he didn't engage the choke. Don thought to himself how silly he forgot and got back behind the wheel. He pulled the choke halfway out, stepped on the starter pedal, and vroom! The old Chevrolet's stove bolt six engine sprang to life! The two of them took a quick ten-minute ride on the rural dirt roads near their home.

Tiger was happy that morning as he pulled their 1941 Chevrolet, or as Aunt Fiery would say… "Forty-one," back into the garage. Their ride was just enough to blow out the soot and carbon from the engine's carburetor and calm Tiger. Right then, he realized their pup loved being in that old car. When he arrived at work, Don had a message from Ann which read: Meeting at Aunt Fiery's tomorrow, 1:00 p.m., can you make it?

He returned Ann's call, and Sarah answered, saying, "The idea for tomorrow's meeting was my Ammygam's, I mean Aunt Fiery. She told gammy, my grandmother, she is so happy telling you what she still remembers and how good she feels after meeting with you. My grandmother told me she is seeing slight changes in our aunt's health and is worried about her."

He looked at his calendar and said, "Tomorrow at 1:00 p.m. is okay with me."

As he hung up the telephone, Don was told Michael from corporate security was waiting to speak with him. They needed to discuss the delivered "fireworks". The two men spoke for forty-five minutes. He told Michael in confidence the reason for the explosives, the prototype device they were working on, and how he needed the security department's help protecting the project. The director's positive comments and commitment were encouraging for Don. He spent the rest of his day preparing for Monday's board meeting.

The following afternoon, Ann was upset at being late for their scheduled 1:00 p.m. meeting at the Blair House. While he drove, he saw his wife open her journal to Saturday, May 1, 2004, and write on the page "Meet Aunt Fiery." It surprised both of them when they entered the building that no one was waiting for them. After signing in, the receptionist instructed them to wait in the foyer. They wondered if they had the correct date and time, which Sarah told them.

But it was not longer than five minutes before they saw Lucy slowly wheeling her aunt down the corridor. With a smile on her face, Fiery gave each a friendly greeting. She was delighted to see Ann. On Fiery's lap, he noticed another diary or journal and wondered if that too would find a home with him. They chose a private table near the window. Don placed his recorder in the middle of the table. Fiery struck up a conversation with Ann, not noticing he turned on the device. Don and Lucy went over to the beverage bar and brought back the usual glasses of water and apple juice for everyone.

Ann gestured for her husband to sit directly across from Fiery and said, "Aunt Fiery was telling me how Alex asked her to marry him after being engaged seven months. That was in January 1941, and Alex wanted to buy a newer car?"

The old woman was smiling at the lead-in Ann provided, stating, "Oh, yes! Alex desired a new automobile, and I wanted to plan our wedding. But Europe was at war, and many had ignored Japan's aggression in Asia.

Some people in the United States suspected we would soon be at war. People purchasing automobiles in 1941 looked for reliability. They also needed a vehicle able to survive an unknown number of years. We wanted the same, plus economical in case of gas rationing, and spare parts had to be available or interchangeable.

"My Alex searched for an auto that emphasized value, and economy with comfort, convenience, and safety. He considered lots of cars, from the luxurious Packards to the economical Willys and Crosleys. Can you believe new Packards came with lap robes that were a carryover from horse and buggy days? They stored these wool blankets on velvet ropes attached to the back of the front seat in case the passengers in the back had cold ankles. Lap robes, how funny is that?"

With that question, she paused and stared out the window at nothing, saying, "Even as late as 1941, many Packard owners had chauffeurs. They reserved most of the creature comforts for backseat passengers. Alex told me of Packard automobiles coming with a whistle that let the gas station attendant know when the tank was full. This actually changed the way people bought gas. Instead of telling the attendant how many gallons they needed, you just said, fill'er up!"

Don thought to himself, how much automotive knowledge does this lady have? And where did she get it?

Without interruption, she continued, saying, "Those who wanted a full-size car at a low cost bought a Willys. They had a four-cylinder sixty-three horsepower engine. It got thirty-five miles to a gallon and had a top speed of seventy-five miles per hour. They nicknamed their engine Go-Devil, and it was inside every Jeep during World War II. The Willys was a basic cheap vehicle. Items standard on most cars like a radio, clock, and lighter were optional on the Willys.

"Crosley automobiles were peanut cars powered by a twelve horse-power two-cylinder engine. They looked like a child's overgrown pedal car and could be driven over forty miles on a gallon of gas. They cost as much as a full-size Ford or Chevrolet and weighed less than a thousand pounds. You could only buy them at hardware and appliance stores, not at car dealerships. I remember Alex asking me how I would enjoy being 'shoehorned' into a Crosley?"

Aunt Fiery paused for just a moment to sip her apple juice. "By March, my Alex narrowed his choices to two manufacturers, Ford and Chevrolet. Living in Dearborn, we felt obligated to own an auto produced by the Ford Motor Company. It was a matter of civic pride. He often reminded me about the old lady who lived in the Dodge hamlet of Hamtramck where he bought his Model A, and how her neighbors took out their vengeance on that car.

"When our friend purchased a Studebaker and drove it over to his father's house in Dearborn, his dad yelled at him, 'I don't want a foreign car parked in front of my house.' They once made Studebakers in Detroit. Then in 1920, they moved their assembly plant to South Bend, Indiana. Funny how twenty years later some people consider Indiana a foreign country?"

Lucy and Ann were fixed on Fiery's words. Don thought his wife looked like a historian hoping to document every detail. He imagined Lucy as a student studying for her degree in automotive history.

Fiery continued saying, "The events between 1934 and 1939 changed our minds about buying a Ford. Security goons for Ford Motor beat up labor union organizers on the Miller Road viaduct… in front of the River Rouge Plant. Henry Ford wanted no part of the union in his assembly plant. Public support soon turned away from their hometown automobile manufacturer. Also, Mr. Ford's overt refusal to back the war in Europe did nothing to change the public's mind.

"His approval of Adolph Hitler seemed obvious. In 1938 he accepted a medal of achievement from Nazi Germany. Members of Ford's inner circle knew he disapproved of Hitler. They just couldn't get their message across to the average consumer. The press castigated Ford for his hatred of the President, not backing the war in Europe, and accepting the medal."

The elderly aunt was definitely on a roll. He sensed he was getting a family history and life lesson rolled into one speech. Fiery wanted to drive her point home.

Now she sounded determined to make a point, saying, "Mr. Ford hated President Roosevelt (FDR). This dislike stemmed back to when FDR was the Assistant Secretary of the Navy. During World War I, the government pressured Ford into building airplane engines. As a pacifist, he refused to make U.S. military planes. But, when approached to design and build an air ambulance, he grudgingly accepted.

"During a test flight of the air ambulance prototype, it crashed, killing the pilot who was a close friend of Mr. Ford. In Ford's mind, Roosevelt was responsible for his friend's death. At the height of the depression, in 1934, he refused to sign on to President Roosevelt's National Recovery Act (NRA) and pronounced his dislike of FDR. The NRA demanded American businesses raise their prices for goods and increase workers' wages while they set regulations for production and hours of work.

"Our government assumed an increase in wages would cause a surge in spending. The more we spent, the stronger the economy. Mr. Ford declined to abide by the NRA, even when threatened with jail. He found the act meddlesome and un-American. He believed it interfered with his company's ability to win government contracts. The Supreme Court later ruled the NRA was unconstitutional."

Fiery stared out the window and continued with her history lesson. She stated, "During the late twenties, Chevrolet overtook Ford as the leader in automotive sales. In 1940 Chevrolet came out with a new six-cylinder engine. It had a patriotic-sounding name: victory-six."

Don thought to himself… at least she's talking about the brand. Now when is she going to talk about our car?

"Alex and I stopped by the Ford dealership in Detroit, owned by Henry Ford's nephew. We contemplated buying a 1941 Ford Super Deluxe. It was wider and heavier than the 1940 model, with stiffer springs for a smoother ride. But, it had out-of-style old-fashion exposed running boards. The salesman quoted us a price of eight hundred eight dollars for the Ford Super Deluxe. I told Alex the car looked 'chubby' to me, and he laughed.

"I found out my Uncle Marty was a salesman at a Chevrolet dealership in Detroit. So, we decided to stop in the dealership and see what my uncle could offer us. The stylish, eye-catching 1941 Chevrolet Special Deluxe impressed us. The vehicle was longer and heavier with a sleek profile. It had a larger chrome grille, a three-speed manual gearbox, and a clutch called a vacuum power shift. It sounded automatic, even if it wasn't.

"The company phased out running boards in 1941. Instead, the bottom of the doors had been flared out. This covered a step into the interior, similar to today's modern car design. It was prettier, bigger, and more impressive than the Ford. Alex pointed out another advantage to the Chevrolet. It looked similar to the more expensive Cadillac.

"Their victory six engine had the same horsepower as the Ford v-eight causing my Alex to reckon maintenance costs may be lower with fewer replacement parts to buy. My uncle gave us his April edition of the Country Gentleman magazine. In it was an ad for the Chevrolet Special Deluxe Town Sedan. The ad highlighted each of the car's features. I was sold! Alex was sold! A Chevrolet Special Deluxe would be our first new car."

As she said those words, everyone at the table could see Aunt Fiery's satisfied smile. Don smiled, thinking; finally… she's talking about our car!

Without stopping to catch a breath, the stately lady said, "Uncle Marty quoted us a price of seven-hundred-ninety-one dollars for the 1941 Chevrolet Special Deluxe Town Sedan. Alex asked him: How much could he get for trading in our model A? When we pulled up for an estimate, the fellow at the used car lot cracked, 'Hey, Buddy, we're not doing a scrap metal drive here.' He eventually offered us a trade in value of twenty dollars. We took his offer and kept driving Alex's old rusted-out jalopy until our new car arrived.

"My uncle advised us to get our order in quick because General Motors was moving more and more to building war armaments. He assumed their car prices would go up, and they would reduce consumer production. So I told Alex we should order our new car that very day, and we could drive it on our honeymoon in August. Confidentially, he signed the purchase agreement right then.

"Uncle Marty said our new automobile would be ready in three months. We didn't anticipate the delivery date being a problem and planned to have it for our honeymoon. But, unfortunately, the war in Europe continued to expand, and by April 1941, the American public suspected, but never admitted, war was in our future. We hoped our Chevrolet might be manufactured before they totally switched to building weapons for war."

Fiery looked tired, but her voice never wavered. She mentioned, "At the time, Chevrolet was the largest of GM's twenty-three divisions. They and all other American automotive companies were gearing up for war.

The United States would soon become known as the arsenal of democracy. Chevrolet would play a significant part in molding that phrase.

"In 1941, people with money rushed to car dealerships. There they purchased a record number of new automobiles. Selling over one million vehicles that year made Chevrolet the top car producer. But, with a war on the horizon, everyone knew fewer cars will be made. Prices soon increased almost ten percent. The automakers sighted inflationary pressure and a lack of production supplies. They were committed to building more war arms for England. There was talk Russia will soon receive many of our armaments.

"The car we ordered was the top-of-the-line model. There weren't many choices available to enhance the vehicle. There were sealed beam headlights with chrome trim rings. It had parking lights and a higher quality wool mohair upholstery. Door armrests and a seven-day manual wind-up clock were standard. But I asked Alex if we could order some special factory features."

Now Fiery looked at Don, then Ann, and said, "Next time you sit in forty-one, look at the several additional options I insisted on adding, like the all-weather-air-control system. That combined heating and ventilation with fresh air circulated to every part of the cabin in summer or winter. It worked even with the windows tightly closed. My favorite option is the tissue holder, mounted under the passenger side glove compartment. I sat there most of the time.

"Alex added the chrome bumper tips. They bolted to the ends of the bumpers. Oh, and there was a flying lady hood ornament and the highest mileage four-ply wide whitewall tires. They were expensive, but they were worth it. His favorite option was a top-of-the-line radio with a short-wave band. With the war in Europe, he wanted to hear the latest news from the British Broadcasting Corporation (BBC)."

The prominent smile remained on her face. She continued to say, "With the options, our out-the-door price, including tax and licensing, the vehicle cost $1,008.56. I still have the forty-one's order form and registration in my diary. Alex and I thought we were getting a lot of car for the money. When compared to the similar-looking Cadillac, equipped with the same features costing over $1,400, our Chevrolet was a bargain."

When she made that analogy, Don thought of Joey with his 1941 Cadillac in Traverse City. He smirked and then hoped Aunt Fiery didn't see him. She might have thought he was laughing at her. Instead he found what Fiery said about the cars, similar to what Joey told him.

Aunt Fiery was staring out the window. She paused, allowing a broad smile to grow on her face. Then she said, "He asked me to choose the color. Other vehicles on the road were boring black, brown, gray, dark green, and dark blue; I wanted something bright. So I picked a cherry-colored paint, which also reminded me of the Traverse City Cherries. Our new Chevrolet was ruby maroon metallic."

Everyone at the table could sense how proud Fiery was as she spoke of ordering their new car. Don thought it may be a swell time for a break. He glanced over at Lucy to signal her, but there was no time as Fiery kept speaking.

The old woman said, "Before we left the showroom, Uncle Marty showed us one last feature of the Special Deluxe. He took us around to the front of the car. There he pointed to a small chrome-plated circle cover at the bottom of the grille. Then, he told Alex, if ever the battery failed, here's what you do. Pry off the round plate and insert the wheel lug wrench through the hole. It will engage a bayonet socket on the forward end of the crankshaft.

"A quick turn of the handle started the victory six engine. When the motor was running, the coupling automatically disengages the wrench for safety. That's how Alex learned to hand crank the forty-one. I asked my uncle, with the car's electric self-starter, why do you ever need to use this?

"He responded, 'The number of couples who park with the radio turned on may surprise you. Before they know it, their car's battery is dead.' Then I saw him wink at Alex. He asked Marty, 'How long will the radio play before it depletes the battery?' My uncle said, 'About two hours.' I giggled at Alex, telling him that's enough time.

"In the summer of 1941, I read that General Motors received more government war weapon contracts. Company officials were busy rushing to find factory space. They soon started manufacturing howitzer shells and machine guns for fighter planes. Everyone was working to meet the demands of the War Production Board (WPB). It was the demand of that board… auto production slowdown.

"That decision resulted in the build order for heavily optioned cars to have their delivery date pushed back. That meant our car would come in later than June. Finally, on August twelfth, our car arrived at the dealership." With a slight pause as if annoyed, she continued, saying, "Other salesmen tried to bribe Uncle Marty to release the automobile to them. But he refused, saying, 'This vehicle has a special duty to perform.'

"On Wednesday, August twentieth, 1941, we picked up our car. I never found out why the dealership held our forty-one for nine days before we could take possession of her. But, during that same week, the new United States Office of Production Management ordered automobile manufactures to reduce production again. The die was cast for those factories to move on to a firm war armament building schedule. The Chevrolet dealer informed my Alex he was fortunate to secure this vehicle.

"When the news broke of more production cuts, everyone headed to the auto dealers to buy or upgrade their vehicle. We often suspected someone saw our Chevrolet being off-loaded at the dealership and tried to buy it for a higher price. My Uncle Marty told us they received several inquiries to purchase our car from different buyers. But he put a stop to that, and we remained thankful to him.

"Arriving at the dealership, Uncle Marty told me, 'You're lucky that you are my favorite niece. Look what I had to do to keep your auto from disappearing.' He showed us the four trucks wedged in around it. Alex thanked my uncle for telling him, saying, 'Taking a train to Niagara Falls wouldn't have been as much fun as driving our new Chevrolet Special Deluxe there. What about that other matter?' My uncle answered, 'No one claimed it. So, it's yours.' Many years passed before I learned of that 'other matter.'

"Honestly, I often thought if my Uncle Marty was not our salesman, we never would have taken possession of that car. The porters had prepped and cleaned her beautifully. After signing the final paperwork, Alex took me on a brief ride home. He was beaming with pride over his new car, and I was excited to put the final plans together for our wedding on Sunday.

"On Sunday morning, August twenty-fourth, Alex drove his Chevrolet to my parent's house. At the house, we received a traditional Polish blessing from my parents. At 2:00 p.m., a polka band my parents hired came to their home. Polka music welcomed the arriving guests.

"Oh! It became a gay affair with the band playing before our marriage. Everyone there posed for a group picture underneath the large pine tree on my parent's front lawn. After taking the pictures, everyone walked me the two blocks to St. Alphonsus' for our wedding service. After the ceremony, Alex's mother, Bernice, gave each of us a silver dollar. This was a Polish custom, which she insisted we follow."

Don noticed the glee in Aunt Fiery's eyes and the broad grin on her face as she spoke of this joyous moment from her distant past. Likewise, Lucy appeared spellbound by her aunt's recollection of the event. Glancing at his wife, she too seemed transfixed on the story being recounted.

With a giant smile, Fiery continued, "Merrily, we each put a silver dollar in our left shoe for good luck. We kept those silver pieces in our shoes all day, laughing at the foolishness of it. Friends of ours laughed at the silliness of it, but neither Alex nor I wanted to tempt fate by removing the coin. Teddy, our best man, and friend of Alex's, drove forty-one to the church. He tied old shoes and tin cans to the bumper and painted 'Just Married' with liquid glass wax on the vehicle's trunk lid before he handed the keys to Alex.

"Our reception was at the Knights of Columbus Hall off Michigan Avenue in Detroit. We spent our wedding night in a new brick bungalow off Warren Avenue in Dearborn." With an even broader smile, she commented, "I made my husband carry me over the threshold. When he picked me up, I felt protected by him. That's when he told me a few weeks earlier he bought the property. Holding me in his arms, I kissed him. He grinned and said, 'You're now a new homeowner.'

"While I was in his arms, he fumbled around for the house key and gave it to me. I unlocked the door. As he was carrying me in, another surprise greeted me. He bought me a blond eight-week-old old puppy! He had tied a red ribbon to her oversized black leather collar, and it came bounding up to his feet. My groom put me down in the living room, and immediately the pup came to me, wagging its tail. I knelt on the floor and had to pet that cute little doggy. I asked the puppy, who do you belong to? Alex told me, 'She's your dog.'

"I was so excited! Growing up, I never had a pet and squealed in delight as he laughed at me. The pup was a blond color. My husband declared, 'I had an animal doctor check her so I know she's healthy. The doc identified her as a high-spirited Scottish gundog.' I considered it a cute little runt of a puppy. I asked him, what's her name? He said, 'That's your department. This dog is supposed to be intelligent, friendly and devoted. Just like you!' God, I loved my Alex."

Don looked over at his wife, who nodded in approval, and at Lucy, who appeared in awe at her aunt's story. The elderly aunt could not stop smiling. Happy tears seemed to form in the old aunt's eyes.

She continued her story, saying, "The blond and white fur on the puppy's neck formed a mane. I told my husband she looks like a little tiger, and that was what I will call her. Alex smiled and shouted, 'Tiger, it is.' The next morning, we awoke and started getting ready for our drive to Niagara Falls. I asked him, what are we doing with her while we're away? He explained how he planned with a neighbor to come feed her, give her water, and let her out during the day.

"I told him she could not be by herself! So the puppy had to come with us. He asked me if I wanted to take a puppy on our honeymoon. I justified taking her, saying she could be our practice child. I promised him there on our wedding night we would always be together, a family."

Lucy watched and listened as her aunt continued to speak of her distant memories. Some stories the niece had never heard.

Mrs. Fiery Maze stated, "When I first saw Tiger, her short tail was wagging like a windshield wiper at top speed. She was exuberant, playful, and affectionate. She was everything a dog lover wanted, and she loved my husband and me. The next morning, we packed our two suitcases and placed them in the trunk. Alex grabbed an old quilt and made a bed for Tiger in forty-one's backseat.

"When he pulled out his pocketknife, I didn't know what to expect. He went to the Chevrolet's rear bumper, cutting off the strings of old shoes and cans attached to it, and threw them in the garbage can. The three of us piled into the car, leaving for our family honeymoon at Niagara Falls.

As Alex drove towards the Ambassador Bridge to cross into Canada, I mentioned we forgot to do something.

"He asked me, 'What did we forget?' I informed him we never named our new car. Alex said, 'A name?' I told him, yes, a name! I explained to him I knew he didn't have a name for his Model A, but this car was our special dream car… and we needed a name. Oh! I told Alex I had a name for his old, dilapidated jalopy, especially when it broke down.

"I used very colorful language to keep that rusted Model A in line. Alex asked me, 'What name do you suggest'? I said to him, well, it's not a Ford, so Lizzie is out. Back then, Model Ts were called Tin Lizzie, and many people referred them as Lizzie.

"My parents always named their cars, Betsy. He said, 'That won't do. I've got it; 1941 is proving to be a banner year for me: a new car, a new wife, a new dog, a new house! So, to honor this year, let's call her forty-one?' I humored him by responding, well, at least I rated higher than a dog and a house. Tapping my hairbrush on the dashboard, I said, I dub thee 'Forty-one.'

"I will never understand how that little puppy did it. But just as I christened the car, she jumped over the front seat and landed between the two of us. Let me tell you, all the years we owned that dog, the only place she ever sat was on that front seat between my husband and me."

Ann reached across the table and placed her hand on Don's. She looked at him, and he could almost read her thoughts. He sat there thinking Fiery had a pup called Tiger, and so do we. And… they each had a best man named Teddy. Don's brother, Theodore, was their best man. They always referred him to as Teddy, never Ted. Don thought, was this a "Godwink?"

Still, with a smile, Lucy's Aunt Fiery continued, "Alex took the cigar Teddy had given him from his pocket and put it in his mouth. He said, 'Let's check out this cat's eye lighter and see how it works.' He pushed in the knob and waited until it glowed like a cat's eyes when shined by a light. Then, lighting his cigar, he cracked open his driver's side vent window. He asked me, 'Do you know the reason for these air vents and how they're used?' I told him for venting air, I guess. He said, 'No, they're for the front seat passengers so they can tip their ashes from their cigars or cigarettes out the window, without them being blown back in their face.'

"I told him I don't smoke. But I do like to stick my feet out of the window during the summer when we're driving. Opening my small vent window, I took off my sandals and put my head in his lap; with Tiger on my hip, I stuck my feet out the tiny window of our honeymoon car. That's when I realized my life would be a special dream with my love, my husband, my Alex."

Aunt Fiery stopped speaking and just stared out the window. But she never saw the scenic view of a perfect dark green lawn that extended 100 feet from the building to a wetland. Grass and marsh surrounded three sides of Blair House. Or, the marshland cattails, prairie cordgrass, and the green foliage that appeared to extend another 600 feet to what turned out to be a line of cottonwood, willows, and maple trees. A peaceful country picture normally seen on the front of greeting cards.

He knew she wasn't looking at the view… she was looking into her past and remembering happier times as a tear flowed down her cheek.

When Aunt Fiery spoke, her words were faint, "I often thought forty-one had providence or a divine purpose. It was through fate or destiny that Alex and I ended up with that 1941 Chevrolet Special Deluxe sedan."

Lucy understood her aunt needed a break. So she interrupted her aunt, saying, "Aunt Fiery, you forgot your bracelet. Let's go to your apartment and get it."

Ignoring Lucy, Fiery turned to Don, saying, "I haven't been down that road… in a long time."

Don gave an approving smile, asking, "Are you okay, or do you want to stop for the day?"

The elderly lady responded, "I could use a brief break, but then can we go on? I have much to tell you about forty-one."

He smiled, responding, "You take your time. We'll be right here waiting for you to return."

When Lucy and Fiery left the table, Ann said, "Lucy told me her aunt needed to take some medication. They'll be back in twenty minutes."

He watched his wife take her red leather daily journal out of her large purse and open it to today's date, May 1, 2004. She wrote on the page, 'Aunt Fiery spoke until 2:10 p.m. then she needed a break.' He smiled, thinking of the words, May Day, on the journal's page. The time on his telephone when he checked read 2:04 p.m. and said nothing of the difference.

He reached for his recorder on the table and turned it off. Don leaned back in his chair, wondering where Aunt Fiery's story would lead him?

Chapter 16

Beyond Belief

While waiting for Lucy and Fiery to come back, Don and Ann explored Blair House and its amenities. They were waiting at the table, wondering what Fiery might say next when she returned wearing a beautiful and what appeared to be an antique gold bracelet on her left wrist. Don estimated he had three more hours of recording time remaining, but he doubted their meeting would last that long. He turned on his recorder, moving it closer to the center of the table, not wanting to miss a word of her story.

Aunt Fiery took this opportunity to pose a question directly to him, asking, "Am I boring you? I really hope not!"

He responded, "Not at all; I love listening to you. In fact, I'm certain everyone is enjoying your memories as much as I do. Thank you for sharing with us. Can I tell you something about me you may not know?"

Fiery's face lit up, and she leaned into him as if to hear an illicit secret.

Don continued, "Actually, there are two things. First, you mentioned your wedding reception was at the Knights of Columbus Hall. I'm an officer in our Knights' Council. I recently attended a training class at the same hall where you and Alex had your reception. Also, I wanted to inform you we were Appleton Street neighbors. I grew up on the north side of the street. How is that for a coincidence!"

"Yes, I thought so," she stated. "I remember your parents as I'm sure they knew of me. The day you were born, I saw your mother when she crossed the street in front of me. I was bringing forty-one home from the mechanics. That was the last time I drove forty-one, and later that day, your father nearly ran into the taxi taking Lucy and me to the train station. Many years later, I remember seeing you playing in the street with other children… we have so many coincidences to consider."

Don's mind swirled as he thought… she just confirmed the maintenance receipt I found in the Chevrolet's trunk, dated the day I was born! He remembered the receipt looked like his birthdate, but now she confirmed the date and the last time she drove the car.

Seeing his puzzled face, Fiery changed the subject saying, "Sometimes this apple juice is just too sweet. That's why I put some water in it."

To give himself time to absorb what she said about driving her car, Don asked, "What is your favorite flavor?" Then thought to himself, what a dumb question to ask.

Without hesitation, she declared, "I love the cherry juice, but they don't have it very often."

"So, how does the color of the cherry juice compare to forty-one's paint?"

She answered, "The color is nowhere near the shade of my car!" Not missing a beat, she continued right where she left off before their break. "When Alex and I took delivery of forty-one, the hue was a bright red similar to a Traverse City cherry. At the dealership… Oh! Wait a minute, I forgot to mention something Uncle Marty didn't tell me until 1950 about that day. Alex visited my uncle two days before we picked our car up to make sure everything was okay. When he got there, they couldn't find forty-one on the car lot.

"Finally, one salesman admitted he hid the vehicle on the overflow lot, hoping to sell it on the sly for a premium price. To make sure that didn't happen again, my uncle and Alex moved our sedan to the main lot, hiding her among the trucks. As Alex was inspecting her for any damage, he became furious when he found something inside and brought it home.

"Can you guess what it was? Someone had left their Scottish hunting puppy in our car! Alex told my uncle, 'If they want it back, have them come see me.' Then to protect forty-one, Uncle Marty hid the truck keys, blocking our Chevrolet in, so it couldn't be moved. I was glad no one ever claimed the little runt! I loved Tiger almost as much as my husband and forty-one!

Ann gently squeezed Don's hand as if to say, can you believe this? He was still thinking about his mother walking in front of the car she was driving… and he now owns. Aunt Fiery didn't notice them as she removed a book from the table, placed it on her lap, and glanced at a couple pages. Her tone took on a younger sounding quality as she continued, "We left for our honeymoon and drove through Canada on our way to Niagara Falls. We had a rough time finding any open service stations after dark, so we stopped in Woodstock, Ontario, for the night.

"There, we found out the Canadian Government had restricted the sales hours on gasoline, forcing stations to close at night. This was supposed to reduce fuel consumption by their citizens." Fiery looked at Lucy, saying, "With our minds focused on our wedding, we forgot Canada was at war. Rather than risk running out of gas in the dark, we pulled into a local motor court. As we waited at the registration desk, someone noticed our just married sign on forty-one's trunk.

"We wondered why people blew their horns, waved, and grinned as they passed. Alex whispered, 'Oh! I forgot to wipe that off the trunk lid.' A little while later, the wife of the motor court owner knocked on our front screen door. She smiled as she stood there with a fresh-baked chocolate cake, saying, 'I brought this for you to help celebrate your wedding. I hope you enjoy it. With sugar rationing, I didn't have enough for the frosting, so I made do with what I had.'

"We thanked her for the wonderful surprise. Then, before going to sleep, I sliced the cake, and we each took a piece. The frosting tasted strange… real minty, and kind of funny. Alex replied, 'This isn't like any mint frosting I've ever had!'

"Then it came to me, I know what it is! It's Pepsodent toothpaste. She made us a cake with toothpaste frosting — who would have thought? I asked Alex if he thought we still needed to brush our teeth before we went to bed?"

Everyone at the table laughed, and someone shouted, "Toothpaste!"

Aunt Fiery grinned at their surprise and went on, saying, "My husband commented, 'You have to give her credit though; she sure made do with what she had.' The next morning before Alex loaded our luggage, he used a wet rag to wipe the just married message off the trunk."

Don could see the happiness in her smile and hear it in her voice.

She continued, "Then we filled up the car with gas. When done, we set off towards Niagara Falls for our adventure. Tiger was lying between us as my husband spoke of different things. He captured my attention when he said, 'You know there's another option your Uncle Marty didn't tell us about. A man at Buhl Sons discovered the long intake and exhaust manifolds on these engines are ideal for warming and preparing food.'

"This fellow from Oklahoma told Alex, while he was saving money to buy an automobile for his move to Michigan; he looked underneath a lot of hoods hoping to find the perfect engine to cook on. His family had gone through the dust-bowl and were refugees who went to California searching for work and couldn't afford to stop at diners to eat. So when they couldn't find much firewood in New Mexico and Arizona, they had to improvise.

"His father had the brilliant idea to use the heat given off by their car's engine to prepare the food. Hard times followed their family to California. Arriving, they discovered too many people and few jobs. They heard farmworkers were needed in Michigan's Berrien County fruit belt, so they saved a few dollars and headed there. Along the way cooking their meals on the car's engine was the only way they survived. When they arrived, the cherry harvest was in full swing, and he couldn't find work. His dad just wanted to support his family, so he hitchhiked to Detroit, hoping for a job at Ford Motor Company, but he ended up with a general worker position at Buhl Sons."

She paused for a moment before saying, "Now the man's son carries a roll of foil, wire, wire cutters, and a pair of pliers with him wherever he goes in case he needs to cook a meal in a pinch. My Alex told me to double wrap the food in foil so it wouldn't tear or have a hole punched in it when driving over a bump. To my surprise, he had wired a half-gallon metal juice container to the exhaust manifold so we could warm up a can of beans. It was getting near lunchtime, and we needed to stop for gasoline. So, we decided to put this trick to the test.

We found a service station with a diner next door and thought… how perfect! We bought four pieces of fried chicken, two dinner rolls, a pint of potato salad from the diner, a can of pork and beans, and a couple of bottles of Coke from the gas station. Alex said, 'It's important to punch a tiny hole in the can's top to let the steam out. If you don't, it will explode like a hand grenade!' Then we double wrapped the chicken in the foil and wired it on the valve cover because we only wanted to keep it warm… since it had been cooked.

"The two bottles of Coke were placed in between the radiator and the grille to chill them. About a half-hour later, we stopped for lunch under a tree by the roadside. Alex grabbed a small clean towel from under the driver's seat and told me to be sure to use it so I wouldn't burn my hands while I used the pliers to remove the foil packets. He was right; they were hotter than you could imagine!

He pulled the beans from the juice can holder and showed me the steam escaping from the hole in the lid. Then, he opened the tin with a church-key… that's what we used to call can openers. I cut up chicken for Tiger, and the three of us enjoyed a wonderful picnic. That food tasted like a home-cooked meal! When we arrived at Niagara Falls, Alex drove forty-one up to the cabin he had rented. We spent the next four days exploring.

"I always liked Alex! But over those few days, I truly came to love him and learned what that meant. It felt so good loving him. I learned how to appreciate the things Alex did for me and loved what I discovered about him."

Don heard a sad quiver in Fiery's voice. She paused to take a deep breath before saying, "I photographed Alex with Tiger's head sticking out of his raincoat on the Maid of the Mist tour boat near the falls. After five days, we had to pack up and go home. I was looking forward to my life as his wife in our home… together. Every morning while he shaved, I made breakfast for him and me. Afterward, he washed the dishes while I took Tiger for a quick walk. As we were coming back, Alex was pulling forty-one out of the garage.

"I always drove forty-one to work so Alex could get extra sleep because he spent his entire shift on his feet, but in the evening, he insisted on driving home. I enjoyed our life, the predictability of those days, and my time with Alex… God knows how much I loved him… and he loved me."

Fiery paused as if lost in thought, Lucy became concerned. "Are you okay, auntie?" she asked.

Ignoring her, Fiery continued, "As 1941went on, Great Britain and Russia applied more and more pressure on our country. We all knew war was coming, and I realized that someday soon, our beloved routine would drastically change… forever. But, for the time being, I reveled in our wonderful married life. If Alex had a Sunday off, we would take a ride to Hines Park. We watched Tiger running through the woods stirring up rabbits — she was a real hunter and always came back whenever we called her. I so loved our Tiger!"

"Each day on our journey home from work, I stared out the window looking for married couples walking closely on the sidewalk. I tried to imagine the lives they built and wondered how they stayed together in both good and bad times. We would see a special elderly couple who slowly strolled along, supporting each other. The man had his right arm around her waist, and her left arm circled his waistline.

"Both were frail and, without the other, could never have made their walk. I often smiled at Alex and said, that's us in fifty years. Sometimes I'd ask him to stop and see if they wanted a ride, but he didn't want to intrude on their time together. One day we didn't see them anymore, and I've always regretted not stopping to hear their story."

Ann noticed a melancholy look on the aunt's face as she abruptly changed the subject. Saying, "On a Monday afternoon in late September 1941, the Buhl Sons Company was hit with a wildcat strike. As a contractor for the Lend-Lease Act, the government forced the company to order mandatory overtime and six-day workweeks. This schedule became a real burden for many employees, and the union steward ordered a walkout. With the plant shutdown, Miss Graves told everyone in our department to go home and call in each morning to check if they settled the strike.

"Alex went to the plant the next day, but as he waited to cross the blockade line, he witnessed something that changed his mind. The picketers took out their vengeance on one of the journeyman's car, slamming their signs into the fenders and doors, chipping the car's paint. Alex at once turned forty-one around and headed home. He called his boss from home and told him he wanted to work, but he wasn't crossing the picket line."

The elderly lady's voice became solemn as she recounted what happened during those depressing moments, saying, "Alex's boss told him to call every day for an update. When he put down the phone, Alex said to me, 'Let's take Tiger and drive up north for an impromptu fall color tour.' The next morning, we called work and realized they scheduled no meetings for the next three days… there was no end in sight. So, we took advantage of this unplanned vacation. Right away, we packed up forty-one, left the city, and headed for Northern Michigan.'"

With that statement, a broad smile appeared on her face. Fiery said, "We took our time and stopped at a roadside park for the night, arriving the next morning at the boat dock in Mackinaw City. We waited twenty minutes to board the ferry that took us and our car on the trip through the Straits of Mackinac. There was no bridge between the upper and lower peninsula back then. We bought a large can of beef stew from a nearby shop and a half-pound of homemade cooked egg noodles for lunch.

"Alex punched a pinhole in the container of stew and placed it in the tin canister on the exhaust manifold. He said, 'Good, now we can have lunch at the Soo Locks in Sault Ste. Marie!' We found a park near the locks, lifted forty-one's hood, pulled out the can, opened it, and mixed in the noodles. The three of us, Alex, Tiger, and I, enjoyed a wonderful lunch as we watched the freighters going through the locks.

"From where we were sitting, we shook hands with a real-life ship's captain when his vessel's bridge came level with the sidewalk. After lunch, we headed for Tahquamenon Falls, where we hiked around the paths to the waterfall. We so enjoyed those moments. The forest, woodlands, meadows, wildflowers, and the entire region was special to us. It was our piece of heaven, and I never wanted to forget those moments.

"A snapping turtle that was sunning itself on the path intrigued Tiger. We laughed as she cautiously sniffed the turtle and tried to play with it. Then, not having much luck with the turtle, she turned her attention to the meadow. We were sitting under a large hemlock tree, on a blanket from our trunk, as we watched our pup chase all the rabbits she could find.

"A small bunny the size of a softball was so scared that it circled the entire meadow, turned in our direction, and ran smack into Tiger, knocking her down. I don't know which of them was more surprised! Alex and I laughed so hard tears were running down our cheeks! Tiger needed a nap after that and laid near us.

"It was then, under that hemlock, Alex amazed me by bringing out a paperback copy of the Song of Hiawatha. He read to me how Henry Wadsworth Longfellow's character, Hiawatha, built his canoe along the waters of Tahquamenon River. I loved the sound of my husband's voice as he read to me… and only to me. I never wanted to leave this magical spot. So, we moved forty-one over to the hemlock grove and pitched our tent there. Then we tied Tiger to the bumper and took a honeymoon nap."

Don saw Lucy's jaw drop and Ann sniggering as both imagined what the elderly lady meant.

"After our nap, we walked over to the river, and Alex taught me to fish. I was fishing while he continued to read out loud from the paperback, telling me of the Ojibwa Indians who fished, farmed, and trapped in this area. The Ojibwa people named this piece of heaven after the color of the river water… Tahquamenon meant 'dark berry', and that's precisely what I observed. And then it happened, I caught a fish!

"Or, the fish caught my line. I was so excited I screamed! Tiger didn't understand what was happening, and Alex thought I lost my mind. I don't know what was louder, my screaming or Tiger barking! My husband scrambled to help me, nearly dropping his book in the river and had to save it and me from ending up in there too!"

Fiery's face beamed as she said, "I was so proud we could have my fish for dinner. I didn't want to stop. So, Alex passed the time by leafing through the paperback, finding passages that interested him and read them out loud to me. In the late 1800s, he told me lumberjacks downed millions of trees and used the river to get them to the mill. He had just gotten to the part about the cedar swamp leaching tannin into the river and turning it to the color of steeped tea… when I caught my second fish! As twilight was coming, we headed back to camp.

"At our campsite, Alex stoked the campfire to life while I cleaned my two fish. After cooking and eating our fresh catch, we agreed this was the best fish dinner we ever had! The day was exciting, and that evening we fell asleep to the faint sounds of the waterfall flowing from a distance with Tiger snoring softly between us. During the night, Tiger burst out of the tent when she heard an invader near our campsite.

"I stayed safely in our tent while Alex went after her. The bright glow of a waxing gibbous moon provided enough light for him to see our pup stop dead in her tracks near the meadow's edge. She stood there bewildered, finally realizing this wasn't her backyard. Not knowing what to do, she waited for him to save her by gently placing a rope leash on her collar and guiding her back to the tent.

"She was up most of the night making low ruff-ruff noises, telling all the forest creatures that she was on guard. I woke up at dawn, surprised to find both Alex and Tiger missing. I panicked for a minute, then found him with a pail of water washing his Chevrolet while the pup was busy happily chasing more rabbits. My husband washed or polished a part of that car every day. I sometimes resented the attention he gave to forty-one, but he thought I was the one being silly.

"He told me he could never love a car as much as he loved me! And, ever since that trip, we always stored our blankets, camping equipment, table, chairs, dog bowls, cooking utensils, pliers, and tinfoil in forty-one's trunk. Our car's entire life story is in that trunk, and we used everything in there."

Faintly laughing and shaking her head, Aunt Fiery declared, "We were young and crazy then… young and crazy." Don thought she had to be tired, but she continued without hesitation, "On Saturday morning, we drove to the nearest town, Newberry, finding an open store with a public pay telephone so we could call work. We then had to make change to make our long-distance phone call. The information we received was that the workers tentatively settled, and we had to be at work Monday morning.

"We talked of leaving, but we were having such a wonderful time… we decided to stay one more night. Near midnight, Tiger woke us up with a loud growl and bounded out of our tent. My husband looked so funny chasing after her in his undershorts! With the moon shining bright, Alex could see someone's silhouette in the tree line, and the pup running full speed towards them. But as she got near the figure, Tiger stopped and headed back to him. They spent the rest of the night keeping a large campfire going, making sure I slept safely.

"We broke camp at dawn and packed everything into forty-one's trunk. I drove over to Saint Ignace as my two adventurers slept in the front seat. When we arrived at the ferry dock to cross back to the lower peninsula, I learned we had a forty-minute wait. Our ferry's name was the City of Petoskey. It held one-hundred cars… we were number fifty-four in line.

"With spare time, I walked to a nearby grocery store and bought two colas, a can of beef stew, and a package of noodles for lunch. But when I got back to forty-one, I noticed a delicious aroma in the air coming from the car parked next to us. The couple was eating hot pasties… you know, those small meat pies popular with the Yoopers in Michigan's Upper Peninsula. They smelled so good I couldn't resist them. So, when Alex and Tiger returned from their walk, I told him I wanted some real Yooper food.

"My husband looked at me, smiled, kissed me on the cheek, saying, 'Anything my darling wants.' That's when he and our pup set out to find a vendor selling those treats. They returned just before we sailed with three hot pasties. I double wrapped them, and he put them on forty-one's manifold. We started the car and boarded the ferry, agreeing to eat our pasties during the ferry boat ride.

"Monday, we returned to work, and Alex was again working mandatory twelve-hour days, six days a week. In the office, we worked six days a week too, but our days were only ten hours long. Our days were busy and exhausting. The only free moments we had together were when we drove to work. With his long hours, Alex still thought of me first and wanted me to drive forty-one home in the evenings while he caught a ride home from his pal. He didn't want me to come back to pick him up when his shift ended.

"We felt guilty leaving Tiger by herself for such a long time. So, we paid a neighbor's teenage daughter one dollar a week to come after school and take her for a walk. Her mother told us how much the girl loved taking care of our dog and making money too! Before we knew it, December was here."

Fiery's face and tone changed when she mentioned December, and everyone at the table wondered what she was going to say next. Then she said, "On Sunday, December 7, 1941, we planned to go to the early Mass at Saint Alphonsus, but my Alex forgot to wind the alarm clock. We slept in late. Even with our full day planned, we managed to attend noon Mass — this was our one day to spend all our time together.

"We were looking forward to cutting down our first Christmas tree as a married couple. Our plan was to drive to a Christmas tree farm in Irish Hills, owned by a machine shop retiree from Buhl Sons. We also wanted to gather broken pine branches to make a wreath for Alex's father's grave. Driving west on U.S. Route twelve, I noticed a roadside diner merrily decorated for Christmas. I pleaded with Alex to stop and have a festive brunch to put us in the holiday spirit.

"Brunches were an import from England and started to become popular in the United States in the late 1930s. As we drove into the parking lot, I told Tiger to be good, and we would bring her a treat. Unfortunately, our pup had other plans, and when I opened the passenger door and stepped out, she tried to escape. When she finally settled down and curled into a ball on the front seat, I covered her with a blanket and locked the door. After we finished, Alex snapped on the radio while I fed Tiger a couple slices of bacon I had saved for her.

"We didn't hear the announcer's actual words, but the tone of his voice was so edgy, so full of emotion, we froze motionless in the front seat. It was too unbelievable; he reported the Japanese had bombed Pearl Harbor, Hawaii… I thought it couldn't be happening; this was beyond belief! Even though the attack was 5,000 miles away, I felt vulnerable and terrified. Home is where I was safe, and I couldn't wait to get there! So, we turned around and went home. My fear soon turned to rage. I screamed, how dare the Japanese attack us!

"No one in the United States saw this coming. We listened to a reporter explaining how one battleship exploded. Then, Alex switched forty-one's radio to the shortwave band. On that band, he found the British Broadcasting Corporations news channel. He remarked, 'I'm sure glad we bought this radio.' The voice of the English newscaster sounded happy when he announced the attack on Pearl Harbor to his British audience.

"With utter disbelief, Alex and I looked at each other. Then, the reporter made an off-the-cuff comment, which got me mad. He said,

'The United States is finally in the war!' He must have forgotten many Americans were also tuned in to his broadcast. When we arrived home, we parked in the driveway and sat there listening to the news reports from Hawaii. We couldn't stop listening!

"Alex worried about his step-cousin Eddie. He was a Seaman Second Class aboard the Arizona and three years younger than my husband. They were close, hanging around together in the years before Eddie joined the Navy. Eddie told Alex he enlisted because he wanted to see the world, but, in reality, he needed a steady job. Two days before Christmas, we received word Eddie was one of the 1,177 sailors who perished on the USS Arizona. His body is forever entombed in the ship, and he will never come home. At church on Christmas Day, we each lit a candle in his memory."

Lucy interrupted, saying, "Aunt Fiery, it's almost time for dinner, and you've spoken long enough for today."

Evidently, Fiery wasn't planning to stop, but she agreed, saying, "Well, I was just getting to the war and the Homefront. Perhaps you're right, I am getting tired. I'll get to that… another time."

Don and Ann thanked the elderly Aunt Fiery for sharing her stories and waited while Lucy wheeled her back to her room. He casually removed his recorder from the table and placed it in his pocket. When Lucy returned, Don asked her if she thought these meetings upset her aunt.

Lucy chose her words carefully, saying, "Honestly, at first, I was concerned. But now, I believe these chats are helpful. My aunt is happy, and that's good. I grew up living with her and never heard her speak the way she has these past weeks. I didn't realize how much she loved her husband… or that car. And, I never paid attention when she spoke of Tiger. She has confided in you and told you more than anyone else I know, except for her girlfriend, Sylvia. I've been trying to figure out the reason."

On the way home, Don asked his wife if she noticed the book on Fiery's lap.

Ann responded, "It's funny that you should ask. Halfway through her story, I looked at her journal and realized the pages were so faded, I couldn't see any writing… she was speaking from memory."

Tiger was waiting at the door when they arrived home, and Don allowed her to run outside on the side lawn, where she started chasing things only she could see. She suddenly laid in the grass, looking tired. She studied him, looked over to the woods, and then to him. Don thought, is something wrong with her? I'll have to mention this to Ann. His brain then switched to the things Fiery said, thinking, who remembers a ferry boat's name or phase of the moon on a date in 1941? He knew she really was a remarkable lady, but he still wanted to prove her facts.

Ann disapproved of his plan when he discussed it with her and said, "You shouldn't question Fiery's events. Sometimes older people change the facts to match their memories. She's a wonderful woman with delightful stories! You may embellish things too when you're eighty-seven years old!"

Despite what his wife told him, Don chose six statements to verify. With his laptop open and listening to Fiery's recorded dialogue, he first searched for the day they picked up their Chevrolet at the dealer. Fiery claimed August twentieth, 1941, was a Wednesday. Perfect! Next was their Sunday wedding a few days later, on the twenty-fourth. Yep! That was right!

Third, he focused on the City of Petoskey and the Straits of Mackinac. To his surprise, there was such a ship, and it held one hundred five cars. She was only off by five cars! He discovered the State of Michigan established the car ferry service in 1940. It traveled between Mackinaw City and Saint Ignace until 1957.

It took him a half-hour of searching to find any information on the Buhl Sons Company strike in 1941. He found many articles on union unrest and strikes in Detroit. Finally, after much internet searching, he discovered in late September, there was a strike at Buhl Sons. The old woman was correct!

Then he remembered her mentioning Alex reading Longfellow's "Song of Hiawatha". Now, according to Fiery, the poem had an association with Tahquamenon Falls. So Don searched the internet for the poem and a link to the falls. It was in the poem's seventh chapter, Hiawatha Sailing. There he came upon a connection. Hiawatha built his canoe by the rushing Tahquamenaw… not Tahquamenon as in falls.

Longfellow set his poem in Michigan's Upper Peninsula. In the poem, Hiawatha is in love with the beautiful Minnehaha. She lived on the southern shore of Lake Superior, where the Tahquamenon River flows into the lake. His search showed the Ojibwa nation people were native to the area. Fiery was right again! Oh! What the heck, he thought. I'll check the moon's lunar phase in late September 1941.

After searching for a 1941 calendar with the moon phases, he exclaimed loudly, "Lo-and-behold!" It was a waxing gibbous moon the day before they departed the falls. The same night she claimed Alex and Tiger noticed a bright moonlit shadow. He finally conceded Aunt Fiery was spot on with her facts. Changing his focus for a moment, he downloaded his digital recorder to a folder on his computer's hard drive. He could not contain his excitement, so just before bedtime, he confessed to his wife what he had done.

She could only smile at him, saying, "I told you not to question her! You should stop looking for the negatives and enjoy the positives surrounding her."

It annoyed Don to know his wife was right and said, "Well, I don't understand how she remembers dates and events the way she does. Wait… what was her dog's name?"

Ann looked at her husband and laughed, saying, "Donald… every veterinarian, like me, knows Scottish hunting dogs. They are of great beauty, devoted, friendly, and intelligent. And, if you haven't noticed, let me tell you now. Her girl dog, Tiger, is the same Golden retriever breed as your girl dog, Tiger!"

Tiger, hearing her name, started running back and forth around the room, wanting to play.

He said, "Look what you've done! Now I have to take her outside to calm her down. Come on, let's go, girl!"

As if she understood his words, their dog ran into the coatroom while Ann continued, "Don, what are the odds we both have a Golden retriever with the same name? I never saw her dog, but Fiery sure described a purebred to me."

Tiger came bounding back into the family room with a leash in her mouth. She looked up at him with her adolescent eyes and tail wagging, as if saying hurry!

Ann remarked, "I told you the breed is intelligent. Don, don't you see all these coincidences?"

As he walked out towards the coatroom with Tiger close behind, he shouted in denial, "What? No, I don't!"

Chapter 17

The Homefront

The grass around Don and Ann's property was turning a bright green on this first Sunday in May. During the night, downed power lines shut off their electricity, and everyone overslept, including their dog. As he wheeled his portable generator out of the garage, Tiger was at his side. Once it started running, it provided electrical power to select outlets in their farmhouse. After Tiger's stroll in the yard, they entered the house, where he could smell the breakfast coffee Ann was brewing.

It was near 9:30 a.m. when the phone rang. Ann answered the call. After completing her telephone conversation, she said, "That was Sarah. She apologized for not being at yesterday's meeting. Her grandma Lucy asked her to visit today with her Ammygam at 2:00 p.m., and she invited us to visit with her."

Fiery's stories captivated Don, so he decided preparations for the board meeting tomorrow could wait. Ann called Sarah back to let her know they would be there. They learned the entire east side of their town was without power, and with limited electricity, to the house, they skipped breakfast at home. With enough time to attend Mass, have brunch at a South Lyon restaurant, and meet Sarah at the Blair House, they left for church.

They arrived at the Blair House, ten minutes early… before Sarah. They found Aunt Fiery in the dining hall with other residents. Seeing them, she smiled and waved them over to her. At the table, she introduced them to her friends and to Katherine. Their reason for gathering was to celebrate Katherine's ninety-fifth birthday!

The birthday girl quipped, "The cake says ninety, but my friends know I lie about my age!"

They spoke to the quick-witted Katherine and her friends, as Don heard Fiery telling others in the group, they were her special relatives. He smiled, realizing this was something special. Soon each received a piece of cake, and the birthday girl made sure Ann had one decorated with a bright yellow sugar frosting flower. After a few minutes, the short celebration was over, and the residents returned to their rooms. The Blair House's staff came over, cut the remaining cake into pieces, put them on small paper plates, and placed them at the beverage bar.

Aunt Fiery signaled for Ann to push her to her apartment. Don brought several glasses of juice and water to their familiar card table near the window while waiting for them to return. Don placed his digital recorder on the table close to where Aunt Fiery would sit; seeing them returning, he switched it on. As the two women approached, he listened to Ann commenting on how nice all of Fiery's friends are.

Without hesitation, the elderly woman said, "There are delightful people here." She paused a moment and looked sad. Her great-great-niece had not arrived. She then remarked, "I'm sure Sarah will join us as soon as she can."

Aunt Fiery, with her amiable smile, glanced at the book on her lap and to each of them, commenting, "I am so happy you want to hear my stories. These are all true, you know? When you were last here, I stopped when the Japanese bombed Pearl Harbor in December 1941. We planned cutting down a Christmas tree that day and never did… everything changed."

Don thought to himself, how long ago did Fiery think our last visit was? Had she forgotten it was only yesterday afternoon?

Fiery continued, "Arriving home, we parked forty-one in our dark driveway. Neighbors came over just to listen to the broadcast news on our shortwave radio. Everyone was silent until the British reporter said, 'The United States is finally in the war!' That got us mad. Everyone became angry, so Alex changed the station. We listened to other reports from Hawaii. On Monday morning, December eighth, we felt a bond among our co-workers to win the war… at any cost. Gone were the arguments promoting isolationism. Now everyone wanted to get involved in Europe's conflict.

"We aren't making parts for the Lend-Lease Act to help Great Britain and Russia anymore. Our country, the United States of America, is who we're working for and helping now! We each understood this was 'our' war. Mr. Buhl knew he had to rally his troops. He had his department managers call all the employees together.

"Mr. Buhl waited until his employees gathered around him. Then he shouted, 'Whatever we can do to defeat our enemy, we will do it correctly and swiftly. We can win this war! Let's unite to make these parts so they will build those airplanes. I'm counting on each of you to do your part.'

"After his brief pep talk, there was a loud cheer, and everyone sang God Bless America. Many workers were crying and wiping away tears as they quietly headed back to their workstations. Soon word spread, President Roosevelt (FDR) will address both Houses of Congress, and they would broadcast his speech live on the radio. The few radios in the company's complex were brought out to the warehouse's largest open space. Antennas had been haphazardly strung. As FDR spoke at 12:30 p.m., workers from the entire plant were clustered around the radios.

"The President in a brief speech declared war on Japan. There was total silence as each of us tried to decipher what the broadcast meant to our own personal lives. Early that Monday morning, Alex's oldest brother, Smitty, stood in line at the recruiting office in downtown Detroit among the throng of men and boys at least ten years his junior. He had called his boss, Jonesy, the night before, saying, 'I'm quitting my job… to re-enlist in the Army.'

"Smitty's wife, Marge, was pregnant, and they had a two-year-old toddler named Stanley, Jr. As an honorably discharged soldier, he had a draft status of four-A. Many thought it was irresponsible of him to re-join. He had done his duty! When anyone asked why he signed up again, he'd declare, 'Don't you know we're at war?'

"Smitty was told to report the following week to the American Lady Corset Company in downtown Detroit for induction into the army. They were more than happy to have him, and they assigned him to the old WW

I Army Recruit Training Center, formally known as Camp Custer. He would train new recruits in artillery basics at this expanded army camp in Battle Creek, Michigan. The night he was packing to leave for camp, Alex stopped over to wish him good luck. He reminded Smitty how the Sunday after World War I ended, their father sat them down for a man-to-man talk… they were only seven and five years old.

"Their dad told them, 'Always be proud to live in America. You can be a success or failure here… but it's up to you. If or when this land ever needs your help in keeping America a great country, give it your best effort.' Smitty asked him if he remembered the remorse on their pa's face when he said, 'I only wish I had served.' Then how he cried because he never served in the military. Alex told his brother how he recalled their dad crying.

"Later, while driving home, Alex told me he kept telling himself that he was no coward. For the first time in his life… he understood we were financially getting ahead. Alex felt like his life with me had just started, how we now had a mortgage we were responsible for, and if Uncle Sam wanted him to serve, he would have to call him. He watched his brother leave for Fort Custer. After seeing many of his friends enlist, my husband gave serious consideration to joining the military. However, his boss told him: 'It will be a great loss to our company's war effort if you joined'.

"At the beginning of the war, many factory employees enlisted in the armed forces. This resulted in countless new workers in the plants. On the shop floor, there was a need for speed during production. But the many new employees operating those machines caused a high rate of accidents. So they gave valued skilled workers like Alex a military deferment.

"Younger men working in the defense plants could never quite shake their doubts regarding their military service exemption. They served their country on the Homefront, but that was never enough. It seemed everyone's attention in the United States was fixated on the war in Europe. Every night we sat inside forty-one in our driveway listening to the latest news with Tiger wedged in between us, getting her ears scratched.

"Sometimes, when the shortwave signal was weak because of storm clouds or dry air, Alex strengthened the signal by adding an external antenna he built at work during his lunch hour. He made two welded brackets in the shop to hold a three-quarter-inch pipe. He attached the brackets to our garage's copula. Next, a ten-foot length of a three-quarter-inch galvanized pipe was inserted in the brackets. The pipe had a wire connected to it with an alligator clip on the wire's other end. He raised the forty-one's antenna to its highest position of ninety-three inches from the ground. The wire's clip was attached to the tip of the car's antenna, and he slowly and carefully backed the car up until it pulled the wire taut.

"With our new antenna extension, we could clearly pick up the BBC broadcast from London. In pleasant weather, neighbors seeing his jerry-rigged set-up invited themselves over to hear the latest news. People stood next to our vehicle while other neighbors sat on the lawn. Some even walked over to our house carrying folding chairs and their dinner plates. Together we listened to that day's BBC broadcast. On a stressful day, Alex lamented, saying, 'Why did we ever buy this shortwave radio?'

"In reality, most everyone in these gatherings found solace reminding them they were not alone. Good or bad, no matter what the day's news was, neighbors always left our driveway feeling united. We had the sole purpose of winning and ending this war. As a way of thanking my husband, neighbors helped him put the antenna away nightly. Each evening the antenna went up, it also came down; Alex never wanted to chance a stray lightning bolt striking the pipe and possibly burning our garage."

Aunt Fiery was so engrossed in her own story, she never noticed Sarah joined them at the table. Don saw a small brown paper bag in Sarah's hand. The wrinkled old bag appeared to have been opened and closed at least fifty times.

The elderly woman continued staring out the window, then speaking as if she was nearing a deadline. She said, "The United States was at war. So the auto companies moved to produce arms full time, instead of cars. This occurred after the War Production Board (WPB) limited car manufacturing on January first, 1942. Car parts that used chrome, aluminum, or stainless steel were then made of plain carbon steel. Those parts were then painted gray, black, or any other color available. Those other metals were redirected to the war effort by the WPB. Engine components were then made of cast iron components. This was similar to the automobiles manufactured before the 1930s.

"The public referred to these engines as blackout specials. They were less powerful when compared to the 1941 engines and not as efficient. Then in early February 1942, domestic car production was completely shut down. At the same time, the government also introduced stricter requirements for new car sales.

"People eligible to purchase a new auto had to be vital in maintaining public safety or the war effort. The list included doctors, police, fire departments, and critical war workers. Strangely enough, on that list were traveling salesmen. By mid-August, things changed again. Available 1942 models could only be sold to the U.S. government.

"Well aware of the need to conserve forty-one, Alex made certain she was always properly maintained. When our Chevrolet turned six months old, he drove her to the service station he used to work at. There she received her first tune-up, and the employees took notice. When the auto was up on the grease rack, Gus, the station's owner, marveled at the tires. He told my husband, 'Those tires are the best ones on the market; they're guaranteed to last for 20,000 to 30,000 miles. He warned Alex to take good care of them, saying, 'Make sure you have them inflated to the highest pressure written on the tire.'

"Gus told him he should rotate his tires every thousand miles. The station's owner continued to reveal how scarce brand-new tires were… how he only had six of them in stock, all mismatched. The used ones he had were bald. Others he had were so dry rotted they couldn't be recapped. Alex asked him, 'Are you sure it's that bad?'"

Don interrupted Fiery, saying, "Aunt Fiery, you've been talking for a while; why not take a break?"

She looked angry as he interrupted her thoughts but soon smiled when she saw her Sarah sitting at the table.

She exclaimed, "Oh! Honey… it's so nice to see you… Sarah. Thank you for coming. You being late worried me… did something happened to you?"

Sarah got up to give her Ammygam a kiss and loving hug, after which she handed her aunt a wrinkled paper bag. She then whispered to her elderly relative. Sarah then apologized to everyone for being late and returned to her seat.

Fiery smiled and remarked, "You are right on time. I was about to say how our government started rationing tires, rubber products, gasoline, and other things." Then, glaring over at Don, she said, "That is where you stopped me!"

She looked at Sarah, saying, "Now Gus was the proprietor of the service station where my Alex used to work. When my husband brought our forty-one over there for servicing, the station's owner educated him on how the government started rationing tires. This was about March 1942, when the Japanese invaded the Dutch East Indies and captured the rubber plantations. Their hostile action cut off most of the United States' sources of natural rubber. Gus's tire supplier blabbed to him, 'Don't look for new tires coming in anytime soon. Rubber is critical to our country's war effort.'

"His customers were pestering him for any tires he could get new or used. The station owner even toyed with the idea of wooden wheels. Alex understood and trusted Gus. So, he told him, he knew where there was a hoard of at least a hundred tires hidden in the woods, six years ago.

"He told Gus most were brand new when they were placed there. He told him how the pile of rubber tires happened to be there, saying, 'Remember when Ford introduced the V-8 in 1932? Those vehicles were some of the fastest. When a hotshot driver stomped on the gas pedal, the car's rear-drive wheels spun so fast it shredded the tire's cords into what looked like spaghetti.'"

Fiery was back to her old self, smiling and staring out the window, saying, "Whenever my Alex told a story, he always started at the very beginning." She chuckled to herself. "My husband told Gus they made those tires with cotton cords causing the tires to shred… they couldn't handle the torque. So in 1935, they started making tire cords out of high tensile strength rayon, which solved the problem.

"So, Alex told Gus how he helped his friend Teddy at his dad's junk hauling business get rid of those cotton cord tires. Teddy's dad had a job at Ford hauling away the debris that accumulated behind the Engineering Building. In their scrap heap were tires. They had been removed from test cars and replaced with the new rayon cord ones. When we lugged the rubbish into a dump, the owner wouldn't accept the tires. He told them no matter how deep you bury them, they'll work themselves back up to the surface.

"Ted's father was determined to get rid of those tires. So, on a dark night, they took them to a heavily wooded section in the middle of Rouge Park, now called Edward Hines Park. In that remote area, the boys laid the tires neatly in two rows, two high. It was autumn, and Ted's dad said the falling leaves will cover them in no time. Alex was certain they are there. Alex told Gus, 'Teddy's pa is now absentminded with Teddy in the Navy; I'm the only person who knows the location.'

"Gus found himself excited and told Alex if the tires are there, he would make it worth everyone's effort. After all, cotton cords tires are better than nothing. Besides, he didn't think there would be a problem. So the next night, the two of them, along with Alex's stepbrothers, Babe and Roger, had gone to the park with them. They used Gus's old Dodge stake body truck.

"Careful not to attract attention, they used flashlights and small lanterns to find the right spot. Alex and Babe told me how they dug through piles of composting foliage and sticks, pulling out twenty-four matching tires. Many discovered were in pristine condition. The fallen leaves had been protecting them from the sun's harsh glare.

"The remaining tires were too damaged or dry rotted and could not be used. As it turned out, Gus's son wanted the bad ones. The following weekend he and members from his troop hauled out of the woods all the remaining tires. The troop took them to a rubber scrap drive where they earned a penny a pound.

"Babe and Roger each received a ten-dollar bill for their help. Gus gave Alex his pick of two tires and even stored them at no cost, just in case we needed them. The government only allowed car owners to keep five tires per vehicle… any extras they confiscated, so we couldn't keep them at home. Gus gave Alex free lubricating for a year and installed the traffic light prism on her dashboard for free.

"During the war, we were lucky enough not to have any tire trouble, but we checked the pressure and rotated them as directed. Often people patched and re-patched their tires. They were as valuable as gold and much more difficult to acquire. Few of our friends even lined the insides of their tires with newspapers to make them last longer.

"It was rumored, to save on gasoline, the government would soon be implementing a mandatory thirty-five miles per hour, victory speed limit. Around April 1942, your Uncle Alex read in the *Detroit Times* that the U.S. Office of Price Administration (OPA) was going to begin gas rationing. It was to start in mid-May 1942 in seventeen eastern states. By the end of the year, the entire country would have rationing.

"After reading the article, Alex asked me, 'How about we take one more road trip before the regulating of gasoline takes effect?' Hoping this would get our minds off the war, I suggested we go camping at Tahquamenon Falls. He requested time off from his supervisor, reminding him he had only taken Sundays off since they settled the strike in October. They approved Alex for taking off two weeks later, a Saturday with the following Monday. Miss Graves approved the same days off for me.

"We left Friday after work and drove that night to Mackinaw City. At the dock, we slept and waited for the ferry. In the morning, we bought coffee and donuts. I reminded Alex we should get lunch ready to eat at the Soo Locks while we watched the freighters go through. He opened forty-one's hood and punched a tiny hole in a can of chili before placing it in the container attached to the exhaust. We double wrapped two hotdogs in foil, scrap meat for Tiger in another foil, and wired them to the manifold. I had finished dicing up onions when the boat pulled up to the dock.

It shocked us as we entered Sault Ste. Marie. The town was nothing like we remembered it from eight months earlier. Few knew ninety percent of the nation's iron ore used for making steel came through the shipping channel. There was a strong military presence, and we saw several barrage balloons floating over the locks on long steel cables. The balloons were there, stopping the enemy from any low-level bombings of the locks, reminding us we are at war.

"The situation made us feel like hiding. I remember commenting to Alex... so much for forgetting about the war! I told my husband we should skip lunch, fill forty-one up, and head for Tahquamenon Falls. We ate dinner at a roadside park along the way and rented a motor court cabin before going to the falls. Tiger barked and chased any animal she saw while we hiked in the area.

"We found our hemlock tree, and Alex set up our tent, table, and chairs under it. We rested in front of a small campfire where Alex held me close and told me he loved me all over again. After several minutes, he stood up and walked into the grassland with Tiger. With the two of them frolicking in the ankle-high grass, I sat there enjoying the view and life's simple pleasures. We left our camping gear there overnight, returning to the motor court to sleep.

"The next day, we returned to our campsite where we hiked, played, and relaxed. Finally, we could put the war out of our minds. We often wondered if we had seen the end of our isolated, idyllic way of life that we loved so much. While driving home on Monday, I asked Alex why there were no barrage balloons around Ford's massive River Rouge Plant where tanks were made. He told me it was probably because there was a lot of air traffic around Detroit. I told him we would just have to keep our fingers crossed, and he gave me a nervous smile.

"Our home on Dearborn's eastside was very near the Ford Rouge factory that produced war arms. We worried that the Rouge plant would surely be a target if the enemy bombed the United States. Misses could hurt or kill us. I remembered reading in the *Detroit Times* that many Honolulu civilians, living as far away as ten miles from Pearl Harbor, died during the attack — killed by bombs that fell short.

"They positioned airplane spotters in the four-story tower of Fordson High School. It was comforting to know they were watching. Rumors said they had a telephone directly connected to the Rouge Plant. If they spotted enemy bombers, this would give the plant a ten-minute advanced warning. Whenever we drove past the high school, I always looked for the spotters, but I only saw them once.

"Gas rationing started in mid-May that same year for the eastern part of the United States. The idea was by rationing fuel, the country would save on domestic rubber products, including tires. They gave most people the common A sticker, but Alex secured the more desirable C sticker. The sticker needed to be displayed on the vehicle's windshield lower right corner. The C sticker allowed the car owner to buy eight gallons of gasoline per week."

Sarah interrupted, asking, "Ammygam, you mean, you could only buy so much gas?"

"Oh!" She replied, "If you had an A sticker, they only allowed you to buy three gallons a week. Your ration book had to have a stamp for each gallon you purchased, which the merchant removed. Now, C stickers were issued to many professional people and some essential war production workers. Underneath the sticker, you'd find a tab for the person to check their occupation. There were seventeen occupations listed on it. You needed a sticker and the ration stamps to buy fuel or oil and reserve any available tires to buy. And none were available."

Don noticed that Aunt Fiery was clutching her diary to her bosom, as if she cherished the moment in her thoughts. Her eyes turned to the journal in her lap. She looked at the book before turning to the window, saying, "Wherever Alex parked forty-one, people would come over to look at his windshield tag. They were curious about his profession. He didn't appreciate this invasion of privacy.

"In late May, Alex signed up for Civil Defense duty and patrolled our neighborhood at night. He looked for any light coming from windows and doors. During blackouts, windows had to be covered, so no light showed. That was the law. Lights, we were told, could help give an enemy bomber his bearings.

"My mother placed heavy bath towels over her curtains as she was afraid they weren't thick enough and might glow. You could get into trouble if any brightness showed. Mom didn't wish to get a visit from her son-in-law, telling her she was violating the blackout rules. Alex had a friend who was in the Army's radio repair school, so when his pal came home on leave, Alex asked him to mount a rare twelve-inch outdoor loud-speaker behind forty-one's grille.

"He soldered a wire from a microphone to the audio section of the radio and wired one of the radio's push-buttons to switch it on. When Alex spotted any illumination from a house's curtains, he got on the microphone, warning the inhabitants to shut off their lights. His amplified voice came booming from the car's grill. The house went dark almost immediately. Alex and I had fun watching people on the street, looking for the sound's source. Now those were the times I enjoyed being on patrol with him."

Aunt Fiery looked over to her great-great-niece, saying, "Now, Sarah, it may interest you to know that the government required each adult to register for a ration card. You used the stamps when you shopped, and the merchant removed the stamp when you purchased a specific item. The sadness and tragedy caused by the war made you learn to enjoy the positive things that happened. There was a sporting atmosphere and team spirit in our community, reminding me of when I played baseball. This occurred when the neighborhood women gathered to trade ration stamps.

"Alex's mother raised chickens, so we didn't need our meat and egg stamps. I traded those for flour and sugar. The government's OPA (Office of Price Administration) ordered the merchants not to accept loose stamps. Shoppers avoided this by saying the stamp had fallen out of their book, so many shopkeepers still accepted them. Merchants wanted to keep their loyal customers when the war ended and accepted the stamps that 'fell out' of their book.

"Another positive thing coming from the war's rationing were the victory gardens. Almost everyone had one… it was your patriotic duty. My house was on a small city lot with a patch of ground behind our oversized garage. But that dirt was so miserable, weeds seldom grew there. So with a generous supply of chicken poop from Alex's mom, Bernice, we coaxed potatoes and pole beans to thrive there."

Clutching the journal tightly against her, Fiery continued, "Alex insisted we grow potatoes. When he was young, his father told him, 'Grow potatoes. You'll never starve.' That vegetable saved his family from starving when he was a boy. At harvest time, we loaded up forty-one's trunk with potatoes, beans, and an ample supply of apples from my parent's two apple trees. We drove slowly through the neighborhood with the car's trunk open as we traded with the neighbors. Everyone grew something different, and we traded with them. Those homegrown fruits and vegetables gave us a mesmerizing Homefront spirit of patriotism."

"By mid-1942, metal scrap drives were in full swing. It was on a Saturday in July when Alex drove to his mother's home. He had a load of old newspapers from work he wanted to give to his step-brother, Roger. Also, he called to see Babe before he left for Marine boot camp.

"He parked forty-one in front of his mom's house and saw his dad's old Victrola sitting on a patch of grass in the backyard. On the ground was the drive motor. Alex assumed Roger had removed it as a donation for a scrap metal drive. Government officials encouraged school kids to turn in anything made of metal, from rusty chicken wire to idle or broken equipment. My husband was fuming by this desecration of their father's memory and was about to chew his brother out.

"Suddenly, Roger bounded out of the front door running towards him. He was a member of the National Junior Salvage Corps. Members of the corps went from house to house, seeking metal, paper, and rubber items for reuse. He excitedly showed Alex his new oilcloth chevron that he had just finished sewing onto his shirt. Roger explained to Alex how he got it at school yesterday, making him a Junior Commando because of the scrap he turned in. My husband smiled broadly at his brother and thought to himself his father would have approved of donating the Victrola's motor to his country."

Don interrupted her, asking, "Aunt Fiery, I'm enjoying your accounts of how you and your husband used to live. It sounds like the Homefront was difficult living during the war, but do you mind if we took a brief break?"

She gave Sarah and his wife an amiable wink, saying, "Honestly, ladies… we should tell the man to hold it! But I am glad he suggested it… for I'm the one who needs a breather."

Everyone laughed and agreed. Aunt Fiery signaled to Ann to wheel her from the table. It was then he saw the tears in Fiery's eyes.

She looked over at him, mentioning, "Now don't you go away. I have more to tell you."

Looking at her, Don smiled, saying, "I'm not going anywhere."

Ann stopped a moment to say something inaudible to Sarah. The young woman got up and joined them. He watched the three ladies leave the room. Don sat there alone, considering everything he had heard, and gave the lady credit for her courage. He understood not everyone could tell their life's story to strangers like him and Ann. Then he sat back in the chair, asking himself, what makes me and Ann so special to Fiery?

Chapter 18

God Willing

When the ladies returned from Fiery's apartment, Don was not to be found. He had decided to return to their car and replace the batteries in the recorder. He didn't want to miss a word of what Fiery had to say. As he approached the table, he ignored Ann's disapproving stare for being late.

Dripping with sarcasm, Ann commented, "At least you could have told us you needed to go outside."

Don ignored Ann and walked over to Aunt Fiery, giving her a hug, saying, "I'm sorry for keeping you waiting. I had a telephone call."

Aunt Fiery smiled at him, saying, "I was telling Sarah during the winter of 1942, we went to the plant, came home, ate dinner, listened to the BBC news, and got ready for the same thing the next day. There was nothing to do to break this routine, and I started missing my simple pleasures. The only fun thing I did was drive forty-one to work. Alex wanted to store forty-one for the winter to save her for after the war. But standing in the cold, waiting for a streetcar, didn't appeal to me. Besides, forty-one's hot water heater kept my feet toasty warm. Our car-sharing club had six of us riding to work in forty-one every day, and the other passengers always appreciated their special ride to work.

"In 1943, the United States entered its second year of the conflict, and allied battle victories had been few. We continued listening to the BBC every evening in our driveway… more and more neighbors joined us. One time, the police were driving by, saw the sizeable crowd in front of our house, and stopped to investigate. They stayed for the entire broadcast and even helped Alex take down the antenna at the end.

"You may think this silly, but by June 1943, with the war raging on and no end in sight, I really missed getting sliced bread at the bakery. Few people remember they banned bakers from slicing the bread they baked. Then suddenly, they removed the ban. But our bakery couldn't get the rolls of wax paper to wrap the bread. So, the baker continued to sell whole loaves only, leaving his customers to slice their bread at home. I missed my sliced bread."

Sarah declared, "I never knew that."

Ann glanced at Don giving him a disgruntled look. Then, she turned to Aunt Fiery smiling and saying, "I can't imagine why wax paper wasn't available!"

Aunt Fiery quipped, "And, I wanted my sliced bread!"

Don teased, asking, "I can see if they have sliced bread in the kitchen?"

He could tell his joke didn't amuse Aunt Fiery as she commented, "Just wait, young man. Some day they may ban something you enjoy, one of your life's little treasures… like hot water, and you won't have it! Then you'll remember my words and understand what I mean."

She peered out the window and clutched the journal; to her bosom. Don noticed her gold bracelet was back on her wrist, and he wondered why it had not been there before their break.

The elderly lady continued explaining, "By mid-May 1943, Alex was still working six full days a week. After church on Sunday, when the weather warmed, the three of us, Alex, Tiger, and I, would drive over to Belle Isle. We strolled along the river's shore or rented a canoe, always finishing the day cooking on our car. It was crowded, and to get a good spot, you had to show up early. This became our only break from the war.

"One Sunday in mid-June, as we were unpacking, a middle-aged man with a broad smile walked over and asked Alex how he liked his car. He introduced himself as Willie and told us he had a 1941 Chevrolet, the coupe model, pointing to a mint green vehicle parked in the lot on the other side of the grass. Willie explained it was his prized possession, and he loved the hydraulic drum brakes. I listened as he told Alex, 'Them brakes are better than adjusting bands all the time, but it's a job to check the fluid!'

"This information stunned my Alex. I knew he was upset! Having owned the car for two years, he never checked the brake fluid. Willie continued shaking his head, saying, 'This sure ain't in the owner's manual.' "He took my husband over to forty-one's driver's door and opened it, saying, 'Let me show you the secret. Undo those screws.'

"Once that was done, Willie's dark hands peeled the carpet back and pointed to the trapdoor. He pried open the flap and said, 'there's the master brake cylinder. Unscrew the plug to see the fluid level.' He finished by saying, 'If it's low, add brake fluid.'

"Alex thanked him as Willie placed everything back as it was. He now wanted to share our secret with him and said, 'I bet I can tell you something you didn't know about your car.' I watched him open our car's hood, grab a rag, and pull out the canister of steaming pork and beans from the juice can holder on the manifold. Willie exclaimed, 'Wow, that'll sure come in handy; thanks for teaching me that!' They spoke for twenty minutes and laughed a lot.

"They spoke twice more that month, talking about their cars, the war, and both having a draft exemption. As we drove around Belle Isle, we always looked for his green Chevrolet. The last time we saw him, Alex shouted out the side window, 'Hey, Willie, how you doing?' He smiled, waved, and yelled back, 'Swell… Alex!' I always wondered what happened to him?"

Don watched as Fiery grabbed and held the gold bracelet on her wrist. It seemed to be incredibly important to her. But why? The elderly lady changed the subject, commenting, "Many of our friends and relatives had old jalopies that broke down regularly. Sometimes they called me to help them out. Of course, at times, it was inconvenient, but I turned no one down. What I meant was occasionally they asked me to drive them somewhere, which I didn't mind because I truly loved driving our Special Deluxe Chevrolet."

Fiery's voice changed, and she struggled to speak of this memory. "The U.S. had been fighting nearly two years, and my Alex experienced guilt not being in uniform. The public's prying eyes and stares full of contempt bothered him. Many of their husbands and sons went to war and were never coming home. It was unnerving to him. He told me, 'We should only leave the house in the evening.'

"I tried to reassure him he was doing more than his part with his work at Buhl Sons and Civil Defense duty, but my words fell on deaf ears. Finally, I told him, don't worry about me! If you want to enlist, the decision is yours. Alex understood I can take care of things here. He didn't like it when I explained his essential war worker deferment to my friends.

"My case was weak… when you considered some of their loved ones had been wounded or captured in some prisoner of war camp. Others were listed as missing in action, and even more killed in battle."

Tears flowed freely down Fiery's cheeks. Sarah left to get some tissues for her. The elder woman watched as she returned with a small box.

She paused, taking a tissue, and wiped her cheeks, saying, "Thank you, Sarah, this is the same size box I bought for forty-one's tissue dispenser." Catching her breath, the old aunt stopped to ponder her words. Finally, she stated, "I told my friends I'd rather have a hero who died defending his country for a husband than a living husband who was a coward by avoiding military service. You'll never know how those words haunt me… how I regret saying them and still do." Softly Fiery repeated, "A hero who died defending his country or a living husband who was a coward." She sniveled and paused, then he heard her crying.

Don assumed she was trying to justify something she spoke of so many years ago. But, deep down in her heart, she couldn't.

Fiery displayed a brave smile and said, "My Alex told anyone who spoke to him about his exemption from the draft and that his work was essential. He never argued with them if they rebuked him. He accepted the conditions, position, and status they gave him, but inside him, a conflict raged. What could he do to best serve his country? Where would he make his finest contribution? In November 1943, he had to give up his Civil Defense duties. Like every other skilled worker at Buhl Sons, he worked ten to twelve hours a day and eight hours shifts on Saturday and Sunday."

"The workers were well paid for their long hours. They harbored no resentment towards the company. Morale, at that point, wasn't even a word in their vocabulary. Alex's draft classification was 2-B. With the war continuing, the military needed every able-bodied man they could find. So, the government changed the selective service laws. This meant Homefront men would have their draft status changed. Regardless of their job, marital status, or number of dependents, classifications changed. Alex's became 1-H, making him eligible for armed forces.

"It was in late January 1944, Alex's supervisor came to him saying, 'We've done all we can to keep you here. We can't afford to lose you, but we haven't been able to change your draft status. So, we thought you ought to know, they may draft you.' Alex told me he was relieved by what his boss said. But, when he relayed the conversation to me, I sensed in his voice that he was apprehensive."

Fiery wiped a single tear from her cheek as she spoke, "I told him let's get his military service out of our way, so we can get on with our lives. Alex agreed with me, replying, 'You're right.' The next day he drove downtown to the draft board, gave up his military deferment, and joined the army. Alex traveled in early March 1944 to Detroit's Michigan Central Depot by taxi.

"Alex always hated goodbyes, making his mother, step-sister, step-brother, and myself promise we wouldn't come to the train station to see him leave. As he approached the loading platform, he wondered if he had made the right decision. Many of the recruits leaving were being comforted and caressed by their mothers, wives, or girlfriends. I'm sure he felt so alone.

"Later, he wrote me how he remembered helping his mother clean those same Pullman cars every day after school fifteen years earlier. To clear his head, he walked outside on the platform, and watched the traffic at the entrance to the station. Suddenly, he recognized our maroon 1941 Chevrolet Special Deluxe in the parking lot unloading space with its hood raised. He told me he felt his heart race and his pulse quicken. Darting through the crowd, he looked for me — and only me."

The aunt dabbed her cheeks with a tissue and looked directly at Ann, saying, "Alex was one of the best for teaching me tricks. He said, 'If you ever need to park quickly, and there aren't any spots available, just coast to the closest curb space and open forty-one's hood.' My husband knew any rational police officer wouldn't give a parking ticket to a frantic woman alone with car trouble.

"He wrote on the train how he searched for me. Finally, he caught a glimpse of me, but I had my back to him. Hastily, he walked up to me, grabbed my shoulders from behind, spun me around, and hugged me. Alex surprised me, and I looked up at him through my tears. I told him I hoped he wasn't mad, but I just had to come and see him leave. He grinned and teasingly responded, 'Yeah, I ought to wring some sense into you.'

"Before I could answer, he said, 'Hey, I've only a moment… give me a kiss to last the duration.' I told him I'll give it my best shot, and I gave him a kiss like I did when we were at Tahquamenon Falls. God, I loved that man! We kissed for a minute or maybe longer. I remember thinking, was it long enough? We didn't break that last kiss until the conductor yelled, 'All aboard!'

"We continued to embrace and linger on the platform until the last possible second. Alex looked into my eyes and told me how much he loved me. He didn't let go of me until the porter picked up the boarding step. He ran and had to hop onto the departing train. He turned towards me while on the stairs and shouted over the noise, 'Hey, I just remembered this will save me postage.' He pulled a wrapped package from his overcoat pocket and tossed it in my direction.

"I caught it with one hand and pretended to throw it towards him like he was the first baseman. My Alex always loved when I did that! He quickly found a window seat, and I walked alongside the slow-moving train, blowing him a kiss. I seized the moment, knowing a long time would pass till we were together again. We watched each other until he was out of sight. I knew then our lives may never be the same.

"I unwrapped the pocket-sized package he had thrown to me right there on the platform as the train disappeared down the tracks. The top of it read, Lachman & Co., Dearborn, Michigan… the same jewelry store where he bought my engagement and wedding rings. I found this gold bracelet inside with the inscription: To my Darling Fiery, no matter what, we'll always be together; Love Alex."

Fiery placed her hand over the bracelet she wore as she said, "My eyes were swollen from all the crying I had done. Slowly, I made my way back to our vehicle and found a policeman peering under forty-one's hood. The officer stared at my face, saw the tears streaming down my cheeks, and asked if I needed any help. Nervously, I told him no thanks. My husband told me what to do.

"With my hanky, I wiped my tears and pretended to tweak something under the hood before slamming it shut. I got behind the wheel and started the engine. With a half-smile, I looked at him and pulled away. I saw him standing there staring in my rearview mirror with his mouth open in astonishment as I headed for home."

Aunt Fiery sipped some juice, and Ann asked her if she was okay.

Without hesitation, Fiery said, "Oh! I'm fine." Somberly, she continued, "I haven't been down that road — in a long time." She paused, then continued, "Alex wrote me a long letter about his experiences onboard the train. He was emotionally drained when he settled into his seat. The recruits aboard his coach appeared young to him and didn't look old enough to sell newspapers on a street corner.

"One by one, each person came up to him and introduced themselves, thinking that because of his age he was an officer. They asked questions like, 'Sir do we get to eat on this train? When are we getting off? Do you mind if we smoke?'

"Alex never let on that he was a boot recruit like them. He watched each trainee put on a brave front while saying how proud they were to serve their country. They laughed, joked, and talked about where they might go and everything they may see. But it became quiet when they realized what may happen to them when they went to war.

"Suddenly, the conductor rushed in and shouted that they were pulling onto a rail siding. A troop train heading for an embarkation point had priority and needed to pass. Alex peered into the windows of the slow-moving coaches as it passed. The first soldiers he saw were two military police sitting with three somber-faced guys dressed in civilian clothes. He assumed they were Absent Without Leave (AWOL) GIs. Soldiers referred to themselves as GI, which really stood for government-issued.

"Some were examining an M-1 rifle, while others played cards. Alex spotted a solitary soldier with crutches straddled across a bench seat, and nearby a GI stared blankly out his window. Mixed in were sailors sleeping in the aisle on their duffle bags. Behind them were many army guys passing around the latest posters of Betty Grable, Ann Sheridan, and

Rita Hayworth. The Marines were all business, sharpening their KA-BAR knives. A grinning sailor was holding up a hand-drawn poster with the words, *you'll be sorry*, written on it for everyone on Alex's train to read."

Fiery was unrelenting in her speech, saying, "In that first letter he wrote to me, he told me how he saw soldiers writing letters home on folded cardboard cups and flattened small boxes. He thought to himself, those poor guys, they don't have any paper! The U.S. had a severe paper shortage… even books were in short supply. Alex admitted, he wasn't prepared to handle what he had seen on that priority train.

"Someone asked, why are they doing that? Another answered at their last stop the Red Cross ladies passed out donuts and cups of coffee through the train's open windows. When they got to the next city, the guys would throw out the cardboard boxes and containers with their names and addresses on them, requesting the girls write to them.

"Sometimes, they asked them to send a note to their folks, saying they traveled through the town and were doing well. They assumed the heavy paper stock kept their messages from blowing away. The ladies picked up those messages after the train left the station, fulfilling their requests… well, that's what they hoped. My Alex couldn't tear himself away from the real-life drama playing out in front of him."

Don observed how the memories of her husband's letters revived her spirits. He sensed a thrill in her voice as she described Alex's adventures.

She said, "The new recruits stood and watched the drama; several pretended not to watch… not wanting to face their destiny. Would the AWOL soldiers rejoin their units or spend the rest of the war in prison? Had the GI on crutches been injured in a training accident or wounded while rushing a Nazi bunker? Were the sailors homeward on leave because their ship sunk and they were the only survivors? Those Marines… had they been the heroes fighting the enemy at Guadalcanal? Was the gloomy soldier a battle fatigue victim from what he'd been through, or was he trying to adjust himself so he could go home?

"Alex sat back, deciding to think of less complicated matters. Things he could control. Something like, if he remembered to pack the can opener for our picnic drives with forty-one. The Army sent Alex to Fort Custer in Augusta, Michigan, for basic training. There he had time to see his older brother, Smitty, who was waiting for his orders and embarkation to Europe.

"He complained about the method of getting in line for everything, and lines were everywhere. Lines to fill out forms, lines to get a haircut, lines for chow, lines to get your uniform, and they never seemed to end. Alex stood his place at the back of those columns when often a clipboard wielding Sargent moved him to the front of the line. He knew his brother was pulling strings for him but never informed the other GIs. He was glad to not have to stand in line all day.

"Rumors floated around camp about his preferential treatment. One story said he was the governor's nephew… another a drafted major league baseball player. But his favorite myth was that he was a captured Nazi agent with American roots. That buzz alleged they offered him a swell deal, but the catch was he had to join the U.S. Army."

Everyone noticed Fiery's jovial smile. She continued saying, "That rumor claimed he had worked for the Allies and returned to Germany to keep himself out of a prisoner-of-war camp. Most supposed he was of German descent. Alex's friends were eager to accept the spy rumor. My Alex wrote letters about the comical and tragic incidents that occurred while in basic training.

"He became interested in learning how to sing and harmonize with other men. Now that's funny! I couldn't believe it, my Alex singing a song! In the evenings, a group of GIs gathered outside the barracks, or by the latrine and sang songs together. Everyone thought he had a wonderful voice. I often played the piano for him, and not once during the six years we were a couple… did I hear him sing!"

Fiery's voice became solemn as she recalled one of the tragic events. She recalled, "Alex wrote of a young corporal who drove a Chevrolet-built Army six-by-six cargo truck to pick up a platoon of soldiers. They had been out on overnight maneuvers. Somehow, he got bad directions and ended up at the wrong location. He waited for hours until they arrived. Not wanting to be late for his date with a girl in town, he took a shortcut to the base.

"His quicker way brought them to an open grassland that, unbeknownst to him, was being used for howitzer target practice. The artillery observer called a ceasefire on the range but was too late. As the corporal drove through the field, two artillery rounds hit the truck. One soldier was killed and four severely wounded. So sad… their poor families.

"After basic training, they sent Alex to Camp Lee, Virginia, for assignment to the Quartermaster Corps for education as a company clerk. He wrote, how during an eight-hour pass, a group of them stopped at a bar in Richmond. There he met a native son and Hollywood motion picture star, Joseph Cotton. When he was home between movies during the war, Mr. Cotton liked to befriend troops from the army post, often buying them drinks. He would let them ask him questions about his career and listened intently to their fears for the future.

"He spent a few hours with my Alex and his friends over a few beers. Mr. Cotton paid attention as Alex spoke of me and his life in Detroit. In just a few short hours, Joseph Cotton had become my husband's favorite movie star. When he returned to the barracks that evening, he wrote to me of his meeting."

Sarah noticed her aunt's voice was getting hoarse and inquired if she could get her something other than juice and water.

Looking at her young niece, she asked, "Am I talking too much?"

Everyone at the table chuckled. Ann seized the moment. She complimented Fiery on her ability to remember so many details of her past. Don understood his wife was speaking on purpose to allow Fiery a moment's rest.

But Fiery interrupted them, declaring, "Well, at my age, I remember what a beautiful time I had and lived with my husband. God willing, we will again live the life… that was taken away from us."

Her remark puzzled the three of them, but no one asked her to explain.

Fiery continued, commenting, "Now where was I, yes… everyone remembers the men going off to war, but they forgot the women who stayed at home, alone. My husband went to war, leaving me with an automobile to service, a dog to care for, and a two-bedroom house to maintain. Soon ladies from my department at Buhl Sons moved in with me. Their rent checks nearly covered the mortgage payment. When more renters came, I made double and triple house payments.

"In late May, Alex had a seventy-two-hour weekend pass. He took a train from Richmond, Virginia to Toledo, Ohio, while I drove the fifty miles from Dearborn to Toledo. When I arrived at the station, Alex was already there waiting for us. He was sitting on a bench in the sunlight in his new uniform. It was the most handsome that I had ever seen him! When Tiger caught sight of him, she jumped out of the passenger window, ran to him, and hopped on his lap, wagging her tail and crying with delight. I stopped forty-one right next to him and ran to him. Frantically, I hugged and kissed my husband.

"Goodness, I was excited to see him! I knew then how much I loved him, by how my heart ached for him. I wanted to hold and kiss him forever. Unfortunately, our reunion had blocked a car, and we had to move.

"I handed him the forty-one's keys, asking him if he would not mind going home to Dearborn. He wasn't hard to sway when I told him we would have more privacy elsewhere than at home. I explained how we had a full five-gallon gas can in the trunk and how each time I filled up, I added a little fuel to that spare container. His eyes were looking into mine, but I stayed on the topic, telling him how we had ration stamps for eight more gallons. I described my plan to go over to Cedar Point in Sandusky for the day. Then I kissed him."

It was then Don noticed Fiery making a gesture towards Sarah. She went over to her Ammygam, who whispered into her niece's ear. The young woman then excused herself, heading off toward Fiery's apartment. Ann mumbled something to Fiery and appeared to be blushing from what the elderly lady quietly replied. Soon both were laughing. It wasn't long before Sarah returned with another journal and box of candy.

She put the box on the table in front of her Ammygam and handed her the book. The young girl unwrapped the box, opened it, and offered everyone a candy. Sarah then placed the open candy box in the middle of the table as Fiery contently nibbled on a chocolate.

When finished with her treat, she commented, "Thank you, Sarah, I needed a sweetie. So where was I, oh yes, Cedar Point? Ann, let me tell you when I mentioned to my husband that our time would be more private at the amusement park than in our house, he said, 'Swell! That sounds great to me… off to Sandusky it is.' Cedar Point was a small amusement park on the south shore of Lake Erie. I think it may still be there.

"It was sixty miles away and a nice two-hour drive. I hoped it would remind us of our picnics on Belle Isle. I wanted Alex all to myself. With Tiger sitting in between us, he had driven only a few miles when I suggested he pull off the road.

"I leaned over and pulled the hood release lever. He asked me, 'What's the matter? Do we have car trouble, or does Tiger need to go?' God, did he look handsome in his uniform! My brain wandered. At the train station, I forgot something and seeing my husband, I was ready to forget… again.

"I tried not to let him distract me, as I explained how we needed to turn over the fish. He said, 'I thought I smelled something cooking, but I didn't know from where it was coming.' I asked him to come take a peek at what he taught me and raised the front hood. To his astonishment, I loosened the wire with my pliers and removed a large foil packet attached to the exhaust manifold. I turned it over, using a clean rag from under the driver's seat, and rewired it.

"Next to the packet was the container with a can of wild rice steaming. Alex didn't realize how difficult it was to buy meat. I pointed out chicken meat was scarce too, and how his mother had only three hens left that produced eggs. As Catholics, we always had fish on Fridays, and I mentioned to him how I was trying different new recipes. I explained how I could only buy two nice-sized fresh lake trout filets last night, which I marinated for hours in oregano and lemon juice with pepper. I closed the hood, and we continued towards Cedar Point.

"An hour later, I asked him if he was hungry. He said, 'I sure am!' I even remember how handsome he looked saying those words… I almost forgot where I was. It wasn't long before we discovered a private park on the Lake Erie shore's side of the road and pulled over to eat lunch with a view.

"As I was opening the trunk, he grabbed me, spun me around, and kissed me. I told him he better stop that, or we'd never eat. I took out our folding table, two chairs, a picnic basket, and a small rug for Tiger. Smiling at him, I popped open the hood to get the fish and rice. Then I retrieved a cherry pie from the trunk and placed it on the warm manifold. My Alex's favorite dessert was always cherry pie."

Fiery noticed friends of hers had come into the room. She offered everyone at their table another piece of chocolate and then asked Don if he would mind taking the candy box over to her acquaintances, offering each a chocolate. Don went to each table and offered the candy. As each friend took a sweetie, Don noticed each one give Fiery an appreciative wave. He returned just in time to hear her comment, 'employees always eat the open boxes of candy.'

She put down her half-eaten sweetie, looked at him, and abruptly said, "Thank you for doing that. I'd rather my neighbors have a piece than the workers here."

Her curt remark aimed at the Blair House staff caught him by surprise.

Then, as if she never said it, she smiled and continued saying, "You know both chocolate candy and cherry pies contain sugar, which was on one of the first items rationed. Sugar was no longer available from Hawaii or the Philippine Islands. I told Alex's mother that I wanted to bake her son a cherry pie, and she gave me all the sugar I needed. Like a much-expected Michigan snowstorm, his mom, Bernice, saw the conflict coming… she prepared for war. When England declared war on Germany in September 1939, she started to buy and store sugar just in case.

"Every other week, she would purchase a five-pound bag until rationing started in the spring of 1942. She was always careful not to draw the store owner's attention. Bernice would trade her extra sugar with her neighbors for other food she needed. And, she made sure I had enough sugar to make her son a delicious cherry pie.

"That evening, we rented a cottage at a motor lodge near the amusement park. The following day we visited Cedar Point. There we met an elderly couple who kindly watched Tiger as we spent time together on rides, boats, and playing carnival games. We thanked them later with dinner. They told us they were from Cleveland, and they were celebrating their thirty-eighth wedding anniversary.

"Before dusk, Alex and I walked our pup along Lake Erie's shoreline. We kept an eye on Tiger as she encouraged the local duck population to move off her beach. When she found a small floating stick, she brought it to Alex. The two of them enjoyed frolicking in and near the water's edge as they passed the stick back and forth. I could tell how much Tiger missed him."

Abruptly Fiery said, "Now that was Cedar Point. Do you mind if I finish telling you about our adventure the next time? I'm a little tired.

When I get like this, I have trouble remembering. I guess this happens when you get old like me."

Don remarked, "Not at all. Promise you'll meet with us again soon!"

She nodded yes, as Sarah helped her remove the bracelet and ring she was wearing, placing them in the ordinary brown paper bag. Don noticed the other item she placed in the bag was a gold key fob. Once the bag was rolled closed, Sarah placed it in her purse. Ann found a young attendant who promised to meet them in Mrs. Maze's room and help her lay down to rest. It had been a full day. He waited for Ann and Sarah to return from taking Fiery to her apartment.

As they walked out of the Blair House, Don saw Ann carrying another journal, presumably to place in forty-one's trunk.

Sarah asked, "What do you think Ammygam meant when she said, 'God willing, I'll live the life taken away?' She sounded so serious saying that…"

Interrupting her, Ann remarked, "She said, 'We'll live the life taken away from Alex and me.' I suppose she loved her husband and always missed him… and her dream, I believe, is to be with him."

Don didn't comment, but thought… does Fiery have something special planned?

Chapter 19

Pittsburgh Reunion

Ann and Don were driving home from the Blair House after their meeting with Aunt Fiery. It was during this trip home, he mentioned there was enough information for him to write his storyboard. He explained how he could now write an accurate and honest storyboard about their 1941 Chevrolet.

With a cavalier tone, he proclaimed, "No need to meet with her again."

Ann became angry with him. She scolded him, saying, "You're committed! You needed to do this… now stay and finish what you started. Listen to her entire story. Besides, if you haven't noticed, she's always speaking to you at these sessions."

Don was stunned to hear what Ann suggested and could only say, "Huh?"

Eager to change her mood, Don changed the subject by speaking about their plans for this year's car shows and how many they might attend. When they arrived home, he put another of Fiery's journals in forty-one's trunk before they even went into the house. Early in the evening, he down-loaded all of his recordings to the hard drive of his personal computer. He didn't want to lose any part of what Fiery told him. To be safe, he copied all his recordings of those meetings to a compact disc.

He wrote himself a note which read: ask Nadine to type out the re-cordings of meetings with Fiery. Nadine was one of the best secretaries at the office, and he understood she sometimes worked two jobs for the extra money. His plan was to ask her if she would like to do this personal typing of his at home, and he would pay her. After he finished with the note, he turned his attention to perfecting his outline for tomorrow's presentation to the board of directors. This proposal would pay their bills, and he needed it to be perfect. He wanted to open with a powerful statement establishing the need for a paradigm shift within their corporation's products and services. However, he knew he also had to address head-on the package of explosives he received.

Don needed two and a half million dollars to fund the final pieces of this new product, which was near a beta trial. Inspiration struck as he remembered the brown paper bag Sarah gave her Ammygam. He knew exactly what to do! Don continued to work into the night.

With only a couple hours of sleep, he woke up early and dressed carefully. He wanted the executives to remember what he presented, not a flashy tie or wrinkled trendy suit. It was important he distracted no one from the matter at hand. Monday, May 3, 2004, at 11:00 a.m., his company's board members convened. Don had fifteen minutes for his presentation, followed by a thirty-minute question-and-answer period.

Don started his presentation at the back of the room, popping a paper bag. With everyone's attention, he stated that is how quickly an explosion happens. Then he explained how this product would save lives and place their company on the cutting edge of technology. How, when implemented, would mark a paradigm shift in their product line. This change in their business could provide the opportunity for unlimited growth and profits.

The one-and-a-half-hour session turned into a passionate three-hour debate. Don was on his game as he answered questions that came at him fast and furious. The chairperson ended the discussion with a vote. When the ballots were tallied, Don's project had won by the slimmest of margins… one vote. That same afternoon, he called a meeting with the department heads. At that meeting, he gave them the good news and planned another meeting the following day. Invited to the Tuesday morning meeting was the director of corporate security, Mick E, the president, Mr. Stone, managers, and employees of the departments involved.

Mick E. started the morning's meeting. He spoke about his department's handling of the explosive materials, assuring everyone how his security team would always be present with the explosives to ensure complete safety. Mr. Stone spoke briefly about the support the project would have from all departments. Don acknowledged the fine work this group did during the development stage. He commended them for the complex tasks they overcame. Those present knew this product could secure their jobs and positions for years.

He worked late at the office that Tuesday evening. As a result, Ann hadn't had a chance to discuss how his presentation had gone until Wednesday at dinner.

He told her, "I opened with a bang using a brown paper bag. I blew it up and popped it, explaining that's how quick a bomb explodes. That got their attention, and from there, I went into my PowerPoint presentation."

Ann congratulated him on his success and listened as he talked of his Washington, D.C. travel plans for tomorrow. Don hoped tomorrow's meeting would be a quick one day in and out. He also casually mentioned future international travel and how he hoped Ann could join him for those trips. Changing the subject, he explained to Ann how a woman at the office named Nadine agreed to transcribe the recordings of their meetings with Fiery, and he would pay her. When Ann heard the amount he was going to pay her, she called him cheap! She told him when you pay her, you double the amount and give her cash. It was important for him to keep his wife happy, and he agreed to do what she said, but also because he wanted to have a hard copy typed correctly.

While eating dinner, Don wanted Ann's opinion on taking forty-one to their next meeting and offering Aunt Fiery a ride. She suggested they consult with Lucy before doing anything. Fiery might not like the car since Johnny O had repainted it.

Don agreed and continued, "It might interest her to see the pooch we have is like hers with the same name. Maybe we should bring Tiger along!"

Right on cue, their dog came running over to Don with a leash in her mouth, ready for an evening stroll. As Don prepared for his mid-morning flight to Washington on Thursday morning, he suggested a meeting with Fiery tomorrow afternoon. Ann mentioned she would check with Sarah and Lucy to see when they could arrange a meeting with Fiery. The following morning, Don planned to work from home. Unfortunately, his flight back home was delayed, and he arrived home near 1:00 a.m. The day's travel had taken a toll on him.

He had forgotten what he asked his wife the day before. Don hoped to relax, staying and working at home. But when he called into his office at 8:30 a.m., his plans changed. At precisely 10:00 a.m., Friday morning, Don met with his key managers for an update on their responsibilities for the project.

While another manager gave a product update, he looked at the written telephone message he received. It read; Fiery this afternoon at 2:00 p.m., call to confirm, Ann. He had complete faith in his team and knew he could easily meet with Fiery. With managers informed, Don spoke of his accomplishment the day before. He ended the meeting congratulating them on their achievements and promised a substantial bonus to each for their efforts.

Don chuckled to himself as he drove to the Blair House, remembering the last part of the meeting. His managers were calling the project X-files after a popular television show. He asked them if they should change it to FI-H-X. These letters had been used to describe the product's properties during the development process. They spent a half-hour discussing their options and voted, only to find themselves tied, three to three. They insisted he break the tie, but he had a better idea.

He went out of his office and stopped the first person he saw. He ran into Sheridan, who worked in their call center, but she was hesitant to come into his office. Finally, Don convinced her it would only take a couple of minutes, and if she got into trouble with her supervisor, she should call him. Looking at the group, he asked, "Sheridan, which name do you think is best for our new project, HI-FI or HEX-FI?"

After hearing her options, she responded, "Actually… they are both pretty clever, but I like X-Fi, with a small i, it's a mysterious name, like the TV show."

He thanked her for her answer and asked her to stay for a moment longer. Don then declared, "Ladies and Gentlemen, I have an announcement. Thanks to Sheridan, our current enterprise under development will be known as… X-Fi, with a small i."

He was still laughing to himself when he found out how Sheridan told anyone in the building, who would listen, how she named the company's secret venture, X-Fi. Unknown to him, this action became a great morale booster for the staff. Before leaving the office, he stopped by her workstation to thank her again. Everyone in her department took notice when the vice-president personally visited her.

Sarah and Ann were waiting for him at their usual table when Don arrived. Ann mentioned Lucy was concerned regarding the length of last weekend's meeting. Everyone agreed to keep it short today.

Sarah chimed in, "I told Gammy you never asked Ammygam any questions. She just talked and talked. The only reason she took a break was that you made her." She paused and looked troubled. While a finger twirled her long hair, she said, "I hope you don't mind, but when we talk of Ammygam's room here, we always call it an apartment. It's not much, but it's all she has now. Gammy wanted me to ask you if you could refer to it as her apartment?"

Without hesitation, they agreed. It wasn't long before Lucy brought Fiery to the room. Fiery's smile grew, and she waved as they neared the table.

As if she never stopped, Aunt Fiery said, "I was telling my niece what a wonderful time we had over the weekend! I shared the story of how in mid-June of forty-four, Alex had a seventy-two-hour pass, and I drove to Toledo to meet him. How we traveled to Cedar Point and met a couple from Cleveland. The rides at the amusement park we rode, while they kindly cared for Tiger. I shared those stories with Lucy."

She gave her Aunt Fiery a smile, making sure she was comfortable and turned her wheelchair to face the window. Then Aunt Fiery appeared to enter her dreamlike state, saying, "Early the next morning with Tiger between us on the front seat, I drove back to the Toledo train station. I knew he wanted me to drive so he could relax, watch me, and concentrate only on me. Alex remarked how we could be apart for an indefinite period and asked me what I would do if he was killed, gone missing, or captured. I told him we'll cross that bridge when we come to it… that ended that conversation."

Don wondered how she did this at her age… starting off exactly where she left off last weekend. She really was remarkable! Fiery again had a different journal, open in her lap, but never referred to it.

Without stopping, she said, "While traveling on the country road, we heard the song, 'As Time Goes By', playing on the radio. I mentioned to him how it was like we were together when I heard that tune; it reminded me of him. How he kissed me. "He looked at me and began singing to the radio's music, 'Moonlight and love songs, never out of date… Hearts full of passion.' Then… as if to make light of the serious moment, he stopped brushing Tiger, tapped forty-one's dashboard with the dog brush, and announced, 'That's it, I declare, As Time Goes By, our official song.'

"When we arrived at the railroad station, we took Tiger for a stroll along the tracks. Alex told me of his first military train ride. He was describing how he watched the boys writing their names and addresses on cardboard and cups. Then we spotted a small piece of stiff paper in the brush. The words were barely legible, but I could read a sailor's address from Kansas City. I informed my husband how I would keep that sheet and write a letter to his parents.

"Too soon, it was time to return to the car. We settled Tiger into her spot on the front seat by scratching her ears. He led me over to the driver's door, where we kissed and hugged goodbye. Alex stepped in front of the car, gently patted the pontoon fender, and simply said, 'See Yaa!' Then he walked away. As he turned for one last look, he caught me crying while Tiger sat next to me with a sad expression on her face.

"Alex stopped, waved, and began singing the lyrics from our song. With his loud voice for everyone to hear, he sang, 'No matter what the future brings, as time goes by.' Goodness, he always knew how to make me laugh, and he had an incredible sounding voice. He sang the whole chorus and only stopped when his train arrived. Travelers cheered when he finished. I sat there in forty-one watching the train leave with the love of my life in it.

"Five days later, I received a letter from Alex saying he had been promoted to private first class and his unit was being deployed to Europe. I couldn't stop crying, but through my hurt, I did something positive. Every letter and note he sent me I rewrote in my journals. I never wanted to lose those words or the dreams we shared.

"I deeply hated the war because it disrupted our family. Our lives shifted so radically from the children we were… to preparing for the unknown. We were at war for three years with no end in sight, no one planned for their future, we had none. We were defenseless and could do nothing about it… my day-to-day living gave me a trapped feeling. My only comfort was praying that God would grant me strength and hope.

"I often wondered if I should've had kids or at least gotten pregnant before Alex left. But he didn't want his child growing up without a father. My Alex lost his dad when he was twelve years old, which was tough enough, but the concept of his child starting life deprived of a father was incomprehensible to him. He saw how his mother had struggled as a single woman trying to provide for him and his sibling. His mother's life would have been easier without the burden of supporting children.

"In one letter, Alex wrote, 'As soon as the war is over, and I'm back home with you, we'll move out to the country somewhere like Brighton. We'll have a farm and raise chickens, goats, and sheep… build a home and raise a family.' I imagined our home would be a two-story white clapboard Cape Cod with a stunning foyer. Behind the entrance, a charming winding staircase leading up to the bedrooms… with three children's rooms. I stored the blueprints in my mind for decades as you do a cherished memory. But war changes all things, even dreams.

"During those Homefront years, I did things just to stay busy and keep my mind occupied. My girlfriend Sylvia, who worked at the DeSoto plant, and I volunteered to work Bond drives around Detroit. I remember driving her in forty-one way out to the mammoth Ford Motor Company factory in Ypsilanti, called the Willow Run plant. They were assembling the B-24 Liberator bomber airplanes used in Europe. The people in charge of those bond drives always liked to team Sylvia and me together because we were both outgoing, good-looking girls who sold lots of war bonds."

Lucy looked over at Don when he signaled, let's take a break to her. She responded with a silent nodding no.

Fiery continued in her dreamlike state, saying, "With Alex in the Army, I had more time in the evening. So I volunteered in the kitchen at the USO in Detroit. Countless soldiers had a layover there while they traveled to their embarkation point. Sylvia would be out front entertaining, or dancing with the soldiers, while I was washing dishes.

"Sylvia enjoyed taking pictures and became the club's unofficial photographer. She never charged for her photographs and often sent them to the boys she could find. Sometimes I even brought Tiger. The guys loved petting that pooch, and she reveled in their attention.

"Living space was at a premium in April 1944, and I was struggling to make the mortgage payment. The government encouraged homeowners to open their homes to war plant workers, but there was one area of mine I would not share… my bedroom. Sylvia and another woman who worked at Buhl Sons shared the second bedroom. They agreed to allow me to take in two more women boarders to help with expenses. Those ladies slept on cots in the living room.

"When Alex bought our house, there was plenty of room with two bedrooms, one bath, a living room, kitchen, and back shanty. But now, with four other women under the same roof, the single bathroom became a major issue. Sylvia proposed having a toilet and sink installed in the coatroom shanty. That back room was a large ten-foot-by-ten-foot space with a secure entryway from the rear porch. The shanty had coat hooks on each wall, and the floor space under the coats was perfect for storing boots or shoes.

"The shanty's second door opened to the kitchen, but with the room not heated, we kept it closed. Sylvia's friend-of-a-friend was a plumber at a war plant. Somehow, she got him to install a heating duct, a new toilet, and a sink with hot and cold running water. In return, I gave her a month's free rent. I never asked my girlfriend what the job cost her, and everyone was pleased with the extra bathroom. We were happy for a week or two with our new bathroom.

"But our happiness was short-lived when the news of the widely expected Allied invasion of Europe at Normandy, France, came across the wires. We hoped the end of war may be in sight, but at what cost… how many of our boys would die? After work on June sixth, my ride-share friends and I went to Saint Alphonsus church to pray. Like other worship places and synagogues, my Catholic church was open twenty-four hours for special prayer services. I'll never forget the look of anguish on the parishioner's faces.

"The next day, I drove forty-one to the market to buy milk, tea, and a few other groceries Sylvia and I needed for a bond drive. While leaving the store, I ran into Mrs. Crabtree, whose only son, a Marine, was killed on Guadalcanal. I offered her a ride, but she begged off, saying she wanted to stretch her legs.

"Loriel, a six-year blonde-haired girl who lived on our street, pulled up to us on her tricycle. She asked Mrs. Crabtree, 'How come you have a gold star on your front window, and Mrs. Maze has a blue one?' My neighbor stared at her and broke down sobbing. Without answering, she turned and ambled towards her home. Little Loriel started to cry and pedaled away, not realizing she had reminded Mrs. Crabtree of her son's death. I told myself if, or when, this situation ever happened to me, I would handle it much differently.

"I sat there in forty-one thinking and crying for the sons, brothers, friends, and fellow co-workers who lost their lives… never to return. They gave their lives in some obscure battle overseas and would never give smiles, hugs, kisses, or grandchildren to mothers like Mrs. Crabtree. She and every gold star mother would never know those joys. We grieved for the families' losses and became numb as more and more bad news arrived. It didn't matter if the bitter information came from the Pacific Theater of Operations (PTO) or European Theater (ETO); those boys were not coming home."

Fiery took a deep breath after saying those words and paused for a moment.

Don interrupted her, asking, "Are you okay?" He looked over at her niece, Lucy. She nodded, which he took as a sign, meaning she's okay.

Fiery declared, "I'm fine — some memories are difficult sharing." Then she glanced at Lucy, "I'm fine… please let this old woman talk. It'll do me good, for once, to tell my story. In August 1944, Buhl Sons won a new government contract making braced framed bulkheads for Liberty ships that transported vital goods, arms, and servicemen overseas. The project called for us to work with Bethlehem Steel and Shipbuilding Corporation.

"To start the job, we required rolls of detailed drawings and metal samples from them. No one wanted them delayed in the mail or lost sitting in a railcar or warehouse. The Buhl Sons' bosses asked my father, Gil, to make the three-day trip to Pittsburgh and get the needed items from

Bethlehem Steel. His boss told him they asked him because he was the most experienced. But, in reality, he knew he'd be the one least missed.

"Dad could take someone along to help. He immediately thought of me, hoping the trip would take my thoughts off the war. Trying to get rail passage to Pittsburgh proved futile. We had to change and wait for trains in either Crestline or Toledo, Ohio, which added days to the planned three-day trek. My father suggested he drive there.

Prior to the war, driving the two hundred eighty-six miles to Pittsburgh was no big deal. "But, with gas rationing and the victory speed of thirty-five miles per hour, the trip seemed next to impossible. The government adage was: Don't travel unless your trip helps win the war. The movement of armaments, munitions, and military personnel was the top priority… not civilian travel vacations. Dad convinced the big shots it would be cheaper, faster, and more help to the war effort if he drove there. He explained that I had a newer vehicle and its tires were in excellent condition, plus I had a C gasoline ration sticker on the windshield.

"My father's bosses approved of him driving to Pittsburgh and gave him an X gas ration sticker for the trip, which allowed him to buy unlimited gallons of gasoline. They only issued those stickers to rich people, politicians, members of the U.S. Senate or Congress, and in special instances to those with high mileage jobs. At the same time, my Alex sent me a letter saying he was in New York waiting to ship out. Without hesitation, I penned him back, telling him the date I expected to be in Pittsburgh, and asked if we might meet there for dinner.

"I never realized that New York was three hundred miles from where I would be, which disappointed me. But before dad and I left, I received a letter saying he would try to arrange a forty-eight-hour pass, and take a train to Pittsburgh. Thanks to his friend from Pittsburgh, Alex included instructions on where to find him at the railroad station. I kept my fingers crossed things would work for us and hoped for the best. Alex's commanding officer pulled a lot of strings and granted him an unheard-of seventy-two-hour pass.

"The planning for our trip to Bethlehem Steel was like preparing to invade Europe. Automobile restrictions demanded commuter vehicles had to be fully occupied or loaded. In addition, drivers had to obey the thirty-five mile per hour victory speed law. My father loaded rolls upon rolls of old Buhl drawings in forty-one's back seat. He did that in case someone stopped and questioned us. Dad was never one for camping, but I still packed my camping equipment in the trunk, just in case we couldn't find somewhere to stay."

Don noticed his wife and Lucy having a quiet conversation across the table. Aunt Fiery never heard them and continued her one-sided discussion. Then he detected a faint smile on the old woman and for the first time, saw the beautiful face she had in her youth.

Fiery continued saying, "We left early in the morning. When we drove over the Pennsylvania state line, a trooper on a motorcycle pulled us over. He spotted my Michigan license plate and became suspicious of an automobile from so far away. Dad showed him our official business letter from a general. The state trooper appeared satisfied and allowed us to continue when he saw our X gas ration decal.

"Stopping only for fuel and nature calls, the two-hundred-eighty-six-mile trip had taken us over nine hours. We arrived around noon. Dad told me he didn't need a helper. I could have kissed him. With a hug and a quick goodbye, I drove straight to the downtown Penn Station.

"When I reached the station, I couldn't find a parking space available, so I pulled over at the loading area. With my X sticker adorning the windshield, I dared any law enforcement officer to give me a ticket. I didn't even bother to raise forty-one's hood before heading in. I was too excited and ran into the station. Inside the depot, there were many servicemen, and I found Alex's train had arrived a half-hour before me. I thought I would never spot him when I remembered his mom, Bernice, telling me, 'If you ever want to spot my son in a large crowd, look for the boy with the roundest head.'

"So, ignoring the catcalls of 'Hey Baby,' and 'Red, over here,' I continued walking and looking for a round-headed soldier. Low and behold, his mother was right! I spotted him from behind, sitting reading a newspaper. I placed my hands over his eyes and said, guess who? He responded, 'Wait, give me a minute. I'll get it?'

"Alex shouted out different girl names… but not mine. I told him… if that's the way he felt, I'd take forty-one and go home! I knew he was teasing, and he understood I was pretending to be upset. That's when he got up from his seat, turned around, hugged and kissed me, stopping only to catch our breath. Then he whispered, 'Let's drive where we can have some quiet naptime.' I knew what he meant by naptime."

Don looked over to see Lucy glaring at her Aunt Fiery as if she never heard her speak so openly. Sarah, appeared surprised never imagining her elder relative a beautiful young wife. Ann's jaw dropped open when she finally realized what 'naptime' meant. Don believed it was time for Fiery to rest and wished to interrupt her... but to no avail, she was in her subliminal state of mind. Smiling to herself, she kept speaking, not missing a beat.

She continued saying, "It surprised Alex that I had found him so easily. I jokingly exclaimed, if it wasn't for your round head, I'd still be looking for you! He came back at me saying, 'Oh, that again, you've been listening to my mother!' We walked out to the jammed parking lot, and I told him where I parked. He didn't see any cars with their hoods up in the loading area and predictably remarked, 'You should have opened the hood!'

"I pointed to the X sticker on the windshield. 'Whoa!' He said as he tossed his small duffle bag into the backseat. A police officer standing nearby nodded at Alex, who waved back while other commuters just stood there and gawked at us as we sped away.

"He asked me, 'Where are we going?' I explained how I had to meet my father at 7:00 p.m. tomorrow and mentioned my idea of camping somewhere. We decided to head east into the country. We stopped at a wayside diner for a fried chicken dinner. That was the best chicken dinner I ever had!

"On the jukebox, he played our song, 'As Time Goes By,' and we danced right there in the middle of the restaurant with everyone smiling at us. When we drove away from the restaurant, the light rain became a steady downpour. Then he said to me, 'Let's drive forty-one until it stops raining.' While driving, he had me under his arm, with his other hand on the wheel... I held onto him, never wanting to let go. While it was still raining, Alex swung forty-one onto a lonely, seldom used county road.

"After a while, he steered our auto off the country road to a relatively flat space. He parked under a canopy of large mature oak trees, next to a wooden fence that boarded a pasture. Alex smiled at me... only at me, and lovingly said, 'Let's not set up the tent; we can sleep in the car. We'll spread out in the backseat.' From the trunk, I took out two twelve-quart pop shells; you know those big wooden soda boxes. We placed the old Buhl drawings on the back floor and put the boxes upside down on top them. Not knowing how cold it could be, I brought several quilts for the trip.

"We made a welcoming, cozy bed in the back where we could stretch out. I knew Alex liked gin rummy and asked him if he wanted to play. He declined, not wanting to sit outside in the drizzle. I told him to follow me, and I opened the rear trunk. Once we had moved everything to the front seat, except our cool box. I climbed into the trunk and begged Alex to join me.

"He was such a good sport! We used the cooler as a table for our cards. I had a pad of paper and a pencil on top to keep score. I dealt the cards, and we played rummy while listening to the raindrops bouncing off the trunk's open lid. During our games, he spoke about his life in the army, the good and the bad. He told me how much he missed me and loved me.

"It surprised me when he mentioned how he enjoyed singing with his buddies, telling me it helped him to forget the war and how much he missed me. I decided it was time for a snack and surprised him with a couple bottles of cola, crackers, grapes, and a neighbor's homemade cheese. I had gotten the cheese by trading my homegrown potatoes with her. As I went for a bottle opener from the front seat, Alex yelled out, 'No need for one!' I turned to see him open a bottle of soda using the car's hinge. Can you believe it? I scolded him not to hurt forty-one and came back with the opener.

"We stayed dry and comfortable in the trunk's open space and soon became sleepy, listening to the tapping of raindrops falling from the trees. I placed our white porcelain washbasin under the driver's side door with a bar of soap. There was also a two-gallon water jug on the driver's side floor with four clean folded towels on the front seat. By then, the rain had stopped, so I moved the water basin to the front pontoon fender and handed Alex a new toothbrush I bought for him. Then he asked me something strange. He wanted me to take his old toothbrush home and keep it safe for him."

With those words, tears streamed down Fiery's cheeks, and she motioned to Lucy that she needed a break. Then, being polite, the elderly aunt excused herself.

Sarah was silent as she watched her grandmother push her Aunt Fiery out of the room. She looked over at Ann, remarking, "I've been visiting Ammygam once a week for my entire life. She's said nothing like this to either Gammy or me." Then, looking directly at Don, she asked, "Do you think they're real… Ammygam's stories?"

He only shrugged his shoulders.

Sarah looked at Ann, then turned to Don, asking, "Do you feel there's some kind of bond between her, that old car, and you?"

He nervously grinned at her saying nothing… but inside, Don was thinking the same exact thing.

Chapter 20

X Sticker

While Fiery was resting, Sarah gave Don and Ann a glimpse into her Ammygam's health status. She spoke about her Ammygam's health declining and how the Blair House doctors asked them not to have her exert herself. They felt these meetings were putting stress on her because of her advanced age. Don saw the two women returning to the table.

As they neared the table, everyone noticed a big grin on Aunt Fiery's face as she whispered, just loud enough for them to hear her say, "I brought some sweeties."

Sarah opened the box and offered some to each person before placing it on the table. After a minute, Lucy glanced at her aunt, asking if she wanted to continue. Fiery smiled while she ate her piece of candy, enjoying the fact that she was again the center of attention.

She looked at Don as if speaking directly to him, saying, "Now I stopped when dad and I had traveled to Pittsburgh on business and Alex met me. Yes, and we went camping for the night in forty-one. The backseat is where we settled, mainly talking of our lives apart. We shared the moment in each other's arms.

"I broke our romantic moment when I told him I was going for a nature walk. He confided… he was too lazy to get up. I scolded him, telling him that he would have to make an effort if I was doing it. Outside, he went one way, and I went the other. I had completely forgotten about having no bathroom, and my options in the pasture were few. So I straddled the farmer's split-rail fence and took care of business."

As she said those words, Lucy put her head down and shook her head as if embarrassed by her aunt's frank language. Fiery slowly turned her wheelchair from the table to look outside. Her eyes gazed out at nothing, and she seemed transfixed in her own world.

Fiery continued saying, "When I returned to the car, I took a quick sponge bath using the washbasin on the fender that had filled up with rainwater. Before getting back into forty-one, I told my husband he'd be proud of me. He laughed and held me tight, telling me he couldn't be prouder. We talked some more, lying there holding each other. A while later, he leaned over the front seat and turned on the car's ignition.

"He wanted to listen to soft relaxing music. But, in a moment, he forgot about the radio and returned to my arms. I thought we were the only people on earth when he kissed me. We could barely understand the cold radio. As it warmed up, the announcer distracted us, saying, 'You're listening to WJR from Detroit, Michigan.' I remember thinking that can't be… we're in Pittsburgh.

"The broadcaster introduced the next song, sung by Rudy Vallee… our song, 'As Time Goes By'. I was in my Alex's arms when he pushed back from me, looked into my eyes, telling me he loved me and would return to me. I never forgot how he smiled at me."

Fiery wiped a tear as she opened the book on her lap and said, "It was then I heard the introduction verse to our song for the first time. Alex whispered and sang every word in my ear. Softly he sang,

'This day and age we're living;

This cause for apprehension;

This speed and new invention;

And things like third dimension…'

"For that moment in time, we hid together between heaven and earth. I was protected in his arms and his kisses were only for me. When we broke our kiss, we continued to embrace, and he looked deep into my eyes and in a voice barely above a whisper, with the radio, he sang,

'You must remember this

A kiss is still a kiss

A sigh is just a sigh

The fundamental things apply as time goes by;

And when two lovers woo…'

"I found myself still lost somewhere in time. Now and forever, I was his. I don't remember hearing anything else until Alex moved an arms-length from me, stared into my eyes, and sang what I believe is the last chorus of our song.

'Moonlight and love songs never out of date

Hearts full of passion, jealousy, and hate

Woman needs man, and man must have his mate

That no one can deny;

It's still the same old story

A fight for love and glory

A case of do or die

The world will always welcome lovers… as time goes by.'

"I held him close to me as he fell asleep. I continued talking to him about our life after the war, although I wasn't sure he heard me. Groggily he interrupted me, asking if it was still raining? I told him no. In his sleepy voice, he mumbled, 'Roll down all the windows, let in that wonderful country air.' I did and turned off the car's ignition. While holding on to him, I fell asleep.

"I slept a little that night but remembered when I woke up in the morning cows were sticking their heads through forty-one's open windows! They woke us up early, jostling their heads in front of our faces, expecting to be fed. Let me tell you, I was terrified! They must have thought we were fodder!

"Waking up in your car with big brown eyes looking at you and mooing loudly is horrible! Not to mention the awful smell of their breath, just six inches from your face. I yelled for Alex to save me from the cows; I was yelling… the cows, the cows! The first thing he said was, 'Don't bother me, I'm on leave!' But he woke up long enough to push their heads out the windows. Then I rolled them up.

"He said, in his sleepy voice, 'Cows eat hay… not people.' And then… my hero closed his eyes, and went back to sleep! So, with all the excitement, I headed outside, but the cows followed me along the fence line. There was no sitting on the pasture's rail for me that morning!

"When I returned from my walk, I again laid down in the backseat and watched Alex sleep, or so I thought. My man, my love, my husband, my Alex… was lying there with his eyes closed. Then, suddenly, he opened his eyes and smiled at me. He moved on his side and leaned into me. I waited for him to greet me with his loving and amorous words.

"With his serious tone, he said, 'Who let the cows in?' We couldn't stop laughing. Our time together was so short, and I wanted to make sure Alex didn't forget me while he was overseas… I pulled him towards me. I greeted him right then with a passionate good morning kiss.

"I was getting out of the car's backseat to start breakfast when he grabbed and pulled me to him, so my back was against his chest. He whispered in my ear, 'Never sell this car. We'll do this again, at least once a month.' I knew exactly what he meant.

"Wanting to see his reaction, I spun around saying, 'What, visit Pittsburgh?' He was gracious enough to laugh at my little joke and leaned in to give me another good morning kiss. I returned it… only to swoon and surrender to the spell he weaved around us. When he released me, I asked my Army man if he was ready for breakfast. He blurted out, 'Yeah, but I don't want to drive into town, and the wood outside is wet; it'll be hard making a fire.'

"I reminded him we could cook on our car. Enthusiastically he asked, 'What're you going to make?' How about eggs, bacon, and rolls was my response. His mother, Bernice, gave me six precious eggs that I carefully removed from the cooler. I proposed he warm up forty-one's manifold for four minutes and then shut her off so that I could safely place our food on it.

"He mentioned, 'I've been eating powdered eggs for so long, I've forgotten how fresh eggs taste.' I brought out a modest slab of bacon, which Alex sliced into six strips. I made two small baking dishes from sheets of metal foil, bent the edges up, and placed them on the car's manifold. I put the bacon in one of my homemade pans and waited while my husband started the engine.

"As the pork cooked and the fat melted, I added two tablespoons of bacon grease to the other pan resting on the manifold. I carefully cracked three eggs in a bowl and poured them into the greased pan. I wanted to cook his eggs sunny side up, so he could count them and see they were real. Alex turned the radio on and listened to the news while I prepared breakfast.

"In another packet of foil, I placed rolls putting them on the valve cover to warm up. My Alex couldn't believe what I was doing and remarked, 'You're becoming quite the master chef at car cooking. You really are amazing!' I mixed up powdered orange juice in a camping tin cup and put a small can of water on the manifold for his tea.

"He watched everything I did and how I did it as if trying to commit this day in his memory forever. Then, with a grin, he exclaimed, 'That engine never smelled so good. You couldn't cook like this driving down the road.' We cleaned forty-one and washed the dishes after our meal in case I had to use them on the way home. The rest of the morning and early afternoon we spent hiking through the woods. We saw a herd of deer frolicking in the meadow and laughed as we snuck up on a flock of wild turkeys waddling in single file along a pond's shore.

"As he drove back to Pittsburgh, we stopped at a hamburger stand with a welcoming look to it. The proprietor noticed us walking in and was exceptionally chirpy, showing us to a booth. The other patrons stopped talking and just stared at us. After we ate, the owner asked us how everything was and thanked us for eating there. He said, 'I know you folks can afford to eat any place you want, and I really appreciate you stopping here. I would like to thank you and give you both a slice of boysenberry pie… on the house.' The pie was delicious.

"Alex whispered to me, 'It's the power of that X sticker. It never ceases to amaze me.' After we left the diner, Alex turned into a filling station for fuel. He pulled up to the pump and instructed the gas jockey to filler up. I thought he wanted to test out the X sticker's mystique again. The attendant looked at us suspiciously; with his stuttering voice, he asked, we wait a minute.

"We were sure he noticed our Michigan license plate and the X sticker. He returned with the gas station owner, a short portly man who condescendingly asked Alex, 'Your X sticker… son? Can you show me paperwork for it?' I pulled my letter from the glove box signed by Mr. Buhl and countersigned by an Army two-star General. It described the reason for the unlimited sticker as vital war business. The man's demeanor did a one-hundred-eighty-degree turn, and he almost tripped over himself, explaining how sorry he was for the inconvenience.

"He explained how he was only doing what the government's OPA told him to do! The station owner said, 'We never had a private stop here driving a car with an X sticker.' My Alex, in his most dignified manner, shared his secret with the manager, saying, 'Well, that's understandable, my good man. I had to remove my bars because I'm traveling incognito. Now not a word of my transaction for six months.'

"The proprietor only replied, 'Yes sir, thank you for understanding.' Then he yelled to his gas jockey, 'Horace, dammit, can't you see this official is on a mission and in a hurry. Fill his tank up right now!' The owner walked over to Alex's window and spoke to him confidentially, 'You have to forgive him, he's a little slow, but he's the only help I can get. The war, you know.'

"Alex, unable to stop his ruse, spoke in his exaggerated voice, 'I understand completely, my good man. Your boy, have him check the oil, radiator, and the pressure in my tires. Oh! And I will need a voucher for my purchase today. Be sure to show the number of gallons on your receipt. Back in Washington, I'll tell them you're doing your part. What is your name?'

"The man was flabbergasted as Alex looked over to me, saying in that important tone he was using, 'Make a note of this person's identification and his station's address.' I opened the glove box and removed the pad of paper I used the night before to keep our Gin Rummy score. In the notepad, I wrote his information while I tried not to giggle. When they were through filling our vehicle with fuel and checking the car's items, Alex paid the proprietor and received his requested receipt.

"The station owner again thanked him for understanding. He and his attendant waved goodbye as we drove away. Alex put the sheet of paper with the station's information on it in his pocket and said, 'As a company clerk, I am the war department. So, I'll send him a thank you from PFC X sticker.' We spent a few minutes laughing about what just happened as he quipped, 'It's the power of the X sticker!'

"Alex missed one turn, driving back to Pittsburgh's Penn Station. It was when he asked me, 'Left turn at this intersection?' I answered right!

Meaning yes, turn left, and he actually turned right. I loved how we laughed together, and he always made me look good. It was his way of respecting and romancing me.

"We arrived at the terminal and parked in the loading area when we discovered Alex's train was late. It would now arrive at 6:30 p.m., which gave us extra time together. We sat listening to the radio while trying to talk of the things we would do when he returned, hoping to distract ourselves — but it didn't work. Minutes later, he turned it off, and I reminded him we had an hour before the battery died. Alex could only say, 'I know.'

"He began singing, 'As Time Goes By,' and I started to cry. I tried to sing along with him, but that only made me cry harder. My husband kissed me every time he sang… a kiss is still a kiss. When his train pulled into the station, I thought only minutes had passed. He waited with me until everyone got off.

"Wrapping my arms around him, I tried to stop him from getting on that train. I clung to Alex in forty-one's front seat until the last person disappeared from the platform. Through my tears, I stared at him, and he told me he must leave or he would have to stand all the way to New York. Then he showed me his collapsible cane one of his buddies had given him before going overseas. Alex commented, 'I used this coming here, and the conductors on the full trains always found me a seat.' I told him I hoped it would work for him this time too!

"I stopped sobbing long enough to hug and kiss him while he slowly opened the driver's door. Alex got out of the car and walked towards the station, reaching the depot's entrance. He swung around, and ran to the front of our car, where he paused, kissed his right hand, and lovingly touched the flying lady hood ornament. Looking at me he shouted, 'Never sell this car, I'm coming back for you, and forty-one with Tiger.' He turned and ran to his waiting Pullman, where he found a seat. From his, window he kept smiling and waving goodbye to me. I watched as his railcar pulled out and disappeared beyond the horizon. He said he would come back for me and forty-one, and he will."

Fiery looked directly at Don while she wiped a tear from her cheek. She turned back to the blankness she saw out the window and continued, saying, "I stared at forty-one's flying lady ornament and recognized right then she was special. In my mind, I replayed how he kissed it and imagined him kissing our child in the same way. My Chevrolet automobile, at that moment, ceased being a shiny hunk of metal with wheels taking me everywhere. It became a real member of our family, and I vowed then never to sell Alex's car!

"Suddenly, a noise from the train station brought me back to reality, and I remembered I had to pick up dad! I arrived at Bethlehem Steel's Ship Building offices' with only a few minutes to spare. Outside the office entrance, dad was talking with two other men. When he saw our car, he waved to me. Soon he said his goodbyes and walked over. He looked tired but got in behind the wheel, ready to take us home. It was as if he knew I wasn't in any shape to drive.

"As he maneuvered out of the parking lot, he asked how my time with Alex went. With that simple question, I burst into tears. While sobbing, I tried to explain how we had fun playing cards, sitting in forty-one's trunk in the rain, walking in the woods, and cooking breakfast on our car's engine. I struggled to convince him they were happy tears, but I doubted my dear father believed me.

"Every minute spent with my Alex was the best of my life. Those were forever my memories to cherish. We crossed into Ohio at the twilight hour, and the temperature in the car was quite comfortable for driving. Dad had just finished telling me of his meetings and the people he met. My father wanted me to know, just in case anyone questioned me back at Buhl Sons. He also thought it would be good to stop and fill forty-one's gas tank if service stations ahead of us were closed.

"When we stopped at a single pump gas station, dad bought us four sandwiches and soft drinks at a nearby open grocery store. I never realized how emotionally drained I was from saying goodbye to my husband. My dad understood it, so he volunteered to continue driving while he ate his peanut butter and jelly hoagie. I soon fell asleep. We were a few miles south of Toledo when dad, too sleepy to drive, pulled off the road, which woke me up.

"I told him I was fine to drive the rest of the way home, so he slept. We arrived at my parent's home just after five that morning. After dropping dad off, I continued onto my house. As I drove into the backyard, I saw

Tiger with her leash on, lying on the porch. I was mad! My renters, I thought, left her outside when they went to work!

"I found a note on the kitchen counter telling me how Tiger ran away during her evening walk on the day dad, and I left. They had searched for hours for her that evening and the next evening while we were driving home. Tiger was missing the two days I was gone! Not knowing what she had gotten into, we greeted the sunrise together in the backyard.

"There, she received a soapy bath and a proper rinsing with the garden hose. I was angry at her for running away. However, I forgave her when she looked at me with her brown puppy-like eyes. Then I dried her with one of my better bath towels.

"At eight, I called Miss Graves and explained how we had been driving through the night to bring the blueprints and sample steel parts back to Buhl Sons. She told me to stay home and rest today while informing me they would pay me for the day! She then asked me if I thought our trip was a success. I told her, after meeting with the right person, I considered it a tremendous achievement and a great success.

"With the unexpected holiday, I realized I was alone in my house for the first time in months. I couldn't wait to take a proper bath with unlimited hot water and no interruptions. Tiger laid on the bathroom floor, sleeping while I relaxed in the warm tub and reminisced of my day with Alex. What I truly loved about him… was how he adored and romanced me. He was my dream… always making me the most important thing in his world. It was then when I discovered a bruise on my left calf and smiled, thinking it had to happen while we were napping in forty-one's backseat.

"That evening, I wrote my husband telling him how I missed him and how good it was to be with him in Pittsburgh. I penned him on Tiger's adventure and apologized for not bringing her to see him. But, I knew he understood when I explained how I wanted him all to myself."

Seeing the tear coming down her aunt's cheek, Lucy interrupted her saying, "That was far in your past! Auntie, you should forget about it! Let me take you to your apartment where you can rest."

Fiery responded with a sharp tongue, "It was a long time ago when I camped with your uncle on that country lane! Why is it we never appreciate the good times until they're gone? And, I do not wish to relax… I'm enjoying myself! Allow me to tell my story to Don and Ann. If you don't want to listen, go sit at another table so you can't hear me."

Everyone was shocked. They never imagined Aunt Fiery speaking in such a coarse tone. It surprised Don how she put their names together. He thought she had forgotten who they were.

Then Fiery apologized, saying, "Lucy, I'm sorry, honey! Please stay and listen… my time with your uncle in Pittsburgh was my dream come true. I hope you understand this was a special time in my life."

Don watched as Lucy shrugged her shoulders and waved her hand at her aunt, signaling for her to continue speaking.

Fiery smiled at her niece and said, "It took three weeks for Alex's letter from New York to reach me in Michigan. In it, he confessed how upset he was with my Uncle Marty, our car salesman, for not delivering our Chevrolet to us. He wrote how he visited the dealership the Monday before our wedding, which was two days before we took delivery of forty-one. Alex discovered the dealership's owner had planned to sell our vehicle to someone else for a premium price.

"He complained to my Uncle Marty and the owner to no avail. It was only when Alex threatened to involve a magistrate, and the soon-to-be government's Office of Price Administration (OPA) did the owner release our car. Alex had a bill of sale and could prove he purchased the fully equipped Chevrolet. The owner was mad at losing the premium he would have been paid and angrily shouted at Alex, 'Pick it up Wednesday! If it's here one more day, I will sell it!' I never realized how close we really were to losing our precious car.

"In that same letter, he informed me, they scheduled his outfit to ship out on the *Queen Mary*. Did you know, when England declared war on Germany, they retrofitted that luxury ocean liner to serve as a troop transporter? She was bigger and faster than all the other passenger ships built before her, and the government painted her gray. Those who sailed on her called her the *Grey Ghost* because of her color and her speed.

"Before becoming a troop transport, she had grand cabins with the finest carpets, furniture, and oil paintings and carried 3,000 people in pure luxury. Not wanting the troops to destroy their ship, the owner removed all her amenities. Those they couldn't remove, like the wood staircase, were covered in thick leather, so no one carved their initials in it. These changes allowed her to carry over 15,000 servicemen and the crew.

"When Alex crossed the north Atlantic, in September 1944, Allied Powers had made great strides in controlling and destroying the North Atlantic's U-Boat dangers… making the trip much safer. The speedy *Grey Ghost* could outrun a German submarine. But, we found out later, there were a few times she crossed unescorted. The ship my Alex was on docked uneventfully somewhere in northern Scotland in just five days. Alex wrote how happy he was that his ocean travel was over and done! I laughed when he said he had no sea legs and was unnerved by sailing on the large ocean with no land in sight. A few weeks later, he wrote from his staging point, someplace in England, never giving their locations before he was shipped to the European continent."

Don nudged Lucy, who he suspected was still irritated from the scolding she received from her eighty-seven-year-old aunt. She looked at him, and he silently signaled a break? Lucy mimed to let her aunt speak longer.

Fiery continued saying, "It was mid-October when I wrote Alex the awful news regarding his precious Tiger. I wasn't certain if I should write him, but he always wanted me to be honest with him. In my letter, I explained how a few weeks earlier, everything happened so quickly as we returned from our evening walk. Tiger wanted to investigate something in the backyard, so I dropped her tether, letting her go ahead of me onto the grass. I gawked as I watched her jump over the hedge and run away from me.

"By then, darkness set in, and too late to ask our neighbors to help search. The girls, my boarders, got our flashlights and spent two hours looking for her when we ran smack dab into Mr. Volk. He took over for Alex and was our neighborhood's air raid warden. Proudly, he wore his black helmet with a big white 'W' on it while he yelled at us, 'Put that light out!'… and 'Turn off your flashlights!' He was serious, but later we laughed, thinking we scared him.

"The following day, I awoke early to search for her; I didn't go too far before I found her. There she was, lying on the back porch with her leash still attached. Sleeping next to her was a male Scottish hunting dog

I had seen in the neighborhood. I quickly got the hose and sprayed him with water so he would go home. I wrote to Alex wondering if we might have puppies.

"Once Alex was in Europe, our letters overlapped, and the tone of his letters changed. He'd ask me how I was coping on the Homefront? How his friends at Buhl Sons were doing? He even asked me to say hello to Miss Graves for him. Alex attempted to make his letters cheerful, comical and wrote of the rumor… that the war would be over by Christmas. But, I had this feeling something was wrong.

"Another letter from somewhere on the continent included a tale of how his sergeant told him to grab two enlisted men and help carry cases of liquor from a truck into the Officer's Club. The Captain was in charge of the club and realized Cokes and Grape Nehi, no matter how cold, would never keep the officer's spirits up. They needed a good supply of liquor. One private helping Alex was from Kentucky, and he introduced him to the captain. The private, from Kentucky, understood how to distill fine bourbon. He and the officer in charge soon became fast friends.

"They even went into business together, and the officer supplied the private with empty whiskey bottles from the bar. The enlisted man filled the bottles with good-tasting bootlegged liquor and gave them back to the captain. Alex understood… neither man questioned the other exactly how or what they did. When he left for his assignment in Belgium, he heard their partnership was still going strong.

"I still didn't know if my Alex received the letter about Tiger because in his next one he didn't mention her. He wrote how he met a sergeant with the same last name as ours. My husband never let on he changed his name and told the sergeant he came from a long line of degenerates, alcoholics, and just plain riffraff. The man replied, saying, 'There's a good chance we're family!'

"Shortly after meeting each other, the sergeant died in a freak accident. An electrical cable from a diesel-powered generator was laid across a dirt road. At one place, the cable passed through a large puddle. Trucks, jeeps, and tanks traveled over it and had worn away the cable's insulation. When Sergeant Maze stepped in that puddle, he was electrocuted. After that, Alex avoided puddles!

"In early December, Alex wrote about our dog telling me not to worry and to let nature take its course. He sounded swell, and I laughed when he said raising puppies was great practice for raising our children. He was fighting a war and telling me to raise a litter of puppies. What was I going to do with them? And then it happened…"

Fiery stopped speaking and stared out the window with a blank expression. Don turned to Lucy and saw tears in her eyes; he didn't understand why she was crying. With a trembling voice, Fiery broke her silence, stating, "Do you mind if we continue another time? I want to inform you of events which happened and affected my life; however, I just can't speak the words…"

Ann watched as a single tear rolled down the aged woman's perfect cheek. Sarah took a tissue from the box on the table and handed it to her Ammygam.

Don said, "When you're ready, you inform Lucy or Sarah, and both Ann and I will be here."

She put a brave smile on her face, saying, "Thank you for understanding."

His heart was heavy and his voice solemn when he responded, "I do. And, God willing, we'll meet again real soon." He walked around and knelt in front of her chair. His frame looked enormous compared to her, and gently he hugged the frail woman. In her ear, he whispered, "See you soon."

Before Lucy could whisk Aunt Fiery away, she waved goodbye to everyone. Don took his recorder from the table, and started to rise when he spotted Sarah's puffy red eyes, and wondered why she was crying?

He listened as she spoke to Ann, "I never knew these things about Ammygam. I visit with her all the time, and she never talks this way." Then, trying to make light of the discussion, she continued saying, "It must be Mr. Bryniarski's personality, something about him that makes her speak of her private life. Or… is it her old forty-one that he owns?"

Lucy soon joined them at the Blair house exit. They departed together. While walking to their cars, Sarah's words haunted him. He was thinking about how she thought he or a car might be the reason for her Ammygam's blunt honesty. He wondered how Sarah thought either could be the reason.

Sarah's words started him on the road to understanding just how dear the 1941 Chevrolet Special Deluxe was to Alex and Fiery. He thought of how Fiery described Alex kissing the car's hood ornament in Pittsburgh. Don now realized how attached Fiery was to forty-one. He also knew the reason she never sold the car… it was her family.

As they approached their automobiles, Don noticed Ann's hands were empty and now asked himself why Fiery hadn't given her a journal for their trunk? He started to ask himself more questions, like was that her last book? Is it one she couldn't part with? Was her story near its ending? With his brain churning, he could only wonder and ask himself… where would these questions lead them, and where would he find the answers?

Chapter 21

Million Tears

Sunday, May ninth, 2004, was Mother's Day. Ever since their mothers passed, Don and Ann honored them by visiting their graves on this special day. This simple act gave them much comfort. On their drive, his wife remarked how she considered Aunt Fiery part of the family now. "Well, I consider Aunt Fiery family to us. After all, she was the original owner of forty-one. Oh, and why don't we drive forty-one over to the Blair House one day? We might even take her for a ride to lift her spirits."

Don considered it for a moment. When he was ready to respond, Tiger started growling from her place in the back seat of Don's work car. Surprised by the noise, Don spoke of the recent change in Tiger's behavior. She wasn't as playful as she used to be; she walked slower and wasn't always eating her food. Putting on her doctor's hat, Ann reminded him she had given their Golden retriever a complete exam just a month ago at the clinic. Your dog is maturing and should be two years old about mid-August. No dog stays a puppy forever.

Ann turned and spoke to Tiger, saying, "Tomorrow, you're coming to work with me!"

Their dog gave her a funny look as Ann recounted Tiger's last visit to the office. It was March twenty-fourth. I was having a broken window repaired that day. Ann turned to Don, saying, "Your dog almost jumped out the open window frame. The workers removed the shattered pane and went to their truck to bring in the replacement.

One of our young high school interns, Abigail, caught your pup halfway out the opening. Your dog and Abigail were both lucky the glass shards didn't cut them." Silently, Ann counted her fingers. She then looked back at Tiger, saying, "We'll see?"

When they arrived home, Ann told him she would walk Tiger while he parked his car in the garage. That evening, while sitting in their den, she asked him if Tiger had run away recently?

He responded, "Never. Is everything okay?"

Ann had her suspicions but assured him all was fine as she watched Tiger try to cuddle with him. Then, a short while later, she moved over to Ann, looking for more affection.

Ann changed the subject, reminding him of the Memorial Day Parade in Howell (Michigan). It was only three weeks away. She suggested saying, "After we've finished, why don't we take forty-one and Tiger to see Aunt Fiery?"

Instead of answering her question, he reminded her of all the traveling he had to do in the next three weeks. He would be busy helping promote his company's new airport security system, now internally named X-Fi.

"I'm confused," she said. "Are you talking about the TV show?"

Don declared, "That's perfect! We were hoping to confuse our competition with that name, and you just confirmed how they would think." Continuing, he said, "The best part is we left the H out of the product name."

Ann challenged him, "So what's so secret about this system, and what does it do?"

Don started speaking like a boy in a toy store, saying, "I can now tell you… patents have been applied for. Our government asked three companies to develop a better way to detect explosives. Our team developed a Hyperspectral X-ray with Fluorescence Infrared imaging, which is an amazing scanning machine. We can identify every type of explosives except black powder. And we do it at an ultra-high rate of speed. This product is perfect for scanning luggage, people at airports, buildings, entrances, basically anything you can think of; we've got it covered! The black powder bug needs tweaking from the software, which we should accomplish this week."

It was obvious to Ann this was his expertise and his passion. He told her how the name Wi-Fi commonly refers to wireless local network technology. He explained how the X-Fi uses Wi-Fi technology for all of its software updates. This made their machine easy to change as security requirements change. He also spoke of how much lighter their machine was compared to the competition's first generation. Don also told her of their plans to develop a handheld scanner.

He laughed, saying, "Our competitors won't know the difference between X-Fi and Wi-Fi. I just need to make sure everyone writes the project's name correctly with a capital X hyphen, capital F, and small i. Of course, that will cause more confusion. Oh! I may travel to Sydney, Australia, sometime next month. I'm not looking forward to flying halfway around the world, but I'll wait to hear what the airport trade association decides."

More confused than ever, Ann tried to recap what he just said, "So, you're playing with X-rays or files, but you're not a TV show. You might go to Sydney to speak about these X things. If there's nothing else you need to tell me, maybe you can answer my question. The one about taking forty-one on Memorial Day to see Fiery?"

He responded, "I should know more tomorrow. Okay, if I don't go to Sydney, Australia, we'll take the Chevrolet to the Blair House and Tiger too."

The next day he was busy at work planning trips to Washington, D.C., on Wednesday through Friday for the next two weeks. With a free moment, Don made time to answer Nadine's questions on the recordings she was transcribing for him. She needed him to identify the unfamiliar voices on his recordings. He identified Fiery, Lucy, and Sarah's voice for her.

Before leaving, he gave her a disc from their Friday meeting. On her way out, she stopped and complimented him on the X-Fi project. She mentioned how the employees understood this project would keep the company in business for years. Nadine also said she never felt so much positive energy surrounding a product before. He thanked her for the unsolicited positive comment and assured her it was a team effort. Don included her by saying she, too, was part of the team that made it happen.

That evening when he arrived home, he was excited to tell Ann the good news. The X-Fi development team was disbanding, and he would now have less responsibility. The decision-making process for the product was moving over to the marketing and manufacturing departments. He looked forward to this day! But arriving home, no one was there, not even Tiger.

He was busy heating leftovers for their dinner and had been home two hours when Ann and Tiger finally arrived. Tiger couldn't wait to get to the dish of food Don prepared for her.

Ann, in a disgusted tone, yelled, "Well, blame it all on Sydney!"

He eagerly responded, "Kitten, good news! Sydney is not the issue. They have postponed it!"

She responded, "In a month, you'll have your hands full, and Sydney is the problem!"

Not understanding, he declared, "Listen — if you want to go to Sydney, we can arrange it — we'll make it a vacation!"

Calming down a little, she said, "Don, I'm tired. It's been a stressful day, and I'm hungry. I'm going to take a shower, and I'll enlighten you about Sydney after I eat."

To him Sydney was a mere journey for international business, and Don wondered what was troubling her. He couldn't stand to see her upset. He kept quiet until Ann was ready to talk to him.

Halfway through her dinner, she looked at him, questioning, "Don, do you recall, when Tiger went to work with me in March?"

He responded, "Not really."

"I told you it was the day we had the clinic's window replaced?"

He nodded in agreement with her.

Ann continued in an aggravated voice, stating, "Well, Abigail, the young high school girl who works part-time, was working. It was when Tiger almost jumped through the open window frame. I asked Abigail to put our dog in the number four cage until the window was finished. That fourth pen is one of our inside and outside runs with an animal door. Here's the issue. It turns out an overnight patient, Sydney, should have left that morning but didn't leave until early afternoon."

Don interrupted Ann, asking, "So, this has nothing to do with Sydney, Australia?"

Annoyed, Ann responded, "Donald, I'm struggling to tell you Abigail, our high school employee, put your female dog in pen number four with another dog, Sydney, who was probably outside in the run. When she discovered Sydney, the male Golden retriever, and Tiger were in the same cage, she immediately moved Tiger. But, at that point, they had already been together for an hour. None of the staff witnessed them doing the deed, but they were definitely in the same dog cage with time!"

Don, being Don, did not understand what his wife was alluding to, replying, "So?"

As professional as she could be, Ann explained, "Don, I did an ultrasound on our dog today, and I counted eight pups. I expect them to arrive at the end of the month. I assume Sir Sydney is the sire."

When a crow flies, between Brighton Township and South Lyon, Michigan, the distance is near nine miles. His wife was sure the residents at Blair House, including Aunt Fiery, heard Don's bellow, "WHAT! HOW THE HECK DID THAT HAPPEN — WE'RE SUING SOMEONE — THAT'S… " His tirade lasted awhile, going on, and on, and on… he stopped only to breathe.

Ann needed her husband to relax and understand that there was a much larger issue than Tiger's puppies. So, she said, "Sir Sydney Bothwell, the third, is a registered Golden retriever stud. Your hound, with no papers, appears to have mated with a pure breed without permission of the owners. Do you realize the legal trouble we may be in at our veterinarian hospital?"

Still fuming, he responded, "Well, who can I sue for this mess… you?"

Ann replied, "Don, calm down! This is serious! On Thursday, I'm meeting with Sydney's owners and Abigail to see how we can resolve this before the litter is born. They could claim, I deliberately told my employee to place Tiger with Sydney. Honestly, I did not know their dog was still there."

As he slowly came to his senses, he grinned, saying, "This gives us something to share with Aunt Fiery, Tiger's unplanned pregnancy. I think she might be amused by it!"

Sydney's owners were very understanding at Thursday's meeting. They didn't want Abigail discharged and only requested the pick of the litter if their dog was the sire. It relieved Ann as she averted a professional disaster. She explained how their attorney would draw up the formal agreement, and once signed, they could put this behind them.

On Friday, Ann asked Sarah if she could arrange for them to see her Ammygam sometime on Sunday afternoon. After a telephone call to her grandmother, Lucy agreed and even suggested that it wasn't necessary for either her or Sarah to be present at their visits. Fiery was comfortable with Ann and Don, and this would give her more visits if everyone came at different times. Lucy's only request was that they notify her granddaughter when they would be there.

On Sunday, they arrived at 12:30 p.m. and were pleasantly surprised to see Sarah waiting for them at the Blair House entrance.

She said, "I didn't want to miss the wonderful stories Ammygam only tells to Mr. Bryniarski."

When they entered the room, they noticed Fiery waiting for them at their usual table. Smiling, she went into great detail and explained the delicious lunch she had. Ann spent the first few minutes of their visit telling her of Tiger's pregnancy and how it happened. Fiery grinned and laughed at the story, but Ann thought she detected a tear in her eye. Unnoticed by the others, Don had placed his recorder on the square table.

There was a brief pause in the conversation when Sarah said, "Ammygam, last week when you were talking, you stopped saying, 'And then it happened'? What did you mean by that? Can you start there?"

Her great-great-aunt beamed. She looked directly at her, saying, "In early December, I received a letter from Alex. He wrote, 'We are all changed by this war, and maybe so is everything on the Homefront. I will come back to you!' He may have had a premonition. Or, now understood the challenges for me, raising Tiger's puppies, when she delivered them.

"I told you how she ran away and came home with a boyfriend. After a trip to the local library, I figured she'd have her pups between mid-December or early January. That winter night was chilly, windy, and miserable. Tiger and I had been walking for twenty minutes. We were on our way home around 8:00 p.m." It was then Fiery paused for a moment. She looked at Sarah, smiled, and said, 'And, then it happened.'"

Fiery turned her chair to the window's prospect and continued, as if speaking to herself, saying, "I never understood how it happened! One minute the two of us were on our normal evening walk, and then were home. I was daydreaming of Alex when an icy shiver ran down my back.

I felt a slight tug on Tiger's leash and let it go. The next thing I knew, she walked away. Tiger just walked away! I thought she hid somewhere to deliver her pups. With the help of my boarders in the house, we searched for hours. We checked everywhere but never found her.

"The following morning, we searched again before going to work, with no luck. That afternoon, Monday, December eighteenth, Miss Graves had a surprise Christmas brunch for her employees. She was determined to have holiday spirit in her office. We were all surprised and appreciated her special brunch treat. We understood Mr. Buhl wasn't happy when he heard of our lunch celebration. At exactly 11:00 a.m., a catering truck delivered us beverages, sandwiches, and holiday pastries.

"Now remember, Tiger walked away the evening before. Everyone at Miss Graves' brunch was full of Christmas spirit. I tried my best to enjoy the moment, but I couldn't put anything past her. She took me aside and questioned me: what was wrong? I explained to her my problem of losing Tiger last night, and she said she was very sorry to hear that. Then she asked me if I had heard from Alex.

"I mentioned he enquired about her and wanted to know if you're having trouble starting your car. Miss Graves laughed, remembering how he assisted her and started her automobile in the cold weather. I told her he was somewhere in France, near Belgium, and she asked me to say hello to him in my next letter. That evening, many neighbors on my street helped in the search for Tiger. We even tacked handwritten pieces of paper on telephone poles in and around the surrounding neighborhoods.

"Over the next two weeks, we continued to search for her and became nightly companions of our air raid warden, Mr. Volk. I always thought I would find Tiger on the back porch with her litter. Honestly, I wasn't looking forward to her having puppies, but I never wanted to lose her; I loved that dog. So how could I tell Alex I lost his dog?

"I was certain she would return… with her litter of puppies, but she never did. She was part of our family. What bothered me the most was I never learned what happened to her."

Don observed Fiery lift her hands from the journal on her lap, grasp the bracelet on her wrist, and press it to her bosom. He saw tears forming in her eye and watched the gold key fob dangle from her closed palm.

Fiery sighed and took a deep breath before saying, "December 31, 1944, was a Sunday. Like most Sundays that year, I was scheduled 7:00 a.m. to 11:00 a.m. The end of the year in southeastern Michigan is always gloomy, with pewter-like skies and a bitter stinging wind. The drive to Buhl Sons that day was terrible, and I was cautious. A light rain-snow mix had fallen during the night, making the roads a slushy, slippery mess. I was halfway to work when it started snowing again, making the drive worse.

"The sleet and ice on the road reduced forty-one's traction on the pavement, and I had to drive slowly to keep the car from spinning out of control. I told my ride-share co-workers that we would be late because I'd rather drive slower and not get into a wreck. Silently I prayed… may Alex forgive me if I smashed up his pride and joy. We were twenty-five minutes late for our shift. When we finally pulled in the Buhl lot, we saw a Western Union delivery boy in his olive drab uniform. He was carefully maneuvering his small motor scooter towards the front entrance.

"The morning went quickly. With my shift ending, I was getting ready to leave when Miss Graves stopped by my desk. She asked me to come with her. I explained I was sorry for being late, but the roads were a mess. As we walked, I told her I'd make up my missed half-hour tomorrow because I wanted to attend today's noon Mass at Saint Alphonsus. Miss Graves told me not to worry. She was glad I made it safely, and she stressed that Mr. Spencer wanted to see me.

"It was then I noticed her eyes were red and her face swollen. I understood she was ill and thought that must be the reason she looked terrible. I remember asking her if her cold was any better. She pulled a hanky from her pocket and wiped away tears. Then, solemnly she replied, 'No, now I feel awful.'

"We continued down the hallway, past Mr. Spencer's office, to the conference room at the end of the hall. I wondered why I was 'doing the walk.' Employees at Buhl Sons coined the phrase. They used it to describe the next of kin being led to or from the room where they were informed of their serviceman missing, wounded, or killed in action. During World War II, the government usually notified relatives of a serviceman's misfortune by sending a telegram to their home address.

"Back then, when you heard the putt-putt sound of a motor scooter in your neighborhood, you saw people peek out their curtains. They watched to see where the young Western Union messenger and his scooter would stop. Everyone prayed it was not for them. Nobody wanted the Grim Reaper's long boney finger to point at their family. In rare cases, those telegrams went to their workplace. During the past three years, I watched several men and women 'doing the walk' with a stunned ashen look on their faces.

"The conference room had white cardboard-covered windows with an exit door leading to the street. Earlier that Sunday, I saw a slender young lady escorted into the room. Soon after, I heard muffled screams radiating from behind the door. I prayed, please God, don't let that ever happen to me.

"But when I entered the conference room, I instantly knew I made… 'the walk.' Mr. Buhl himself was there, along with Mr. Spencer, and my Pastor, Father Tom. Before they could say anything, my stomach lurched, and my knees buckled as I fell to the floor. I remember feeling two people lift me up and set me in a chair by the table.

"Mr. Buhl spoke, explaining a telegram had come for me at my house after I left for work. He said, 'Your next-door neighbor told the boy where you were.' He told me how he had intercepted the Western Union messenger boy when he arrived at the company and hoped I didn't mind when he took the telegram from him. It was then Mr. Buhl said employees were an extension of his family, and whatever problems they had were his problems too!

"He asked me if I wanted him to read the telegram, and I nodded yes. In a solemn voice, he read, 'The Army Department deeply regrets to inform you that PFC Alexander Maze was killed in action on seventeen December, Ardennes Forest, Belgium. Harris, The Adjutant General.' Father Tom hugged and blessed me. Miss Graves did her best to offer condolences, but she was sobbing uncontrollably.

"Mr. Buhl spoke in a kind, caring voice… 'I can honestly say to you, Mrs. Maze, that I will never forget your husband, Alex. It was just a few years ago when he cooked hot dogs in the rain at our company picnic. I told him then I appreciated what he had done for me, the company, and our employees.' To this day, I still remember Mr. Buhl saying, 'I personally tried to keep Alex out of this war and keep his draft deferment at 1-H. I'll always regret that I couldn't stop the government.' Then I looked at him and realized his tear-filled eyes were all red.

"Mr. Buhl was composed, but I could tell he had been crying earlier. Mr. Spencer and Father Tom had tears streaming down their faces. Miss Graves was sitting in a chair next to me; her head was buried in her folded arms on the table as she sobbed hysterically. Oblivious to everyone around me, I slumped on top of the table and listened to myself repeating, I can't believe it… I don't believe it… it can't be true.

A few minutes later, I started to laugh, and remembered screaming… THIS IS LUDICROUS! This is some kind of mistake! Alex wasn't even in the infantry; he promised he'd be home after Christmas! Mr. Buhl was worried about me, and someone asked me if I needed a ride home. I told them I had my car, but I wanted to go to my parents. Father Tom said, 'Her parents live near the rectory; I'll drive her car to their house and walk home from there.'

"Glancing back at my priest, I asked, who's doing the late Mass? He responded, 'I've planned for Father Egbert to handle it.' Then, as though talking to myself, I whispered, Oh! How are the people I rideshare with going to get home? Miss Graves lifted her head off her arms, responding, 'I found them all rides.'

"Later, I found out she was the one who broke the news to my parents and contacted Father Tom. He had hitched a ride with a parishioner who lived near the Buhl Sons complex to be there with me. Miss Graves brought me my coat and hat, helping me to button it. I was numb; I couldn't or refused to process the information on my husband. Miss Graves hugged me real tight, and I heard her start to sob again. My pastor held me by my arm and led me out the door to the street.

"Walking up to forty-one, I said, here's my car, Father. He replied, 'My, that's a beautiful automobile, Fiery.' He always called me Fiery. I told him, yes, Alex and I both love it… it was then it hit me… my Alex was gone and wouldn't be coming home. Finally, I began to cry. Father Tom helped me into the passenger seat, and I reached for a tissue from the dispenser under the glove box. On the way to my parent's house, I thought of the last time I sat in the passenger seat… my husband was driving.

"I sat there staring at my gold bracelet… the one he threw to me as he was leaving for boot camp. I read and reread the inscription: To my darling Fiery, no matter what, we'll always be together; Love Alex."

Don watched as Fiery moved her hands to her lap and looked at the bracelet adorning her wrist.

She continued saying, "Father Tom pulled my car up to the curb in front of my parent's house. My parent's large pine tree on their front lawn was covered with ice and snow. The boughs hung down like the long shimmering white sleeves of a wizard overhanging their sidewalk and white picket fence. The tree seemed to beckon me while my mind replayed the scene of Alex jumping over that fence, clicking his heels on a bright summer day. Father Tom jolted me back to reality when he tried to open the passenger door and help me out of forty-one, but I resisted.

"My eyes became fixated on my feet, as I thought forty-one was Alex's car. I'm with him now… whenever I'm in it. The snow was falling in large quarter-size flakes as both of my parents waited for me on their front porch. I rolled down the window and yelled, I forgot my boots! They each tramped through the snow to the car's door, helped me out, and the four of us made our way up the stairs inside their house."

Fiery glanced over at Don, and he saw her forbearing face with her hand clutching the gold bracelet. The same bracelet Alex had given her so many years ago. She looked so unhappy with an understandably sad face.

She affirmed, "If you're wondering why I'm not crying, it is because I have cried a million tears before… there aren't any more tears left, only a heavy heart."

Don noticed Sarah and Ann with teary eyes and commented, "We might pause here or call it a day?"

Fiery took a sip of her juice and forcefully shook her head no. She responded, "I'm fine… I prepared myself to talk about this today."

Sarah wiped tears from her eyes and cheeks with a tissue and asked, "Ammygam, are you sure you're okay?"

Aunt Fiery chuckled, saying, "Every time I go down this road, it is bumpy, but then I guess it always will be. It's a part of my life and our story together." She studied each women's face, then turned to stare out the window, adding, "Before my husband left, we talked of the possibility of him not coming back. But I never expected or imagined it would happen to us, never this way.

"It was later in the evening, when I thought I was through grieving that I finally called Alex's mother. When his step-sister Violet answered, I could barely speak and started sobbing hysterically. Somehow, I got a few words out, telling her of her step-brother's death. I heard Violet scream for her mother to come to the telephone.

"When his mother, Bernice, picked up the receiver, a great calm entered me and told her what had happened. I listened to her heavy breathing; she was quiet, saying nothing. As I read the Western Union telegram to her, I struggled and almost broke down. I listened to my own words for the first time, speaking the dreadful news. When I finished reading the telegram, I wondered, did I just admit my husband was dead?

"Then, I remembered his mom was on the telephone; I asked Bernice if she was there? There was a pause, and a moment later, she started crying. Then she bellowed, 'My son, my son, I lost my Alex! My Alex is lost!' That's when my self-control abandoned me, and I felt myself trembling uncontrollably. I only controlled myself long enough to tell Violet I was staying at my mom and dad's place.

"I worried about his mother screaming and realized she lost a child, a son, a person she had given life to and knew for all thirty-one years of his life. How does a mother survive this loss? I had lost a husband, a best friend, the love of my life, a person I had known for eight years. I was comforted when I recalled they were the best years of my life.

"That evening, Bernice and Violet visited me at my parent's, where we wept together and consoled one another. I cried with her a week later when I saw the single gold star banner displayed in her window, symbolizing a relative killed in the war. I returned to my home Monday afternoon and found myself alone. There I was, in what was our house, now my house with no husband and no dog to comfort me.

"It was a frigid January day, but I didn't care as I made my way to the garage and opened forty-one's trunk. Inside were those two large wooden soda cases. We kept our small picnic and camping things in them. I started going through the items, removing them from the shells, when I came across a bottle top opener. I cried… and then laughed.

"Alex always forgot to bring an opener. I think that was the first time I noticed one shell labeled FANTA, the other Vernors Ginger Ale. I don't know why I began noticing and remembering those silly mundane details. Like the pliers we used to wire the food in place, double foil wrapping the meat, a card table, a cool box, wood folding chairs, tent, and the church-key.

"I was still in denial, and tears rolled down my cheeks. Finally, I forced myself to peer into the backseat. Then I removed the blankets we used to cover the seats and placed the wooden shells upside down on forty-one's rear floor, and made the bed. I intended this to be similar to when we were last together. It was a few months ago when we slept here in the country. I wanted to travel back into my dreams when my Alex held me in his arms.

"That day forty-one became my vehicle to take me to that other time. A time when Alex and I laid together right there where I was lying. When he had embraced me in his arms, and we talked of our future after the war. I laid in that backseat for hours remembering, crying, and realizing that I would never hear his soft voice or see him… ever again."

Aunt Fiery paused a moment, her eyes glassy, looking as if they were ready to flow tears.

Sarah interrupted, asking, "Why don't we take a break, Ammygam? Mr. Don needs a minute to stretch his legs."

Fiery broke from her dreamlike trance, responding, "Sarah, please ask one of the staff at the front desk to come and help me." Quietly, she continued, "I need to take a bathroom break." Then in a louder tone, she spoke directly to Don, asking, "Do you mind if we take a short recess?"

He agreed, saying, "Yes, let's do that… unless you'd rather we return another day?"

Don solemnly thought to himself this was the first time she suggested a recess instead of a break. He smiled, thinking she must consider us family, as she spoke openly of visiting the bathroom.

Fiery answered, "No, I only need a moment. I want to finish this chapter of my life."

Both Sarah and Ann started to wheel Fiery to her apartment, but she stopped them and asked a staff member to intervene. The two women returned to the table, shocked that she wanted a staff associate to help her.

Ann remembered something and commented, "Don, on your car's back seat is a box of chocolates. Do you mind getting it for us?"

As he rose to leave, he noticed Ann and Sarah's swollen, watery, and red eyes. Fiery's story had deeply saddened all of them. Walking outside to his car, he shook his head, pondering Fiery's loss. Within two-weeks, she lost her beloved pregnant dog Tiger and the love of her life, Alex. He thought to himself, how had Fiery and forty-one survived?

Chapter 22

My Things

Don found the chocolates in the backseat of his car and returned to the Blair House. On the short walk back, his mind wandered to the similarities between Fiery's story and his own. Many meetings ago, she had mentioned the best man at their wedding was named Teddy. By coincidence, Don's best man was his brother Teddy… a nickname he had called him since childhood. Each had a Golden retriever called Tiger. Both dogs were pregnant, but hers walked away. He vowed, from now on, to keep his Tiger on a leash.

He met Sarah at the entrance to the meeting room and gave her the box of candy.

She said, "Doctor Ann told me your Knights of Columbus Council appointed you Grand Knight. Congratulations! That must be a big deal."

He responded, "It's an honor just to be nominated… being elected is huge. Now I'm responsible for chairing our monthly meetings and fundraising to support the charitable work of the Catholic Church within our community. We also do events that support the youth of our community. They elected me to serve a one-year term, but most Grand Knights serve two terms. So we'll see how I do."

At the table, Don realized he had left the recorder on during their recess. He didn't want to confuse Nadine when she transcribed his meetings, so he returned the device to the start of the break. He then spoke into the device, saying, "Time 1:22 p.m., Sunday, May sixteen, middle of our fifth meeting with Aunt Donna… I mean Aunt Fiery. No, make that Mrs. Fiery Maze, Sarah, my wife Ann, and myself."

Fiery appeared tired as she was wheeled back into the room. Don discretely turned on the recorder and moved the aunt's journal closer to her place at the table.

Her face brightened when she saw Sarah opening the chocolates, asking, "Did you bring sweeties for me?"

It wasn't me, Ammygam. You can thank Mr. Don and Doctor Ann for this treat."

Fiery savored her sweetie, and soon the three women were talking about their favorite flavors.

Looking directly at Don and Ann, Fiery exclaimed, "Thank you for remembering me."

He watched as she selected another chocolate. She placed it with care on the napkin in front of her, and Don nodded his approval.

She looked at him, stating, "I'll have that piece later."

Ann leaned over and whispered in Fiery's ear, "Don't save it; enjoy it. You can take the leftovers to your apartment and eat them whenever you want."

Don made a mental note to thank his wife for bringing the candy. Fiery reached for the bonbon in front of her and took a nibble.

She watched Sarah eat her treat and commented, "When your grandmother was a little girl, I loved taking her to the candy store. I would give her five pennies and wait as she wisely and carefully selected her choice of penny candies."

Sarah was astonished and said, "Candy only cost a penny back then?"

As if on cue, Fiery finished her sweetie, grabbed her diary off the tabletop, opened it, leaned back, and turned her wheelchair to face outside. Everyone knew she was ready to continue her tale. Without asking the others if they were ready for her, she said, "During the next four days, I spent most of my time lying on forty-one's backseat bed. My best friend, Sylvia, knew that car was my connection to Alex. She couldn't stand to see me hurting. So she came out to the garage with hot soup, hot chocolate, hot tea, hot sandwiches, trying to make me drink and eat. But all I could do was cry.

"On my second straight day outside in forty-one, Sylvia came home from work and literally carried me into the house to get warm. We spent that Wednesday night alone in the kitchen talking; what she really did was listen to me. I told her it was my fault Alex had been killed. Boldly, I had proclaimed for anyone to hear, 'I would rather have a dead hero for a husband than a live coward.' Now those words haunted me, and I wished I had never uttered a word.

"I talked of the last time I saw my Alex and what he told me, 'We're never going to sell this car.' I talked for hours while she patiently listened as I argued with myself. I was numb, numb with fear of the unknown. It was my friend Sylvia who truly came to my rescue that night. Not only did she listen to me, but she also made me listen to her when she told me I was bitter. At first, I resented her calling me that. Sylvia explained I wasn't a bitter person, but I was bitter because I had no control over how my life had changed.

"Initially, I argued with her and told her how I was the one who shamed Alex into joining the Army with my cruel words. Suddenly she recited the phrase, 'Always be proud to live in this country. And, when this country needs your help in keeping America a great country, you should give it your best effort.' She asked me if I remembered my husband saying those words his father had said to him? I remembered…

"Sylvia recounted the scene in our living room when Alex said goodbye to her and our friends. She paraphrased him, saying, 'This is our country, and we're going to save it, and not speak German for the rest of our lives. We will die to win this fight. Everyone should do their duty for one reason, TO WIN THIS WAR! My job has changed, and I will work to fight and win this war.' She convinced me my husband had to go to war, not for me, but for his father!

"It was then I realized, some gave more than others. Bernice and I both surrendered a loved one. What greater sacrifice could a family make than surrendering a loved one for such a noble cause? It was then I vowed to snap out of my bitterness and make him proud! We spoke until 2:30 a.m. Thursday morning, and before going to bed, I did something important. I wrote a note for Sylvia to give to Miss Graves, it read; I will start work on Friday, Fiery.

"During the weeks that followed, my numbness diminished. Every night I walked, thinking that I might find Tiger or one of her pups one day, but that never happened. I found out what probably happened to my husband by reading the newspapers. During the first few days of a battle, Nazi Germany attacked the Allied forces in the Ardennes Forest.

"Many non-infantry soldiers were hastily assigned to quickly formed rifle platoons for emergency action. They needed to plug the holes in the Allied lines. Then, on December sixteenth, wintry weather hit, grounding our planes, and the Nazis attacked. Those lean, green, and untested Allied troops slowed them down. The Allies bent but didn't break.

"That's how this attack became known as the Battle of the Bulge. In the course of that fighting, my love, my Alex, was killed. They buried him in the American Battle of the Bulge cemetery near Neupre, Belgium. During the second week in January 1945, I had our pastor say a funeral Mass for Alex at Saint Alphonsus.

"During the homily, Father Tom said, 'How wonderful it is for a man in this land to give up his life, so democracy endures for others.' My sister Maureen, who was sitting next to me, nudged me, saying, 'Isn't that comforting?' Right there in the pew, I brusquely responded, 'That's just bullshit!' I resented the fact that my husband had to die and couldn't get over my guilt as I encouraged him to enlist.

"Our friends asked why I had allowed Alex to join the Army when he still had a 1-H deferment. They were certain he would never had been drafted. The war in Europe they felt would end by May or June. Their remarks only made me feel more guilty. For months, I told myself he was missing, in a hospital separated from his outfit, or heaven forbid a prisoner of war! I was unwilling to accept his death those first months and continued to deny it for many years.

"I was so used to thinking of our lives, our car, our dog, and our family. Now it was only forty-one and me. Tiger and Alex had left me; why didn't they take me with them? For weeks, months, and years after he died, I went to the garage and laid in forty-one's backseat.

"I found my solace there, in another era… a place with no tomorrow. Where Alex and I, husband and wife, two people in love and with Tiger, made happy family memories. Our car was the only family I had left."

Now Fiery glanced at Sarah with a patient smile and then at Don and Ann, saying, "I want to show you something. You see this?"

With those words, she held up her hand and dangled a worn gold round object. They eyed the object, trying to determine what she was holding.

He said, "Is that an old coin?"

Ann chimed in, "No, it's a… a thing that hangs from your pocket!"

Fiery remarked, "Yes, my fob. My husband gave it to me with a key for forty-one."

Don was startled. What is she doing with a key when she lives in a nursing home? So, politely, he asked if he could inspect the object.

Aunt Fiery responded, "I normally don't let anyone else touch this, especially the staff. Most of the employees are honest, hard-working people, but the others, those scoundrels, will take anything of value. The management here never listens to us when we complain or report them. The thieves disguise themselves as nurse's aides. They come and go, toiling at different nursing homes, where they pinch items from the residents they want or can sell."

Fiery's comments surprised Sarah, and she gave her a scowl as she declared, "Ammygam, you know that's not true. You have delightful friends here. They're always ready to help you!"

Not wishing to be manipulated, Fiery looked for support from Don and Ann. With none, she said, "I didn't say they were all unpleasant. I meant to imply only one or two are thieves."

Don noticed the exasperated expression on Sarah's face and quickly changed the subject interjecting, "May I look at your fob?"

Fiery grinned proudly, answering, "Only if you promise to give it back. And, I'm only letting you hold it to see if you recognize anything."

She handed the item to Sarah, who then gave it to Don. He displayed a smile of appreciation as he took the fob and examined it. He held it in his hands while looking at the object. The fob appeared similar in size and shape to a fifty-cent piece but gold with a single worn key dangling from the chain. He noticed the writing engraved on the fob and immediately recognized the sentimental value this object held for Fiery.

As if reading his mind, she said, "Yes… it used to hold all my keys, and now I have just one. For years I fell asleep holding it in my hand, dreaming of forty-one taking me to that place. Now they won't let me keep it here." With her last statement she scowled at Sarah.

Not understanding her comment, Don gave the object to Ann and jokingly said to Fiery, "So, you still have a key to forty-one?"

Ann looked up after hearing his question and handed the fob to Sarah, who returned it to her Ammygam.

Fiery placed her index finger to her lips and whispered just loud enough for those at the table to hear, "Shh! The key is my secret!"

They each laughed, thinking she was making a joke. Then Ann asked, "Would you mind us visiting next Sunday about the same time?"

She responded, "Oh! I would love that."

While the conversation was going on, Sarah handed Aunt Fiery a wrinkled brown paper bag. He watched as she leisurely removed her bracelet, placed it in the brown sack, and stared at the young girl with a question on her face.

As if knowing the question, Sarah answered, "Yes, Ammygam, your fob, and ring too."

With the items safely in the bag, Fiery wrapped the top closed and unwillingly handed it to her.

Fiery directed her next comment to Ann, saying, "I would love to see you next week. I so enjoy your company. Oh! And I have more to tell of Alex's family."

Ann took the box of chocolates, closed the lid, and placed it on top of the journal in Fiery's lap.

Aunt Fiery grinned and replied, "Thank you." As she noticed Don looking at the brown paper bag in Sarah's hand and remarked, "I told you, leave nothing here of value. The staff, you know."

Don smiled and whispered, "I know… the staff. Thank you, again, for telling us so much about your life, forty-one, and for allowing us to visit with you next Sunday. I want to thank Sarah for joining us, and please thank your grandmother, Lucy, for allowing us this personal time with Aunt Fiery."

Fiery acknowledged his compliment with a broad smile.

Sarah suggested, "Ammygam, may I take you back to your apartment?"

Her Aunt looked tired as she nodded yes. Before wheeling Fiery to her apartment, Sarah asked, "Doctor Ann, do you mind waiting so I can walk out with you?"

Ann nodded her head yes, as she leaned over to whisper a parting remark in Fiery's ear, chatting for a minute or two. Don, meanwhile, walked over and gave her a gentle hug, thanking her again for what she shared. While going to Fiery's apartment, Sarah stopped at a table to greet three women, kissing each on the cheek. They watched as Fiery offered each of them some chocolates. Each of the women turned and waved thank you to the Bryniarskis as they selected a sweetie.

They returned the wave and, under her breath, Ann quietly criticized him for giving a farewell type speech, like something he might say at work. He apologized, informing her that wasn't his intent. Instead, he told her how emotional the encounter had been for him. He explained that he never thought Fiery would speak of her husband's death while telling forty-one's story.

Don, being Don, couldn't resist getting the last sarcastic word and thanked Ann for the lesson. Ann wanted to respond to him but saw Sarah returning and held her tongue.

In the parking lot Sarah commented, "Ammygam was tired and is most likely napping by now. Thank you both for listening to her. You know, today was the first time I ever heard her talk of her husband dying. Wow, I think I'll go home and cry!"

Driving home, he mentioned his thought of bringing forty-one to Blair House for Fiery to see. He suggested Memorial Day, and his wife agreed. Don explained how Aunt Fiery's stories had touched him, and he now realized their vintage Chevrolet wasn't just another automobile. The car was special. He felt inspired to carry on her legacy. Not understanding the abrupt change in her husband, she begged him to clarify what he meant. The next twenty minutes he spent describing the admiration he developed for Fiery after listening to her life story.

Don's sudden hesitation about driving forty-one to car shows and not wanting to take a chance on damaging the auto stunned Ann. He asked her what she thought of possibly lending their 1941 Chevrolet Special Deluxe Sedan to a museum in Washington, D.C.? The museum was looking for funding for its new WW II Homefront exhibition. His change of heart pleasantly surprised Ann, and she suggested he contact their attorney, Bruno.

Ann mentioned Bruno needed to investigate any organization they may consider. Their top priority, now, had to be the safety of forty-one. Later that evening, Don reminded Ann of his business trip on Wednesday. He made sure she also added to her calendar his business trip for the following week on Wednesday, May twenty-sixth.

Ann looked at Tiger, then wrote in her day planner. Ann paused and looked up from her planner, "Tiger really misses you when you're gone on these trips. She's not the same when I'm the only one around. Oh, one more thing! When Nadine is finished with her transcribing, I would love to read her notes, okay?"

Don agreed as he downloaded today's recording of the meeting to his computer and made a disc for Nadine. The week flew by. On Thursday, Don was disappointed to call his wife and tell her he would not be back until Saturday morning. He asked how things were going and asked about Tiger. She confidently answered with her best veterinarian voice by saying Tiger was fine and right on schedule to deliver the first or second week of June.

Friday at work, Sarah greeted Doctor Ann with a brown paper grocery bag, asking if she would take this bag of clothes to her Ammygam on Sunday. She explained her grandfather was having health issues, and her Gammy Lucy had been caring for him and had no time for a visit this week. Sarah also had plans and wouldn't be able to visit. It delighted Ann they would have some alone time with Fiery and that they were trusted to deliver a package and eagerly agreed. Sarah mentioned they're now on her aunt's visitor list and only needed to call Blair House when planning to visit. The staff would notify Fiery to expect them.

"Ammygam," she remarked, "Truly enjoys speaking with you, or maybe it's your husband."

Ann laughed, saying, "You may be right… she does seem to like Don."

Ann asked Sarah what the bag contained. Sarah explained she didn't know, so together they looked. Inside, they found what looked like 1940s women's clothes, including brown slacks with a matching thin belt, a bright red long-sleeved cotton blouse, and a light brown sweater.

On the bottom, they found a pair of woman's vintage work shoes. Under the shoes was a man's large flannel shirt. On top of the shirt was the familiar-looking wrinkled brown paper bag containing Fiery's gold bracelet, ring, and key fob. Puzzled by the odd selection of items, Ann asked Sarah who chose these items.

She responded, "Gammy packed the bag according to Ammygam's wishes. She instructed my grandma not to put them in a box, as boxes draw too much attention. This had to be done just right." Now with an odd look on her face Sarah said, "What's funny; these are the only clothes she made us take from her house."

Sarah went on explaining how Fiery told her grandmother they were traveling to the falls. Lucy didn't question this as the Blair House occasionally scheduled day trips for their residents. However, it had surprised Lucy that her aunt had decided to go on this trip. Sarah described how it was years since her great-great-aunt had been on a scenic tour; she defaulted to the Blair House's decision if her Ammygam was okay to go.

Early Saturday morning, Don's plane arrived at the Detroit airport. Before heading home, he went to the Brighton sign shop, picking up the posters he had printed. He had ordered them the week before and hoped to show them to Fiery tomorrow.

They were up early the next morning and attended early Mass. After church, Ann wanted to check on Tiger before going to the Blair House. She explained Tiger was acting strange, and she was a little worried. Arriving at their farmhouse, they found her fine and happy to see them. Don put Tiger on a leash and walked her around the yard as his wife prepared breakfast.

Before they knew it, it was time to leave. As Don and Ann were pulling out of the driveway, Ann remembered she had forgotten to bring the bag Sarah had given her. She made her husband go back, and he retrieved the paper sack from her car. She explained how Lucy packed it for her aunt as he drove. Fiery was waiting in the dining room when they arrived.

She was facing the window at what Mrs. Fiery Maze considered being 'their table' and didn't notice them until they walked over and said hello.

Ann placed the brown grocery bag and a small box of expensive chocolates on the table. Don proudly leaned his large signs wrapped in white paper against one chair. Fiery was genuinely pleased to see them as they greeted and hugged her. Then he placed his recorder next to the candy, noticing a worn journal was already in Fiery's lap. She thanked them for the chocolate and peered into the paper sack as if taking inventory, wanting to make sure nothing was missing.

Ann stated, "I was to remind you inside is a smaller bag containing your bracelet, ring, and key fob. Sarah told me those were for your trip."

Fiery ignored her comment and said, "Oh! Thank you for bringing my things." Then more quietly, she declared, "I will not wear my bracelet today. They might see it, you know, the thieves!"

Hoping to change Fiery's mood, Don picked up his signs wrapped in the heavy white paper. The posters were forty-eight by twenty-four inches, enclosed in transparent plastic, making them weather and waterproof. As he unveiled them, he explained the car shows and how he intended to use the posters. Don desperately wanted her approval and spent a moment reading the poster to her. He read:

"1941 Chevrolet Special Deluxe (The Honeymoon Car)

"Alex Maze purchased this Chevrolet Special Deluxe brand new in March 1941. He took delivery of this automobile on August 20, 1941. Five days later, on August 24, Alex and Donna Maze of Dearborn, Michigan, were married. They drove this car on their honeymoon to Niagara Falls.

"The couple enjoyed driving this Chevrolet. In early 1942 World War II halted the production of civilian passenger automobiles. Alex and Donna were glad they purchased the car, and their friends were envious they had a new Chevrolet.

"From 1941 to 1944, Alex drove this Chevrolet to his job as a tool & die maker at Buhl Sons Corporation, a war armaments manufacturing plant in Detroit. In January 1944, Alex joined the U.S. Army. At the age of thirty, married, and holding a job as an essential war worker, he could have kept his deferment; instead, he chose to serve his country. On December 17, 1944, he was killed in Luxembourg during hostile action, in what would become known as the Battle of the Bulge."

He explained how he would display the sign near forty-one's grill at the auto shows they attended. Although she never said it, Fiery had little interest in the posters. But she took a moment to quiz him of his plans to show forty-one. He confessed they had only a single show planned this year, next week's Howell Memorial Day Parade. He mentioned their plans to bring her car to Blair House, asking her if she approved.

She eagerly commented, "It's nice of you to reunite me with forty-one; we can go home. Now, when is that day?"

Don answered, "That will be eight days from today. Not tomorrow, next Monday."

They watched as she moved her wheelchair to gaze out the window, saying, "That car will always have a place in my heart." Then she spoke, spending fifteen minutes telling them about all the people who wanted to buy her forty-one. She described how new cars were scarce when the war ended. She explained how people worked so much overtime in the war armament factories they had lots of money to spend. These car-starved people offered to pay cash for her car, most times offering more money than Alex originally paid for it.

Over the next ten years, she consistently declined their offers. Individuals thought she was selfish not selling forty-one, but she never responded or told them her reason. Aunt Fiery spent another thirty minutes telling about her bitterness for the war and how it changed the government. Her scorn reached the boiling point when she read in the *Detroit Times* that the U.S. was sending aid to Germany.

Fiery went into great detail regarding the irony of the Marshall Plan. She and most of her friends did not support rebuilding Europe. The B-24 and B-26 airplanes were the very planes she and Sylvia built to win the war. She watched them now being scrapped to rebuild the country we defeated. Fiery offered her unsolicited opinion on our country's leaders. She felt they were more interested in saving their political careers.

Their speeches were of how nice it was to help the country that killed millions. She told how the politicians spoke flowery speeches to cover up the stink of their deeds. They did little to help the American people, according to her. She understood the balance of power was similar to before the war, except today, Russians are the enemy.

Fiery told them how she reached rock bottom as she considered her situation. Her husband was dead, and not one damn thing had changed! This ate away at her, and her grief became self-destructive. But finally, she held herself by devoting her time to volunteering at the veteran's hospital, seeking friendship with other women who lost their husbands in the war.

Not stopping with her post-war stories, she exhausted another fifteen minutes on her father retiring. In May 1946, her parents moved to Appleton Street in Dearborn Township. They purchased an old farmhouse in the country with three bedrooms, indoor bathrooms, and a small chicken coop. How could they sell her childhood home and leave to raise chickens? She felt abandoned and laughed when they told her they would live out there but still remain parishioners of Saint Alphonsus. Every Sunday, they had to drive six whole miles to church!

Tears were in her eyes when she spoke of Alex and the big decision she made in March 1948. She had saved the installment checks from her husband's $10,000 government insurance policy. Fiery planned to use the money to have his body moved from France and shipped back to Michigan. She had Alex's remains re-interred at St. Hedwig Cemetery in Dearborn in September 1948.

Before his reinternment, she made preparations with the local undertaker to open his coffin and place his Purple Heart ribbon inside. The government had given this to her for his sacrifice. That day she gave his mother, Bernice, her son's actual heart-shaped gold medal. Fiery explained how she would never forget the sound of his mother Bernice crying! That day, they cried again.

Fiery described how she had enough money to buy an impressive headstone and reserve a burial place next to him for herself. She explained how her husband believed in a circle of life and how people you really love never die; their spirit lives on. She knew they would reunite in her afterlife. With more tears, she told them how, within three short months of 1948, she buried both of her parents and re-interred her beloved husband.

In her casual tone, she said, "My Alex will come for me driving forty-one. He'll have Tiger, and together we'll go home!"

Ann responded, "What a beautiful dream."

Her words broke Fiery's concentration, and she turned to Ann with a smile.

Ann continued, "I believe it's time for a sweetie!" Reaching for the candy on the table, opened the box offering a piece to Fiery.

She agreed, saying, "Yes, a brief break." She selected a chocolate and whispered, "Thank you."

After finishing her treat, she sat back in her chair, and Don immediately noticed her change. She didn't peer out the window, and her voice had a casual tone. Fiery now recounted the story of how Lucy came to live with her. With a melancholy tone, she explained in great detail her sister Maureen's failed marriage and her struggle with mental health. Fiery described moving in with her parents in 1947, how they adopted Lucy, losing both of them the following year, and how she stopped driving forty-one.

With a happier tone, Fiery spent twenty minutes describing how she drove forty-one; one last time because of a tree falling on her garage. She paused, then looked at Don and told him how forty-one stalled in front of his parent's house, how his mother walked in front of her car touching and kissing forty-one's hood ornament as Alex did. She remembered the day as Monday, June twenty-second, 1959, it was the day Lucy and her traveled by train to Florida for Sylvia's wedding.

Aunt Fiery continued to speak for another thirty minutes about her best friend, Sylvia. She recapped her friend's life, relationship with her family, and her death, after which she paused with tears in her eyes.

Ann seized the opportunity to suggest, "Aunt Fiery, you've been talking for a while. Maybe you can save your other stories for next week?"

Fiery looked at her, saying, "Yes, you're right, I've been blabbing too long. But just let me finish my thoughts."

She explained how sad she felt when her niece Lucy told her it was time to move into a nursing home. It was when she no longer could cook for herself and how she reluctantly agreed. She wanted them to know that she never sold her parent's house or forty-one.

Fiery said, "It was this place they're thieves they took my things from me, all of them." Fiery appeared unhappy and discouraged when saying those words.

Changing the topic, she asked Ann to put another of her journals in forty-one's trunk. Then she asked Don to leave the card table, folding chairs, and Alex's camping equipment in the car, explaining she wanted to see them one more time. Ann promised her, as long as they owned forty-one, her possessions would remain with the car. She heard Ann's words, and her face lit up with an enormous smile.

Don wondered if he might use her things at an auto show. Perhaps he could show how they cooked on the manifold. Fiery waved at a Blair House staff associate and asked to be taken back to her apartment in five minutes.

The staff associate departed when Fiery remarked, "We each have to leave this world sometime. When I do, you can remove my things from forty-one's trunk. And when I leave, the employees here are going to remember me."

Don saw her wipe tears from her eyes when she asked them each for a hug. Ann placed the box of chocolates on her lap and embraced her, thanking her for sharing the stories.

Don embraced her and reminded her they would see her next Monday with forty-one. She softly spoke to him, saying, "I haven't been down that road in a long time. Thank you for listening; you helped me so much." Then in an uncommon tone, she remarked, "I look forward to seeing forty-one next week, and Don, I'll help you when you're in a tight spot, with no damage." The slight grin on her face barely showed when she stated, "Be patient, going up and down, one, two, three."

He watched as the nurse's aide came and wheeled Fiery back to her apartment. He was more confused than ever. Then he felt sad, not remembering if he said goodbye to her. He did remember telling her they would bring forty-one here next Monday, Memorial Day. Before placing his digital recorder in his pocket, he spoke into it for the purpose of Nadine's transcription.

He said, "This concludes our sixth meeting, with Donna Fiery Maze on Sunday, May twenty-third, 2004. Attending were Mrs. Fiery Maze, Ann Bryniarski, and myself, 2:30 p.m. adjourned."

While driving home, he made a mental note to ask her on Memorial Day what she meant when she said, "I'll help you when you're in a tight spot? No Damage?" He was perplexed. When could she help him?

Chapter 23

They're Gone

The last flight from Washington, D.C. to Detroit on that Wednesday night was one to remember. Don and three team members were returning with a signed contract for the first eighteen X-Fi machines. Seventeen of them would go to the busiest airports in the United States, the other to Washington National to detect explosive devices. Don was proud of what they accomplished and thought this product could take the corporation's stock public making him a wealthy man. However, these thoughts came to an abrupt halt when the plane shook violently and threw unsecured items around the cabin.

This wasn't normal turbulence, and his brain immediately shifted to his own mortality, to Ann, and thoughts of Fiery. He wasn't ready to lose any of these! He replayed Fiery's theory of life in his mind. Her belief was we have no control over when we are born or, to a certain extent, when we die. According to her, the only person we are guaranteed to spend the rest of our lives with is ourselves. So, she rationalized, we better get along with ourselves!

Don was always grateful for everything he had achieved, but at that moment, he realized he needed to enjoy who he was. He needed to change and start appreciating those around him. Trying to take his mind off of what was happening with the airplane, he pulled out Nadine's transcription she had given him as he left the office yesterday. The transcript was of Sunday's meeting with Fiery.

Quickly scanning the notes, he stopped when Fiery started speaking about her best friend, Sylvia. How the two young women had met, Sylvia being almost famous, working on war bond drives, volunteering at the USO club. Don's attention was suddenly drawn to a date on the page, June twenty-second, 1959. The day Fiery drove forty-one for the last time, she saw his mother, and left for Florida to attend her friend's wedding. Not to mention it was the day he was born! He asked himself, was this another coincidence?

The plane continued to bounce, and Don kept on reading to distract himself. When Sylvia's fifth marriage failed eight months later, she sold the restaurant and moved back to Michigan to be closer to her sons and grandchildren. She loved being active and meeting new people, so she began attending senior citizen dances near her home in Farmington. Fiery couldn't believe it when Sylvia married and divorced two men she met at these dances.

Although her pal had more money than she ever needed, her friend became a miser. She told Fiery she remembered being a six-year-old girl, wondering where her next meal would come from. Not wanting to be that girl again, she never spent any of her money. Sylvia's oldest son only came over when he wanted money, and her friend became bitter.

Her other son, Jim, was different. He constantly looked in on her and expected nothing. But Jim's kids always asked their grandmother for things they wanted or money to buy those things. Again, when Sylvia stopped giving, her grandchildren ended their visits.

As Don read, he remembered seeing Aunt Fiery get misty-eyed when she told them how in December 1990, Sylvia fell and broke a hip. Sylvia appeared to be doing well when Fiery first visited her in the hospital. She was in good spirits and expected to be released the following week when Fiery left for her planned trip to Chicago. But her health took a turn for the worse. Upon returning from her trip, Jim called, saying his mother had picked up an infection, and she was dying.

Fiery immediately returned to her friend's bedside. When she entered the room, she was shocked at what she found. Sylvia was unrecognizable in her hospital bed. Her best friend was a frail, pallid, old woman with white hair, eyes closed, mouth open, and moaning. Don couldn't take his eyes off the transcript and went on reading Fiery's words.

Jim's wife entered the room and smugly declared her husband would finally get the money he deserved. Fiery joined her at Sylvia's feet, watching the girl stare at her mother-in-law. Then Sylvia's daughter-in-law said, "Not a beautiful way to die? I never liked her, and she never liked me. Can you believe it, she married seven times?" After being in the room only a couple of minutes, the daughter-in-law left, declaring, "I'll leave you girls alone so you can say your goodbyes."

Fiery was glad to see the woman leave and whispered in Sylvia's ear: "I'm sorry for this, but thank you for being a swell friend my entire life. You are the best girlfriend I ever had."

The next day Jimmy called saying he was clearing out his mom's house and found a card table and chairs with Fiery's name written on them. He asked her to please come over and take them. He was there waiting for her, at his mother's home. Jim had thrown out or donated most of his mother's belongings and had already sold the house. In the living room stood three boxes, all that remained of her friend's possessions. He boasted how an appraiser was coming over to see the antique figurines and her jewelry.

He offered Fiery a box containing framed photos of her friend and Jim's family. To save them from the dumpster, she took them home. Five days later, Jimmy called, telling her his mother had finally died.

After hearing the mournful words, she went into the garage, moved away forty-one's tarp, opened the door, slid into the passenger seat. She described pulling a tissue from the dispenser to wipe her eyes. Then, staring out the windshield, she thanked Alex for making the correct decision not to leave her with a child. She then said a silent prayer for her friend, Sylvia, the woman who saved her.

The plane shook and dropped what felt like one hundred feet just as Don finished reading the transcript. Fiery believed God had a unique plan for each of us. She told them how she lived her life as healthy as possible while preserving memories from her past. She kept up with the present while keeping an eye on the future and explained how she always tried to help bring happiness to others.

Don remembered the way Fiery described Alex. He was a real guy who believed in God, was proud to be an American, someone who loved his country and the world he lived in. She spoke of how much she and her husband enjoyed each other's company. She reasoned Alex's spirit was within forty-one, and that's why her Chevrolet special deluxe never let her down. If a car could be a loyal friend, forty-one was hers.

Don considered her words as the plane bounced. Perhaps it was the plane shuttering that made him wonder what could make him and forty-one the happiest? What should he do? He came to realize that an antique automobile such as forty-one helped others relive their lives, learn the history of another time, and that car now had a written record of the lives of ordinary folks. It became plain to him he needed to tell Fiery's story to others almost as important as it was for her to pass on her story to him.

He considered writing a book of two working-class people who used, enjoyed, and loved their auto. But then he realized the best way to share forty-one's story may be to loan the car to a prewar museum. He could never sell her! Don always wanted to have control over what happened to their antique 1941 Chevrolet. He made a mental note to ask Fiery how she would feel, knowing her precious car was being seen and shared with so many other people?

He reflected on her words to him at their last meeting when she said, "I hope I don't cause you trouble up and down, one, two, three." Although he didn't understand her message, he was more troubled not remembering if he said goodbye to her. Then he wondered if he had said something to make her mad. Soon he brushed the thoughts away, reasoning she was probably tired. He hadn't noticed how much time had passed until the flight attendant announced their final approach to the Detroit airport.

The plane landed and was taxing to the terminal's gate when he recalled Fiery believed in the afterlife. There Alex, their dog Tiger, and forty-one would reunite with her. He snickered to himself, wondering what dreams he may have at eighty-seven.

It was near 11:30 p.m. when he finally arrived home. Tiger welcomed him by wagging her tail, jumping over him, and getting her leash; she was ready for a walk. He located Ann in her favorite family room chair with her red leather journal and one of Nadine's transcripts in her lap. She was resting her eyes. When he went outside with Tiger, the closing door startled Ann.

She walked over and into the garage to investigate, where she found her husband standing behind forty-one. She joined him there. Still half asleep, she held his waist as they walked on their asphalt driveway. Don laughed as he watched Tiger sniff her way in the yard and frolic happily on the grass. When they reached the dirt road, they stood there in the moonlight, greeting each other with a hug and kiss.

He turned to Ann, saying, "I had a dream forty-one was in an exhibition hall."

Ann was half-asleep when she commented, "We'll talk tomorrow."

They strolled up the driveway, where she gave him a gentle squeeze and headed into the house and to bed. He stayed outside for another fifteen minutes before he could convince their pooch, it was time to sleep. On Thursday evening, as they lounged in the family room chairs, he broached the subject of donating forty-one to a museum. Don admitted he enjoyed driving the 1941 Chevrolet but was now afraid something was going to happen like an accident.

Then he confessed to Ann how he now considered the antique automobile was not really theirs. Ann looked at him puzzled as he explained how he felt they could never enjoy or love that auto the way Aunt Fiery did. He again mentioned loaning it to a museum with Fiery's approval.

She stated, "You need to speak with our attorney and explore all the ramifications of such a serious decision."

He responded, "I've spoken to Bruno several times. I even gave him a name of a museum and person I met in Washington to investigate. He told me the museum and person were legitimate."

As their discussion continued, Don revealed what was bothering him. He wanted the 1941 Chevrolet Special Deluxe to stay in the state. After all, forty-one is a Michigan car, and she should remain here.

"If you're serious," Ann said, "Forty-one's last show should be the one at the Traverse City Cherry Festival, a month from now. Our friends Bill and Kathy always treated us so nicely when we were there. So it would be a fitting tribute to have the car's last public showing at the Old Towne Car show."

He added, "I'll speak with our attorney tomorrow about a loan contract to a museum if he has time." He reasoned, "I told Bruno, we need to be certain after we loan or donate it; they have to display her and not store or sell the automobile." Ann agreed, saying, "We both want to preserve the car for Fiery's sake. But I don't think we should say anything to her of our plans."

He acquiesced to her, for now. Then, their discussion turned to the weekend and what they needed to get done. Don reminded his wife how he hired Matt, the son of a friend, to clean and wash forty-one on Saturday. He explained how he wanted it to look especially grand for Monday's parade, but mainly for their visit to Aunt Fiery.

All the while he was speaking, his wife was keeping a close eye on their dog. She thought Tiger would have her litter in a week or two. She asked him to stack the spare wire cages in the garage in the shape of a square pen to keep her pups together. He promised to prepare the birthing area.

At work the following day, he understood everyone was anxiously looking forward to starting their long holiday weekend. At nine that Friday morning, he brought his directors in for a quick conference. He told them that their non-essential employees may leave at noon and would be paid for the entire day in the meeting. The workforce welcomed this surprise. Somehow, they soon discovered the decision had been made at a board meeting thanks to Don's insistence.

Before leaving the office that afternoon, he checked in with his wife at the clinic. Sarah answered the phone and thanked him for visiting with her Ammygam last Sunday. She told him of her visit the day before and how her aunt mentioned she looked forward to seeing forty-one Monday. He felt good hearing her say those words. But, in her speech, he sensed something wrong, asking her if there were other concerns?

She took a moment to describe her Ammygam's cough. Explaining how the Blair House doctor considers it a common cold, but her grandmother, Lucy, didn't like the sound of the cough. He inquired of her great-great-aunt's overall health. Sarah assured him she was well and reminded him to give the Blair House a call on Monday before going so her aunt could be ready when they visited.

She mentioned, "My aunt showed me the clothes, fob, ring, and bracelet you brought and told me she was going to wear them on her journey home." Sarah laughed, saying, "I think she says one thing and means another. Ammygam is dreaming. I checked with the front desk.

With the current threat of terrorism, they have no trips planned. Oh! Just a minute, the doctor is out of her client meeting."

Ann picked up the telephone and listened as he told her of their half-day off and that he was heading home. She urged him to check on their dog when he came home. An hour later, he found Tiger as playful as ever, displaying no sign of delivering her pups. Saturday morning, Matt arrived early to detail forty-one and put a car wax coat on her. After five hours, Don was so impressed with the young man's work he asked him to return in a week and detail his 1959 white Ford convertible. Since being hurt in an auto accident years earlier, Matt's only income was detailing cars. Don paid him cash with a generous tip.

After he left, Don stood back to admire the antique automobile. Clean and shining, he thought, this is what Fiery and Alex admired decades ago. Tiger followed his gaze and appeared to give her approval. He hoped Fiery would approve! The following morning after Sunday Mass, Don did a few overlooked chores around the house and outbuildings. Then he went into the garage and cleaned a space in the corner, Ann suggested, arranging the spare animal cages to make a square birthing pen for Tiger and her expected pups.

When his wife came out, she placed forty-one's tarp inside the enclosure because Tiger always enjoyed laying on it. A two-by-eight-inch wood board five-foot-long blocked the opening. This allowed Tiger access to the pen while keeping her anticipated puppies safely within. A large cardboard box completed the area. Ann gave their pooch time to inspect the area, and she seemed to approve.

The only thing Tiger hated was her leash, so Don tied a fifty-foot nylon rope extension to it. The extended cord allowed her to roam further away while tethered. It was nearly eight in the evening when they finally stopped to admire their work.

Before going inside, Ann looked over forty-one and commented, "It looks nice! I hope Aunt Fiery thinks so too!"

Both were exhausted and relaxed in the family room. They sat down to discuss their plans for tomorrow's Memorial Day Parade and their visit to Fiery. They agreed to leave no later than 7:30 a.m. tomorrow. After a hectic day, it was near 10:00 p.m. when they went to bed.

As she soundly slept, Ann's one hand extended out over their bed's edge. She awoke feeling Tiger's cold, wet nose pushing her fingers and heard her whine, wanting to go out. The clock on the bedside table read, 1:11 a.m. She attempted to wake her husband to tell him his dog needed to go outside, but he didn't respond. Half asleep, she glided her feet into his convenient slippers and put on his thick white terry-cloth robe before trudging down the stairs.

At the backdoor, she secured the leash to the dog's collar and tried to remove the leash's rope extension but was unable. They went outside through forty-one's now opened garage door, and Tiger scurried out into the yard. Ann followed the dog, not noticing the yellow cord untangled, allowing the pooch to walk further onto the grass. It was a beautiful night to be outside, cool but comfortable.

Holding the brightly colored rope with a firm grip, she lumbered over to a lawn chair and sat down, waiting for Tiger to finish. Wanting to be cozy, she pulled the robe's hood over her head, laid back, and was soon asleep. In her dream, Ann heard the male voice call, "Come girl, come on, Tiger." She felt a slight tug on the rope and let go. Confident Don had taken Tiger inside; she fell into a deep sleep.

The clock read 5:23 a.m. when she returned to the bedroom. She was mad at her husband for letting her sleep outside. She immediately woke him to discuss her displeasure. Half-asleep, he did not know what she meant. Ann was sure he had brought Tiger inside the house. While getting dressed, he again told his wife, he didn't even know they had gone outside.

Now they worried, so they searched the entire house and garage, including the birthing area. But Tiger was nowhere to be found. It was a half-hour before sunrise when they began exploring the yard and surrounding woodland, only to find the yellow nylon cord on the lawn. Ann suspected she had wandered away to give birth to her litter. The couple continued to search for over two more hours before realizing they were late for the Memorial Day parade.

They were now forty-five minutes late in leaving when she reminded him they should have left at 7:30 a.m.

Ann commented, "If you want to skip the parade, let me know now! Dogs have pups, all the time. Tiger is capable of defending her pups in the woods. We can keep the garage open for her. But right now, I need to shower!"

Don decided they would go to the parade if Ann was quick washing up. While Ann showered, he looked under shrubs, bushes, trees, and even in their barn. Ten minutes had passed when he returned to their farmhouse to make coffee. As he entered the house, Ann was just coming out holding two travel mugs of coffee.

While he pulled forty-one from the garage, Ann locked the garage's entry door into the house, closed forty-one's bay, and opened the door, exposing her car. Her thought was neighbors seeing the car would think someone is home while Tiger could access the garage when she returned. Each kept an eye out for their pooch as they drove away. It was 9:14 a.m. when they arrived at the staging area. Don checked them in and was assigned position number twenty-three. A team of volunteers quickly directed them to their assigned spot.

With the morning's confusion, he realized they hadn't eaten breakfast, his wife only had a piece of toast, and both of them had forgotten their cellular telephones. Don calculated he had twenty-five minutes before they would start moving, giving him just enough time to get them a snack. So, he walked over to the local gas stations, where he picked up two cups of coffee and the last edible bagel sandwich. It was then he remembered he didn't attach the posters he had made to forty-one.

Hurrying back to the car, he handed Ann the coffees and sandwich through her open window and went to the trunk removing the two large signs. Next, he attached a now magnetized poster to each side door of their automobile. Don slid behind the wheel with only a second to spare when he was signaled to move ahead.

His wife asked, "What were you doing back there?"

He smiled and chuckled, "I put the magnetic tape Matt gave me on the reverse side of the posters and placed one on each door."

The parade halted just as they turned onto Grand River, and Ann used the delay to leave the vehicle for a quick look at the posters. She complimented him on how well they looked on forty-one. Then, the procession started moving again, which was their cue to roll down all the car's windows and turn the heater on high. As veteran parade participants, they knew this helped dissipate the car's engine heat, helping to prevent it from overheating. Today Don and Ann appreciated the car's heat as it was an overcast day with temperatures in the mid-sixties. The couple smiled and waved to the crowds lining the street as they rode in the parade. He reminded his wife to watch for children going after the candy thrown from the floats ahead. He never liked the idea of throwing candy but knew the children loved it. Halfway along the route, a slight mist fell over everyone.

While driving the event route, they discussed the possibility of permanently loaning forty-one to a museum. Somehow their conversation always returned to Tiger and where she might be. They were both eager to resume their search for her but agreed they should first eat at a restaurant, rationalizing it would be quicker than making something at home. With the parade over, Don stopped for gas. The twenty dollars he spent moved the fuel gauge to three quarters.

He drove several side streets before arriving on East Clinton Street, a block from the Grand River diner. Once parked, they rolled up the Chevrolet's windows in case of rain and placed the posters in the trunk. From there, it was a quick walk to the crowded diner. When Ann entered, several patrons recognized her and said hello. The well-dressed doctor thought to herself, thank goodness I took a shower and changed.

Then she looked over at her husband. He looked dirty, disheveled, and upset. If this were hunting season, he would easily be mistaken for a hunter who spent three days at a remote camp deep in the woods without bathing. Ann introduced him to a few people, to whom he was cordial, but he was hungry. Don wanted to eat and go home. He had to find Tiger!

When they left the restaurant, they soon realized they had walked the wrong way to their car. Turning around, they walked in the opposite direction but still couldn't find their car. Desperate to find their auto, they decided to circle the block going in opposite directions, just in case they made a mistake. Halfway around, they met each other. Expressing their shock, they continued to walk in opposite directions, now thinking the worst.

Their full circle completed, they met up once more. Each was now certain this is where they parked her. Don thought this couldn't be happening to them! This kind of thing didn't happen in their town! Topping things off, Don couldn't find his car keys; what a day, ugh!

Don and Ann walked ten minutes to the police station. While walking, they kept looking, hoping to find their 1941 two-door ruby maroon sedan parked along their route. Don listed out loud his reasons someone should never steal his vintage Chevrolet. Hard to start, difficult to drive, no power steering or power brakes, it had lots of blind spots, and those skinny wipers barely removed the water from the windshield when it rained, and that's only for starters.

They arrived at the municipal building to find themselves first in line. It was a slow day for the police department. They partially filled out the forms but would need to return tomorrow to complete the missing information. While they were there, Ann insisted they fill out a lost dog report hoping it would help them find Tiger.

At the station, Ann used the payphone to call the Blair House, wanting to let Fiery know they wouldn't be able to visit her today. She asked for Mrs. Maze; the individual informed her that she wasn't there. Ann left her a message and assumed Lucy took Fiery to see another doctor, forgetting today was a holiday. The police department kindly provided the Bryniarskis with a ride home. While riding in the cruiser's backseat, Ann spoke of how Aunt Fiery would react when she found out somebody stole her beloved car. Her comment made the officer ask if her aunt may have taken the automobile? They laughed, explaining Aunt Fiery lived in a nursing home and was eighty-seven years old. As if thinking aloud, Don commented, "I can't understand why anyone would steal an antique auto that is so difficult to start and drive."

They arrived home, finding the garage looking empty with no forty-one and no Tiger to greet them. He circled the house, calling for their pooch. With no response, he went inside their farmhouse and put on his boots. He returned outside, searching the woods and wetlands near and beyond their property. He met his spouse an hour later on a woodland trail while she too looked for Tiger!

Ann stopped a moment to apologize for thinking he left the keys in their vehicle. In the excitement, she had forgotten he had locked the car and, for safekeeping, gave her the keys. Each went on their separate ways, knowing they could cover more ground that way. They met up at home three hours later. When neither had come back with Tiger, they worried.

That evening he called a local radio station asking them to make a public broadcast concerning their lost dog. The station's broadcasted message never generated a response.

Ann printed flyers announcing a reward for finding their dog. Don continued to look in the woods and wetlands. Meanwhile, Ann delivered lost dog notices to neighbors, local businesses and even tacked them on telephone poles. Finally, when it was too dark to continue, they retrieved forty-one's registration and title. Together they drove to the Howell police station. There they completed the paperwork for their stolen 1941 automobile. Unfortunately, their worry over losing a cherished pet and their beloved antique auto on the same day took them away from their normal daily routine.

The next morning, before sunrise, Don and Ann again went out looking for Tiger. They returned home after two hours. Ann printed more lost dog flyers before leaving for work. He took those leaflets and walked up and down the streets near their home, placing one in every mailbox he came upon. When he ran out, he returned home to get ready for work. It was June first, and he had a busy day scheduled.

He called the office to let them know he was running late and then noticed it. Their answering machine's red light was blinking, signaling six messages arrived. The first five were from yesterday. Each was inaudible and sounded like someone crying. The sixth message was this morning from Ann. She asked him to call her at work.

When he returned her call, he expected to hear Sarah answer, but Ann was the one who answered. Her voice sounded serious, which concerned him.

She then said, "I have terrible news."

His mind started swirling! Was Tiger dead, or was forty-one smashed up in an accident? He never had time to answer himself.

Ann continued, "Aunt Fiery died yesterday morning at 1:23 a.m."

Stunned, he sat on a kitchen chair, shaking his head. He took a moment to reply, asking, "What happened? Oh! I am so very sorry. Why didn't they let us know?"

His wife replied, "Don, Sarah tried to call us yesterday but couldn't leave a message. She said, 'When she went to speak, she started crying.'

But listen, there may be a bigger problem. They can't find Aunt Fiery's remains. A ninety-five-year-old resident named Katherine passed away three hours before Aunt Fiery.

"They assumed the crematory picked up both of the women's bodies. Fiery had prepaid her burial expenses. You know her last wish was to be buried next to her husband, and the Blair House staff never notified her chosen funeral home to pick up her corpse. Sarah and Lucy are there now, trying to resolve this mess. I know they could use your help!"

He heard the emotion in his wife's tone.

She continued, "No one knows where her remains are!"

He reassured his wife he would stop there before going to the office to see if they needed his help. Don arrived at Blair House within the hour. There he found Lucy and her granddaughter, Sarah, in conference with the director. They were glad he arrived when he did, and they asked him to join them. The director was insisting Lucy, being Donna Fiery Maze's guardian, needed to sign a document. Supposedly, this gave them her permission to investigate the matter.

Upon reading the paper, Don found it was a standard "hold harmless" agreement. It would release Blair House and its employees from all wrongdoing. He requested the director excuse them for a few minutes. They moved to the meeting room, where they often met with Aunt Fiery. There he listened as Lucy told the entire story from the time she received the call informing her of her aunt's passing until now.

Sarah said, "Not only is Ammygam's body missing, so are her clothes and possessions. Including the items you brought her. Mr. Bryniarski, it's as if Ammygam was never here!"

He asked them if they wanted his help, and both readily agreed. It was then he advised them not to sign the document. They returned to the director's office, where he asked if they had notified the law enforcement agency. The director told him that such measures were unnecessary. Don informed the man he would report this matter to the state police, requesting it be treated as a missing person report.

When they rose to leave, the director tried to appease them by giving him a photocopy of Mrs. Maze's death certificate. While they stood in the Blair House parking lot, he called his attorney, Bruno. Don explained the incident and events to Bruno's secretary. She confirmed a 3:00 p.m. appointment for the following day.

As he spoke to the secretary, Lucy started crying, saying to Sarah, "My aunt's only wish was to be buried next to her husband. Now, I can't even do that for her!"

He agreed to meet with them tomorrow in Bruno's office. Don then departed for his office, getting there just in time for his meeting. That evening he, Ann, and a few neighbors combed the woods for their dog, but they didn't find a clue. On Wednesday afternoon, Don, Lucy, and Sarah met with Bruno and two of his associates promptly at 3:00 p.m. They told their story and included the written details of her aunt's funeral arrangements. It was then Lucy became emotional and broke down crying.

He agreed his firm would represent Lucy and called the Blair House's director. The man advised Bruno he couldn't discuss the matter and referred him to their legal department. As they were leaving, his attorney pulled him aside. He told him of inquires he had received regarding the loaning of their 1941 Chevrolet, asking him to call later in the week when he knew more.

Sarah overheard their brief conversation and commented, "Oh, Mr. Bryniarski, you're donating Ammygam's auto to a museum; how nice is that." Lucy whispered in Sarah's ear, prompting her to ask, "When we have a memorial service for our aunt, could you bring her old car? It would be such a wonderful tribute to her and her life."

Don understood he was in trouble! He hoped the family never found out what happened. How could he answer her? He paused, biting his lip, then explained over the next fourteen minutes how he was no longer in possession of Aunt Fiery's former and their beloved 1941 Chevrolet Special Deluxe Sedan. It shocked both women when they heard Aunt Fiery's vehicle had been taken. Lucy started to cry again; it was too much for her.

Don started laughing, stating, "Lucy, if you don't laugh with me, I'll start crying too!"

She stopped and smiled at him as she wiped away her tears.

Meanwhile, one associate came out of her office with a newspaper saying, "I think your automobile made the tabloids."

There, on the front page of the Livingston County paper, was forty-one. It was a picture taken at the parade, probably the last one of the car. Don thought to himself; this conference should have been about Fiery and not their stolen 1941 Chevrolet. He felt he had forced more sadness on Lucy and her grieving family.

After their meeting, he checked with his secretary, then went straight home. He changed his clothes and started looking for his Golden retriever when it struck him. Tiger had disappeared the same morning Fiery passed away! A dear friend, the car she once owned, and his dog — they're all gone. Was this another coincidence?

As he trudged through the neighbor's wetland, he didn't worry about forty-one. No one could ever show that car; even driving it would bring attention to both the car and driver. He was confident in a few days the police would catch the thief. As for Aunt Fiery, her passing created great sadness; she had become a surrogate grandmother to him. As he ambled through the bog, he said a prayer for her, hoping she was at peace. It would be the first of many…

But his pooch, Tiger, that was something else. He was determined to locate her and her pups no matter what it took. He just had to find her!

Chapter 24

Strange Presence

Three weeks later, Lucy stood with Don and Ann on the steps in front of Saint Alphonsus Catholic Church. Donna Fiery Maze's memorial Mass had just ended. She had been a registered member of the parish her entire life. Her niece, Lucy, thought it only fitting to have a service there in her honor. Fiery's body was still missing, but Lucy wanted to celebrate her aunt's life with a solemn service. One her aunt would be proud of.

They waited for the few sorrowful mourners to exit the church. While waiting, Lucy brought Don up to date on Bruno's investigation. His law firm had brought in both the local and state police right away. Her aunt was officially pronounced dead by a Blair House doctor. He was the only person who viewed the body, which caused the authorities to be suspicious. The Michigan State Police discovered other unreported similar cases. The investigators had some theories and were keeping every option open.

Don listened to the resentment in Lucy's voice when she spoke of the unknown persons at the nursing home who treated her aunt so carelessly. Another reason for their grieving was both she and Sarah couldn't fulfill her Aunt Fiery's last wish to be interred next to her husband. Ann tried to console Lucy, but she abruptly changed the subject, asking about their lost dog and if they heard any news of forty-one. She told her how excited Don had gotten when the police reported someone seeing their car in Dearborn Heights, but nothing came of that report.

When the few other mourners left, Don invited Sarah, her grandmother, Lucy, and their two neighbor friends to join them for lunch. They kindly declined his offer. He wanted to remember this day as Fiery's memorial Mass and never said today was his forty-fifth birthday. After saying goodbye, Ann and Don drove the eleven miles to Hamtramck. There they dined at their favorite polish restaurant, Polonia.

While they were eating, each spoke of how sad they were, having experienced three major changes in their lives on the same day within twelve hours. Don lamented over the loss of Aunt Fiery, a friend whom he admired, and continued on about their 1941 Chevrolet, a car so special to his friend, and smiled when he said he was glad he didn't have to tell her what happened. But their Tiger walking away was personal and saddened both of them the most. He described these three events as coincidence, but his wife told him it was divine providence. Then Ann asked about his attitude and how he has remained so upbeat.

He answered, "People are so much friendlier when you smile at them. They don't know or care about your troubles, so I figured I might as well smile." Don paused a moment before saying, "Kitten, to get us out of our melancholy mood, we're going to do something fun!"

With that remark, he made Ann bring out her day planner and started discussing their next car show. They agreed to show his 1959 white Ford Galaxy convertible at the Old Towne Classic Car Show in Traverse City on Sunday, July Fourth. Ann proposed going there a few days early. They could then explore that part of the state and display his Me-Car.

He also asked Ann if her schedule would allow her to attend two conventions with him, one in late September in Nashville, the other in Australia during October. Don reminded her it will be springtime in the southern hemisphere. He then recommended they tour the country, sightseeing for a week or two.

Smiling, she remarked, "That's an extended period for me to be away from the clinic and my clients."

He grinned at her, saying, "It'll be great! When will we get another chance to see Australia?"

Days became weeks, and there was no word of Tiger or forty-one. They left for Traverse City on Friday, the second of July, in Don's Me-Car.

His 1959 Ford was much more modern than forty-one, and Don enjoyed the drive. They spent Saturday with their friends Bill and Kathy, reminiscing old times and catching up on what had occurred over the past year. The couple was interested in their meetings with Fiery and were sorry for what happened to their auto.

On Sunday, Don and Ann took turns watching their Ford while the others toured the exhibits. Neither wanted to take the chance of their 1959 Ford disappearing. He made the most of this opportunity by passing out informational flyers announcing the theft of their 1941 Chevrolet. His friend Cadillac Joey even took extra flyers to pass out at other shows during the season.

While looking at the 1930's automobiles, he saw the body shop guy from whom he bought forty-one. He went over to Johnny O and reintroduced himself. The two guys had a cordial conversation concerning the 1941 Chevrolet, and Don explained what had happened to the automobile. He clarified how much he enjoyed owning the vehicle. Then he inquired about Johnny's reason for not being upfront regarding how long he owned the Chevrolet. The body shop owner explained how he didn't think Don would have spent the money buying her if he knew the truth.

Don remembered what the fellow mentioned to him during the sale and asked him again why he sold forty-one? Johnny O was about to answer when his wife interrupted them. The body shop owner introduced her and requested she answer Don's question.

With a blunt voice, the woman declared, "I always sensed that car had a strange presence. One day I saw this guy near the car, he was dressed in really old work clothes and was holding a light brown puppy by his flannel shirt. When I asked him what he was doing, he walked around the corner, and was gone. That night I dreamt of him stealing the Chevrolet. Isn't déjà vu the other way? You know, dreaming first. Well, I had enough weird feelings and told Johnny it was me or his hot rod."

Finished with her story, she explained to Johnny where she would be, said goodbye to Don, and left them to carry on their conversation. They both laughed at his wife's comment. Then Johnny O gave Don information on a classic car parts dealer, telling him to give the man a call and say, Johnny O recommended you. He'll let you know if someone is dismantling your Chevrolet and selling it piecemeal. When he heard those words, Don's heart sunk. He couldn't imagine such a fate for Aunt Fiery's forty-one. It made him sick just to think about it.

With the show over, the couple set out the next morning on their self-guided tour of the western Michigan shoreline. They were in no rush and enjoyed the scenery. Then Don commented on how he wanted to write a book using the recorded transcripts of their meetings with Fiery as the central storyline.

Ann encouraged him, saying, "That would be a wonderful tribute to a beautiful woman. She bonded with many people during her lifetime. She was a resilient person with grace, passion, and love. I don't just mean for her car, but for life itself!"

Over the next few days, they visited several lighthouses on Michigan's western shore. The first stop was the Grand Traverse Lighthouse in Leelanau State Park and then over to the one at Mission Point. They stopped at other lighthouses on their way to visiting the cities of Charlevoix and Petoskey. He insisted they visit Hemingway Point on Charlevoix Lake before going home.

While driving home, Don confided in his wife. He told her he always wanted to visit the Keweenaw Peninsula in Michigan's Upper Peninsula. She agreed to put the location on a future to visit list. Don then reminded her he needed to make airline and hotel reservations for the two conferences. Ann informed him her schedule was clear for the September conference, but she was still working on clearing the time in October.

Smiling, he turned to his wife, saying, "Wonderful!"

Over the next four months, he spent his free time listening to his recordings made in meetings with Aunt Fiery. He shunned Nadine's accurately typed transcripts, for whatever reason. Instead, he handwrote detailed notes of what Aunt Fiery said. His notes for this project had to be written only in blue seventy-page spiral ruled notebooks.

When Ann questioned him about his reason for not using the typed transcripts and his computer, he abruptly responded, "They're not always correct, and I do it my way!"

After that, she no longer offered constructive criticisms or comments on his choice for a book name, which was, Memories of a Honeymoon

Car. To her, that name just didn't fit. By the time they left for Nashville, he had already filled two spiraled notebooks. At the convention, she learned he was the keynote speaker on Enhanced Airport Security; and, during dinner, learned her husband's new project was infrared topographical imaging. Ann was glad she was there to share in his accomplishments.

After the Nashville conference, they received a call from their insurance agent. It had been three months since someone had stolen forty-one. The agent was calling to complete and pay their claim. Their attorney, Bruno, had advised them to leave their claim open for a full year and made a logical case for his recommendation. If they settled and their car recovered, the insurance company could file for a salvage title and be able to sell the vehicle to anyone. Don and Ann wanted to keep control and ownership of forty-one… out of respect for Aunt Fiery, at least for now.

Ann cleared her calendar for two weeks in October and found herself flying with Don to Australia for his convention. When they landed in Sydney, they had a one-day layover there. With limited time, they took a two-hour guided tour of the city, choosing to act like tourists. Early the next day, they traveled to Canberra, the nation's capital, where Don's conference took place. While there, he attended a three-day security conference.

Ann occupied her time by participating in activities planned for the guests. In the evening, they met for dinner and socialized with other attendees. But, it was on the conference's first day that everything changed. Two different companies contacted him. Each wanted to manufacture the X-Fi product in Australia. Late that night, Don spoke on the telephone with Mr. Stone, his company's president. They talked about the possibility of permitting another company to manufacture their product.

Don soon favored the idea of licensing their X-Fi product, and so did the board back home. With Mr. Stone's approval and Don's recommendation for which company to work with, he negotiated a high-level agreement in terms. They would allow their attorneys to work out the details. Unfortunately, because his internet connections were so unreliable, he had to fax every document to Michigan. This time-consuming paperwork caused Don and Ann to start their vacation a day later.

With the conference ended and his work completed, they continued their vacation touring the continent. Messages from Mr. Stone interrupted their holiday when he asked Don to fly to Brisbane on business with his wife. They stayed in the city two days, even though he had a three-hour licensing agreement meeting. His travel agent changed their travel plans, and they flew out of Brisbane to the United States and home.

While they were traveling home, Bruno had left them a message regarding forty-one. When they contacted him, he told them of an inquiry he received. It was from a museum with a proposed World War II Homefront gallery. A recent federal grant had provided the museum with the gallery's seed money. The female staff member he spoke with told how they were now searching for artifacts. She said the museum considered their 1941 Chevrolet an ideal fit for their gallery.

The woman wanted to discuss their 1941 Chevrolet, knowing it was stolen and not recovered. Don and Ann were interested in learning their terms. They permitted Bruno to explore the possibility of loaning the vehicle. Later, they discovered the museum was not in Michigan. Their deliberation was quick and did not consider the location to be a deal-breaker.

Christmas had come and gone when Don welcomed in New Year's Day 2005. He had completed his sixth spiral notebook and now typed over sixty thousand words for his, *Memories of a Honeymoon Car* book. After several failed attempts to have his book published, Don explored electronic books, printing on demand and self-publishing his book. But each was in their infancy. So, he put his novel on the shelf, intending to return to it someday. But before doing that, he paid to have ten copies printed for himself, just in case he never returned to the project.

Aunt Fiery consumed a fraction of Don's free time during the last nine months. The reality was more of his free time was consumed being the Grand Knight of his local Knights of Columbus Council. He volunteered many hours for his council's meetings and charitable events. At his council's March meeting, the membership nominated him for a second term. It was at this same meeting that his brother knights voted for him to represent their council at the Knights of Columbus, Michigan State Convention.

Since November, he had gone to Brisbane, Australia, twice more for business, and he was tired of traveling. He tried to convince his brother Knights to let someone else attend in his place, but they insisted he represent them at the meeting. The Michigan Knights held their annual convention at the Grand Hotel on Mackinac Island for over one hundred years. Most knights considered this a prestigious event. Don was not looking forward to attending the convention. To him, it was another meeting added to a succession of business meetings.

The conference was scheduled to begin the Thursday afternoon before Memorial Day and would end that Saturday at noon. Ann thought they should attend and afterward spend four days in the Upper Peninsula. Ann began planning their mini holiday, making sure they would have a chance to visit Copper Harbor, which sits in the northern point on Michigan's Keweenaw Peninsula. It was two weeks before the convention when Ann looked at renting a car.

Her reasoning for a rental car was to have that vacation feeling. She found they could rent a high-end automobile for one week at no cost using his airline travel points. She knew Don would love driving and riding in a luxury automobile. Ann planned to pick up the vehicle on Wednesday evening, the twenty-fifth of May, the day before they left, to surprise Don.

She planned to start the four-hour trip to Mackinaw City early Thursday morning. They should arrive around nine, park their rental car in the ferry's lot, and board the ferry to Mackinac Island. A horse-drawn carriage on the island would take them to their hotel. After Saturday's closing ceremony, Ann planned for them to drive the six hours to Houghton. The city is on Michigan's Keweenaw Peninsula. Ann had already reserved a motel for their two-night stay. Sunday, she planned they visit Copper Harbor and the mining museums along the way.

Early on Monday, Memorial Day, she planned the six-hour drive across the Upper Peninsula to Sault Ste. Marie. She had booked a luxury suite for them at a casino hotel that they could use as their base. From there, they could visit the Soo Locks and other historical sites. On Wednesday, June first, they would travel home, returning the rental car that evening. Unfortunately, the rental company spoiled her surprise when she needed Don's permission to use his airline points, which he gave without hesitation, and was now looking forward to going.

On Wednesday, the twenty-fourth of May, Sarah drove Ann to the car rental agency. It was half-past seven that evening when she picked up the car, making sure she listed Don as an authorized driver. Don was waiting for her when she arrived and approved of her choice of cars and was ready to pack it with a bag of snacks, a cooler with drinks, and a suitcase with casual clothes. They had a special luggage bag for their formal wear necessary for the convention.

That evening Ann packed her red leather journal, Nadine's notes, and the stamped envelope addressed to their insurance agent. That letter contained the forms and title to settle their claim on forty-one. Earlier, they had agreed to mail the claim on June first. Don took his laptop and a copy of his book, thinking he may have time to read and improve his earlier writing. Before going to bed, Ann forwarded their home telephone number to her cellular telephone, in case there was an emergency at the clinic.

The next morning, Ann grabbed the keyring that had the house and all of their keys on it, putting it in her purse. She told her husband, "I'm taking this in case the electric garage door doesn't work when we return."

Don laughed, remembering the day a power outage stranded them outside their own home because neither had a key. It was five in the morning when they left. Ann drove the first few hours, giving Don a welcomed chance to sleep longer. Then, after they stopped for breakfast, he took over the driving duties while Ann began reading his book. She had learned to speed read in college and quickly scanned the printed version she had never seen.

She stopped and asked, "So, Alex Maze, Fiery's husband… his actual name was Maeselowski?"

Her husband nodded a yes, and continued driving north on Interstate seventy-five to Mackinaw City. His wife resumed her reading of the hardships women like Fiery made on the Homefront. Ann couldn't believe how women endured shortages of everything and made sacrifices, including losing their husbands, family members, and friends. His words made her think about how deeply he lamented the loss of their dog, their antique 1941 Chevrolet, and a dear friend Fiery Maze all on the same day.

He wrote of Alex finding a Scottish Hunting pup inside his brand new 1941 Chevrolet Special Deluxe. How Fiery named their new addition Tiger on the day they were married. Don described how many years later, he discovered the same breed puppy in the car and called her Tiger before they ever met Aunt Fiery. She continued reading. When pregnant with pups and ready to deliver, each of their dogs walked away. Neither was ever found.

When Ann read those words, she angrily commented, "That's wrong! You don't know that we'll never see Tiger again."

He responded in a stern voice, saying, "Look, it has been a year. I think wild coyotes behind the house got her and her litter in the woods. You know how aggressive those animals are."

Ann rapidly countered with, "It won't be one year until Tuesday, and I'm not giving up hope! Dogs go missing for years and sometimes return home; she may surprise us! Oh! And remind me to mail this letter to our insurance agent on Wednesday, so forty-one's claim can be closed."

Still reading, Ann discovered how much Don cherished Aunt Fiery and how she truly enriched his life. His words expressed how he relished driving their pre-World War II classic Chevrolet with their dog at his side. She put the book aside when they reached the ferry's parking lot in Mackinaw City.

She looked at her wristwatch, commenting, "It's nine-forty-five. We're right on time."

The next three days were busy for them. Don attended the business of the convention while Ann took part in the ladies' programs. They both enjoyed the pomp and pageantry of the event. One of their favorites was the ceremony where the Sir Knights wore black tuxedos, silver swords, colorful capes, the feathered chapeaux reminiscent of ancient sailors. It was a beautiful sight. The conference concluded late Saturday morning with the Knights in their formal regalia and their spouses attending a special Mass.

The couple arrived at the Mackinaw City ferry dock around 1:30 p.m., packed their rental car, and began their mini-vacation. He told his wife he would drive over the five-mile-long Mackinac Bridge, and then they could switch drivers in a few hours. Along the way to Houghton, they stopped for a Yooper lunch of pasties.

They checked into their Houghton motel around 2:30 p.m. Ann was glad she had made the reservation in advance, as there were no vacancies. That evening the couple enjoyed dinner at a restaurant overlooking the Keween-aw Waterway. After an early brunch on Sunday morning, they made the one-hour trek to Copper Harbor. Both enjoyed the tour of the lighthouse. Don ascended to the top, where he waved at her from the lighthouse's catwalk.

On their way back to Houghton, they stopped at a mining museum, learning about the industry and Michigan's copper history. Before checking out the following morning, they had breakfast at the motel. They wanted to leave for Sault Ste. Marie so they could avoid the Memorial Day Parade. Neither wanted to deal with the street closures and parade participants. Don drove while Ann re-read his book, but this time slower. He noticed her making notes in her red journal.

When Ann laughed out loud, he asked, "What's so funny?"

She responded, "I just read where Aunt Fiery said, 'The Blair House will remember me.' I thought that was funny."

He laughed too. The couple spoke of what has transpired over the past months. The scandalous news of Blair House executives and their scheme with an out-of-state crematorium. How they carelessly disposed of human remains and profited by their actions. State police charged a few Blair House employees with possession of stolen property and stealing from residents. Much credit for uncovering the scandal went to their attorney, Bruno.

His lawsuit prompted the state police to investigate. He had sued both the nursing home and Blair Investment Group, causing BIG to move residents to other locations and close the beautiful Blair House facility.

Don commented, "They may never find her body, but I guarantee you every employee that used to work there remembers Aunt Fiery."

He loved the way their rental car drove. He continued driving, only stopping for gas and lunch. They arrived in Sault Ste. Marie with hours to spare before they could check into their hotel. So, they visited the Soo Locks a day early, spending the first hour in the visitor's center. After that, they sat on a bench outside, watching large lake freighters rise and descend, making their passage through the waterway. The amazing sight fascinated both of them.

Ann commented, "I remembered hearing Fiery say, in your book, that in May 1942 she did this same thing with her husband and forty-one. Is that the reason we're here?"

Don considered his words before replying, "I'm not sure, but I felt we should visit here… ever since Aunt Fiery died." He looked at his spouse, asking, "Does that make any sense?"

They sat there talking of the woman they knew a short time, her husband, Alex, and Tiger, the love they shared, and how they too loved their vacations in the Upper Peninsula.

He joked, saying, "If we had their Chevrolet with us, I could cook you beef stew!"

They both laughed. Later they checked in at the casino's hotel, where they arranged to stay for two nights. Although neither gambled, they enjoyed the lounge's evening entertainment. The following day, they planned to visit other historical sites in the city, but they changed their plans at breakfast. Instead, they decided to check out of the hotel, do their sightseeing, and then leave for home that evening. Ann checked out when they finished eating, while Don packed their rental vehicle, and they set off to tour Old Fort Brady on Lake Superior State University's campus.

It was near 9:30 a.m. when Don parked their car at the fort's entrance. As they got out, Ann's cellular telephone rang. Placing her purse on the car's hood, she searched for her ringing phone. But by the time she found it, the ringing stopped. Ann thought it odd the caller's identification information didn't register.

A moment later, she received a voice mail message. When she retrieved the message, it was from a deputy sheriff named Al, asking her to call him as soon as possible. She engaged the speaker on her phone and replayed the message before calling the number back.

It surprised both of them when a woman answered, saying, "Luce County Sheriff's Department."

Ann identified herself and said she was returning a call from Deputy Al. The woman asked her to hold a moment and transferred her call. Then, a commanding tone declared, "Deputy Sheriff Maeselowski speaking, how may I help you?"

She again identified herself, mentioning she was returning his call.

He thanked her for returning his call so quickly and continued in a firm tone, stating, "I need to ask if you can account for everyone in your party?"

Ann replied, "I don't understand what you're asking?"

The officer said, "Are any of your family members or friends missing?"

She looked at her husband confused, and into her telephone, announced, "No, not to my knowledge. What's going on?"

Ann's cellular telephone kept cutting out, so she moved to another spot in the parking lot, hoping it would improve the call's quality. With no luck, she took her cell phone off speaker and walked to the car. There she placed her purse on the hood, pulled a hotel pen from it, and began writing on the hotel receipt.

The only words Don heard her say were, "No, don't… I'll call you right back. I need to speak with my husband." She opened the passenger door and sat down in the seat. She looked dumbfounded and signaled for him to join her. Once he was inside, she said, "That was the Luce County sheriff's department. They found her."

Don's face lit up as he asked, "They found Tiger?"

Ann responded, "No, Don, they found forty-one! Can you believe it? They found Aunt Fiery's 1941 Chevrolet Special Deluxe!"

Chapter 25

I'm Home

Ann continued to explain her conversation with Deputy Al while Don sat there in disbelief. "Backpackers found forty-one abandoned near a lake this morning. The deputy wanted to know if anyone in our party was missing. They thought someone might have drowned or become lost. He didn't know the car was reported stolen until I told him."

Don questioned, "What? Where is the car now?"

Ann commented, "I guess in the woods somewhere near water. He was starting a search until I told him no one was missing."

He asked, "Where is he?"

His wife was busy looking for their road map responding, "Newberry, Michigan. We can meet him there tomorrow at the Sheriff's office."

Don looked happy and anxious, saying, "Where in the heck is Newberry?"

They searched the rental car for their Rand McNally Road Atlas. A minute later, they found it under the driver's seat. They soon discovered Newberry was in Michigan's Upper Peninsula, about an hour and a half's drive from where they were. Ann was so excited she immediately called the deputy to see if they really had to wait until tomorrow.

She said, "Al, we're over here at the Soo Locks in Sault Ste. Marie. Do you have a minute to speak with my husband, Don?"

Ann handed her cell phone to her husband, and the officer explained he hadn't seen the vehicle and could only relay the information reported by the hikers. He told Don he was planning to go out there about eleven and invited them to join him. The deputy explained he needed to remain at the station until eleven because they were short-staffed, it being the day after a holiday.

Al agreed to wait until they had seen the car before calling a tow truck. Once Don was off the phone, they drove the sixty-seven miles to Newberry in a speedy fifty-five minutes. Considering the road conditions, he thought that was pretty fast. When they arrived at the Luce County sheriff's department, they rushed in the door and met the officer. Al said the hikers had trouble identifying the automobile because of its age. Don's heart sunk when he heard those words; maybe it wasn't forty-one after all.

Al told him his office ran the license plate in the state's computer system, and that was when they found his wife listed as the vehicle's owner. The deputy spoke of how this could be a simple recovery with no insurance business involved, but he needed other proof of ownership besides the car's registration. Ann thought for a moment, searched her purse, and produced the envelope she planned to mail tomorrow. With the officer present she opened the letter addressed to their insurance company. Inside was the 1941 Chevrolet's title which she handed to him.

After a brief inspection of the title, Al commented, "I need to verify the serial number on your title with the one on the vehicle. Let's go see if we can find your car!"

The deputy advised them they could leave their car at the station and ride with him. Ann sat upfront. On their ride, Al inquired how they received his call if they were in Sault Ste. Marie. Ann explained she was a veterinarian and that she forwarded their home telephone number to her cell phone in case of an emergency while they were on vacation. Don told him of his joy owning their 1941 Chevrolet and the possibility of donating it to a museum. He explained how this was their plan before someone took the car. Now they weren't certain if anyone would want her.

They traveled north, then east for a half-hour when the officer slowed and made a U-turn. He continued for five minutes before slowing and again turning around. He explained he was looking for a landmark and was happy when Ann spotted the rusted Chippewa County line sign. Again, Al made another U-turn, crossing back into Luce County. After making this last U-turn, he continued to drive even slower.

The deputy apologized, commenting, "Thank you for being patient going up and down, one two three, but it's somewhere near here."

Ann declared, "What did you say?"

He replied, "It means, I'm sorry for taking you up and down the highway, like this."

"No!" She responded, "You said one two three, what does that mean?"

He laughed and continued looking past her at the field. The deputy answered, "This is one two three!"

He noticed the quizzical expression on Ann's face when she asked, "The road?"

Al sensed her confusion and remarked, "The highway we're on is one two three. Well, that's what we call it. The road we're riding on is Michigan State Route one twenty-three."

She turned in her front seat, looking back to see if Don made the connection. He was just getting ready to speak when the patrol car went off the roadway onto what appeared to be an overgrown snowmobile trail. After a short while, Deputy Al stopped his cruiser.

He glanced over at Ann, saying, "If my directions are correct, we have to hike from here."

With him leading the way, the couple followed. After a walk, they arrived at a bend where the high grass walkway became a narrow footpath. Soon the pathway turned again, revealing in the distance a ruby maroon-colored 1941 Chevrolet Special Deluxe Sedan. It was parked near a meadow under some large trees. It looked like a picture you would find in Country Gentleman Magazine. Don smiled as they got closer and closer to the automobile.

The closer he got, the more he liked what he saw. He noticed the trunk was open and immediately began inspecting the auto, stopping only to show the officer where the serial number was located. Al confirmed the numbers. This was their vehicle! While Ann and the deputy were in deep conversation, Don scrutinized the automobile from the front bumper to exhaust pipe, while listening to their discussion.

The car's galvanized pail and rags were by the rear wheel, looking as if someone had just washed the sedan. She was sparkling clean! The deputy was busy explaining how technically this was and wasn't the park, but close.

Ann asked, "What recreation area are we near?"

Pointing to the meadow, Al said, "Tahquamenon Falls State Park is right there."

Finished with his inspection, Don realized the car was in the same condition when they took it a year ago. He wondered how the elements hadn't rusted this car? He noticed the trunk was empty except for his two parade signs. On a whim, he walked beyond forty-one down the grass-covered path, about sixty feet beyond where the trail turned left, leading into thick undergrowth and woods. There, he stopped and stared, astonished by what he saw.

Don yelled, "Are people allowed to camp out here? How about in the 1940s?"

The young lawman chuckled, saying, "There are no campsites here. As for the forties, I wasn't born yet. This morning some people were telling me this was the best camping spot before the state park opened in 1946."

As Al was speaking, Ann remembered the keys and took the keyring from her purse. She stepped past the car, walking to where her husband stood and saw what he was looking at. Deputy Al joined them. There, just off the path, hidden by the undergrowth, was a campsite with an older tent, table, and two wooden folding chairs. A gust of wind blew, surprising them all. Ann and Don looked at each other, neither uttering a word.

The officer whispered, "Did you hear that voice?" Without waiting for an answer, he rushed into the woods to do a thorough search of the area. When the deputy returned, he looked at the camping equipment and inquired, "Is this your stuff?"

Don ignored him and ambled over to the fire pit, where he found the smoldering remnants of Fiery's journals. The pages were ashes, but he could distinguish pieces of the bindings. He called Ann to look at the smoking remains. They recognized everything! Including the nearby Vernors and Fanta wooden pop shells. Don picked up a long stick from the ground and poked at the few red-hot ashes, which caused them to burst into flames, consuming the remaining bindings.

Ann stared at the fire, then turned to the deputy, commenting, "Those items never belonged to us."

Al had moved over to the table and was examining the vintage cooking utensils, saying, "Two people were camping here. We'll have these things removed when they take your vehicle out."

Ann handed her husband the ring with their keys, whispering, "Here, see if one of these works?"

He took the keyring, searching until he found the correct one, and walked over to forty-one. Inside the automobile, he sat and went through the starting procedure. Holding his breath, he turned the key. Vroom! The engine started! He let the auto idle while he walked around the car, inspecting each tire, making sure they were fully inflated.

Don moved over to the deputy, asking him, "If you're okay with it, I'm going to drive her out of here?"

The deputy replied, "It's your automobile. If you can, that would be great. We'll treat this as a simple vehicle recovery and remove it from the database. But you must return to the sheriff's office to complete the paperwork and claim your other item."

Don readily agreed, asking Ann if she wanted to ride out with him? There was no need to ask her twice, especially since she was seated in the passenger seat. Don waited for the officer to walk halfway down the path before he slowly removed his foot from the clutch, moving forty-one forward. Ann paid special attention as he carefully maneuvered down the narrow trail.

She watched as he stared at the rearview mirror and saw his startled face when he slammed on the brakes, stalling the car. He stopped so abruptly that a plier, screwdriver, paper bag, and rags flew out from under the bench-style seat. The sudden stop caused Ann to slide forward off the front seat, bump her left shoulder on the dashboard, and land on her left knee, looking straight into the passenger's side-view mirror.

Don jumped outside from the car and ran to the vehicle's rear. Ann stared at the mirror and what was behind them. That moment, she felt as if time was being played out in slow motion. Then she blinked, and time resumed to normal. Composing herself, she stepped outside of forty-one, where all she saw was her husband coming towards her.

The officer suddenly realized they were no longer behind him and came running back, yelling, "Is there something wrong?"

Don waved to the deputy, signaling they were okay and continued to drive out at a snail's pace. Meanwhile, Ann placed everything from the floor in between them on the bench-style seat. She witnessed Don repeatedly glancing in the rearview mirror. During his lifetime, Don was never able to explain how he drove forty-one out of the woods without once touching a branch or tree leaf to the sides of their car. He stopped before getting on the highway, asking the officer to check if his brake lights worked. It was then he noticed the fuel tank read three-quarters full.

Al had Ann ride with him to the sheriff's station, letting Don lead in forty-one just to make sure there were no mishaps. The ride back to the municipal building seemed much quicker than when they were looking for forty-one. There the officer completed the paperwork, coming out only to ask for Ann's owner's signature on several forms. Afterward, Don and Al did another safety inspection on forty-one. When they entered the building, she heard the officer say their license plate expires tomorrow. As he walked by, the deputy handed her the completed paperwork.

The date and time stamp read May 31, 2005, 1:23 p.m., exactly one year to the minute since someone stole their auto! Ann knew Don would want to drive forty-one home tonight, so she called the rental car company looking for a drop-off point near them. There were two locations nearby, one in Sault Ste. Marie and the other in Mackinaw City. Ann chose to drop the car off in Mackinaw City and confirmed their office would be open when they arrived.

She was waiting for her husband and Al to finish up when she noticed a small four-year-old boy coming out of the office. He sat on the opposite side of the long wooden bench, and Ann saw he was crying.

She strolled over to him, sat down next to him, and smiled, saying, "Hi! My name is Doctor Ann. If you tell me what's wrong, maybe I can help!"

The child sobbed, heartbroken, and barely managed to reply, "People brought in a dog. He likes me, and my sister Maggie too. I named him Butch, and he wants to stay with me! But my daddy says he has to go home with his owners."

While she was consoling the lad, Al came inside, went directly into his office, and came out with a black plastic garbage bag. Don ambled into the foyer holding a rag and two burned hot dogs wrapped in foil and a container of stew with a hole in the top. Before placing them in Al's garbage bag, he showed them to Ann.

Don commented, "Someone played a joke on us. I found these on the car's engine!"

Ann grinned as Al left to dispose of "the garbage". It was then she noticed a girl about six years old trailing behind her husband.

The deputy came back to grab the girl's wrist, stating, "Come on, let's get this task over with Maggie. Lewis, you come, too."

The children followed their father into another room off the lobby. Don and Ann discussed their travel options as they waited for the deputy to return. They agreed Ann would follow him to the rental car office on the hour-and-a-half ride to Mackinaw City. Once there, they would decide if they wanted to drive forty-one home.

Ann was sitting on the dark wooden bench with Don standing next to her when the youngsters returned with a Golden Retriever pup attached to a length of rope. When the dog saw them, it bolted directly to them. The pup started wagging its tail, jumping up and down on Ann and then on Don, begging for attention and affection. The couple was speechless when they saw the dog. When it tried to jump on the seat, Ann sat on the floor grabbing the pooch.

She tried to calm the spirited young hound as it laid down, rolled over, and tossed its paws in the air. Moving to the room's opposite side, Don knelt on the floor. The pup noticed his movements and immediately sprinted over to be played with and petted. Then it turned, running over to Ann where it slid on the slippery floor, landing right on her. She again grabbed and held it for a moment, trying to calm the dog.

While Don stood up and came over to Ann, she examined the canine. She noticed the children's gloomy faces as the deputy explained to them how the backpackers discovered the puppy on their car's front seat. The hikers didn't want to leave it alone with anyone around, so they brought it in when reporting your vehicle.

Al sounded contrite as he remarked, "I hope you don't mind, but our family cared for your pup the last few hours. It was easier than putting it in a kennel."

Ann looked at the children, Lewis with tears streaming from his eyes and Maggie ready to cry. She asked them to come over to her as she untied the rope from the pooch's neck and retied it in a loose loop. While the pup's tail kept wagging, she picked it up, and they locked eyes; Ann smiled. The children thought for sure she was the pup's owner!

In a gentle voice, she spoke, "What we have here is a three-month-old pup, pure-bred blond Golden Retriever. This breed is intelligent, friendly, and likes to play with little boys and girls. We own a dog just like this, but our pup is a boy; this is a girl, which means this couldn't be our puppy." Lewis was smiling with delight as Ann continued saying, "Butch is not a girl dog name, so you'll need to call her something else."

Maggie broke out into a bigger smile, sassing to her brother, "See, I told you so!"

Ann put the dog down and handed her the rope with the dog attached, saying, "You better ask your dad if you can take your puppy home."

The children and pup didn't wait for their father's answer; instead, they ran to the front exit. But at the doorway, the tail-wagging puppy stopped for a moment. She turned towards Ann and Don with her brown puppy eyes appeared to say goodbye.

They noticed a slight tug on the pup's rope collar and heard Maggie calling from outside, "Come on, girl. C'mon, Tiger!" Her voice was so loud it echoed into the building.

The tail-wagging Golden Retriever pup turned to the door, jumped over the threshold, and disappeared from their view.

Ann tried to judge her husband's reaction to what just occurred and thought it was like hers. She declared, "We need to leave… now!"

They signed a waiver denying ownership of the dog and left the police station. Traffic was light, and their trip to Mackinaw City was uneventful. Arriving in the city, Ann was still tense from driving the five miles over the Mackinac Bridge. In the city, they refueled both cars, transferred their luggage to forty-one's large empty trunk, and dropped off the rental car.

Before getting on the highway and heading for home, they ordered takeout dinners. Once on Interstate seventy-five, Don kept the car's speed at sixty, which meant it would take them over four hours to drive home. To save time, they ate dinner as they drove. Ann didn't enjoy trading her air-conditioned luxury ride for the pre-World War II vehicle but thought it best they stay together. She was glad they found forty-one. Neither were ready to discuss the events they had experienced earlier in the day.

They had been traveling for an hour and a quarter when Ann completed writing notes in her journal. She closed her book, placed it on the seat between them, and announced, "Well, I'm finished!"

Don quickly responded, "So am I!"

He explained he would take old U.S. twenty-seven south to Grayling, allowing the faster traffic to pass them. With those words, he turned onto the highway's exit ramp at Waters, Michigan. This allowed the very long line of faster traffic behind them to speed ahead while they traveled the Interstate's parallel road at a slower, more comfortable speed.

It was then Ann asked, "How is the car driving?"

He replied, "Good. I just don't want to push her too hard. Anything over sixty miles per hour makes her groan, and the noise is unbearable."

After a brief silence, he spoke at length about how forty-one felt different. Mechanically, the car was running fine, but somehow it just didn't feel the same. She asked how he felt about loaning forty-one to the new Homefront Museum? Commenting on how easy it would be since Bruno had already drafted a tentative agreement. Don hesitated, then abruptly remarked he didn't know what he wanted to do, especially after today.

As he spoke, Ann gathered the trash and food containers, placing them in one bag. The pliers, screwdrivers, and the old rags went back under the seat. The small, crumbled brown bag looked familiar. She placed it in her lap.

Don hoped to change the subject, asking, "What did you talk about with the deputy on the way back to the station?"

She replied, "Actually, he wanted to learn about your 1941 Chevrolet. I told him how it was kept in Dearborn for many years. Then he started telling me about his family, who were originally from that city. He told me his father's name was Stanley and his grandfather was Smitty Maeselowski. Don, Smitty was probably Fiery's brother-in-law!"

Ann took a deep breath before saying, "Here's what's interesting. His father Stanley Maeselowski moved to Newberry, Michigan, in the 1970s.

Al's young son told me his proper name is Alex Lewis Maeselowski. The reason they call him Lewis is that his dad's name is Alex. That's our Deputy Al. Do you get it? Fiery's husband's name was Alex Maeselowski before he changed it to Maze. I think they are related!"

Ann was staring at the heavily weighted brown bag in her lap all the while she was speaking. When she looked inside it, she was surprised by what she saw. Ann continued in a somber tone, stating, "When you have a chance, pull over for me." She briefly paused before saying, "Deputy Al told me what he heard in the woods. He asked me if I…"

Don interrupted her asking, "I just saw a sign. In a mile, we're coming to a roadside park. Can you wait till then?"

"Yes."

He soon slowed the vehicle, turning it into what appeared to be a 1940s-era wayside park with restrooms. Ann got out of the car and walked to the front bumper, all the while clutching the brown paper bag. Don shut the car off and got out to join her. Ann's face was pale, and she appeared shaken and nervous as she sat leaning against the car's large front fender.

He questioned her, "Are you okay?"

"No, I am not! Something happened today, something you don't want to talk about or admit. Did you tell little Maggie what to name her new dog?"

He vehemently answered, "No!"

"Well, didn't you find it strange when Maggie called her puppy, Tiger?"

He replied in a cavalier tone, "It's just coincidence… nothing more than that."

"Coincidence, my foot!" She yelled as she went to the car, retrieving her red leather journal.

After searching for the correct page, she read aloud, "I suppose it's a fluke that Fiery and your family lived on the same Appleton Street in the Village of Dearborn. The last day she drove forty-one is the same day you were born. Do you remember Aunt Fiery telling us while on the way home forty-one stalled and stopped in front of your pregnant mother when she thought she ran out of gas?" Not waiting for his answer, she pointed to the car's front hood. Ann continued, "Fiery told us how your mother kissed this hood ornament, the same way her husband did when she last saw him. Their best man's name was Teddy, and so was ours. And let's remember her husband found a Golden retriever puppy in his new automobile, and so did you."

With no one else in the wayside park, she yelled, "And what do we discover with those children at the sheriff's office? The same breed and gender pup, only three months old, Fiery's, yours, and their pup, all found in this vehicle. So, call me in three years when their pregnant Golden retriever dog walks away from them as Fiery's and ours' did! How are you going to explain that? Another coincidence in your life?"

Don tried to calm his wife, but she continued ranting, declaring, "Oh! And it's a fluke we came upon that campsite at Tahquamenon Falls set-up with Fiery's and Alex's equipment. Who burns someone else's journals? Don't forget the food you found on the car's motor! Who does that? Remember Fiery telling you, 'We'll help you in a tight spot, and be patient going up and down one two three.' Well, I didn't get the memo telling me that was the state route where we would find forty-one, did you?"

Ann took a deep breath, looking as if she was ready to cry. But she continued on reading from her journal, "Let's consider Alex, her husband, how he registered the car in Fiery's name as you did for me. Oh! And who introduces you to Aunt Fiery, my employee, Sarah. Who knew Sarah was Fiery Maze's great-great-niece? Then she names our dog, the same name as Fiery's dog, Tiger. Finally, you described before how when you first saw forty-one, it almost crashed into you. With all these events happening, how can you still say it's a coincidence? Are they small coincidences or a damn big one!"

Ann slammed her journal closed and glared at him. She was still clutching the small brown paper bag when she asked Don, "When we were at Tahquamenon Falls, what did you hear in the woods? And how did you drive forty-one out of those woods? Do you really suppose you're that good of a driver? Or, did you have help from above to make forty-one float like that?"

He responded, "When I was driving out, I did imagine there were people behind us. But let me assure you, Kitten, when I got out, no…"

Ann was looking around the 1940s style rest area, shaking her head when she interrupted him, saying, "Look at this place. Doesn't it seem strange to you, we're here with a car that actually belongs in this time period?" Not waiting for his answer, and again pointing to their Chevrolet, she said, "And look at this car! It looks like it did when we finished the parade, exactly one year ago today. Where was it for the last year?"

In a calmer tone, Ann revived her case, stating, "The deputy told me what he heard in the woods, and it gave me the shivers. When he was walking by himself in the woods, he distinctly heard a man's voice say, 'Everyone should own a Model A.' I didn't tell him Fiery's husband would say that to everyone he met."

Ann watched her husband's reaction, seeing a nervous smile only a wife would notice.

She continued saying, "When that first gust of wind blew, Al heard a woman's voice saying, 'I'm home.' Don, I heard that same voice! When you were driving out and suddenly stopped, I landed on my knee, looking right into the passenger's side-view mirror. In it, I saw a young couple behind us down the lane, a man in a flannel shirt holding a puppy and a young woman wearing a red blouse like the one I took to Fiery. Don — they were waving goodbye to us. When I got out, they were gone."

With that, Ann leaned over, hugged her husband, saying, "I don't know what's happening… but it's no coincidence."

Don searched for words, slowly saying, "I saw them in the rear-view mirror. When I stopped and got out, I watched them walk into the forest. The flannel shirt man, I have seen before, always with a puppy, and the girl did look like a young Aunt Fiery. I think, I wanted to see them to complete the dream Fiery had, and finish their story. But then reality sets in, and I tell myself none of this is real."

His wife angrily pushed him away, yelling, "If that's what you think, explain this brown bag? Back in the woods, when you stopped suddenly, it rolled out from under the passenger seat!"

Handing him the bag, Don looked inside and slowly let the objects flow into his palm. There he saw Fiery's one-carat diamond wedding ring, gold bracelet, and her worn golden fob with forty-one's key. He studied the objects and said nothing. Carefully, he placed the jewelry back into the paper bag and put it in his shirt pocket, saying, "We'll return these things to Lucy Graham, so they'll stay in her family. No car thief would leave these items."

Don took a deep breath and continued in a somber tone speaking directly to the car, "Where did you journey this past year? I sure don't know! I think, Fiery planned these past twelve months her whole life, and this was exactly how things were supposed to end. Wasn't it?"

With that he opened his arms wide and Ann moved in to hug him, again. After a moment, he whispered in her ear, "I'll call Bruno tomorrow about the museum's loan agreement. Whatever we experienced back there was good and no coincidence. Now — let's go."

They drove the long way home on the rural country roads. Many minutes passed before Ann interrupted the repetitive road noise to ask once more, "How is the car driving?"

"I've been thinking about that. I always felt something magical driving this car, but that's gone. Now it feels like this is the last time I'll be behind the wheel. Does that sound odd?"

Instead of answering Ann presented him with another question, "Do you think – back there in the woods – that was the dream Aunt Fiery always hoped for? You know with this car and what we may have seen?"

Turning briefly to look at his wife, half-smiling, he answered with his own question, "Do you believe in true love and forever?"

With a soft broken voice Ann said, "Yes, and I would like to think we're part of their story!"

"You were and we are. We'll always be connected to Aunt Fiery and this car she called, Forty-One."

THE END

Their Campfire
"The dream lives on."

ACKNOWLEDGMENTS

To Judith Forfinski and Robilynn Farren, for their continued inspiration, helpful critiques, and sincere honesty throughout the writing process, encouraged this individual to continue the dream. Their kind help during the writing, editing, and rewriting stages gave this author hope for completion. jmf

A special thank you goes out to all the individuals interviewed over the many years, including the real Mrs. Maze and her niece. Your time, contribution of stories, and honest statements made this book possible. The time spent with you was special for us. Thank you all!

To the anonymous young women, who overheard the authors speaking and told them how their car story was really about Fiery's love for her husband. We heard you and hope we expressed your thoughts on these pages. A sincere thank you.

To our proof and beta readers, Brenda Embrescia, Louise Mediate, Bruno Mediate III and Ronald Volk. My profound gratitude goes out to each of you for your time and helpful comments. Your honest reviews made going down this writing boulevard a little bumpy at times. But your candid words were appreciated and helped to pave a smoother road. Thank you all.

I would like to thank Denise and John Nalepa, the John Michael Nalepa family, the Matthew Mixa family and Michael Dobish. Your kind words, inspiration and guidance along this journey will never be forgotten." jaf

The authors wish to thank and acknowledge our copyeditor Tessa Potgeter for her fine work and dedication to this project. To contact her for your project email: tmariepotgeter@gmail.com.

We thank Jess and the team of individuals at Spiro Books in Franklin, Tennessee, for their work on the book cover design and interior formatting of this novel. Your work was appreciated.

The authors recognized the song *"As Time Goes By"* was written by Herman Hupfeld and copyrighted in 1931 by Warner Bros. At the time of this publication, the authors continue to seek permission to print the lyrics of this song.

A final heartfelt thanks goes to John and Robbie Farren. Without their love and dedication to their good friend who was called home and the "God winks" they received, none of this would have been possible. I am eternally grateful! jaf

The authors would like to acknowledge other companies and organization we contacted while writing this novel. Your time, comments, guidance and in many cases, the responses given were appreciated. They are:

ASCAP Music Licensing, New York, New York;

BMI Music Service, New York, New York;

Ford Motor Company, Media Center, Dearborn, Michigan;

Knights of Columbus, New Haven, Connecticut;

Music Services, Brentwood, Tennessee;

Newberry Area Chamber of Commerce, Newberry, Michigan;

SESAC Music Licensing Division, Nashville, Tennessee;

Tahquamenon Falls State Park, Paradise, Michigan;

The Henry Ford – Greenfield Village in Dearborn, Michigan;

Traverse City Area Chamber of Commerce, Traverse City, Michigan;

Warner Bros. Burbank, California;

Warner Chappell Music, New York, New York;

WMG Warner Music Group, Los Angeles, California;

Warner Media Licensing, New York, New York.

ABOUT THE AUTHORS

Ronald "Ron" Forfinski (1959–2019) was born in Dearborn, Michigan, the son of Polish American parents. He attended Schoolcraft College and Lawrence Institute of Technology majoring in engineering. Ron lived an interesting and almost eccentric life, which included a passion for classic cars. It was that passion which inspired the beginning of this novel. He also enjoyed volunteering his time to his Knights of Columbus Council and Assembly, where he chaired meetings as Grand Knight and Faithful Navigator, respectively.

Ron and John

John Farren is a native of Cleveland, Ohio, who served his in the United States Marine Corps during the Vietnam era. After his military service, John attended evening university classes while working in the telecommunications industry. In 1990, he moved to Ann Arbor, Michigan, working in his company's college and university division. There he served as Regional Sales Manager, until his retirement. He then became more active in the Knights of Columbus rising to the leadership position of Grand Knight and Faithful Navigator within his Council and Assembly.

It was during this time John met Ron, and the two became good friends. When John and his family moved to Florida, the two authors and their families often vacationed together. It was during one of these vacations when their collaboration began on Forty-One's Journey. John's family and Ron's widow remain close friends to this day.